MORE PRAISE FOR

The Care and Handling of Roses with Thorns

"Even readers with black thumbs will be enchanted by the bramble beauty that is Galilee Garner. Dilloway has culti-vated a fascinating plot in the rich science and magic of flower breeding. A story about family and the ways in which the unex-pected blossom is often the most cherished. This novel is a rose personified."

—Sara McCoy, author of *The Baker's Daughter* and
The Time It Snowed in Puerto Rico

"Believable situations with well-drawn characters make this novel as lovely as the roses Gal tends. Dilloway's second novel is a captivating study of how love and understanding nurture our lives. Engaging, enlightening, thoughtful, this is a winner."

—*Library Journal*

"A tender, moving story that shows how family not only has the capacity to wound, but offers us the possibility to bloom again."

—Shilpi Somaya Gowda,
bestselling author of *Secret Daughter*

"Galilee Garner is as prickly, thorny, and gracefully sweet as one of her prize roses."

—Tiffany Baker, *New York Times* bestselling author of
The Little Giant of Aberdeen County

"A touching, moving story . . . Margaret Dil͏ ͏ ͏ ͏ed, talented writer."　　　—Darien Gee͏ ͏ ͏ ͏ ͏ ͏ ͏ ͏ ͏ad

"Dilloway's rapturous ne͏ ͏ ͏ ͏ ͏ ͏ ͏ ͏ ͏ ͏ ͏ ͏ ͏ who shows what happens ͏ ͏ ͏ ͏ ͏ ͏ ͏ ͏ ͏ before us, we risk bloomi͏ ͏ ͏ ͏ ͏ ͏ ͏ ͏ ͏k is an understatement."

͏ ͏ ͏ ͏ ͏ ͏ Leavitt, *New York Times*
bestselling author of *Pictures of You*

continued . . .

The CARE

and HANDLING

of ROSES *with* THORNS

———

Margaret Dilloway

———

BERKLEY BOOKS

New York

THE BERKLEY PUBLISHING GROUP
Published by the Penguin Group
Penguin Group (USA) Inc.
375 Hudson Street, New York, New York 10014, USA

USA I Canada I UK I Ireland I Australia I New Zealand I India I South Africa I China

Penguin Books Ltd., Registered Offices: 80 Strand, London WC2R 0RL, England
For more information about the Penguin Group, visit penguin.com.

Berkley trade paperback ISBN: 978-0-425-26097-5

The Library of Congress has catalogued a previous edition of this book as follows:

Library of Congress Cataloging-in-Publication Data

Dilloway, Margaret.
The care and handling of roses with thorns / Margaret Dilloway.
p.   cm.
ISBN 978-0-399-15775-2
1. Roses—Breeding—Fiction.   2.   Aunts—Family relationships—Fiction.   I. Title.
PS3604.14627C37   2012   2012009276
813'.6—dc23

PUBLISHING HISTORY
G. P. Putnam's Sons hardcover edition / August 2012
Berkley trade paperback edition / July 2013

PRINTED IN THE UNITED STATES OF AMERICA

10 9 8 7 6 5 4 3 2 1

Cover image of "Woman" by Lee Avison/Trevillion Images;
cover image of "Roses" by Shutterstock.
Cover design by Rita Frangie.

ALWAYS LEARNING   PEARSON

To Deborah, for the inspiration

To Keith, for the faith

Some people are always grumbling because roses have thorns. I am thankful that thorns have roses.

—*Alphonse Karr*

Winslow Blythe's *Complete Rose Guide* (SoCal Edition)

March

This month is when you will see the benefits of the severe pruning you gave your roses last month. Sometimes a little tough love is good. Greenhousers may see blooms early in the month, while the rest of us will have to wait until the end.

Now spring is nearly here. Your roses will need a great deal of nourishment after the hard winter. Use a general fertilizer (20-20-20) to give them a solid start with strong foliage.

The first critters of spring make their appearance now, out in force after the winter rains subside. Organic gardeners, arise early and pluck all the snails from the roses. Try out ladybugs for natural aphid control, or handwash your roses. Poisons should be used according to directions; keep out of reach of the kiddos and furry friends.

1

For a moment, I think I have made a mistake. My tweezers pause and shake over the yellow rose. I have already stripped the petals to expose the stamen, which will release the pollen from this father plant. But is this the rose I had put aside earlier? Or did I want the white rose with orange-tinged petals, with a bloom so open it looks more like a daisy? These parents are known only by their codes: G120 and G10. I double-check in my rose notebook. G120. G10. I do not breed the plants without writing down this information. That way, I can re-create an outcome, or adjust by breeding with another plant. My memory has been suffering lately, though I refuse to acknowledge this aloud. I adjust the lamp, calm my twitching hands, and continue.

I am a rose breeder. Not just a rose grower. Most rose hobbyists grow only roses that other people have already perfected. I invent new varieties.

Breeding roses is not something I do for fun. Not solely for fun, anyway. It's the kind of fun most people classify as "drudgery," but then again, I'm not like most people.

Roses are my hobby, and what I want to be my vocation. Someday, I hope, I will wake up, find a prizewinning rose peeking out at me in the greenhouse, quit my job, and devote myself to roses full-time. My pastime inspired me to dig up my nice neat suburban lawn and plant a wild thorny mass. A homeowner's association would have booted me long ago.

You would have to be nuts to want to do what I want to do with these roses. Which is, to make a never-before-seen Hulthemia rose and bring it to market. One that will be prized for its scent and distinctive spots and stripes. If I can produce this rose in my little garden, I will take it to one of the smaller rose shows. If it wins a prize, I might be brave enough to enter one of the larger shows, like the American Rose Society convention show. If a rose of mine wins Queen of Show, it would be like a Barbizon modeling school dropout winning Miss America. It would give me the confidence that my rose was worthy of a pricey patent, a process costing at least two grand before attorney fees.

My greatest hope is to get a rose into the American Rose Society test gardens, where a few select new roses are grown in different climates to see how they fare for two years. Of these, the rose society selects one or two varieties as the best of the best.

How long are my odds? Consider that a big rose company, with endless resources, will come up with hundreds of thousands of new seedling varieties every year. Of these, only two or three make it into the market.

And consider me, Galilee Garner, an amateur with an extra-large yard and perhaps a few hundred new seedlings, at best, trying to compete against professional growers. It doesn't look very good for me, does it?

However, there's something more important at work here. Luck. You can't overestimate the importance of luck. It's like playing the lottery. Sometimes, a person playing one dollar in the lottery wins it all, while the person who spends one hundred dollars a week for a year walks away with nothing.

Take the man who bred the Dolly Parton tea rose in his Michigan basement. He was growing all sorts of rose hybrids when he found an ugly little red-orange seedling with only twelve petals at first bloom, not the twenty you might expect. Just as his hand closed around the seedling to yank it out, he thought to smell it. And its smell was incredible.

He left it alone. It grew into an enormous sixty petals, inspiring its name, blossoming into one of the most popular roses ever. That man retired off the Dolly Parton, I believe. All because of luck.

And I grow roses that need a lot of luck. I didn't pick the easy roses to breed, the sort you can find in any old garden center or big-box store. I love the Hulthemia roses. They are difficult and obstinate, thriving when I introduce them to an impossible variety of conditions. Like any rose grower, I have my own particular methods of doing things, my own fertilizer formulas, my own routine. I pay as much attention to temperature as an ice cream maker does in the middle of the Sahara, though I know one day my successful seedling will have to survive in a variety of punishing climates. I apply the exact amount of water and fertilizer necessary, at exactly the correct times. When fungus appears, like powdery mildew or black spot, I attack it before it spreads to other plants. I set loose ladybugs to eat those little green aphids, the tiny bugs that have plagued roses since before the time of Moses.

And as long as no other event occurs to throw them off course—which doesn't happen often, in my mostly protected greenhouse—they do wonderfully.

Difficult and obstinate. Thriving under a set of specific and limited conditions. That pretty much describes me. Maybe that's why I like these roses so much.

A student of mine described me in these words—difficult and obstinate—on the Rate Your Teacher website my school's headmaster, Dr. O'Malley, set up. A silly website. Another place where everyone is the expert, but no one knows the real story. A website I imagine the headmaster and parents clucking over while they sip their coffee at Headmaster Coffee Break. "That Ms. Garner," they probably say. "Won't she ever learn?"

Obstinate. I was impressed with this anonymous student's word choice and by the apt description. If this student put as much time into my biology class as he did into writing this review, maybe he would have passed. I suspect the student is a "he," because the student added as a postscript, "Constant PMS. Get over it." Females take exception to such accusations.

Most people are surprised by my rose hobby. I look more like I'd have a secret science lab in my basement, a torture chamber, perhaps, than a rose garden. Visually, there is no good explanation for my rose obsession. Roses are frilly and soft and sweet-smelling, which I am not. If you saw me in the teacher lineup, our faces bathed in harsh light against the black height lines, would you pick me for the rose lover? No. You would pick someone like Dara, the art teacher, with her carefully messed halo of Botticelli curls. Or Mrs. Wingate, the English teacher, whose fluffy circle skirts sometimes remind me of roses in their layers and frilliness. Not plainspoken me, squinting unmercifully back at you, my eyes barely visible behind my round gray-tinted lenses. A garden gnome without the jolly expression.

I am short, due to the childhood onset of my failed kidneys, an inch under five feet on my best day. I have never been called "pretty." More like, "she looks pretty good, all things considered." My face is always puffy. My skin, while not glowing, at least has been spared freckling from the sun, thanks to my sunblock and hat diligence.

If you looked at the rose more than superficially, you'd see why I am drawn to them. Florists strip those thorns for you so you don't stick your fingers when you buy them, while some breeders have engineered the bite right out of them, creating smooth-stemmed varieties. I personally wouldn't try to strip mine down for anyone. I love roses, thorns and all. People should learn to take care.

My house is in Santa Jimenez, a small community inland of San Luis Obispo, in central California. It's a great place to grow roses, with fairly mild winters and early warm springs. We have a mix of houses, from small tract cottages, to working farms, to mansions of the well-to-do where we get many of our students.

I live on the outskirts of town, on a long and narrow rectangular acre of land. My house sits near the front, my land stretching out behind it. I would have preferred a square so my neighbor wouldn't be as close.

It's a far different place from where my sister and I grew up in Encinitas, down in Southern California. The lots were postage-stamp-sized, and you could not only spit on your neighbors but say "Bless you!" when they sneezed. My parents still live down there in the same three-bedroom ranch they bought for a song back in the day.

A muffled rap sounds at the vinyl door. The greenhouse is vinyl, glass being out of my price range currently. I push my golden-wire-rimmed glasses back up my sweaty nose.

"Come in." I'm not very much concerned with strangers. I've been on my own for far too long to worry about anything except what is right in front of me.

It's my friend Dara. Dara taps on her bright yellow plastic watch. "You're not ready." Her curly hair is bound up in a ponytail. I move my own dark brown bangs off my forehead, out of my eyes. We met in the teachers' lounge of St. Mark's School, nearly three years ago, when Dara was new to the school.

I had asked Dara for help drawing the Hulthemia I'm trying to breed, since my sketches are little better than cave drawings. She responded by creating a watercolor painting of my dream flower, so beautiful that I had it framed and hung it on my bedroom wall. After that, Dara asked to see more roses, and would come over to my garden just to sketch. Then Dara asked me for photos of DNA sequencing to use in some of her conceptual art projects. Before long, she was dragging me to see artsy films and I was dragging her to popcorn flicks. Our friendship has taken off over the years. She is my closest friend.

Today, in my greenhouse, her face is red and two semicircles of sweat are forming on her midnight blue silk blouse. It's March, unseasonably hot this day as Southern California sometimes gets, but I have not noticed the temperature, even out here in my sweat lodge of a greenhouse. Where we live, the summers cook to over a hundred degrees, and we are too used to air-conditioning. The results are people like Dara: unused to real air, they get overheated and cannot handle it. Humans are not meant to live in overly controlled climates. I've kept my temperatures as close to natural as I can, given my health restrictions.

"You're interrupting me at a very crucial moment," I say

to her, though I am in fact almost done. "I'm making a new rose baby." Dara says roses are a Freudian substitution for my lack of love life. I tell her I can't miss something I've never had. Well, there was once that fellow biology student I met in college. I thought all our late study-dates and joking banter were something more, but he saw it differently.

"Are you ready?" Dara does look like she's about to swoon, so without moving my arms I kick another stool on wheels toward her across the concrete floor.

Dara could be my twin sister, if twins were polar opposites of each other. While I am small, she is tall and long-limbed. Where I am thin, with hanging skin that makes me look two or three decades older than I am, she is muscular and firm. My hair is nearly black, and hers is that gold blond people try to get out of a bottle. Add to this that she is the art teacher at the private Catholic school where we teach and I am the biology nerd, and we're perfectly yin-yang. The only matching thing between us is our feet, both size ten. The big feet look better on her height; even I, the non-artist, can tell that.

Of course, she would never deign to wear the practical sneakers I own, while I would fall over if I tried to wear her spiky-heeled, pointy-toed shoes that the Wicked Witch of the West would choose. "It's what they say to wear on *What Not to Wear*," is her response.

"They're telling you *not* to wear it. It's the name of the show," I always say, teasing her. "Besides, I don't believe in cable. It's expensive, and life's too short."

To this she rolls her eyes, as though she's my young teenage sister instead of a colleague only four years younger than I.

"You're going to be late." She leans her elbow on a table

and points her sweaty face toward the fan. "I'm surprised you're not dead out here."

"I could have driven myself." I transfer the stamens, now free of petals, into a clean glass jar. Later, the anthers at the tops will shed their pollen, which I will then collect and transfer to the mother plant.

After I set the pollen from the father rose into the mother rose, I will leave it alone. In fall, if I'm fortunate, the mother rose will ripen into a rose hip, containing the seeds. I cut this seed pod open and put them into peat moss, then put the seeds in the refrigerator to induce dormancy. Next spring, I will plant these seeds, and from this new variety will hopefully spring a magnificent new rose, with the best traits of its parents.

THE MOTHER IS A HULTHEMIA of vivid magenta, with an equally vivid crimson sunburst in its very heart, bleeding outward toward the petals. Hulthemias are not widely known to consumers; they are relatively new and the most difficult type to grow. Most amateurs simply don't try to undertake their breeding. These blossoms are round, like an old-fashioned rose, but the center opens up to reveal the welcoming yellow stamen and the distinctive dark blotch at its heart. "Blotch" is not the prettiest word to describe the color, but it's how breeders refer to it. The blotches are usually red, but can also vary from deep pink to purple to orange. It's always darker than the surrounding petals.

If they look different from any other rose you've seen, it's because they are. They are not a true rose. These roses are hybrids of flowers called *Hulthemia persicas,* which the Persians considered weeds, with barbed vines running amok.

In 1836, an accidental Hulthemia hybrid growing in the Luxembourg Gardens in Paris caught the attention of rose breeders. They coveted the red hearts for regular roses.

It took one hundred forty-nine years to get there. The first Hulthemias, including that specimen in the Paris garden, were homely and infertile. It wasn't until the late 1960s that an Englishman named Jack Harkness, of the famous Harkness Roses, was the first to get a breakthrough. His friend Alec Cocker decided that if the flower could exist by accident, it could exist if he bred it. He got more Hulthemia seeds from Iran and gave some to Harkness. In 1985, Harkness finally got a Hulthemia variety that could reproduce: Tigris. These early Hulthemia were crossbred with true roses, a project taken on by multiple other breeders, and eventually we got what we have now.

There are specific attributes a Hulthemia needs to be successful with the casual rose grower. People want a rosebush that will not get too gigantic for their small backyards. They also want a fragrant bloom. They want a rosebush that will produce dozens of blooms over and over again throughout the season. This repeat blooming is something that was only fairly recently bred into our modern roses, obtained from Chinese roses. The French began to cross Chinese roses with European roses around 1798.

In short, the consumer, as always, expects the impossible. At a mass-market price.

To date, this Hulthemia doesn't yet exist. Whoever is the first Hulthemia grower to bring this kind of consumer-friendly plant on the market will make a fortune. Her (because I plan to be the winner) name will be sung by the rose-breeding bards.

Of these assets, fragrance is the most difficult thing to

come by. It's been bred out of modern stock. Generally, rose breeders wanted hardiness and disease resistance at the expense of fragrance, which ensures growers can massively produce and ship roses all over the world, at any time of the year.

Fragrance tends to appear more randomly, not always linked to a recessive gene, not always predictable. For example, if a rose's grandparents were all fragrant, it doesn't mean the grandchild will be. Perfumed roses also tend to be more delicate, and most casual breeders do not want to attempt them.

I have a repeat-blooming Hulthemia on my hands, a fifth-generation plant I've created after five years of crossing its ancestors. Last year, it bloomed in the spring, summer, and fall, generating bloom after bloom as I clipped it. I'm going to take it to a rose show in San Luis Obispo next month.

I haven't officially named the rose yet. It is only G42 to me, an orange Hulthemia with that crimson center. This year, I hope to have the scent as well. If it does make it to trials, it will be known as the "Gal."

The rose is top secret, occupying a special spot in my greenhouse. My father, a retired contractor, built this greenhouse for me from a kit during a visit five years ago. Here I have workbenches, built to my modest height, and a rolling seat. No bees are allowed inside, though a few, like the aphids, find their way in. Bees are not my friends. I am the only one who will pollinate these roses. I am their mad scientist.

I have always been somewhat of a mad scientist, beginning in my teen years when I bred roses as a science project. In one season, I was hooked. I turned my parents' garage into a de facto breeding center. Though none of my creations were unique enough to go to a rose show, I could never stop. The hobby is addicting.

Now, with Dara perspiring next to me, I clean my tweezers with a sterilized cotton ball and alcohol and return them to their plastic case, where they rattle with the other tweezers. "But now that you're here, you might as well take me."

Dara grins and pops pink bubble gum. "You can't get home alone."

I smile at my friend and punch her lightly on the arm, tomboy-style. "Thanks, kiddo." I don't know what I'll do if Dara ever gets her own life.

"Let's get going." She shifts her water bottle in her hand. I know she wants to take a drink, but she remembers I cannot have any liquid before the procedure, and so she won't. Dara is too polite like that. She shouldn't be. Yet I do not encourage her to take a drink, because it really will make me thirstier. My mouth is dry and sticky and I wipe my chapped lips with the back of my hand.

I point to the black notebook on the table. "Brad's coming in today. Remind me to leave the greenhouse key under the mat." Brad is the football team quarterback, the starting pitcher on our baseball team, the student body president, and inexplicably the best student in my AP Biology class. As his required community service project for high school, Brad helps me with the roses. Brad is, of course, my favorite student, on some days the only reason I make myself go into the classroom.

Brad has the ability to remember the Latin names for things, the groups, the subgroups, the phylum and the subphylum, and the grouping. He does this as easily as some young boys do baseball statistics. He has an attention to detail I appreciate. Our brains work alike, though I would never tell him so. I considered naming the rose after him, though I decided not to. Roses aren't usually named for men. No man wants to buy his wife a bunch of Brad roses.

It's because of students like Brad that I got into teaching in the first place. Shaping young minds and all that. It's fun, as long as they're willing to be shaped. That and the summers off, plus the early day, make teaching perfect for me. It leaves me time to tend to my roses, in spite of my other problems.

"Come on," she says, extending her hand to help me up, though privately I think she's the one who needs help, clad as she is in an impractical, impossibly tight pencil skirt.

"I'm pretty sure your skirt is against school dress policy." I get up as she totters back.

She rolls her eyes and pops her gum again. "It's called 'style.' You should get some."

"Form follows function, Dara. An art teacher should know that." I shut the greenhouse door and lock it. From the other side of the fence, I see my neighbor, Old Mrs. Allen, watering her lawn in her black silk kimono robe with her big black straw hat, looking like an extra from a silent film. From here, I can see the red slit passing for her mouth. I lift my hand in a wave and she almost waves back, then remembers who I am and lowers her hand with a scowl. The stinky fish emulsion I used on the roses caused a police visit to my door last year, courtesy of her. The neighborhood kids call her the Old Witch. If I were a kid, I probably would, too. I wonder what the kids call me. Nutty Rose Lady?

I smile at Dara and slide into the front seat of her car.

THOUGH SHE KNOWS THE DRILL, Dara insists on staying put in the waiting room. I check in with all the seven layers of hell security slapping wrist tags on me like they're tagging wildlife. Then again, I wouldn't blame me for running off. The hospital's been my second home since I was a kid. Two kidney transplants and years of dialysis will do that.

The paper pusher, who must be new because I've never seen her before, pauses in her typing to actually take me in. "Galilee Garner?" She can barely spit the name out.

"Yep." I sit back on the hard chair. "You can call me Gal."

Galilee is the name my parents chose to saddle me with after a hippie trip to the Holy Land back in the 1970s. The Sea of Galilee.

By the time I was two, it was clear I was not a Galilee. "Galilee" rolls off the tongue, a musical of notes, meant for a curly-haired little girl in pink dresses with bows. Not me. So they called me Gal for short.

My older sister had it much better. Becky. No one has ever misspelled my sister's name or asked her to repeat herself.

"You all right?" the woman asks, eyeing my sallow skin, my tired eyes, the scars on my forearms.

I nod. I make hospital workers nervous, if they don't know me. If I go to the emergency room, I get pushed to the head of the line, even if someone else's leg is sitting in a cooler beside him. I have that look about me, I guess. The look of impending doom.

The woman asks me all the standard questions about where I was born and what my insurance is.

Today, in the *Miami Vice*–like waiting room, there's an elderly woman with hair resembling light pink cotton candy swirled atop her head, and a middle-aged man with an impressive potbelly, who belches every minute or so. I wonder if the hair is pink on purpose, or if her red-haired dye job didn't do the work.

Then there's Mark Walters, an older man who is holding *Road & Track* up to his face because he forgot his reading glasses. Everyone calls him Mark Twain, because he sports a full white handlebar mustache and has a head of wild white hair. I think he looks more like Einstein. He's always wearing some uniform of white, as if he fancies himself an angel. Today it's white jeans, a loose white V-neck shirt that shows his white chest hair. I wish he'd cover up. Even from here, across the room, I can smell the Old Spice aftershave. It makes my nose itch.

As if he feels my eyes on him, he looks up from the magazine and winks, one bushy eyebrow almost covering his wrinkled eye. This does not embarrass me. I'm always staring sternly at people, particularly at my students. A nurse comes in to fetch him. I recognize her as Nurse Sonya, a large Russian woman who seems to take about as much joy in her work as an undertaker.

"Mr. Walters, you're looking fit as a fiddle!" she singsongs.

My eyes pop wide open.

"A fiddle that's been left out in the rain at the beach, perhaps." His voice is raspy, his breathing a little strained. He gets up slowly and she holds out her arm.

Mark. Mark is here because he did not take his blood pressure medication. He was too busy eating steak and boozing it up to bother. Lost his liver first, got a transplant for that. And now, because he caused his own kidneys to fail, he is on the waiting list.

And he just got higher priority than I.

I was born with reflux. This means the flap at the end of the passage from the kidney to the bladder didn't close properly. My mother could not change my diapers fast enough, I made so much urine. Constant bladder infections were the result, then kidney infections. By the time the doctors figured out what was wrong, when I was four, one kidney had already withered away. The other one, already on its way to failing, went when I was twelve. My mother was the first donor; that one lasted for twelve years. The second was from a cadaver, someone who checked the box on their driver's license. That one lasted only four before my body decided it was definitely a foreign object. I've been on dialysis for eight years.

Dialysis basically cleans your blood, like a kidney. You're hooked up to a machine attached to a vein, and all your blood pumps through and gets filtered. There are different kinds of dialysis, but I do the kind where I have to go in every other day. You can do dialysis overnight or during the day. I do dialysis overnight because it's simpler and I can sleep. If you skip a treatment, you will feel like you have the flu and your brain will stop working so well. If you stop dialysis altogether, eventually your organs will all shut down and you'll die.

There are more than half a million Americans on dialysis. Theoretically, people can survive for a very long time. It depends on the accompanying problems of a patient. During the first year of dialysis, twenty percent of dialysis patients die, half within the first three months. These folks most likely have more pressing problems, like high blood pressure or diabetes, which caused the kidneys to fail in the first place. Infections are another issue; your immune system is nonexistent, so a little cold can turn into a deadly problem.

The odds of death go up with each year you spend on dialysis. In year two, the survival rate is sixty-four percent. Year five, thirty-three percent. By year ten, it drops to only ten percent.

I am approaching year ten statistics.

Thus, it's vitally important to get a kidney as soon as possible, but there simply aren't enough to go around. People don't line up to donate kidneys like they do to donate blood.

Today, I'm at the hospital for a blood flow test, to show how well my blood will move around a new kidney. The doctors would not want to give me one of those precious kidneys, only to have it expire because it can't get any blood.

I take my place in the waiting room chair. The same nurse returns to take me back.

"You ready, Ms. Garner?" Nurse Sonya is already walking away.

I try to think of a joke, something to make her laugh. Nothing comes to mind. I've seen Sonya for the past five years, and she's never commented on more than my blood pressure and pulse.

I decide to hell with it, and her, and Mark. I don't care. I shuffle along behind her, painfully aware that my gait is no better than Mark's, though he's at least thirty years older.

2

It is newly dark when Dara brings me home, the air chill. A California chill. People from the East would be wearing shorts; I have on a heavy jacket. I thread my hands together on my lap. Dara and I have been avoiding talking about the test. We generally do not speak about the severity of my situation. If I dwelled on that garbage, I'd be more of a basket case than I already am. I say it anyway. "If I ever have to do that again, it'll be too soon."

The MRA test I'd just had was more like a medieval torture chamber than a modern medical exam. First, they injected me with a protein-based dye. Then they strapped me to the top of an iron frame and stuck me in the machine. Turns out I'm claustrophobic, because it wasn't long before I was hitting the panic button. They gave me a sedative, so I was able to lie still for the ninety minutes I had to listen to the machine whirring around, hoping no one had left metal in the room that would go flying. The only way I got through it was by closing my eyes and visualizing my rose breeding. It worked. I came up with an idea for a new parent combination to try out when I get the seeds this fall.

"You got through it. You always do." My friend glances at me.

Dara pulls onto my street. I'm glad to see the lights blaze in the greenhouse and a beat-up faded red Honda Civic is parked on the street. Brad's silhouette is inside and the hose rushes water.

"He's here late." Dara frowns. "Doesn't watering at night make fungus?"

"Drainage is what matters. As long as your soils drain well, you can water at night." He was supposed to be out and done by six. It's seven.

We make our way up the front walk as the lights turn off and the greenhouse door closes. Brad bounds up, his teeth shining in the porch light, the bright light of his cell phone shining open in his hand.

"Sorry. Practice ran late." He flips his hair out of his face, worn in that fashion requiring such constant flipping, one bang over one eye. It's a little girly-looking to me. Brad himself is almost too pretty for a boy, with a finely turned nose and very light green eyes marked by lashes so black it looks like he's wearing eyeliner. He's got the strong chin of his father, though, and the big ears, which offset the femininity.

Brad Jensen is a scholarship student. At some schools, this might mean he would be an outcast. At our school, he's the most popular. Hardworking, bright, and polite. Everything you want your kid to be. Every mother of every girl he's dated has practically adopted him. No one begrudges him his scholarship, not when his mother died in Iraq when he was a toddler and he's being raised by his single dad, the school janitor.

"I'd rather have you home studying than here too late." I

take my key out, fumbling for the lock. Dara watches for a second before taking it out of my hand. "Hey, I can do that."

"Don't want to wait all night." She undoes the deadbolt.

"It's no problem, Ms. Garner. I told you I'd do it and I did." Brad shakes his hair back again. I really don't know why the girls love it so.

"You should get a haircut. You'll see better." I go inside. "Good night, Brad."

"G'night." Before I get all the way inside, his car has started.

"That kid. What isn't he interested in?" Dara turns on the light. "Do you know what he was talking to me about in study hall? French cinema." She snorts. "As if he knows anything."

"Trying to impress you, I expect." Dara's the prettiest and youngest teacher at the school, a mere thirty-two. Of course all the boys have crushes, though she is never anything except professional. I put my hand on the hallway wall, making my way to the bedroom, past the very clean and nearly unused powder room. If you're on the kind of dialysis I am, you don't have to pee. Ever. The one convenient thing about it. "He's a very well-rounded kid," I continue. "I think he'll have his pick of colleges. I'm only sorry he's graduating."

She goes ahead of me. The bedroom is pale green with pink accents. The bed is my four-poster from childhood, with a white canopy I've replaced with gauzy white curtains. I've spent more money in here on bedding than I have on my living room furniture. It's the place where I spend the most time.

She turns down my covers. "There you go. All ready." Dara sags against the door frame.

Suddenly I realize how tired she must be. Almost as tired as I am. "Thanks for staying with me, Dara."

"I'll stop by and see you tomorrow." It is Friday night.

She's got too much to do as it is. I am time-consuming. "No. I'll be fine. I've got cans of chicken soup to eat."

"You're ridiculous if you think I'm not checking in."

I wave her away. "Get along, now."

I hear the front door latch as she leaves.

The red light is blinking on my machine, and I know it's my mother before I check. I am not ready to talk to her. I get up and turn on the strong outdoor porch lights that lead the way into the greenhouse.

I should be lying down; a sedative still runs through my veins. But right now, I feel more relaxed than doped, and I want to do just a quick check on the roses.

The greenhouse is divided into different sections. At the short wall opposite the entrance, I have a desk, with shelves of my notebooks detailing my parent plants and how they were bred over the past decade.

In the middle of the greenhouse, I have three shallow boxes, four feet wide by six feet long, containing potting soil and topped with peat, which looks like white pearls sitting on top. These are my seedling boxes, where I sprout my new roses.

Farther down along the walls, I have tables of my older potted roses, the parent plants, spaced carefully apart from each other to prevent accidental pollination, two and half feet apart to ensure proper air flow. Each one is carefully tagged on the pot and cataloged in a notebook as well as in my computer.

And then I have my top-secret rose, the repeat bloomer, G42, in its special spot on my worktable. Though I'm hoping for fragrance this year, as a repeat bloomer it will be enough to get me into the market.

Outside, on my property, are rows and rows of my flowers. These are also categorized. Nearest the greenhouse, separate from the others, I have pots of my rootstock. After you get a good seedling, you take it and graft it onto rootstock to generate more of the exact same kind of seedling. Then you try growing these outside to see how they do. Not all will do well outdoors; a good many will die off. Some will return and surprise you in unexpected ways.

Then I have other roses grouped by type, mounded together with dirt paths in between. Though Hulthemias are my favorites, I have all manner of roses out here: hybrids, teas, climbers. Some of these are my second favorites: English roses, David Austin roses, big-headed and fragrant, almost like delicate cabbages.

My landscaping is functional and farmlike, not an aesthetically pleasing garden. Many casual rose growers plant other flowers that will bloom when the roses finish. Freesias with heady fragrance or ranunculus bobbing on their stick stems are popular. I don't bother.

Out here is where the bees roam free, where I let nature take its course, more or less. In November, birds eat the rose hips and crap out the seeds during their migratory flights. I've thought of placing a tracking device in the rose hips to see where they end up.

There, I unlock the door and survey the scene. The hoses are put away, the water is off, the pruning shears are placed back on the pegboard hanger. I turn off the lights and lock the door, making sure the key is not under the mat.

Now my sleepiness hits me. I go back indoors.

It's dark inside. The only sounds are the refrigerator

humming and my own breathing. I make my way through the unlit house into the bedroom, taking a carefully worn path so I don't run into any furniture. I switch on the dim bedside lamp and regard the blinking light of the answering machine again. I take a breath, dialing my mother back on speaker as I take off my shoes and socks and change into my nightshirt, a long football jersey handed down from my father.

"Hello, how are you?" I ask when she picks up. My voice sounds unnaturally loud in this house, and I fight the urge to whisper.

"Fine, thanks, and you?" This we must go through, no matter how many times per day I speak with her. "Let me call you back." She hangs up and so do I. Mom does not want me to incur long-distance charges.

The phone rings. "How did it go?" Mom tries to sound cool, but underneath, worry vibrates as plainly as tight violin strings wail.

"Dara took me. I'm fine." These are two things Mom wants to hear: that I'm not alone, and that I am all right.

"Will they make you do the IVP test?"

"I don't have any results from this test, Mom."

The MRA test was a last-ditch effort to measure my blood flow. The best way to get the results is through an intravenous pyelogram, or an IVP test, and I'm allergic to the dye. I've gotten a CO_2 test, where they pump carbon dioxide through you: results inconclusive. And now this MRA. If the MRA doesn't work, the doctor will insist on the IVP test, allergic or not.

I change the subject. "How was the library art show?"

"Great. I sold a watercolor. Gal, I can be out there tomorrow morning."

"You sold a watercolor?" I don't want her to visit. "Congratulations! That's major, Mother. How much?"

"It doesn't matter. Do you want me to come?"

This is one reason I left my birth city. If my mother is here, she will be all over me, too guilty and busy to go outside and make her plein-air landscapes.

"It was noninvasive, Mother." I muffle my sigh in my pillow. My parents are going to France soon, to sit in the French countryside, visit Champagne wineries, and eat moldy cheese that would be outlawed here. I am not going to have my mother miss her trip for me, though she always buys travel insurance "in case Gal has something come up."

"Are you sure you're all right? You sound off." If she were here, she'd be making me tea and stroking my hair. For a moment I want her here.

"I'm on a sedative. I'll be more coherent tomorrow." I put my glasses on the nightstand and rub the bridge of my nose. I want to change the subject. "Heard from Becky lately?"

She hesitates, oddly. "I have."

My eyes close. I am so close to sleep that I regret asking, yet I can still detect there's more to come. "What's up? She lose her job again?" Becky is a pharmaceutical sales rep, traveling her region and selling pills to doctors. Like me, she has a degree in biology, and on the surface, she looks like a well-respected suit-wearing white-collar worker, with flat-ironed shiny hair and carefully applied makeup.

"Not lost it. She got a new one. More travel." Now Mom's voice sounds funny. "Riley's coming here to stay with us. After we get back from France."

"Really?" I yawn. Riley is Becky's daughter. Father in and out of the picture, out for good now.

"I'm not sure it's a good idea." Pot lids clang on Mom's

end, meaning she is more nervous than usual, even after one of my operations. "We're to visit Aunt Betty this summer after her knee surgery . . ." She trails off. "Teenagers are a lot to handle."

"Did you tell her that?" Mom lets Becky walk all over her, sending her money whenever Becky goes over budget, which I'm sure is more often than even I know. "Did you say she didn't need to create another new problem?"

Mom ignores this, so I know she didn't say a thing. "I'm sure it will work out."

"Always does, one way or the other. Even if it's badly." I smile at my little joke.

"Ha ha."

My mind drifts. Poor little Riley. The last time I saw her, I was still living at my folks' house. I haven't seen her in, what, seven years? She's fifteen now.

When Riley was a toddler, perhaps two years old, I'd stopped by Becky's town house in San Diego. Becky had been laid off from her first pharmaceutical sales job. At the time, Becky had been a party girl, a pot smoker and drinker, perhaps more. We suspected "laid off" was a nicer term for "let go because you showed up hungover."

I was dropping something off. I don't remember what. The door was unlocked. Her cat meowed at me.

"Riley? Becky?" I moved into the house.

Becky was stone-cold passed out on the couch.

I shoved my sister. She didn't respond. I slapped her face. "Becky? Where's Riley?"

"Uhh?" Becky managed to open her eyes, but could not focus.

Then I heard crying from the backyard. Riley was on the patio, dressed only in a sagging diaper, clutching the nape of the old yellow golden retriever Becky had inherited from her ex. Her eyes were reddened and stood out Christmas tree green, her face was filthy, her arms covered in mud, but she was all right. She held her arms out to me.

I scooped her up and took her over to my parents' house. It was hours before Becky woke and realized her daughter was gone.

Riley went to live with her father after that, and we thought everything was all right. His mother watched Riley while he worked. Becky cleaned up, stopped partying, and saw her daughter regularly. We chalked the incident up to immaturity.

A few years later, Riley's grandmother passed away, and Riley's father got another woman pregnant. A woman who didn't like the fact that Riley's father had had another family before hers. He married her and moved to Boston, and Riley went back to Becky. I understand that Riley's father hadn't offered more contact than his monthly signature on the support checks.

Becky had moved to San Francisco for her new job, at a different drug company. Now, if Becky partied, she made sure to show up to work sober, or at least functional, because she'd held on to this job for years. I'd suspected that though she'd slowed with the alcohol, she wasn't averse to the occasional super-strength pain reliever, palmed out of her samples. I could hear the fog in her voice on the rare occasions when we talked on the phone. Though she pulled in a good salary, she was always, somehow, in financial straits. Her boyfriends had been numerous, and always had questionable job titles like "nightclub promoter."

My mother refused to believe anything was wrong. "Riley would tell me," she would always say. Mom would fly up to get Riley, fly back down with her, keep her for weeks at a time during the summer. I had to think my parents had a stabilizing influence, as had her paternal grandmother, during her very young years. I had to believe Riley couldn't remember her earlier neglect.

"Riley doesn't want to be taken away from her mother," I said. At eight, Riley showed a fierce and undeserved loyalty to my sister.

"Everything is fine, Aunt Gal," she told me on the afternoon of her eighth birthday, when I phoned.

"Look in your cupboards and tell me what's there," I challenged her.

She had responded immediately. "SpaghettiOs, pizza, and a lot of vegetables. A lot of vegetables. My mother makes me eat them."

I caught her out. "You keep pizza in your cupboard?"

"I thought you meant freezer."

And it was always like this, Riley protecting and covering up for her mother, Becky wheedling whatever help she could get out of my mother, without admitting she should have given up her daughter long ago.

I remember this as I stare at the ceiling, listening to my mother make excuses for my sister. At last I say, "What Riley needs is a good education in a stable home. Her mother's ruined her." I think of my colleagues with children. The first child gets free tuition. It had always pained my frugal little heart that I could not take advantage of the program. "She oughta come here. Get a free private school diploma."

"You couldn't handle her."

"You haven't seen me in action with my students." I chuckle. Oh, I'm close to sleep. I think I'm on the beach in San Diego, dipping one toe into the frigid Pacific. "Pollution levels are high," I mumble and slur. I'm dreaming of another high school science project, testing the ocean water.

Her tone softens. "I better let you get to resting."

It's all I can do to hit the End button on my phone receiver. The pain medicine is better than a sleeping pill. The moonlight comes in, dappled through the chiffon curtains, making abstracted rose patterns on the ceiling. I close my eyes and picture my rose family pedigrees. Hulthemia. They rise three dimensionally around me, dancing like I'm Alice in Wonderland visiting those snotty flowers. I smile in my delusion. Maybe I can breed the pink to the yellow. I cross Hulthemias in my head, their offspring reborn as quick as film passing by. Until I fall asleep.

Gal's Rose Notebook

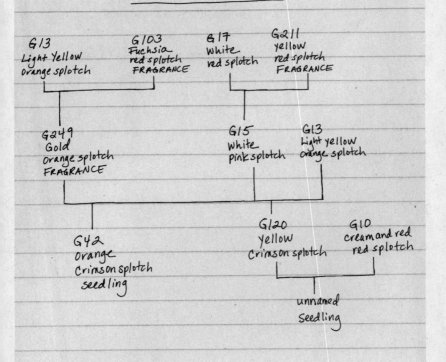

G13
Light Yellow
orange splotch

G103
Fuchsia
red splotch
FRAGRANCE

G17
white
red splotch

G211
yellow
red splotch
FRAGRANCE

G249
Gold
orange splotch
FRAGRANCE

G15
white
pink splotch

G13
Light yellow
orange splotch

G42
orange
Crimson splotch
seedling

G120
yellow
Crimson splotch

G10
cream and red
red splotch

unnamed
Seedling

3

―――――

ON THE MONDAY AFTER MY PROCEDURE, I WALK
up and down the front of my classroom, my sensible athletic
shoes squeaking on the black linoleum. All the science
rooms have black linoleum floors and black counters. At
Halloween, I decorate it to look like a dungeon. I don't have
Bunsen burner gas lines like the chemistry room, but I do
have an array of microscopes along the counters under the
mottled-glass ancient windows. It's a room students tend to
daydream in, on the second floor of the building, overlooking an array of still-bare treetops and the athletic field,
where a P.E. class is engaged in a flag football game.

There are no pictures of saints on the walls, like there are
in the religious studies' room; most Catholic schools these
days are not really very Catholic. There aren't even any nuns
here; not enough to go around. Our priest comes in only
once a month or so, to lead Mass. Otherwise, it's essentially
like any other private high school.

I've worked here for eight years, starting right before my
kidney failed again. I came from a public high school, with
indifferent faculty and even more indifferent students. A
smaller private school was a welcome change.

The headmaster, Dr. O'Malley, looked worried when he first met me at my teaching interview, glancing from the top of my head down to my feet. "How will you keep the kids in line?" he had asked.

I straightened to my full height. "First of all, I come from a public school and never had any problems. I thought this school was intolerant of bad behavior. Second, the tongue is mightier than the sword."

Dr. O'Malley had smiled. "I think that's the pen. And you're right. We do have good kids here."

"I know what you're thinking." I leaned across his desk. "I'm going to get sick, cost you lots of money."

He started to demur, but I held up my hand.

"Let me say this. No one knows what will happen. A perfectly healthy person could get hit by a semi tomorrow. But I guarantee you, no matter how much time I have left, I will leave the school a better place than when I found it." I sat back in my chair, my case presented.

In the end, of course, the board had not found a reason they couldn't hire me. They certainly couldn't say I was short, or unqualified. I have been here ever since.

Today, the class will learn about osmosis. Osmosis has to be one of the simpler concepts to understand, and a fun lab to boot. I've brought in potatoes. We've sliced them up and put them in beakers of water: one plain, one salted, and one sugared. They're supposed to explain why the salted potato got so soft, why the sugared one didn't get as soft, and why the plain one got harder. Osmosis causes water to move toward the salt.

A girl with a red ponytail in a cheerleader uniform raises her hand. The cheerleader uniforms are not too unlike the regular uniforms: a plaid skort and a sweater emblazoned with St. Mark's instead of a white blouse and skirt. "Can we use the same glass for all three?"

I have already gone over the directions, but she had been staring off outside. I turn to the rest of the class. "Anyone know?"

John, a boy wearing a school sweatshirt, clinks his beakers together. "Um, Sarah, how many beakers do you have in front of you?"

The rest of the class titters. If she were a cartoon character, she'd have a giant lightbulb go off above her head. "Oh! Got it."

"I thought cheerleaders were supposed to be kind of smart at this school," the boy mutters, shaking his mop of black curls.

"Hey. There's only room for one smart aleck in here." I tap my fingers on the table in front of John.

He grins sheepishly. "You?"

I nod and smile. "Everyone, if you have any further questions, John will be more than happy to assist. Without commentary."

He blows air through his lips and crunches his shoulders together, but does not say anything else.

They at last all settle down and begin working in earnest on the lab. The class lasts about fifty minutes, and they have almost forty left.

I sit at my workdesk in the back of the class, where I have a good clear view of them all and they can't see me. Despite spending the weekend resting, I feel run-down and hope I'm not coming down with something. A kid near the front coughs and I listen carefully. Sounds like a dry allergy cough to me. After nearly twelve years of teaching, I can tell the difference now. Aware that I was holding my breath against the germs, I allow myself a big yawn.

On the desk is my water bottle, filled with half a liter, half my daily allotment. If you're a patient that still makes urine, you're allowed more than this. It's not much, but it's better than the first time I was on dialysis, when I was allowed the equivalent of only one can of soda per day.

This lack of liquid gives my skin the lizard look of lotion commercials. A bottle of plain white hand cream sits on my desk. In a locked drawer are the pills I'm supposed to take regularly, and my nondelicious, low-phosphorus, low-potassium, dialysis-friendly snacks. Eat too much of these and you could trigger a heart attack. I should market my own diet. The slogan will be, "It's so unappetizing, you'll lose weight." I grin.

I open my rose file on the computer. The family tree of my roses spreads out before me. G42 should bloom any time now; I hope it's sweet-smelling. Its parents were the multiblooming rose from last year and another multiblooming rose. The grandparents of these roses have fragrance. In my strains, the fragrance seems to appear about once every other generation, like blue eyes do in some brown-eyed families. This is what I've intuited, though I'm not always correct. It's always a surprise in the end.

Dara appears beside me, quiet in her black ballet flats. She has no students right now; it's her prep period. A twinge of irritation wells. She shouldn't be interrupting my class because she's bored. Also, I admit, I was doing something I'm not supposed to, thinking about my roses during class time. I click off the screen so she can't see what I'm doing. Dara has been known to lecture about such things before.

"Finally come to learn about osmosis?" I swivel around in my seat. "Or is there a matter of importance I should attend?"

She sits in the hard plastic chair next to mine. "I was walking by and saw you weren't busy." She looks pointedly at the computer screen. "I just had a great idea while I was drawing up plans for next semester."

Teachers really aren't supposed to visit with each other like this. I can see why. All the kids are interested in us, not in their projects. "We can talk at lunch, Dara. Not in front of the kids."

She ignores this. "What if we do a joint project? Biology and art."

"My students can't draw. That's why they're in biology." I wink at the watching students.

She blinks, and I notice how much mascara she has on, and how heavy her eyeliner is. It's run into the small creases beneath her eye. "First of all, plenty of biologists can draw. Plenty of artists can do biology. Who do you think illustrates anatomy textbooks?"

"All right. I was just joking."

"It didn't sound like a joke." She crosses her arms. "Darn it, Gal, this is a good idea. Don't shoot it down."

I realize what I said wasn't just a joke, and if I think it was, I'm kidding myself.

I open my mouth to apologize, to explain myself. The kidney. It's always the kidney. I shouldn't use my illness as an excuse for anything anymore. I should know how to control my mood swings. This lack of water might be drying out my brain. My eyes are dry and I rub them behind my glasses.

I had snapped at Dara the weekend before last, arguing over where to sit in the movie theater for a showing of *Black Swan*. She said middle. I said I didn't even want to see the movie in the first place, therefore we should sit on the aisle like I wanted. I had won. I usually did. That didn't mean I was correct, though.

Dara continues. "The project's conceptual. They don't need to know how to draw. The art students don't need to know biology. Though they probably do." She points to the students. "I see ten students in here who are in my art class."

At this my irritation returns and increases, especially because now everyone has abandoned their work, openly staring to see what will happen. Dara is a popular teacher. The cool teacher who lets them eat snacks during class and go outside to draw. I am the mean one who makes them think and doesn't accept extra credit. "That explains a lot about their scholarship."

Her neck flushes red and blotchy and I know I've crossed the line. Cheap shot, Gal. She stands.

I feel terrible. "Dara."

"Forget it." She leaves, the lining of her wool skirt making a scratching noise.

All the students are watching now, whispering, laughing. A few are shocked at what I said. Staring at me. These kids are wolves. Any sign of weakness and they descend.

My nonworking fistula for dialysis, a piece of plastic tubing implanted in my inner right arm, itches painfully. I want to rip it out of my flesh. This foreign object, battering me. I try to speak, but my voice has a frog, so I take a tiny sip out of my daily water allotment. The students, these children whose greatest daily obstacle has been which type of sugary cereal to choose for breakfast, snicker. It's an overreaction, but I feel like overturning a table suddenly. "Back to work, all of you!" The sound of my voice echoes in this room, bare of softness, and hurts my eardrums. Thankfully, they all bow their heads and leave me alone.

. . .

HOME. A SIMPLE DINNER of a fried-up hamburger, which I made myself to be low-sodium. Tonight I have dialysis. My bag is already ready with its extra toothbrush and fuzzy slippers; my teaching bag, with ungraded papers, sits on top. I always keep the hospital bag packed, like a perpetually pregnant housewife.

I walk my outdoor rose garden, wandering in and out of the paths, pulling a red metal child's wagon behind me to throw in the detritus. I have my rose gardening gloves on and carry my shears, snipping at random tendrils threatening my feet. Brad has taken care of most of the strays. This is one of his jobs. Easy enough. I itch to be in the greenhouse, tending to the rose for the contest, but at this point there's nothing I can do except wait for its bud to open in bloom later this month, to see what I've got. It's like waiting for a chick to hatch.

Near an American Beauty, that pure red rose, a shoot pushes through the organic mulch. I can't tell if it's rose or weed at the moment. It's just a green shoot. If it's a rose, it's not one I planted, but some unwanted accident that will suck up my real rose's nutrients, choking the roots of the beauty. Which is pretty much the definition of a weed. I could pull it out and start it in its own pot, but who has the time? Heck, if I did that for every possible rose, I would have no more pots left. I yank it out and throw it into the wagon pile and continue on.

I BRING MY photo album of roses to dialysis and sit looking through the photos in the waiting room. Here are all the roses of the past ten years, since I got really serious about my hobbies. The Hulthemias stretch back about six years, when I first discovered them.

One of my favorites is a pink one with a nearly maroon-colored blotch. It's my earliest cross. I called it G21. Nothing particularly special, no fragrance. It was simply the first Hulthemia I had created.

"Those are some roses."

I stiffen. Walters is peering over my shoulder, so close I feel his breath on my scalp. I shut the album abruptly.

"I meant that in a nice way, you know." He ambles away, giving me a wink on his way out.

"Gal," I hear my name called.

On my way to my room, I pass Walters's, that rogue who shouldn't even be on the list. He's chatting up Nurse Gwen, as usual. What is it about him that these women adore? I don't see it. He gives me a dapper little wave, and I fight the urge to flip him off with two middle fingers.

Into the bed I go. Nurse Gwen slides the needle into the plastic graft inside my leg. When my arm shunt got permanently jammed, they switched to the leg, and when that got clogged, they used my jugular for a while. One tube into the machine, one tube out of the machine with the clean blood. It sounds horrific to have a needle jammed into your neck, but after all the years of pricking it's not so bad. The tissue inside, I'm sure, is roughened and scarred.

"You comfortable?" she asks. She reminds me of Flo from Mel's Diner, all brassy blond and pink-lipsticked. Her hands smell of cigarettes and baby powder.

I give her a thumbs-up instead of speaking. She makes the room dark.

These hospital beds are as familiar and comfortable to me as my own. The medicinal scent of the sheets, their rough texture, the plastic bars at the sides. I haven't added it all up, but I've probably spent almost as much time in these beds.

Once, when she was ten, my sister, Becky, fell out of a tree and hit her head. It knocked her out. She awoke in a hospital room. My pediatrician, seeing the name "Garner" appear in the roster, rushed over. For once, it was a different Garner. The doctor asked if she knew where she was. "I'm in Gal's bed," she said.

The pediatrician was sure Becky had a brain injury, until my mother had a realization. "She thinks the hospital is Gal's bed, because Gal's always here."

When my mother tells the story, Becky ignores the point. "So the doctor was relieved it wasn't Gal? Just me?"

"Gal's been through a lot more than you," my mother replies. A well-worn explanation.

In the dialysis room, the sound of my artificial organ lulls me to sleep. I don't even wake up when the blood pressure cuff beeps on anymore.

I awake feeling more or less like the old Gal, which is to say, moderately okay. A normal person like Dara would probably feel like she had the flu, but this is my new normal.

When I get back home, fog covers the rose garden. I haven't looked at the weather report to see if it will clear. I unlock the door. The house air is stale and unpleasant, so I open the kitchen window. The sink holds the dirty dishes from my dinner last night. I should have put them into the dishwasher and wish, out of nowhere, that there was someone to do it for me. I boot up my computer and make myself a cup of tea. In the yard next door, Old Mrs. Allen is out there watering again, though clearly she watered plenty yesterday. "You're gonna kill your precious lawn," I say. She's in a black lacy robe with a thick flannel nightgown peeking out from underneath. I step back before she notices me.

I take a sip of my tea. My mother sent it, though it's central California, not outer Siberia. Mom reads up on herbal remedies and sends me crates of vitamins and supplements that have no scientific research to back them up. I used to tell her it was a waste of money, but now I set the boxes in the teachers' lounge and write "Free" on them. They're always gone by noon. No one ever thanks me.

At my desk, my MacBook, purchased at a sizable discount through the school, tells me I have a new e-mail. My heart pounds a little bit harder. It's probably only an alert from the online rose forum I belong to, telling me I have a new message on my Hulthemia discussion thread, but I'm hoping it's something else. I feel my face cracking into a broad smile, so big and out of the ordinary that it almost hurts. It is. It's Byron.

Byron Madaffer, known in the rose breeding circles as Lord Byron. He lives in Texas, on a many-acre ranch with its own airport. His people were cattle ranchers, but also real estate investors. Now Byron's so wealthy, he doesn't have to bother with cattle. He never has to bother with anything he doesn't feel like bothering with. Instead, he grows roses.

He has already won several Queens of Show, sending rose companies into frenzies to acquire his roses and test them out. The most successful is a pale pink rose with orange tips, called Byron's Flame. It's a delicious-smelling tea rose with long stems. If you've ever gotten a dozen roses for Valentine's Day, you'll notice that they hardly ever smell good, or like anything at all. They might as well be silk. Not Byron's.

It has not, of course, escaped my attention that Byron,

with his assistants, has resources I do not. But he has made me believe I, too, can achieve what he has.

I met him at my first big rose show in Texas six years ago. That year, I competed in an amateur category with what I thought would be a winner: a pink hybrid tea rose with white stripes. I called it Peppermint Candy. The previous year, this rose had won a blue ribbon (though not Queen of Show) at the local rose society show. At the time, I thought I was hot stuff, sure to win every competition I entered. I'd saved up my money to travel to this larger competition. I called a dialysis center to make sure I could attend one day during my three-day trip. Then my little rose and I went to the ballroom at a Hyatt in Dallas and waited for the competition.

Everyone talked to each other and not to me. Nor did I try to talk. I simply sat at my designated table, the number 24 taped to my shirt, and waited for the judges to come around.

Of course, what I didn't know was that dozens of different takes on my rose already existed, most of them a thousand times more refined than mine.

One of the judges took it upon himself to inform me of this fact, his casual cruelty made all the worse by his lack of eye contact and his turning away. "You know there's already a rose with this name?" he said. "Come back when you're ready to compete."

If I had belonged to a rose club, like most rose breeders, chances are I would have known. Someone would have pointed it out.

But the truth is, I don't belong to any rose clubs because I don't want anyone telling me I'm not good enough. The questions I ask in the online rose forum are general; I don't show anyone photos of my flowers. I don't want to hear any negative comments. Besides, I'm a loner with already limited time. At that moment, however, I saw the drawbacks of this choice, and hunched down, wishing the floor would open and swallow me.

Byron, almost hidden behind his big rose display a mere two tables down, stood and stared after the judge. I didn't know who Byron was before that day, but everyone talked about him during the show. His cold reputation preceded him like a nor'easter.

He strode over to me, his blue eyes bright like two flying lights coming at me. The color was all I saw. People did the Red Sea thing to let him through. He stood straighter than anyone I had ever seen. He was James Bond. Only handsomer.

He stood in front of my table. "I heard." He sounded more like he was from England than from Texas.

"You want to get your licks in, too?" I did not bother to stand, playing with the yellow ribbon I'd tied around my poor plastic rose pot. It looked limp and pitiful compared to the giant bows everyone else used.

"I've been looking at your rose all day." His blond eyebrows raised into two pyramids. "The petals are ragged. Is this intentional?"

"I wanted it to be frilly." I glanced up at him. "I like frills."

He was silent, turning the rose around. He sniffed it. "Creative."

I heard the grudging praise in his voice. His smile, when he turned it on, was kind. "Since you appear to be finished for the day, why don't you come to my table? We can talk shop."

At that, he picked up my rose and strode back to his table,

me following behind in his wake, still feeling more lackey than queen.

He pointed to a woman with tiny feet and disproportionately large hips teetering toward us. She looked as though she had been beautiful once, her blond hair artificially shiny, but her jaw was beginning to jowl. She had on a bit too much makeup, the foundation several shades lighter than her neck, which made her look like a circus clown. I wondered if Byron had the same internal judgments going on. "This judge is Ms. Lansing. Theoretically married, insists on being called Miz. Husband and wedding ring never seen. She is always nicer to the men than to women." He inhaled. "Sorry fact of life."

I looked around the hall at the numerous men. More men than women take on this hobby. Lots of scientists and engineers. You have to have a certain kind of personality, and patience for the long-term results. "So she spends a lot of time being nice." I suspected she was especially nice to Byron and his broad shoulders. "Why are you telling me all this?"

"Because you need to know."

Ms. Lansing arrived at our table with a brief disapproving smile directed at me, her face melting as she shook Byron's hand. "My goodness, Byron, your roses are looking well. And so are you, I might add." A creamy chuckle sounded at the back of her throat.

"Not as well as you. A true Texas rose." Byron's formal inflections softened to a Southern drawl. I winced at how thick he was laying it on, but Ms. Lansing blushed. She had it bad for him. I couldn't stifle a laugh, which made her look toward me. "This is Gal," Byron said, with a sweep of his arm.

"New assistant?" Her eyes were back on him. Of course. I was as much competition for a man as an armchair was.

"New competitor. Watch out for her." He stepped back with a little nod as she walked on, his accent changing back. "Schmoozing with judges. Most exhausting part of the day."

After we spent the afternoon discussing my Hulthemia lines, how I postulated I would achieve the perfect Hulthemia and which crosses would be ideal, Byron turned to me. "You're very intuitive."

I blushed from my feet to my scalp. Compliments are rare.

His assistants packed up his roses. He shook my hand and slipped his card into my palm, magicianlike. "Please keep in contact."

I expected he was merely being polite. But he e-mailed me first, finding my contact information on the Internet. There aren't too many people named Galilee.

Now we are e-mail buddies, asking questions of each other, sharing information about our roses. Byron, in another state, did not require regular meetings and socialization of me. He is the one networking contact in the world of roses I've met in person.

He sends me seed specimens of interest, "to grow my collection." I reciprocate. Though I of course always keep my best roses secret, as I am sure he keeps his.

His advice about the judges had paid off. At the next show I attended, I knew to compliment Ms. Lansing on her hideous teal suit. While I didn't win that show, she invited me to listen to a special discussion panel of rose breeders for free.

I open Byron's e-mail. Perhaps he's offering me a job at his ranch, finally opening the full-time official rose business he can well afford.

Got a speckled rose. Want to keep the speckling. Any
suggestions?

He has attached a photo of a magenta Hulthemia with
small white speckles all over its petals. Its center is a deeper
magenta. I frown. It is obvious. Byron has an undergraduate
degree in botany; he's no dummy. He will simply have to try
out another cross and see if the speckling holds; some people think that speckling is due to a virus rather than genet-
ics. He also knows I have several speckled roses, none of
which will reappear consistently for me.

Nonetheless, I do not respond at this time. I want to
double-check myself to be sure I hadn't missed something
obvious. Sometimes I get the impression that he asks me
these questions as a test. With Byron, I am loath to make any
mistakes. If he ever made his operation professional, maybe
he'd hire me.

It's time to go to the greenhouse. I must prepare for
today's class, but since I've taught these classes for several
years, I can wing it. Just give me a dry erase marker and a
roomful of students and I'm good to go. I get up from the
desk and immediately feel woozy. Just low blood pressure
from dialysis. Nothing to worry about, unless, of course, I
pass out and hit my head. In which case there's nothing I can
do. I go into the bedroom and get dressed. I won't remember
I haven't eaten breakfast until noon.

4

I WRITE MY QUIZ PREP ON THE WHITEBOARD. My students, all fifteen sophomores in this fourth-period biology class, are being deliberately obtuse. The hormones are affecting their brains. You really might as well give up education from age twelve to twenty.

It's the simplest thing in the world. I write everything that's going to be on the test up here. Then they are supposed to study it. But somehow, some way, the test always surprises a lot of these kids.

"Please write this on your index cards and study them," I intone to the class. Half of them ignore me. Another quarter break out their cards. The other quarter stare at the board, as though they believe they can memorize twenty pages' worth of material without writing anything. "I promise you, if you know these items, you will get an A on the test."

I sit heavily behind my desk. Already I can tell Dr. O'Malley, the headmaster, is going to want to talk to me again after this quiz. I take off my glasses and rub my eyes. It is said that happiness is directly inverse to intelligence. The dumber you are, the happier you are. Doctors say that having a malfunctioning kidney takes away twenty IQ points.

Today I should be pretty darn happy, because not only do both of my kidneys not work, I'm sporting a raging sinus infection, which I'm sure must take away at least ten more. The classroom is not exactly a sterile environment.

As if on early cue, the intercom buzzes from the office. A tinny female voice says, "Dr. O'Malley needs to see you, Ms. Garner."

"Now? I'm in the middle of class."

Dara knocks, then enters. Today she wears a cream dress that has a sweetheart neckline and full skirt with a crinoline, printed with crimson roses. Her hair is curled and pinned back. She's in 1950s pinup mode. I actually see one of the boys blush, his pronounced Adam's apple moving up and down in a gulp. In my opinion, a high school teacher would be better off wearing a burlap sack. Or, at the very least, skirts down to the ankles, and no makeup. "They sent me to cover for you."

I throw up my hands. "This better be important."

"They didn't tell me a thing."

"It's probably a grouchy parent," I say under my breath. I think I'm being quiet, but the entire back row swivels their heads around. Yes, I'm talking about you, Sean McAllister, I think at the first boy. His mother throws a fit when he gets less than an A minus. The boy never turns in half his homework. He doesn't even have the decency to look away.

Dara shushes me. "Gal."

"You know exactly what I mean." I pick up my purse and my water bottle. I salute Dara. "Good luck. Carry on, kids."

I close the classroom door with a click.

Last winter, the school's headmaster called me into his office one bright Monday morning after the report cards went home. This happened every Monday morning after the parents got the first-semester report cards in the mail on Saturday. I think Dr. O'Malley must have written it into my contract.

Dr. O'Malley had chewed on his yellow pencil, staring out blankly to the parking lot, where students sped off in cars that cost more than my annual salary. "You're too hard," Dr. O'Malley said. "We've had complaints. From parents."

I figured these complainers were the same kids who did not write down all the test topics I posted on the whiteboard before the test, failed the test, then had their parents complain to the principal that I was too hard.

"Too hard?" I asked him. "I wrote down what the final was going to be on! How could that be too hard? It's AP Biology, for crying out loud. Why don't I make all the tests open book?" I did not raise my voice. I hardly ever do, channeling my frustration instead into the hard tone Dara said could pierce metal. "These parents want their kids to learn, don't they? That's why they pay tuition. I don't put anyone through unless they earn it."

Dr. O'Malley ran his hand through his still-thick gray hair. The only Irishman I'd ever seen with a full head of hair after age sixty. His naturally fair skin was a mottled red and brown, the result of his spending his youth on the water. "You can't fail two-thirds of the class."

"I can, if they deserve to fail." I put my hands on my hips and became very quiet. At that first interview, Dr. O'Malley had assured me I would not be beholden to helicopter parents who want to give their kids the world in return for nothing, so when they go to Penn or Wesleyan or all the second-tier Ivy League schools our students usually get into, they will not fail out and come back home because nobody ever made them really work. Unfortunately, Dr. O'Malley had begun to capitulate to parental demands more over the years, as the economy worsened and competition for students became stiffer.

Dr. O'Malley sighed and sat on his desk. Even here, he was a head taller than I. I knew he, and the parents, and the board, all regretted my tenure here. But now there was no way to fire me, not without it looking incredibly bad. Not with me and my bad kidney. The only time this disease has been worth anything, I guess.

I smiled up at him without warmth. "Look, Doc, we go through this every first semester. And every year you seem to forget. By quarter three, the kids are used to me. They buck up. Or their folks hire tutors."

He blew air out through his pursed lips.

"You're slipping," I said. "You're lowering the bar."

"I am not."

"Then let me teach my way. My students graduate, and they go to college and they know how to work. They ought to be thanking me. In fact, many of them have." Every year, I get at least two cards from students off at college, telling me that I saved them from flunking out.

O'Malley closed his eyes. "Let's table this discussion for now, Gal."

Finally. "We always do." I left his office without waiting for him to dismiss me.

TODAY, THROUGH THE headmaster's glass windows, I see a dark head sitting in his guest chair. The blinds are partially closed. Even so, his expression of concern is clear. My heart begins hammering. I immediately think of my sister, my parents. Something must have happened to one of them. My worst fear.

He leaps up and opens his office door. "We have a situation."

So it's not a family emergency. I take a deep breath. It must be a different emergency. I go through all the possible kids who could have complained. There are too many, so I give up. I shuffle inside.

Someone sits in the guest chair opposite O'Malley's desk. It is not a parent out for blood. It's a kid, a teenaged girl, with long dyed black hair and too-white makeup on. Raccoon eyeshadow. She wears a polo shirt, orange with a big pink horse on the chest, the collar turned up like it's 1985, with torn and safety-pinned black jeans, flocked pink Doc Martens, and a black overcoat. She looks like the lead singer of the Cure, by way of Ralph Lauren. I'm reminded of the judge from the rose show for a second, in a weird way. Someone wearing a mask, someone who doesn't want us to see who she really is.

"Who's this? What's going on?"

The headmaster sits down and nods at her.

She lifts a hand covered in silver skull rings and spikes. "Hi, Aunt Gal."

My mouth drops open and I can't close it. Riley? My niece, Riley? A thousand jumbled thoughts go through my head. My voice is calm and emotionless when I speak, though.

"Where's your mother?"

"New York, right now. She's on a business trip. Then they're sending her to Hong Kong for a couple of months." Riley meets my eyes and I expect to see fear, or sadness. Her expression is blank. I imagine she's telling herself that everything is all right, that she is in her happy place. Or perhaps she has simply taught herself to be numb to the aftereffects of her tornado of a mother, like I have for my sister. Anger at her mother blooms anew. How dare she? What was Becky thinking? She wasn't, is the answer. There is no point in asking.

"She took the bus here." Dr. O'Malley runs his hand through his hair. This time I actually see three hairs fall out and feel sorry for him. "From San Francisco."

"That's not too far," I say. This must be a dream. I touch Riley's shoulder and the bony knob feels real. I note the fact that my niece is resourceful under pressure. Good for her.

The headmaster looks at me funny. What I said was odd, I realize. Am I trying to pretend that it's normal for a mother to send her only child across the state alone, without telling the person expecting her?

"I'll call her mother immediately." My voice sounds distant. I wonder if I am in shock, or if it's this sinus infection fog.

I walk around the front of the chair so I can face her. Even when she's seated and I'm standing, she's not that much shorter than I am. The last time I saw her, she was a little girl. Now she's nearly unrecognizable. She used to have dark blond hair that looked exactly like Becky's, and dressed in the ladylike clothes Becky bought for her. Every trace of that innocent has been stamped away.

If I had had a daughter, if Riley had been mine, she would be different. She would not be wearing black clothes and she certainly wouldn't be thousands of miles away from me.

I realize I can't remember Riley's birthday without my calendar. It shames me.

"Riley?" I whisper, unnecessarily.

"Yeah?" She angles her face away from mine.

"It's good to see you." I mean it. I think about hugging her and bend over awkwardly, but she twists away, her head back.

Her eyes, purposefully blank, the same hazel as my sister's, darken into a yellowish green as she lifts her head. "Mom said you knew."

"Knew what?" I am racking my brain.

"She talked to Grandma and set it up." Riley clutches the gray-on-gray Hello Kitty tote bag on her lap.

My parents are in France for the next two weeks. I remember the conversation I had with my mother after my procedure. She had said something about Riley leaving her mom—to stay with her, not me. After their trip to France. Not right now.

Had I agreed to something I didn't remember? I might have been medicated when I spoke with my mother, but she'd never have suggested this. Not with my illness.

"Mom said you said I could come here. Free tuition." She breathes in deeply. Under her overcoat, I see she is painfully thin. Her pale fingers tremble. "I guess Mom got it wrong, huh?"

Free tuition. Yes, there was free tuition for faculty offspring. Or legal wards. Had I mentioned this to Becky, ever? If so, it was in passing. Maybe during a long-ago Christmas conversation, yes, I had said casually, "Too bad she's not mine. She could go to St. Mark's for free." And this was considered an open invitation? Assuming things, as she always did. Taking what she could.

I put my hand on Riley's wrist. God, it's so small I could snap it like a piece of chalk. She's more fragile than I am. What has my sister done to her? She should be growing bone mass to guard against osteoporosis. She needs calcium and vitamin D. "We'll figure it out. I'll take care of it."

"You better go on home for the day." Dr. O'Malley stands. "Gal, do you need anything?" I can tell what he's thinking. Gal's family is completely messed up. Should I call the police? Is Gal able to handle this? His face is all sad basset-hound sympathy. I can't stand it.

Riley stands and she's tall, taller than her mother, at least five-ten. She looks like some kind of preppy vampire hunter in those clothes and that hair. "Thank you very much for your assistance, sir." She holds her hand out to the headmaster and pumps his up and down firmly. She straightens her posture and sets her lips, with their faded dark-red lipstick, firmly in a line. "Thank you, Aunt Gal."

"You're welcome." I'm surprised at her politeness. When you see a kid dressed like her, you expect her to be withdrawn and surly. Maybe I should be the one dressing like that. Get me some tattoos. I wonder briefly if she has any, and decide it's not the right time to inquire.

I wait until we're at my house to call Becky. I hope this is sufficient time to calm my nerves enough to do more than shout at my sister. I am so mad I can feel the wax melting in my ears. I decide to make a list of points I will make to her so I don't leave anything out.

Riley flicks her gaze around my small living room. It's shabbier than what she's used to, I know. "The guest room has a queen-sized bed." I hang my keys on their hook by the door. "Make yourself at home."

She nods, still folded into herself, and curls up on the living room couch.

I go into my bedroom and shut the door, hitting Becky's number. It rings twice before she answers. "Hey, did my girl get there all right?"

For a moment I think I've lost my mind, my sister's voice

is so confident and casual. "Becky, what in the name of all that is good and holy is Riley doing here alone?" There. Not exactly a shout, but not meek either.

"Becca. It's Becca now." She lowers her voice. "I don't understand."

I ignore this. "Becky, I was not expecting Riley. We never talked about it."

"Mom said . . ."

"I don't care what Mom said. Mom's not our go-between. Pick up the phone and call me directly if you want to talk to me." I don't believe for a second our mother agreed to this. It would be entirely out of character. The only thing I can think of is, my mother was distracted by her packing when Becky talked to her, and Becky, as usual, made some very grand assumptions about what I'd do.

The very sound of her breathing hurts my ears. "There's only one little problem. I'm about to board a flight for Hong Kong."

I throw my hands up. "She's your daughter, for crying out loud. You can't dump her someplace."

"I'm not trying to dump her. If I don't go to Hong Kong, I have no job at all." Becky takes a breath. "Listen, if you want, call Mom. I'm sure she'll come home from France and get her."

"Don't make Mom solve all your crap. It's not fair."

"She sure solves yours." Her voice rises again. "She'll be at your side at the drop of a hat if you need her. Not mine."

I take a deep breath of my own. I think of Riley out there on the couch, probably listening to all this. How no one wants her. That can't be good for a kid. "Did you talk to her father?"

She snorts. "Now that is funny. That would do no good.

Besides, living with you in California is a lot better than shipping her off to her wicked stepmother in Boston."

I have nothing to say to this. It is incomprehensible. All of it.

"Listen." She takes on the confident, salesperson demeanor she makes her living with. Nothing can touch her in her bubble. I know I am lost. "Just keep her until I get back, okay? Please? She hasn't seen you in what, a year?"

"More like seven."

"And whose fault is that? The phone works both ways, last time I checked."

Touché, my sister.

Becky continues. "I'll send you a check for her upkeep."

That isn't the point. Though I'll need it.

"Gal? You there?"

"Yeah. I'm here." I forgot I wasn't talking. It's a habit I've developed with my sister. She's useless to argue against.

"All right. I'll call when I get in." I hear a baritone murmuring behind her, probably into her other ear, into her neck. "I gotta go, Gal. Thanks."

The dial tone feels like a slap in the head.

I shouldn't have assumed all was well.

I go into the living room. Riley's staring blankly out the window. I am struck by how fast time has gone. She's almost an adult, fifteen and a half. To me, the period I didn't see her means seven or eight new roses, barely enough time for a new rose success. My perception of time is more geological than human.

Her energy somehow fills up the house, makes it vibrate. It makes me tired, frankly. She stretches and shoots a withering look toward me. "Who doesn't have cable in this day and age?"

"Welcome to the home of the last great cheapskate hold-out." I grin. "No cell phone, either. And dial-up Internet."

"You've got to be joking." She leans forward and rubs her temples with her fingertips. "I guess my mother really is trying to punish me."

"I'm not that bad." I want to point out that at least I have my head screwed on straight, but instead I go into the kitchen. What will I feed her? I never have company. "You hungry? I've got minute steaks."

"No thanks." She follows me into the kitchen, opening the old yellow freezer door with a groan. "Ugh. Frozen peas. Minute steaks. It looks like Grandma's freezer."

Now she's acting more like a regular teenager. The type I'm used to.

I choose the simplest food possible, plus a few extra things in case Dara comes over or Brad looks hungry. "She taught me well." I dig inside. "I might have a frozen burrito."

"Can't we get a pizza?"

I give her a stern look. "Didn't your mother teach you how guests should behave? You eat what's put in front of you." I find the burrito encased in a tomb of frozen water. Bean and cheese. I crack the ice off over the sink and stick it in the microwave. "Take it or leave it, buddy."

"Buddy's what you call boys." She sits at my round glass table, putting her fingers underneath it. Who gets fingerprints on the underside of a glass table?

I sit across from her. "You're just like me. Get cranky when you're hungry."

"It's not because I'm hungry. I'm always like this."

"Oh, good. I've got something to look forward to." I'm teasing, but her expression drops and darkens. Oops. She probably never got teased, the way my father teased me and Becky. I punch her lightly on the arm to show I'm playing.

She winces as though I could actually hurt her. "I didn't want to come, you know. But I had no choice. My mother was like, hey, I gotta go to Asia, and Gram's not home, so you're going to Gal's. Who cares that the school year's almost over? Who cares what I think?" She leans toward me. "You know, she didn't have to take that stupid job. She could have looked for a new job at home."

I lace my fingers together. "Not exactly fair, I suppose."

The microwave beeps. Riley gets up and takes the burrito out, putting it on a plate she pulls out after a second's search. "Want half?"

I shake my head. "I might have salsa in the fridge."

"I'm not a bad student, you know." She retrieves the salsa and sits down again across from me, wrinkling her nose. "This expired last year."

"Expiration dates are relative." I sniff at it. Still smells like salsa. No mold. It's all those preservatives. I throw it away to appease her. "What's your favorite subject?"

She takes a bite of the burrito, careful of its heat, and does not speak until she is through chewing. "Art."

"Art. That's nice." I'll have to put her in Dara's class. If she stays long enough to enroll. But what else am I going to do with her, even if I have her just three weeks? She can't sit here alone. "Science is where it's at for girls, though. This country needs more female scientists. Heck, more scientists in general."

She chews, her bored expression speaking volumes.

"Come on. You can be good at whatever you want to be." My standard rah-rah teacher speech, mostly aimed at girls whose scientific and mathematical aims got squashed some-place south of the sixth grade, when they didn't get to be on the Lego robotics team.

"I didn't say I wasn't good at science. I said art was my favorite." She has finished her burrito.

"You'll have to meet my friend Dara. Miss Westley. She's the art teacher."

"I probably won't take art, though." She swipes her mouth with the napkin, leaving a swath of darkness.

I wait for her to continue and she doesn't. "Miss Westley is an excellent teacher."

"They always make you do the art like they want it to be done, and then I get marked down for doing it my way."

I'm not entirely sure what she's talking about. I haven't attempted a real piece of art since I threw out my Crayolas in second grade. My rose sketches hardly count. "I'm sure Miss Westley wouldn't do that to you."

"Yeah. Never mind." She gets up and puts her plate in the sink. "I suppose you don't have a dishwasher, either?"

I decide not to press her about the art. I'm a biology teacher, not a guidance counselor. I point to the dishwasher. "I do like some technology."

She puts the dish in the appliance. "I'm going to hang out in my room."

Good idea. There are purple bags under her eyes that are not a result of the otherwise heavy cosmetics. "Better wash off that makeup first. And you know you can't wear it to school."

"I figured." She slumps off into the bathroom. I hear the shower turn on. I hope she doesn't use my towel. I can't have other people's germs rubbing off on me. It's hard enough avoiding them at St. Mark's.

I sit back in my chair, feeling tired even though it's supposed to be one of my good days. I should probably call my mother on her cell phone in France and discuss what to do with Riley and my sister, but the thought of that makes me feel like I need to go to bed for the next thousand years.

Besides, I don't want to disturb my parents. I know, even if I tell my mother not to, she will cut her vacation short. No one has perished. No one is even ill. This is a momentary bump.

I can handle this.

I have to go out and see if a rose I prepared a few days ago is ready to give me its pollen. It's not something I can skip, nor do I want to. The thought of the greenhouse reinvigorates me. "I'll be out in the yard!" I call to Riley's closed door, and get a muffled response.

I pull on a sweater and go outside. Immediately, the air and the scent of grass and roses and pollen makes me feel better. I count my blessings that I don't have allergies.

My neighborhood is covered in shade trees of varying heights, spreading out as far as I can see, which is not very far, considering the tall houses blocking the view in my suburb. The greenhouse air is balmy and dense, tropical compared to the dry California air. I pull up my stool, turn on my worklight, and consider the anthers in the plastic cup I pulled out a few days earlier. The pollen has built up and looks like orange dust on the anthers.

Meanwhile, the mother plant's stigmas have gotten sticky, ready to receive the pollen. I transfer the pollen to the stigma. Now all I can do is hope for the best.

I go look at the plants I've grafted onto rootstock. These are the plants I've hybridized successfully and am now propagating. Propagating is different from breeding. It's creating more specimens of the rose you want to keep. To propagate, you could also cut off a six-inch stem of the parent at a forty-five degree angle and dip it into some rooting powder. Then you stick it into soil and hope it roots.

There are about twenty-five of the propagated plants in plastic pots, set up on wooden benches. All of these have buds. These are also wait-and-see. Most other regions in the country don't have blooms until June; in California, the outdoor roses start blooming around April, sometimes earlier.

I remember Byron's question. I'll go ahead and send him my answer. For best results, he needs to go back two generations maternally, and use the mother he had then instead of the mother he's using now. I think.

THE GREENHOUSE DOOR OPENS, and I jump a little. I hadn't heard anyone coming. Dara stands there, looking concerned. "What on earth happened to you? Dr. O'Malley showed up and took over. He wouldn't say anything. Just said you and your family were 'physically' all right."

"I am." I write "G101" on a paper tag and tie it around the new rose I've pollinated. "It's my niece. She's here."

"Riley is here?" Dara knows all about Riley and Becky. Dara shakes her head. "Is your sister here, too?"

"Becky is not. Becky's on her way to Hong Kong for her job, apparently." I put the rose back in its proper place, the best seat in the house. "She sent Riley here."

"She can't do that." Dara's voice rises. "She can't drop her kid off and expect you to pick up the pieces."

"That would be expecting my sister to be reasonable. And you cannot expect that from Becky." I stand. "Let's go inside. You can meet her. She loves art, but she hates art class."

"I'll change her mind." Dara follows me in. "Your class behaved well, if you were wondering."

"Of course they did. They're never bad. Just lazy."

Dara laughs. "Spoken like someone on tenure."

"You know I only speaketh the truth. I'm the Oracle of St. Mark's." I take a minute steak out of the freezer, suddenly ravenous. "Want one?"

"No thanks. You should eat leaner meat."

"So they tell me." I take out a frying pan.

"Why don't you sit down and let me cook?"

"I'm fine." Dara is sweet, but sometimes too overbearing. Like my mother. However, if it weren't for Dara, my mother would have far more episodes where she decides to fly up in the middle of the night based on a hunch that I'm sick or needy.

"Anyway, there's more news." Dara sits up, her face lit. "Dr. O'Malley hired a chemistry teacher."

"About time." We've been interviewing candidates forever. At least, since last year. "Which one did he pick?"

"A new guy. Comes from a chemical company in San Luis Obispo." She shrugs. "Everyone's talking. Seems like a step down for someone like him. Step down in pay for sure. And it's not like we live in a glamorous city."

"That is interesting." I flip the steak out onto a plate. Teachers at our school are underpaid, earning even less than public school teachers. "We'll see how long he lasts. At least he can help coach the Science Olympiad team."

I had volunteered to coach Science Olympiad after my first year, because I didn't like how the old coach had done things and our team had come in next to last place for three years in a row. Not a very good showing for a private school.

The team is supposed to have two coaches, one in life

science and one in physical. Ms. Maseda, the physics teacher, dropped out this year. She's close to retirement and suffers from a variety of physical ailments. Plus, she kept falling asleep during the after-school meetings. We made quite the decrepit motley pair, she and I, showing up to meets with one good kidney between the two of us. But we did place third last year.

Sometimes my mother worries about me taking on too many activities. The truth is, the more a patient like me does, the better. All of this keeps me going.

"You're so cynical."

I don't think I'm cynical at all. If I were, I would have given up long ago. "I expect the worst, but hope for the best."

Dara shifts and glances toward the closed bedroom door. "Riley must be exhausted."

"She's slept long enough. I should get her up. Otherwise she won't be able to get to sleep tonight."

"Teenagers sleep. Haven't you seen them in your class?"

"Ha ha."

Dara stands. "I've got to go. I just wanted to stop in and see if you were all right. Let me know if you need more help."

"Going on errands?" I hope she is, so she can get me a gallon of milk. I might even need to dust off my Costco membership if Riley's going to be staying with me. Stock up on soda and chips.

"Nope. Got a date."

A pang of jealousy stabs pitifully at me. I squash it. Just because I haven't had a date in, oh, ever, doesn't mean my friend can't. I'd had more pressing things to worry about, like whether or not I'd survive my teens. "I hope it's not the mechanic. He smells like brake fluid and cigarettes." She has no steady, that Dara; none of them are right for her. Even the ones I'd settle for, she finds some fault with. Heck, any woman would settle for a lot of these guys, the ones who don't drink, who have steady jobs and hold the door open for her and remember to give her roses on her birthday. Someone's always not artistic enough, or not romantic enough, or likes watching sports a little too much. Or he talks too little or too much.

"Not seeing him anymore." Dara winks at me, checks her hair in the white framed mirror by the door. "This is the accountant. Chad. He has excellent hygiene."

"Good." I brighten. "I need help with my taxes."

"He works for a corporation. He's not H&R Block."

"Useless. Dump him."

She doesn't take me seriously. "Remember to feed Riley a vegetable at dinner. I know you don't have many."

"I've got some cans in the pantry."

"Frozen are better than canned."

"She will live."

Dara leaves. I stand at Riley's door, debating whether to knock. I am seized with the urge to peek inside, see whether she's breathing, like a parent home with a newborn. No. Let her sleep.

The contents of her backpack are spread across the coffee table. A Neil Gaiman novel. Some comic books with wide-eyed Japanese characters. A black Moleskine sketchbook, like the kind Dara uses. I flip it open. I expect to see depictions of death, skulls and crossbones, and bottles of poison. Instead, there are dancing cupcakes. Big-eyed cartoon animals. Close-ups of flowers—daisies, a few roses. Very good.

The last is a pen-and-ink portrait. I recognize Becky immediately. It is drawn from above. She is on a pillow, asleep, her mouth open, her long hair spread out as though she is underwater. Fine lines crease at her eyes and between her brows in a frown. Her mouth is open and a trail of drool coming out onto the pillow. If it hadn't been for the drool and the pillow, I would have thought she was drowning. I have to give it to Riley. It is realistic.

Riley leans against the doorjamb. "Are you looking through my stuff?"

"Just this." I shut the notebook. Was I not supposed to look at art? Is that like looking through a journal? I'll have to ask Dara. "Don't leave it out if you don't want people to see it."

She harrumphs and slinks forward to grab her backpack. She's one of those kids who walks along with a slouch, her eyes trained to the floor as though she expects land mines.

I try a compliment. "You're an excellent artist, Riley. You must get it from Grandma."

She rubs sleep out of her eye, smearing eyeliner.

I cluck. "Didn't you wash that off in the shower?"

"I need makeup wipes." She wipes her finger on her sweat pants. "Don't worry. It's hypoallergenic."

"I was more concerned about mascara stains on my pillowcases." I fish a pot of cold cream out of my dresser drawer and hand it to her.

She stares at it like it's a rattlesnake.

I place it on the dresser top. "St. Mark's only allows lip gloss. And I agree."

"I like to express myself. I suppose you've never tried it." Riley picks up the cold cream.

"Everything I need is up here." I tap my temple. "Not on the outside."

"My appearance is a manifestation of my personality."

Riley heads into the bathroom. "I thought you, with your roses, could understand that."

I'm kind of impressed by her use of the word "manifestation." "I suppose I do understand. But roses can't help how they look."

"Because you make them look how you want." She shuts the door.

I HEAD OUTSIDE, intending to lock up the greenhouse. The air is cooling. A gnat buzzes by my face. As I walk to the greenhouse, my clogs crunching on the path, I hear a noise from the roses. To my surprise, Brad is in the garden, pulling weeds on his hands and knees. I'm more surprised to see how many weeds I'd missed. "Hey, Miss Garner." He isn't surprised to see me, on the other hand. He pushes his floppy hair out of his face. The boy hasn't broken a sweat though his wheelbarrow is full.

"Brad. I didn't know it was your day to come. Were you here earlier? I was just outside." How had I missed him, squatting in the bushes?

"Just got here."

I accept this. "Have you heard from any colleges yet?" Brad plays football and baseball, but our school is too small for scouts to bother. Instead, I've advised him to apply for science scholarships, ones for children of veterans and first-generation college students, and whatever else I've ever seen cross my path.

He shakes his head. "Not yet. Ms. Garner? I can't come tomorrow. Practice. So I came tonight to work."

"I have dialysis tomorrow night. Who's going to water the greenhouse?" Tomorrow is their day for watering.

Most people would suggest watering today instead, but Brad knows better. These roses need water when they need it, not sooner and not later. Otherwise you can kill them. "I can get my dad to come."

I think of Brad's dad, the school janitor, heading here after his long hours of cleaning up after the private school kids, some of whose weekly allowances are more than his pay. Mine too. I don't want Brad's dad to do it. "I'll think of something else." Dara, maybe. Or Riley. Of course. Riley's here.

"Riley!" I bellow toward the house. I have a really loud voice for someone so small. It's the kind of voice that cuts through all other noise and chatter. Dara says when I try to whisper, it's louder than most people's regular volume. Never try to gossip with me quietly in public. Everyone will hear.

Riley comes out, her face scrubbed clean of makeup, her dyed hair bound in a neat ponytail. Wearing her Abercrombie sweats with a pink Abercrombie T-shirt, at last she looks more like the niece I remember, more like a little girl, the opposite of what she wants. "Giving that company plenty of free advertising, I see."

"Yeah, yeah." She nods at Brad, who finally gets up from his weeding.

"This is your niece?" Brad wipes his hand on his jeans. "I'm Brad." He smiles in a friendly way, but she kind of looks off to the side again and offers her hand back, floppy as a fish.

"Did the kids talk about it today?"

"You better believe it."

Kids always know more than the adults do when it comes to gossip. "Riley, come here. I'm going to show you how to water the roses tomorrow night."

She nods once, reluctantly. "Um, yeah. Don't I just turn on the hose?"

"They have to be watered the right amount. And they'll need food, so we have to use the sump pump." I consult my rose book, Winslow Blythe's *Complete Rose Guide*. Blythe is an octogenarian rose grower who's written volumes of works. Sometimes I modify what he does, but he often has some good detail. If it weren't for him, I would have used pesticide at full strength on my new blooms, burning them.

"Wait a second." She disappears into the house.

Brad raises his eyebrow at me. "Guess you have your hands full."

It's such an adult thing to say, but typical from Brad. "Do me a favor tomorrow. Help her find her way around."

"Yeah. No problem."

She hasn't reappeared. "Riley!" I yell.

"I needed my shoes. Sheesh." She has put on a jacket. The sky is darkening.

Brad follows us into the greenhouse. I could tell him to run along home, but I figure he'll have something helpful to say. Riley barely deigns to acknowledge either of us.

I get out the measuring pitchers and show her the rose food. I show her how to use the sump pump, sticking one hose into the rose-food mixture and the expelling end out over the roses. "Don't forget to plug it in."

Riley crosses her arms over her. Her stomach grumbles audibly. It's been hours since that burrito. I've got to get her dinner. "So. Is that it? Each plant gets water? What a revelation."

Apparently sarcasm runs in our family. I change the subject, pointing to one of my speckled red Hulthemias. Not unlike the one Byron has. "What do you think about this plant?"

She screws up her nose. "The spotting makes it look diseased."

Brad snorts.

"Thank you for your opinion." I decide to e-mail Byron about it.

"It's true."

Brad scribbles something down in the notebook on the table. "The formula." He rips the page off and sticks it onto the tack board above.

"I can remember. Three cups of food. Water to the line." Riley glances around as if seeing the room for the first time. Her lips purse. "I knew you did this, Aunt Gal, but I didn't know you were so, like, into it."

"It's pretty much her whole life." Brad sits on the stool and assesses my niece. I believe the term is "checking her out." I frown at him, but to my relief Riley does not notice.

"Cool." Her tone says it's anything but. "So, uh, can we go eat?"

I glance toward Brad. He nods. "I'll lock up after I put away the wheelbarrow."

"Thanks." I point to my car. "McDonald's all right?"

"Not really, but I'll eat it."

"Good job not complaining." I unlock the car.

Brad stands in the driveway, waving to us as though he owns the place. Of course he does. He spends so many hours here. If I'm home, I feed him chicken nuggets or pizza rolls and give him soda. I'm like his aunt. But for some reason I feel peculiar. Uneasy. It must be because of Riley and how he looked at her. I'll have to be careful with her. Teens and their hormones. My own were too weakened by illness to torment me.

"Do you have a boyfriend back home?" I said.

"No, I do not. Did not. I don't want one." She crosses her arms. In profile, in this burgeoning evening, I could mistake her for Becky. I don't tell her that, guessing my sister probably isn't Riley's favorite person at the moment, as she is not mine. In school, teachers would ask if I was related to Becky, and I'd always say, "Yes, but only by blood." They would laugh every time. It wasn't long before they discovered I was the studious one.

"That's good. Keep it that way until you're forty."

"How old are you?"

"Thirty-six. That must be why I don't have one yet." I laugh.

"Your jokes are as corny as Grandpa's." She relaxes visibly, stretching her long legs out in my space-limited compact vehicle.

"I learned from the best." We pull into McDonald's.

5

In the morning, I have my tea in the kitchen, listening to the unfamiliar sounds of Riley getting ready. It involves a lot of banging doors and running water and loud music. Finally she appears, and I nearly spit out my tea in surprise. Her hair is in a French braid, and she didn't re-apply her makeup. No makeup at all, in fact, which makes me see the dark circles haven't yet entirely disappeared from under her eyes. A plain white blouse and navy blue pants complete the look.

"I'll get you some official uniforms today." I nod. "Very good, Riley." In time, I hope her dark circles will disappear. If she stays on with me. I'm a terrible fuddy-duddy. So is Grandma, but grandmothers are expected to be, not aunts. Grandma is also generous with giving out pocket money.

"I told you I wasn't an idiot."

Ah, but the attitude hasn't changed. "I never said you were."

"You implied it."

"Good vocabulary, too." I refuse to argue with her. "Take

a compliment when you can get it. You'll soon find out I rarely give them."

At school, I buddy Riley up with my female Brad equivalent: Samantha Lee. Brad would of course be my first choice, but he seemed a little bit too taken with Riley for my comfort. So a girl it has to be.

Samantha has long straight hair, naturally blue-black given her Chinese heritage, that she always wears pulled back, even on the weekends when I see her around town with her equally fastidious parents. "I am the Asian stereotype," she told me once last year. "Good grades, good girl."

"That's what you should be in high school." I liked her immediately. "Stereotype or not. I wish all the kids were like you."

Samantha and Riley eye each other nervously. "Ready?" Samantha says. She actually appears more frightened than Riley, whose reputation probably precedes her, now that I think about it. The girl with the troubled mother who just shipped her kid off on a bus, appearing out of nowhere in the middle of the school year. Of course kids are going to talk about Riley. She's the new bad girl. The one Samantha's parents probably won't even let her hang out with. Though they might because Riley is associated with me.

The transcripts from Riley's old high school arrived this morning. Let's just say Riley isn't working up to her potential. Even in P.E., she got marked down two grades for "refusing to wear uniform."

I am more than a little concerned that a kid who tested into the gifted and talented program has not had an advanced class since the sixth grade. Normally, St. Mark's wouldn't let in such a subpar student. But Riley's not a normal case. I tell Dr. O'Malley I'll whip her into shape.

AT LUNCH, I think about going into the student cafeteria to see how Riley's doing, and decide to leave her a bit of time first. Time to integrate without Aunt Gal breathing down her neck. For some reason, these students are against having relatives come to school. My parents never embarrassed me. But then, as my mother says, I was born to be old.

Dara sits beside me. Today she's wearing a yellow shirt-dress, belted at the waist, with a ridiculously full skirt. Her lips are painted coral, which she carefully blots before taking a bite of her egg salad sandwich.

"Are you wearing a crinoline?" I say, seeing the out-of-place piece of netting poking out from underneath. "When you go retro, you really commit."

"You know you're so jellies." This is her cutesy way of saying "jealous." Some kind of young-person slang Dara tries to stay connected with. I don't even bother. She touches my arm. "Check out the new chemistry teacher."

"Where?" I swivel around. "I don't see him."

"Shush! Keep your voice down."

"Is that him at three o'clock?" I am pointing. He glances our way. Dara gives a little shriek and bats my hand down.

"You're worse than the kids." I appraise the man candidly from our position. "He's bound to look over here at some point, anyway."

He definitely looks like Dara's type, with a dark beard and a sort of pompadour swoop over the top of his head. He wears an aqua-colored button-down, sleeves rolled up, and a pair of black slacks with black and white saddle shoes. He is in reasonably good shape, a bit beefy, but solid.

He glances my way and his cheeks dimple into a grin in the bare spots of his beard. I grin back and feel a silly flush on my face. He is definitely Dara's type, I say to myself. Not mine. If anyone was my type it would be someone like the history teacher, who unfortunately has been married for fifteen years. I mean, unfortunate for me. Not him. I am disgusted at my muddle-headedness.

I nudge Dara. "Looks like the universe just plopped a husband into your lap."

She breathes in and out noisily. "He's a little short."

He's a head taller than me. He's probably the same height as Dara, maybe even a little bit taller than she is. She likes giants so she can wear heels. "Not really. But you know what they say about short men."

"No. What do they say about short men?" Dara takes a sip from her coffee mug.

"I don't know. I was hoping you did." I waggled my eyebrows at her.

She laughs.

"Hello."

It's him. He's standing over us. "Is this seat taken?" He places his hand over the plastic seat next to me. His eyes are puppy dog brown, with long black lashes and black eyebrows.

"It is now." I slide it away from the table with my foot. "I'm Gal Garner."

"George. Morton." He shakes my hand and sits.

"This is Dara," I say, all but forcing her to hold her hand out.

She swallows her coffee. "Art department."

"Excellent. And you?"

"Biology." I push my glasses up against my face.

"Biology and chemistry. Sister subjects," he says.

I shrug. "I think all subjects are sisters, don't you?" I point to Dara. "She's developing a cross-curricular program. Science and art."

"Really?" He turns toward Dara, who nods and gives me a little glare. Pushy Gal. But hey, she's not getting any younger, and she needs to move fast before Ms. Schilling from mathematics snaps him up with her red hair and slinky pantsuits. She is already eyeballing him. And she's short enough to be interested.

I wonder what has brought him here to this small school in the middle of nowhere in particular. To leave his old and probably highly paid position in research. But maybe he was called to teaching. Some are.

He is eating a wrapped sandwich from the cafeteria, reminding me I should poke my head in and see what Riley's up to. Avocado and turkey. The avocado is a little brown.

"The pizza's the best thing on the menu." I throw my trash into my lunch sack. "They cook it off-site."

He laughs, and it's a pleasant one. Thank goodness. I hate whinnying laughs. "Thanks for the advice."

"Let me know if you need any supplies. I'm in charge of that." I stand up. "Mr. Morton, nice to meet you."

"Call me George."

"I hardly know you well enough."

"Gal's old-fashioned. Like 1850 old-fashioned," Dara says.

"One of my many charms." I wink at them both. "Have a good lunch, kids."

I walk off, leaving them to their talk. When I use my back to open the door, I look back. They are talking, Dara's hand tangles and swirls in her hair, her sure sign of flirting. For some reason, I feel a pang. But it's just like the coffee. It's not good for me. So I avoid it.

I spot Samantha sitting with her usual suspects. The kids from the math team, the debate club, the community service club. All the clubs designed to get you into college. And where I want Riley to be sitting.

Finally I see Riley at a table in the far corner of the room. She's eating with Dr. O'Malley. Her art notebook is open before them. He laughs at something Riley says.

Two minutes at this school and she's winning over my boss. I don't know if I should be jealous or thank her. "I knew if I left you alone, you'd fall in with the wrong crowd." I sit down.

"Hi, Aunt Gal." Riley waves. She looks happy. No. More than happy. Sparkling. Much happier than she'd looked this morning.

"Riley was just telling me about your roses," Dr. O'Malley says. "I didn't know you breed them. I thought you just grew them."

"Aunt Gal has come up with brand-new roses," Riley says.

"You should have your biology class do a rose project." Dr. O'Malley leans toward me. This is the most interest the man has ever shown in anything I've done. Always, he's been open and friendly with the other teachers. Dara's even had Christmas Eve dinner at his house, helped his wife bake cookies. He's been known to take the Student Scholars of the Month to get frozen yogurt, to allow himself to get pie in the face at the annual carnival (I buy plenty of tickets to that). But to me, he's been only businesslike and formal. I've always gotten the feeling I'm a worry to him. A burden.

I nod at the Doc. "That would be impossible. It's not part of the curriculum. And I have to teach to the curriculum." My voice shakes with annoyance. He knows this. I can't just do whatever I want in class.

"True, true. Not always my choice, you know." Dr. O'Malley looks considerably cheerier than he had yesterday. He pats Riley on the shoulder. "Nice kid, Gal. And quite the artist. Miss Westley will have a field day with her."

I can take no credit for Riley. But I nod and thank him.

"Let me know if you need help with the guardianship. I did it before, when we took care of one of my nephews." Dr. O'Malley puts his trash on the tray.

"Guardianship?"

"Legal guardianship. Her mother signed a form. It's in with her school records. You just have to sign and turn it into the courts."

Legal guardianship. It sounds so dreadfully official. Of course I would need that officialness. But I feel uneasy. Just how long is Becky planning to be gone?

I'm also a little surprised that Becky remembered to do something official. Of course, she's not totally irresponsible, or she wouldn't be able to hold a job at all.

I glance at my niece, who is nibbling at a green apple slice. It's hard to believe, only yesterday I was not responsible for another human being. Actually, being responsible for me counts as two, or three, people, so what's one more?

Dr. O'Malley bids us good-bye. I turn to Riley. "How did you do that?"

"Do what?" She drinks her milk, leaves her green apple on the tray. "I was sitting here alone, and he came over and talked to me."

"Eat your fruit." I change the subject. "What happened to Samantha?"

Riley pops the rest of the green apple in her mouth and swallows without chewing. "She's not as great as you think, Aunt Gal."

"Really?" I glance toward Samantha, who is looking guiltily our way. "How so?"

"I cannot say without breaking a confidence." She looks pointedly the other way, where Brad is holding court with his friends. He feels her eyes on him and waves. She purses her lips.

"No one's hurt or in trouble?" I prod.

She shakes her head.

"In that case, a confidence is okay." I get up as the bell rings. "I guess I'll let you make your own friends, then."

Her lips twist and she shrugs. I know what she's thinking. What does it matter, if neither of us knows how long she'll stay, or when her mother will get another bug and come back as suddenly as she left? I reach across the table to squeeze her hand. She drags hers away, into her lap.

AFTER SCHOOL, I host a tutoring session for some of my struggling sophomores. This I do in spite of the fact it's my night for dialysis and my blood feels extra, extra unclean, like it's been a week instead of two days since my last visit.

In addition, I have received a message from Dr. Blankenship, left on my answering machine at home and accessed when I called to check it just now. "The MRA tests were inconclusive. We need to discuss the IVP option."

I nearly throw the phone across the room.

Dr. Blankenship believes that my IVP dye allergy is psychosomatic, despite many doctors believing otherwise. She cites one study to me all the time. In it, researchers took people who said they were allergic to IVP dye and those who weren't. They gave IVP dye to both. No one had reactions any worse than the ones they'd had before. If they were truly allergic, the study authors argued, their reactions would be worse.

I consider the study unethical. I mean, who takes people whose throats close up and puts the same allergy-causing substance back into them? Just because a study is conducted at a university by MD's doesn't mean it's foolproof. This is where Dr. Blankenship and I disagree, on the fallibility of physicians like herself. *One* of the points where we disagree, I should say.

There are some doctors who know they are not infallible, who take in all the available information and make sound decisions based on the individual patient. Dr. Blankenship, while having a high success rate with transplants, has a fatal flaw: she thinks going to medical school makes you something akin to a god. In her mind, her reading of a study is more correct than mine.

But I'm the one who has lived in this body, not her. I'm the one who has to live with what she does. After all these years of dealing with doctors, I've seen plenty of mistakes made.

If I don't speak up, no one will.

I would switch doctors if I could. But my limited health plan, and the limited hospital where we are, means she is my only option.

I have to put it out of my head.

The after-school students trudge in. All of them want to be elsewhere. I can't blame them. I'd rather be elsewhere, too.

Riley is standing at the doorway, having stopped by as I'd instructed her, unwilling to put a foot in the room. I ask her if she wouldn't like to stay and get some extra help, too, considering she's missed most of this year.

"I'll go work at the library until you're done. I didn't go to school in outer space, you know. I know things." Riley dismisses me.

"With those grades, you could have fooled me."

"An outer space school would probably be better, because the aliens would have better technology." Riley's backpack looks as though it will topple her.

I smile at her logic. "Unless it's a school in one of our space stations. But you're right. You would probably have to be a superstudent to go to school in outer space." I take my wheeled plastic cart that I use to carry my books to and from the car and give it to her. "Use this. Your backpack's going to kill you."

"Are you trying to make everyone hate me, for real?"

"Of course. I think that's in the parent-figure job description." I grin as the sophomores come into the room, pushing past Riley. "Ask any one of them."

"It's true." It's Brad. Not a sophomore. His hair looks just-washed and slicked back. "I'll drive her, if you want."

I blink at him. "I thought you had practice."

"Tonight." He hefts Riley's backpack as though it's nothing. "You want to go?"

I look toward my niece. I still can't figure out why she doesn't like Brad, except that he thinks she's attractive. She is fifteen, after all; boys will like her. I trust him absolutely. Maybe she likes him, too, and that's why her limbs collapse together like acute angles on a geometry proof gone wrong. It's certainly basically how I'd always reacted to men I liked.

By ignoring them. "Would you like to stay here, walk to the library, or get a ride from Brad?"

Brad moves to reassure her, avoiding eye contact. "It's all right. Samantha's going, too. I am an excellent driver. Your aunt checked."

This is an exaggeration. I don't check driving records of my household helpers. Just criminal records.

There are six students waiting for my help. "Riley? Make a decision."

"I can't." She sounds like she's three.

"If you don't learn to make decisions, they will be made for you. And you might not like the decision made. You have until zero." I begin counting down from ten. "Ten, nine, eight . . ."

She jerks her head toward Brad. "I'll go with him."

I smile. "Wait for me at the library. I'll pick you up when I'm done."

6

MY TUTORING SESSION ENDS AFTER AN HOUR. These students need review and repetition more than anything else. I get out microscopes and slides and have them make flash cards about the cell division stages we'll be having on a test soon, drawing out mitosis and meiosis in color pencil, and telling them they will have to identify each stage on their own.

The halls are deserted. Many of us stay after to prep or tutor, but a fair number also sprint out ahead of the students at the last bell. Unlike many schools in California, such as where I grew up, this one is enclosed and air-conditioned. Besides the heat that peaks in the fall, we also have occasional bad air-quality days.

I am going to Mr. Morton's room. Tomorrow the Science Olympiad team meets, and I will ask him to be the other coach. Though he is brand-new and he could be the worst teacher on the planet for all I know, I cannot handle the team alone anymore. Last month, I had to cancel two practices due to my own illness.

Though I was fine moments before, I shiver and pull my

cardigan closer around myself. It's too cold in here with all the students gone. My heart rate increases. I realize I am nervous about asking him to help out.

He is, thankfully, by himself. When I spring upon teachers who think they're alone in the building, sometimes I see things I wish I hadn't. I have seen Mr. Tang the history teacher trimming his nose hair, Ms. Schilling the math teacher sitting at her desk with her pants unbuttoned and soft belly poking out, and Brad's father, the janitor, singing into his mop as he danced the hallways. I would have made a great cat burglar, because not one of these people knew I was coming, though I made no effort to disguise my footfalls.

One of these late afternoons, I'm afraid I'll come across a couple of teachers in flagrante delicto. I had half expected to see Mr. Morton in here with Dara.

"Hey, there, Ms. Garner." Mr. Morton runs a hand through his chestnut hair and stretches, his arms high in the air. Student papers are spread out before him. On the whiteboard behind him are equations I'm happy to see make sense. His classroom looks neat and organized, bins holding worksheets and books not askew, all pencils in their jars.

"Miss will do." I sound prim, even to my own old-fashioned ears. "Call me Gal."

"Oh, really?" He gets up from behind his desk and comes around to stand in front of me. His gaze is warm. I mean, I think it's literally warm, because my cold has evaporated. "Does that mean you'll call me George?"

"Not unless I slip up." I clear my throat. "I have come bearing a proposition."

His brow wrinkles.

"A good proposition, don't worry." I feel myself blush. "I want to ask you to be the other science team coach. One afternoon a week, a couple of Saturdays as we get closer to the tournament. Twenty-four or so kids. What do you think?"

"I was going to volunteer if you didn't ask." He claps. "Hell, yeah, I'll do it."

"Language, Mr. Morton." I relax back into my teacher role. "This is a Catholic school. You can't say the double hockey sticks word around here."

"Sorry." He leans against the desk, chastised as a student. I feel a bit sorry for telling him to watch his mouth. I notice his shoulders are wide and firm, his belly slightly paunchy. He probably doesn't worry about working out every second of the day. I wonder what he does like to do in his spare time.

Before we can get into any other sort of conversation, the cell phone on his desk buzzes. Dara's photo glows on the touch screen. He glances at it. He already has her picture in the phone.

"I have to go. You should answer it." I waggle my finger at him. "Dara doesn't like to be kept waiting."

"I'll see you tomorrow." He lifts a hand to me, reaching for his phone simultaneously. I am forgotten before I step out of the classroom.

THE LIBRARY IS NEARLY EMPTY when I look for Riley. Not only is it empty, it's empty of my Riley. The librarian doesn't think she's seen her, but then so many kids from all the schools go there, I can't possibly know if that's true or not.

I get back in the car and drive home. I am only ten minutes late for pickup, having stopped by the grocery store to stock up on frozen foods and vegetables for her, which now melt in the car. Where's my niece? Maybe she went out for a walk. Maybe she got kidnapped. Maybe Brad convinced her to go out for a burger. Why am I too cheap to have a cell phone? No more. That will be priority one. Matching cell phones.

This is why my mother has gray hair.

Riley is fifteen. And with Becky for a mother, I'd wager Riley's been taking care of herself for a long, long time. Neither of us is used to having someone around to be accountable to.

Heck, did I even go over rules with her? Come to think of it, do I even have any rules? No, but she should have common sense. I did. Hopefully that got Darwinized through our genes.

At home, I get a leftover burger patty out of the refrigerator and sit on the couch, too tired to get up and turn on the television. A couch spring sticks into my hip. Darn old furniture. The sun goes down on the other side of the house, so the living room is already dim.

I fall asleep on the couch. I don't know how much time passes before the front door opens and closes. "Aunt Gal? Why are you sitting here in the dark?" Riley flips on the light. Outside I hear a muffler roar and a car drive off. Brad.

"You weren't at the library. I couldn't find you." I mean to raise my voice, but I'm too tired. "Where were you?"

"With friends from school." She slinks toward her room.

"With Brad?"

Riley looks down. "We went to Samantha's house. Then Brad gave me a ride home. We were studying."

"Were Samantha's parents home?" I recall that they both work.

She looks right at me. "Yes."

I look at the clock. Eight. I was supposed to pick her up at five. Her eyes are clear, the whites of her eyes white, not red.

She doesn't smell of anything illegal. Her steps are steady. Her clothing is not askew. I don't think she's telling the whole truth, but I decide to let this slide. "I'm glad you're making friends."

"Mmm." Riley retreats into her room.

"Get your homework done?" I call.

"Yeah."

Something else occurs to me, something I've never worried about, but should have. I have to be at the dialysis center at nine and won't be home until morning. I go into her room. Other than her suitcase, it doesn't look like she's living here. "I'm sleeping at the dialysis center, Riley. Will you be okay on your own? Otherwise, you can stay in the recliner in my room. Or possibly with Dara." Not that I've asked Dara if this is all right. I feel panicky. I've overlooked too many important details.

"As if my mother hasn't left me home alone overnight." Riley smiles tightly with her mouth only.

I want to ask her when Becky began leaving her home alone overnight, but I don't want to know the answer, because then I will be even more likely to strangle my sister the next time I see her.

It's almost time for me to go. "Do you want a burger?"

"I ate." Riley stretches out on the bed. "Don't worry about me."

I feel like I'll fall asleep if I try to drive anywhere, so I call Dara and ask for a ride.

She hesitates. "Gosh, Gal, I wish I could, but I can't. I have plans."

"It'll only take a half hour." My tone sounds a bit whiny, even to me. "I'll buy you a burger." Silly Gal. I sigh inwardly. I will have to call a cab.

"It takes an hour, Gal, you know that." Her tone is dry. "Really, I can't do it tonight. I've already had a glass of wine and you know what a lightweight I am. Maybe if you told me ahead of time . . ."

"I hardly ever need a ride. I didn't know ahead of time." Who's she drinking with? Dara is a social drinker. I have a twinge of the psychic and simultaneously my stomach lurches. It must be my need for dialysis. "Are you out with Mr. Morton?" I squeeze my eyes closed, afraid of the answer. She had called him earlier today. It must be him.

"No. Pennebaker." She whispers. Chad Pennebaker is the short-haired accountant.

"I thought accountants were sticks in the mud."

"Not him. He's less dry with a few drinks in him." She giggles at her own joke. I actually roll my eyes. She is tipsy.

"What about Mr. Morton?"

"What about him?"

"Don't you like him?" I feel angry on Mr. Morton's behalf. Such a nice guy, and here Dara is acting as though she doesn't care.

"Gal. I just met the man." She sounds sober at once. Nothing can get Dara like righteous indignation. "We talked for five minutes, tops."

"Yes, yes. I'll let you go." I get off the phone. Dara, of course, has every right to casually date as many men as she wants until she has found The One. The Mr. Right. But it sure seems like her standards are impossibly high. One of these days, she is going to wake up and see strands of gray in her blond mane. All of these nice guys she finds reasons to reject are going to go away and not come back.

I sigh. I can't solve Dara's problems for her. Also, it's not like I do any better. At least Dara is having a good time. I need to call the cab.

Riley comes out of her room, heading for the kitchen. I wave the phone toward her. "How about looking up Yellow Cab? The number's on the bulletin board by the fridge."

"I can take you." Riley's mood shifts yet again, her face losing its anger and taking on an eager openness. Almost like she's morphed from teen back to young child. It's dizzying. "I just got my driver's permit, you know."

My head has begun to ache. "And then you won't be able to get home. Just get me the number and next time you can drive. I'll let you drive me all over town."

"It will save you twenty bucks in cab fare, I bet." Riley is banking on my cheapness and she's right, because I am truly tempted for a second to let her drive me and just stay the night, but I don't. Maybe I can rally and drive myself. It's not too far. I've done it before. I take a couple of deep breaths and then stand up. "It's all good. I'll drive myself."

Riley steps forward. "Are you sure, Aunt Gal? You look kind of pale."

I don't know what I look like, but I do know I feel kind of pale. And dizzy. I sit right back down again.

Riley takes the car keys off the hook by the door. "Come on. I'll get a cab home."

IN THE EARLY MORNING I wait to be unhooked from the dialysis machine, watching the blinking lights of the machines and the blood pressure cuff inflate. The lights are still off in here, but the clinic is now brightly lit and coming to life with voices and laughter. I see Dr. Blankenship walk through the adjoining corridor. She has on sneakers that squeak on the ultraclean waxed floors, instead of her pumps, which means she's prepping for surgery, not office hours. Her white lab coat is clean and pressed, over khakis and a cotton button-down.

She and I had started off on the wrong foot right away when she first arrived here a year ago. The surgeon she'd replaced, Dr. McMillan, had been less concerned with blood flow, and set to move me to the top of the list. But he'd been abruptly transferred, and I wasn't too happy about my new doctor. And she definitely wasn't happy about a patient who voiced her opinions so stridently.

Her gaze focuses straight ahead, so she doesn't see when I wave. If I were a snake, I would have bit her. I know she is doing that on purpose. "Hey, Doc!" I yell. Today my voice carries extra force, now that I've gotten my new super-human injection of regular, clean blood.

She backtracks in the hallway to my door. "Oh, hi, Gal. Didn't see you there." She bats her eyes innocently, smooths down her red bob. Her pale skin looks greenish under the fluctuating fluorescent light. One of the bulbs flickers and hisses.

"That's because you weren't looking." I smile, clutch the scratchy bleached sheet so hard it hurts. "When are you going to have a kidney for me?"

"When you take the test again." She presses her clipboard against her chest and doesn't make eye contact, instead focusing on the closed blinds to the right of my head. It's terrible to have your own surgeon not even like you. But I don't care if we never exchange Christmas cards; I just want a working kidney. "We have to do it because of your leg graft. Otherwise, if we put a new kidney in, your blood flow may be compromised. The kidney will die. You know I can't perform the transplant unless you get a good blood flow test."

She has delivered all this in a monotone, still not meeting my eyes. I've met plenty of doctors with a poor bedside manner, but Dr. Blankenship takes the cake. I spread my hands apart. "I'm giving you my permission to do it anyway. Doesn't that count for something?"

"I know what you're saying, and I know what the protocol tells me to do."

"So I'm damned if I do and damned if I don't."

She squishes her mouth into a smile, wrinkles deepening in her cheeks. "Nothing bad is going to happen to you when you're on the IVP dye, unless you think it will."

I shut my eyes for a second.

I know I am allergic to IVP dye, the same way you would know you were allergic to bees. The first time I had a reaction, I was twelve, and I didn't even know what IVP dye was. My breathing slowed, my throat swelled, and I got a rash on my face. I don't remember much of it, other than what my mother's told me. Besides, my point is, how could I have a psychosomatic reaction to IVP dye when I wasn't even aware they were pumping it into my veins?

The doctor who used IVP dye then told my mother that if I was allergic, and if I had it again, I'd probably die.

"What if the first time you got stung by a bee, you swelled up and your throat closed?" I asked Dr. Blankenship the last time we had this conversation. "Would you go around trying to get stung again on purpose?"

She laughed me off. "This is entirely different. Apples and oranges."

"More like apples and apples," I said. "Maybe Granny Smith versus Red Delicious. But they're both apples!"

Now, as I sit here with my eyes shut, this memory welling into me, Dr. Blankenship tries again. "We can try it and take you off right away if something goes wrong. I am sure it's not the dye. Nothing in our studies suggests that such an allergy is even possible."

The same old song. "This conversation feels oddly familiar, Doctor."

"Good morning, Mr. Walters." Dr. Blankenship's tone silkens. Walters walks by.

Walters pauses. Today he's in pressed white linen pants and a light blue T-shirt, carrying a Panama hat in his hands, looking like he's off to vacation in the Bahamas instead of going to dialysis. "Surgery this morning, eh? Going to have one of those kidneys for me pretty soon, I hope?"

"I bet within the next couple weeks." She's all smiles.

He gives me a courtesy wave. "And how are we this morning?"

"I don't know about 'we,' but I am fine, thank you." I speak through a clenched jaw.

He walks on.

Dr. Blankenship turns back to me. This time, she actually finds it in her to meet my eyes. Hers are a watered-down green, the charcoal circles underneath not quite covered by her concealer. "Gal, please. I want to get you a kidney as badly as you do. But I have to abide by the rules. If you're in danger of rejecting it, then I can't give it to you."

"What about him?" I nod toward Walters's retreating back. "He could drink it to death. Stop taking his blood pressure meds. He did it before. Seems like I'm a better bet."

"I can't discuss another patient's case." Her expression

closes off. She steps back, done with the conversation. "I have to go."

I grimace. I feel myself being pushed down, down, down to the very bottom of the kidney list. I accept the fact that if I don't do this test at all, I will not get a transplant. At least, not from this doctor.

"Listen. I have never had a bad response when a patient is premedicated. We'll put you on a Benadryl and Prednisone drip. We'll use only a tiny amount of dye." Dr. Blankenship studies my face.

"And then I'll get put on top of the list?" This is what I want, to not wait in dialysis purgatory forever.

"You have my word." Dr. Blankenship awkwardly puts her hand over mine. Her hand feels like it needs to be de-iced.

7

It is Saturday. The day is cool. Only a little wind. My house has its porch light on, despite it being mid-morning. My car alarm beeps, and I wonder if it woke Riley. I squeak the door open. Being a guardian is so difficult. Who knew I'd go from zero to sixty in parental anxiety? If I'd had her all these fifteen years, I would have had time to get used to this raw worry, not have it blossom all at once.

I used to long for a normal life, a life like the one Becky had. I used to sit in front of the big mirror on my mother's dresser, thinking I could step through it, like Alice, to a parallel life. One where my kidney reflux was discovered and fixed early on. Where I had gotten married fairly young, and begun having babies with some decent man. I used to want six. Three boys, three girls. I had names picked out for them, all from Greek myth. Cassandra, Alexandra, Penelope. Ulysses, Jason, Hector. I would have needed an accommodating husband with a short last name.

But now, I'm thinking maybe it's better that I didn't become a parent. Maybe I could never have handled it in the first place, based on how I am handling Riley. Not that I have done anything bad.

It's just that I'm used to being alone, doing what I want, not thinking about kids, other than my students. When my students went home, they were no longer my worry. I could think about roses, piddle around in my greenhouse as much as I wanted.

Riley is up and talking on the phone. The television is on. So is the radio in the kitchen, to some rock music with bass I can feel in my bowels. It sounds like pure noise more than music. I turn off the radio and study my niece.

She looks healthy. No signs of partying or illness are in the room. In fact, she appears to have straightened up. She has on thick socks with pictures of roses on them that I recognize as mine. What else has she looked through while I was gone? She turns her head away from me.

I go into the bedroom to give her privacy and shut the door, hearing her say, "I love you too, Mom," before she hangs up.

I reappear, wondering what my sister had to say for herself. "How's your mom?"

"She's great. She loves Hong Kong. Nonstop, like she is." Riley says this without a trace of bitterness. "She's going to bring me some cool souvenirs."

"She ought to just bring you herself, not junk." I sit on the chair opposite my niece and put my feet on the coffee table.

"She needed to take the job." Riley chews on a hangnail, stares out the window. "When she comes back, she says we're going to buy a house. They pay for her housing, so she's saving up."

I somehow doubt my sister has a real plan to save money, but I don't say anything to Riley. "Did she say when she'd be back?"

"She doesn't know yet. The Hong Kong assignment might

be longer than she thought." Riley gets up. "She said it might
be through the summer." She rubs the heel of her hand into
her eyes to stave off tears. "It's a good opportunity for her,
isn't it?"

I see it all then. Becky is no good for her. Riley would be
better off if she cut ties with her mother, said good-bye to all
these years of disappointment, stopped calling her on the
phone. But she won't. She can't, yet. Maybe being here, with
me, will let Riley see the shell that is her mother. This aban-
donment should not be what Riley thinks is normal.

I want to tell Riley all this, but know she's not ready to
hear it.

"It is a good opportunity," is what I say instead. I nearly
choke on these words.

Riley turns back to me. "It was really quiet here."

"Quiet is good. But you can come with me, if you want."

"I got so bored, I cleaned up the greenhouse after I
watered."

I freeze. "You cleaned up the greenhouse?"

She waves a hand. "Don't worry. I didn't throw away any
plants."

I force myself to take deep breaths. Training Brad to
clean up had taken a few weeks, and here Riley has done it in
one evening? I have everything in a particular space, a particular order. If I could have painted a grid system over the
entire greenhouse with spots for everything, I would have. I
do not like this to be messed with. I realize I am clutching
the back of the sofa rather hard, and relax my grip.

"Aunt Gal?" Riley says.

"Riley, it's good to want to help." I struggle for polite
words, when cursing is all that comes to mind. "But how

would you like it if I went into your computer and decided to poke around and clean stuff up?"

"I wouldn't."

"Exactly."

Her face falls. I feel terrible. But really, it's my stuff.

I GO INTO THE GREENHOUSE. Here, it is truly quiet. Only the sounds of the fans. I inhale once, twice. Soil and the spicy scent of the seedlings.

It looks like she's swept and taken out the trash. And dusted; the metal fans are clean once again. Not bad.

I walk to my seedling bins and look over the rows of the Hulthemias. More have sprouted and bloomed. I handle a yellow Hulthemia I've tagged G8. It's got a lot of blossoms and a bright orange center, but no scent. That's too bad. I was sure it would have fragrance, like its cousin. Fragrance is elusive, I remind myself.

I walk to seedling G42. This is the one I'm hoping will be the best of the bunch. It will look like a clean orange flame with a red center, reminding me of bonfires. One bud has opened. It's beautiful, the splotch perfect in the petals like watercolor spilled by a skilled artist. No fragrance, though. Darn.

I should wait another year, see if I can turn out a better rose.

But what if there's not another year?

I refuse to let the thought settle. There will be another year, I tell myself sternly.

The next bud might have fragrance. It might smell more strongly in a couple of days. I am vacillating. This rose has unique coloring that I might not get again. Though I know it could be better.

Every time I look at the bloom, my heart accelerates and I feel giddy. That's got to count for something. Besides, the entry fee for the show I'll enter is only twenty dollars, and it's just over in San Luis Obispo. It's worth it, even if I lose. "Oh, Gal. You're so stubborn," I say, then laugh to myself. I sound like my doctor. Or my mother. I go back into the house and fill out my rose entry form.

8

OVER THE NEXT WEEK OR SO, I PUT THE ROSE SHOW out of my mind. There's really nothing else to do about it, unless a better rose blooms in the meantime, which would always be nice. Riley, it is decided, will make the drive to San Luis Obispo with me for the show.

Riley gets up on time, without the complaining I'd braced myself for, gets in her uniform, and rides to school with me early. I like to get in an hour before school in case a student needs help. Riley usually goes over to Dara's class and draws.

She really ought to be one of the students getting tutoring. Riley is in my sophomore biology class, and whatever she learned at her old school she either forgot or hasn't yet studied. She stares at the slides and cannot make out the proper cells. A blood cell seems to look the same to her as a plant cell. I point out the differences, she agrees, and the next day, she forgets again. Nor can she remember the scientific names for anything.

Originally, I thought she was a visual learner, because she's so attracted to art. Now I think she's a hands-on learner. Her main problem is she can't think in the abstract very well. Anyway, the bottom line is, she could use as much help as she can get in the sciences, because it does not come naturally to her.

"I study on my own," Riley told me when I suggested she come in and get extra help. We haven't had a quiz yet, so I can't say how well she will do in my class. I would be lying if I said I wasn't worried about her.

"Don't be stubborn," I said. "It's not a crime to not be good at science. Maybe you'll be better at physical science."

I bring this up with Dara one day at lunch. "What does she draw?" Riley has not shown me any class artwork, and Dara keeps most of it until the end of the year, when she puts on a show for the parents.

"Mainly people." Dara chews on her spinach salad thoughtfully. "I always say that people usually like to draw either people or landscapes. She is definitely people. But I'm having her move away from representational drawing and experiment with different media."

I have no idea what she's talking about. "So you're making her into a Picasso?"

Dara gives me a quick smile. "Pretty much. Picasso knew how to draw realistically before he went into abstraction, too."

"It's funny. She only got a C in art at her last school. And her citizenship grades weren't so high." I ponder what brought her citizenship down. Talking in class? Not turning in homework? These behavior-based marks, given in addition to letter grades, always seemed arbitrary to me, varying with each teacher. Some teachers even marked the kids down for not participating, for being too quiet. Silence, to me, was not a detriment to learning.

"Maybe no one gave her a chance before, or maybe the smaller school helps."

"I think it's the uniforms." Riley sits at a lunch table with Sam and her cronies. Her black hair has begun to grow out, showing lighter roots. I'm not sure what it will take to bleach it back down, but it's sure to be expensive and time-consuming, so I figure growing it out works just as well. "Uniforms solve everything." I raise an eyebrow at Dara's getup, a hot pink blouse with black pants and a black-and-white-striped scarf.

She waves her hand at me dismissively.

I rest my head on my hand. "Am I not motherly enough?"

"You mean nurturing? Warm and fuzzy?" Dara takes a dainty bite of her carrot stick. "Not at all."

"I can't be what I'm not."

"Everyone can change their behavior, Gal. That's what we ask the kids to do."

"I'm too old to change," I say.

Dara brushes off her hands and gets a grin. I look to where she's looking. Mr. Morton.

He is wearing a purple button-down with small checks and a purple and black argyle sweater vest with his khaki pants. I am not used to seeing men in purple, but he carries it off nicely. I notice all the girls giggling as he walks by, but he is thankfully oblivious. He sits down at our table. "I was thinking we should build a trebuchet for Science Olympiad."

"What's a trebuchet?" Dara cuts in.

"Catapult, basically." I drink my allotted water in one sip. Drat. Still thirsty. I bite into my apple to get some juice. "It's for an event called 'Storming the Castle.'" I nod at Mr. Morton. "I've never done it, but if you want to, then I'm all for it."

Dara looks excited. "'Storming the Castle'? Now that sounds like fun. Shall I make you some medieval costumes?"

Mr. Morton and I giggle and exchange a glance. His eyes are merry. Dancing, even. He says, "I suppose we could, but it's more for the physics applications."

"We'll talk about it at Science Olympiad practice. Are you handy at building? No one around here is. That's why we haven't built one."

He wrinkles his nose. "I can put together IKEA furniture."

"That's better than most. We'll have to get a real builder, maybe a parent volunteer so we don't hit anyone in the head." He and I laugh again.

I glance at the clock. "Time for my meds. See you guys later." I get up to clear my sack lunch, feeling a peculiar flutter in my stomach. Is it caused by Mr. Morton? It can't be. I joke with everyone. I throw my trash away and glance back toward the table, just in time to see Dara lean in, her hand on his forearm, and Mr. Morton laugh at something she says. I had thought he wasn't her type. But then, when did Dara ever have a type? He's better for her than most of those yahoos she dates, I think. Something like anger, or frustration, knots hotly inside. I slam open the cafeteria door a bit harder than necessary as I leave.

Winslow Blythe's *Complete Rose Guide* (SoCal Edition)

April

Happy April! Happy Spring!

Happy Critter Month! Remember to keep washing those rose bottoms every single day. If you do use pesticides, use it at half strength for the new blooms, so they won't burn up.

Weekly fish emulsion will make your roses sing (and make your dogs go crazy! Woo, it is stinky). One time this month, give the roses a big old Super Feed of zinc, iron, and Epsom salts.

9

RILEY AND I BEGIN TO DEVELOP A ROUTINE. Generally, we go home in the late afternoon, after all our school duties are done. I handle the roses, Riley does homework. I make dinner, she does homework. We do laundry as needed. It's a fairly normal life, except for the dialysis. It's kind of nice to have someone around.

On Mondays, we stop at the grocery store after school. I let Riley plan the dinners, considering how she complains so much about them. The first week, she spent two hours on the Internet, looking up gourmet recipes. I take one look at her list (baby arugula, New Zealand lamb shanks, wild Alaskan salmon) and laugh so hard I lean on the shopping cart for support, drawing the stares of the other shoppers. "Riley, dear, we are not the Rockefellers."

"Who are the Rockefellers?" Riley flushes all the way down into her shirt collar.

"We're not the Hiltons," I clarify for her benefit. I hand her the list back. It's written on one of those free notepads that Realtors hand out; Riley has adorned the man's grinning face with horns and a mustache. "Please. Teacher budget."

"But how can I change my menu? We're at the store

already." She crosses her arms and looks like I just told her there's an asteroid plummeting to Earth.

I take a grocery store circular, pushing the cart over to the side so I don't block the strawberry display. "Buy what's on sale. Plan from there. Things I know how to cook, preferably."

We go through the store, choosing dry spaghetti and cans of sauce and pork chops on sale. "This actually isn't so bad," Riley says, putting a half pound of hickory-smoked bacon, wrapped in white paper, into the cart.

"Yep. No one got hurt." I pick up a cantaloupe and have her smell it for ripeness. We check the expiration dates on the dairy, we look on the bottom shelves for the bargain brands, we decide what to freeze for later. I hadn't realized how much grocery knowledge I had, just waiting to be passed on.

I grin at her as we go through checkout.

"What?" Riley says, putting back the copy of *National Enquirer*.

"Nothing," I say, still grinning. "Just happy. Is that a crime?"

"Nooo." She laughs, widens her eyes. "It's just weird."

During the second week of April, my parents come home from their trip, find out about Riley, and drive up even though they should be resting from jet lag. They arrive midmorning on a Saturday, which means they left at dawn. Riley and I hear them and go into the driveway as they pull up. Mom opens the sedan door first, of course. She braces herself on the passenger door to get out and moves slowly toward me. Her right hip is arthritic and will need replacement soon. She's dressed in one of her flowing maxis, her hair all over the place. "Gal," she says, crushing me in a hug. She smells of something spicy, and I sneeze.

"Sorry, Mom. It's your perfume."

"Oh dear." She steps back and looks more concerned than I meant her to. "I'll take a shower right away."

"No, no. It's fine, Mom."

"You look good." She turns next to Riley. "Look at how big you've gotten, my granddaughter!"

"Hi, Gram." Riley submits to a hug and rolls her eyes over Mom's shoulder.

Dad steps out and puts his big arm around me. "Hey, Squirt. Got any projects this weekend that need doing?" Dad always fixes stuff for me while he's here: leaky faucets, crooked pictures, drafty windows. He hates sitting still, for one thing, and for another, I'm hopeless at handyman tasks. I save them all up for him.

I think about it for a second. "There is one thing you could do. A project for the school."

MR. MORTON ARRIVES in an hour, dressed in jeans and a clean Lacoste shirt even though he's here to work on the trebuchet with Dad. Today they'll build a sample, cut the parts for a second, and then Mr. Morton will have the kids build another one during the club. He drives a black Audi convertible, too nice a car for a teacher to own. The trebuchet wood is strapped to the rack on top, a rack meant for skis. He sits in the car for a moment, as if he's listening to the end of some song. Or maybe he's hesitating. I imagine he didn't think I'd make good on my trebuchet project so soon.

Riley bangs open the screen door and leaps down the two front steps. "Mr. Morton!"

"Riley." He smiles easily at her. "You going to help out?"

"I don't want her getting any fingers cut off." I come out-side and squint in the sun.

"That's more likely to happen to me." Mr. Morton grins and holds up a scratched-up fire-engine red tool box. It means he uses it. He and Riley undo the wood.

We go around the back to the garage, where Dad has set up a workstation across two sawhorses.

"Dad, this is Mr. Morton. Mr. Morton, my father. Tom."

"Call me George." Mr. Morton shakes my father's hand firmly.

"By George, you're George." At Dad's corny joke, I glance at Riley to see if she's groaning, but she ignores it. I bet if I'd said it, she would have run screaming down the street. Dad takes the wood from him and sets it up on the worktable. "Gal says you've got plans for this thing?"

"Printed this morning." He spreads the sheets on the table. I examine the diagrams. It's a small catapult designed to launch beanbags into a bucket. Whoever can do this with the most accuracy wins the competition. He glances up at me with a raised eyebrow. "We should have made the stu-dents come over and help."

"Too many cooks." Dad gets out his electric saw. "I don't want a bunch of kids over here in my way. Except for Riley. You're going to measure." He hands her the measuring tape.

"Me? Why me?" She takes the tape as though it were a live grenade. "How long?"

"Look at the plan." I point to the measurement. Three feet, two-eighths of an inch.

She squints at the measuring tape as she pulls it out. "Is this it?" Randomly, it seems, she points to a measurement.

"Are you going to be on the science team, Riley?" Mr. Morton smiles gently.

She looks at me as though she expects me to answer. I do. "She's more of an artist."

"I might try it." She glares at me. "I can do more than one thing, you know."

"I know." I never seem to know what this girl is thinking, except that it is the opposite of me. I don't remember being such a pain when I was fifteen. I never had the whole angsty hormonal teenaged girl thing. I spread the plans out and double-check the measurement. "Riley, you're over too far."

Dad corrects her and she makes the mark.

"Measure twice, cut once," Dad says.

She remeasures. "I can't tell if it's right." She's not even looking at the tape or the drawing. "I think it was wrong before."

"You're not even trying now." I reach for the tape, but she pulls it away. "Let me show you how this thing works and what these little hatch marks mean."

"I know what they mean. Inches."

"No. The little tiny ones. If you knew what they meant it'd be easier."

"I don't want to know. I don't care." She throws down the tape. "Ugh. This is a stupid project."

I glance at my father, who busies himself with another piece of wood. "Just give it a try."

"I can't do everything." Her face contorts like someone sprayed lemon juice into it. I purse my lips. I am used to students being frustrated. I am not used to quite this much emotion involved.

I pick up the tape. "Calm down and try it again. You can do this."

"You do it. I'm going in to help Grandma make lunch."

She tosses her pencil down, runs off. It bounces and skitters away under a shelf of Christmas decorations.

"Ah." Dad starts up his saw. "Reminds me of her mother."

"Unfortunately." I bend over to look for the pencil.

"Allow me." Mr. Morton squats and peers under the shelving unit.

I regret that I never swept the spiderwebs away. "Watch out for black widows."

He gets on his belly and reaches far into the darkness to retrieve the pencil, then wipes the dust off his jeans. "Riley has a low frustration threshold, I've noticed."

"You think?" We go outside, away from the saw noise and from the house, where I suspect Riley is standing with an ear to the window. I tell him about Riley's background and how she came to be here.

"No contact with her father?"

"Used to have. She spent the first few years of her life with him. Basically, now he's a sperm donor and an occasional wallet." I cross my arms. "But my sister chooses to live a certain way. And her kid suffers."

Mr. Morton looks at me full in the face. "It's really good of you to let Riley live here."

I think about when Riley arrived, how my initial thought had been to send her to live with my parents. Then I remember showing Riley the grocery store. I think about what Becky is missing. What she has missed, all this time. I'm not sure I want Riley to leave.

I clear my throat. Compliments tend to embarrass me. I shrug. "She's my niece."

His gaze focuses on the rose garden. I think he'll ask me a question about the roses next, but he doesn't. An expression of sadness crosses his face, more sadness than Riley's story should have mustered. I consider asking him what's wrong, but I don't know him well. I don't like it when people pry into my life, tell me I look tired or sick, want to know all the gory details. I wait. If he talks, I'll listen.

He takes a breath and focuses back to where we are. He grins. "Let's get back to our medieval weaponry."

10

On Monday morning, my mother drives me to my IVP test.

"I don't like this one bit." Mom grips the steering wheel so hard her hands turn white. "You are allergic to that dye."

"I don't have a choice, Mom," I say mechanically. We have been having this conversation for the past twenty-four hours, and longer than that. I am afraid Mom will unleash her full mother bear wrath on the doctor, and then I will never get my kidney.

"They're idiots. Idiots." She is practically spitting. Gone is the artist full of gentility and flowing robes. She has her hair pulled back into a knot and she's wearing her cherry-red velour tracksuit, the closest she gets to a power suit.

"Stay calm, Mother."

"Your doctor needs to be told what's what."

Great. "Please do not challenge Dr. Blankenship. She already hates me."

Mom pulls into a parking space and turns to face me. "Gal. If I had been one-tenth as assertive as I am now when you were little, you'd still have a kidney." She swallows hard.

I pat her arm. Mom will never get over this guilt, this feeling that she should have done more. It's not her fault. She trusted the doctors to find out what was wrong, not let it destroy my kidneys. We will never consider doctors to be infallible again.

Inside, Dr. Blankenship waits. She extends her hand to my mother. "Mrs. Garner, good to see you again."

Mom shakes her hand feebly. "I don't like this. She had this dye done when she was twelve, and the doctor said she would die if they repeated it."

Dr. Blankenship blinks. "We're taking every precaution. Don't you worry."

Mom snorts. "If you had children, you would know that is a useless thing to tell a mother."

Dr. Blankenship is at a loss for words, for once. She breaks away from my mother's glare. I grin a little.

MY MOTHER AND I sit in the waiting room until they are ready for me. This I've never understood about doctors' offices: they tell you to come in early even if they don't plan to do anything for hours.

Mom thumbs through the *People* and *Us* magazines fanned across the coffee table. "I have to say, I haven't heard of half of these people."

"I have, unfortunately." I look for a *Scientific American* or even a *National Geographic*, but cannot find one. "It's difficult to get my students to work hard when you can get famous by releasing a sex tape."

"Gal!" My mother actually blushes.

"Hey, it's not me. It's them." I gesture toward the magazines.

"I'm sure Riley doesn't think like that." Mom picks up an ancient *Good Housekeeping* and cracks it open.

Considering that Riley's mother hasn't even taught her how to grocery shop, I can't imagine Becky offering much guidance in the area of pop culture and morality. "It depends on what her mother's taught her, doesn't it?"

"It's up to you to teach her now." Mom is pretending to read the magazine, keeping one eye trained on me.

"I try." I think I'm not doing such a bad job. Riley is doing well in school, despite my initial misgivings. She is popular with the teachers. Kids treat her well, as far as I can tell. She hasn't complained.

"It has to be difficult, going from zero kids to a teenager." Mom pats my knee. "You know I'll take her if you can't handle it."

I bristle. "I can handle it."

My mother nods. I understand she is offering me an out, the option of admitting I cannot handle the responsibility of a child, even an almost fully grown child. But I am fine and Riley is fine. I think. Doubt swirls up now, a cyclone my very own mother has created in the way only fleshly female relatives can. I actually sigh with relief when the nurse calls my name and it's time for my dreaded procedure.

I am set up on a bed. The nurse prepares the IV drip with Prednisone and Benadryl. Mom sits next to me. "Make sure they don't kill me," I say. I force myself to relax. This is for my kidney. I need this for my kidney. I picture healthy kidneys dancing in my head. My kidney functioning strongly, regenerated into a healthy organ instead of the essentially dead one inside of me.

I'll try anything to get my kidney to work. I traveled to Santa Barbara several years ago to meet a hypnotist who treated me once a week in a glass-walled office overlooking the Pacific. Hypnosis worked well for pain, but nothing happened to make my kidney heal. I went to an acupuncturist over the course of a year and lay with needles sticking out of my back for half-hour increments in a bid to make the kidney restart. I've written to researchers who have grown new kidneys in mice, volunteering to be a human guinea pig; they all said it was too early to try out the procedure on me, that this technology is at least a good decade away. And my mother and I have prayed for help from every saint in the saint lexicon. My patron saint against kidney disease is St. Margaret of Antioch. There are prayer chains of elderly ladies across the U.S. asking for a kidney miracle for me, at the urging of my mother and her cronies, who e-mail chain letters about my illness.

"Saint Margaret, pray for me," I say, probably only in my head, because I'm pretty sure my lips have stopped moving.

I used to wonder if God hated me. Then, around age twenty-four, I had an epiphany. God doesn't hate me more than He hates anyone else. Good people die, horrible people live trouble-free lives. He's a pretty hands-off type of deity. It's the cost of free will. We're not pawns in a game, like in *Clash of the Titans*.

So if this IVP test is what I have to do, so be it. Whatever happens will happen.

"I'm here," I hear my mother say.

The IV goes in. I barely register it.

The Benadryl hits my system and I pass out.

I AM STANDING in my rose garden, only it's a perfect rose garden. No bugs, not even any dirt, just perfect blooms. My house is gone. This doesn't bother me, because the sky is so perfectly clear.

I see my two Hulthemia parents, the ones I started last year. I bend and sniff the mother I used. They are growing out of what should be the ground but is a sterile hospital floor.

Riley stands nearby, holding a black hose connected to nothing. "I'm watering the roses, Auntie." She isn't paying attention to what she's doing, she's flooding the flowers. They will die.

"Stop it, Riley."

She ignores me. "I know what I'm doing."

I try to move, to get to her and stop her. But I am rooted to my position. When I look down, I realize I have no feet. It is quite clear I am becoming a rose myself.

Byron appears before me, his chest nearly colliding with my eyeballs. "Ms. Garner?" He's holding the rose I'm taking to the contest. His eyes look so very very blue, like exotic oceans I have never seen. "Congratulations. You have won the gold medal."

"Yay! I won!" I turn my head and expect to see Riley, my mother, my father standing there. But there's only an empty greenhouse.

I turn back and Byron is gone.

My roses have disappeared.

The rose in my hand grows hotter and hotter until it melts away into ribbons of molten lava colors and I drop it with a soundless cry.

I OPEN MY EYES. I hear my heart pounding in my ears. My mother is shouting from a distance. Dr. Blankenship is at my feet, new lines creasing her face. She is not as young as I thought. A nurse has an oxygen mask pressed to my face.

My first thought is to ask if Riley turned the water off. No, that wasn't real. I wait for the dream to dissipate. Something bad has happened. But I'm still alive.

My eyes feel puffy and my throat aches. I've had another allergic reaction. They have stuck me with epinephrine to resuscitate me.

Mom yells indecipherably outside my room at whoever is keeping her from coming in and breaking the doctor's neck.

Dr. Blankenship puts her thumb and forefinger on her temples. "Fuck," she says, almost inaudibly.

"Doctors aren't supposed to curse in front of patients." My voice is hoarse.

She sags with relief. "You're stable, Gal."

I think about saying *I told you so*, and decide against it. Definitely, I will later. "So, do I get my kidney now?"

Her face is pained. "One thing at a time." She strides over and puts her hand on top of mine. Hers is really cold again.

"Sheesh, Doc, what are you, a vampire?" I flinch but find I am not quite strong enough to move. "I have the rash on my face, don't I?"

She nods. "You're going to be fine. We used just a tiny bit of dye and stopped right away."

"Did you do the X-ray?"

"No."

I sigh. "That was completely useless, then."

My mother finally busts in and runs to my side. "Gal! You're all right."

"Of course." My throat opens up all the way. "Just tired. And cold. Can I get another blanket, please?"

"I'll do it." Dr. Blankenship leaves, glad to be doing something.

"She's feeling guilty." I relax into my pillows. I'm already feeling better.

"Serves her right. What did we tell her?"

"I know, Mom." I'm still groggy, thinking about my dream. The medications will take a while to wear off. I'll probably have to stay overnight. The thought angers me. I was supposed to water tonight, check on the seedlings again to see if any great new blooms appeared. Tomorrow I have to wash the bugs off the blooms. I was supposed to do it today, actually, but I didn't have a chance before my appointment. I hate useless overnight hospital stays. They never let you sleep properly, always waking you up to make sure you're still alive.

"Mom, call Brad and tell him to go do the roses, will you?"

"Is it just watering? Dad and Riley can do that."

"No. Brad knows what to do. Tell Brad." I drift off into sleep, thinking how funny it is that I'm in this life-or-death situation and I'm worried over some plants. "Do it, Mom," I mumble. "Don't forget."

11

My parents stick around a few extra days longer than I'd like them to stick around, my mother looking for clues of my good health like she's Miss Marple cracking a case. Once she even held a mirror under my breath while I slept. I awoke with a start and whacked the mirror up into my nose. "Ow! Mom, what the heck are you doing?"

"Sorry, sorry," she whispered, retreating into the darkness with her long hair flowing around her. If I hadn't known she was my mother, I would have thought she was a ghost.

My father's excuse for staying is that he has not finished the trebuchet. He takes his time on the contraption, a simple project he could have completed with Mr. Morton that last afternoon. I know my mother has put him up to it, because I see him out in the garage, taking long breaks to sit and listen to the ball game on the radio. He tinkers with other things in my garage, changes the oil in my car, hangs some pictures. My mother buys Riley a dresser and desk set from the local Target, and my father is also super slow to put these together.

At last, by the weekend, he has finished with all his

projects, and I take the opportunity to boot them. Politely, of course.

I get them to leave by promising I'll have Brad come over and help with the roses and that I'll get my groceries delivered. As a bonus, I press Riley. "Tell them you'll do all the cleaning and you'll make sure I take my meds."

"I will?" Riley is enjoying having her grandparents here. Gram makes her whatever she wants to eat, or buys it for her. She probably eats two bowls of ice cream a day. Lucky for her, she has Becky's metabolism.

"Not the meds. I'll do that. Just the cleaning." I am whispering to her in the hallway while my mother changes my sheets. She washes them twice a week in ultrahot water so I won't be bothered by dust mites. I tend to be more lax.

"And what will you give me?"

I stare up at my niece. "I shouldn't have to give you anything. This is what you should do because you are part of this household." I haven't seen too much of her since I was in the hospital five days ago. My parents have ferried her to school and back, and if she wasn't at school, she was over at Sam's, presumably studying but probably staring at music posters or something. I overheard her complain about the lack of fun things to do around here, whether or not her grandparents were visiting. My illness is an inconvenience to her.

What my mother said flashes back to me. Maybe Riley would prefer to not be with me, where the threat of sickness is a constant companion. I hesitate, wondering if she'll take it as a rejection. I'll say it. "Riley, if you'd rather live with Gram and Gramps, then I bet you can go there."

She purses her lips. I cannot tell if she's pleased or dismayed at this idea.

I am relieved she has the option now. If she wants to stay, it will be of her own accord. "Until you decide, let's help each other." I hold out my hand. "Deal?"

"Fine." She shakes. Her hand is stronger than it was when she first got here. She has filled out. Her cheeks aren't so sunken. Well. At least I'm doing something correctly. "Gram!" Riley yells. "I have something to tell you. I'm going to help Aunt Gal."

So it is that my parents take off.

SUMMER ROSE SHOWS can be tricky; the seedlings have to be transported in coolers. I prefer the spring shows, though there are fewer of those. On the West Coast, the roses bloom earlier, so the shows begin earlier. I'd never survive in one of the cold weather states, waiting longer for my roses.

On Sunday evening, Brad and I are in the rose greenhouse. He has a tiny blue iPod clipped to his shirt, the white wires feeding into his ears like two leeches sucking out his brain. I can hear some sort of banging noise emitting. I tap him on the shoulder. "Turn that down. You'll blast out your hearing."

He complies with a grin, wiping dirt across his tanned face. "Yes, ma'am."

I go through the seedling rows, deciding which ones I'll throw out. I keep only those I might take to a show, use as parents, or propagate.

I ask Brad to make pots of soil. I use a blend called Queen of Show specially designed for roses, which is compost, peat moss, coir, and sand. It's sold at the local nursery, where I have an account. I send Brad there to get twenty-pound bags and put them into the storage shed. This is the kind of heavy lifting I am not allowed to attempt. Nor would I. I'd only fall over.

Brad makes dozens of pots, so they will be ready for me whenever I need them. I walk through the greenhouse, looking at all the seedlings once more. I pull out the ones with ugly foliage and funky blooms, throwing them into my green trash wheeled container to be turned into compost.

We work without talking. I have known Brad since he was a freshman, and while he is somewhat of a chatterbox at school, he is silent around me. I do not inspire chattiness in people. Even when I get my hair cut, the hairdresser who tells everyone about her mother's appendectomy works quietly on my hair.

My sister, Becky, on the other hand, is the opposite. Everyone and anyone talks to her. Sales is a good profession for her. In theory.

Riley interrupts my train of thought by coming into the greenhouse. She tries to move quietly but trips on a soaker hose and falls, hip-checking Brad's pile of seed pots and sending the expensive soil flying into the four corners of the universe. She gives a little groan, then lifts herself up. I see the fall isn't bad, no worse than someone sliding into home plate during a P.E. ball game. She is filthy, though.

"Are you all right?" Brad laughs, covered in dirt himself. He holds his hand out to her.

"It's not funny. Who laughs when someone falls?" Riley is indignant.

"You're not hurt, Riley. If we didn't laugh, we might be crying over spilt soil." I calculate how much money I've lost. "Maybe you can see if you can save some of that."

"Aren't you going to ask if I'm okay?" Riley waves off Brad, brushes herself off.

"You're okay." I have never believed you should carry on for simple injuries. Slap a Band-Aid on it, kiss it better, and move on. The more upset a parent gets, the more upset the kid. My mother didn't learn how to keep calm until I was ten.

She rights some of the pots she's knocked over. Brad gets a dustpan and a brush. I then notice a piece of now-crumpled paper in her left hand. "I came in to get your signature. I'm doing the science team."

"Next year?" I take the permission slip, staring at it and turning it over in my grimy hands though I myself typed up the form. Riley wants to be on the science team?

"No. Now."

The science team trials are next month, and we have no more room. Besides, Riley lacks the maturity and science skills needed for the team. More kids than we can accommodate want to do it every year. Selection is made by the teachers. I flash back to Riley working on the trebuchet. How easily she gave up. Maybe if she'd put her guts into it and helped out, I would have a different idea.

No. Riley's good at art. Not science and math. It's a fact, just like the fact that I am color-blind though females aren't supposed to be. I try to think of a gentle way to let her down.

"Riley, you can't do it this year." I hand her the paper. "Just concentrate on the art show."

"Mr. Morton said I could, to do the trebuchet. He says there's a hole in the team and since my grandpa built it . . ."

"Mr. Morton said so, did he?" I make a mental note to talk to him. I am in charge of the team. Not him. He should have asked. "He's new. He doesn't know all the rules. I do. It's too late."

"But . . ."

"Riley, you should listen to your aunt." Brad straightens, slapping potting soil off his gloves. I'd forgotten he was there.

She glares at him, then cools her gaze and straightens. "I want my aunt to listen to me."

"Everyone else on the team worked hard to be on it." Brad's lip thins as he sets his jaw. "I'm sure you'll make it next year."

Riley glances at me, but I am not going to defend her. I agree with Brad. I can't help it.

"Well. Okay." She takes the permission slip and folds it into a tiny grimy square and tucks it into her pocket. "May I order a pizza instead of cooking? I have a lot of homework."

If it was up to me, I would open a can of something or other from the cupboard and eat it over the kitchen sink. But I feel bad that I had to turn her down. I rub my neck. "You may."

She closes the greenhouse door carefully behind her. Her head is down. Something in her posture hurts me. I shouldn't feel bad if I'm right. She can't do whatever she wants. She has to earn it like the rest of us.

Her mother never set boundaries for her. No, everything for Becky was, Ask and you shall receive. I'll talk to Riley later.

"Now, Brad." I turn to him. "This is between me and Riley. There was no need to chime in, okay?"

"It got her off your case, didn't it?" Brad sticks a spade into a small pot. "I mean it. I've seen her in study group and she lets everybody else do the work. She just rewrites the notes. She's not going to pull her weight."

I find myself coming to Riley's defense. "She's new, she's behind. You can't expect her to be at the top."

"I don't want her pulling me down, Ms. Garner." He sniffs and wipes at his nose with the back of his hand.

"She isn't pulling anyone down."

"Yet." His eyebrows knit.

This is a new side of Brad I haven't seen, indignantly righteous and not so generous. "Riley's a smart girl. I'm sure by next year she'll be caught up."

"We'll see." He rinses his hands in the sink, wipes them on his jeans. "I gotta get going."

"Wait." I stop him. "Are you dating Samantha?"

"Don't be silly. She's not allowed to date." He looks me in the eye.

After Brad leaves, I sit in a plastic lawn chair for a while, staring at my rows of roses. Riley will not diminish Brad, nor any other student. I'm sure of it. Is that what the kids are saying? Of course, Riley got into St. Mark's only because I am employed there. If she'd walked in off the street with her poor transcript in hand, Dr. O'Malley would have booted her backside to the curb quicker than she could say a Hail Mary. So would I.

I realize then why Brad has me so disturbed. He reminds me of me. And I can't say I particularly like the view.

The pizza truck pulls up, and I leave the greenhouse to its slumber.

LATER THAT EVENING, Becky calls me direct. "Riley hurt herself today," she says without preamble.

I blink, surprised. I've taken my hands out of soapy dish-water to answer the phone and it makes the receiver slippery.

I move it to my other hand, drying the wet hand on a towel. "I don't know what you mean."

"She fell. She told me. You should take her to the doctor." My sister's voice is concerned, clear.

I laugh. She's talking about the fall she had in the greenhouse. "Her pride is hurt more than anything. Riley's perfectly fine, Beck."

"It's Becca. She's not. I can hear it in her voice." My sister is working herself up. Pulling out the older-sister card, though as older sister she has only ever been older, never wiser.

I put the phone on speaker and place it on the counter next to the sink, attacking the greasy pan again. "Hey. If you're so concerned, why don't you come home and take care of her yourself?"

"Some people have a low pain tolerance. You never think anyone's injuries are as bad as yours."

I snort. "That's because they generally aren't."

"I think you should take her in. Or at least write her an excuse for P.E."

"I'll do nothing of the kind. She's not eighty years old, Becky. She slipped and fell and broke nothing except a pot of dirt. If you didn't trust me," I'm yelling into the receiver now, "then you should not have sent her to me."

"Agh." Becky makes a strangled noise. "You're impossible."

"Same to you."

We hang up simultaneously.

I feel my shoulders slump forward. Riley inches into the kitchen, back in her Abercrombie outfit. "I didn't know she was going to call you," she says.

"Are you hurt, Riley?" I examine her again. No limp. No swelling. Only a bruise.

"I don't know," she says.

"You're not."

She shrugs.

I sigh. "I know you're a teenaged girl and all, but can you cut back on the drama a little bit? For me?"

She sniffs, edges back toward the living room. "She said you'd say that."

I guess my sister might know me better than I thought.

12

THE DAY OF THE ROSE SHOW, THE LAST SATURDAY of April, breaks overcast. I hope the gray cloud cover will dissolve into sunshine. I read somewhere that a sign of a weak mind is letting the weather affect your moods, and I'm sorry to say my mind today is as flimsy as an antique negligee. I sit for a minute on the edge of the bed. Picture a sunny day. A perfect day. Perfect roses. Queen of Show. It's not working. My natural surliness is too present. I give up.

I fetch a surprise for Riley, hold it behind my back in one hand. A pink cell phone, just for her. My mother, having heard of my cell phone wishes, added us to her family plan and purchased us two phones.

"Riley!" I rap on her door. "You ready?"

"I am." Riley leaps out, shutting the door in a wink. She is dressed in a pair of black skintight jeans and a floaty white peasant blouse that looks like it came out of my mother's closet, circa 1975. Again with the style change, a chameleon trying to fit in. For a moment I get the impression she's hiding something, but I can't figure out what. Why would I think this? I have no basis. Is my parental radar finally coming online? "Everything all right?"

"Yeah." She meets my gaze and I know she is not telling me the truth.

But I don't want to spoil the surprise. I will break my own mood, I will ignore whatever this girl is hiding for now. "Guess what I have?"

Her relief is almost palpable at the subject change. I take my hand out from behind my back and show her the phone. A little pink cell phone.

Instead of being delighted, she shrinks away. Why does this girl always have reactions I don't expect? "My mom said she was getting me one of those."

"Well, she hasn't yet, so this will do the job." I make her take it. "It's not a fancy phone, but it will receive and make calls."

"Great. Thanks." Her voice is flat.

I suppose Becky promised her an iPhone. We will see if she follows through. I give a little mental shrug. "Let's get this circus into town."

I've been giving Riley some space since our little row over the science team. Mr. Morton's reasoning was that someone dropped out while I was gone, necessitating a replacement. "I will take responsibility for training her," he said when I confronted him about the unauthorized deal in his classroom after school. He crossed his arms.

"We have a waiting list. We call the next person," I said.

His expression changed from defensive to apologetic. "I didn't know about that."

"You didn't ask." People never ask me. They assume. It's like I'm not even in charge. "Science team is very popular around here."

He uncrossed his arms. "My stance would be to accommodate all interested students, not just a few. Let everyone benefit."

"The best students get on the team. The other ones have to wait and be alternates, or try out next year. There are team limits." I don't relish confronting Mr. Morton like this, upending our heretofore harmonious relationship. Every Tuesday, we'd been meeting after school to coach our teams, he with the trebuchet, me with the physiology students. To me, having ten students in my group was enough, plus more than twenty altogether on the entire team in the little class-room. But he had the unlimited energy and enthusiasm of a green teacher. He could probably handle a half dozen more students and be unfazed.

"I am sorry," Mr. Morton said, touching my arm. "I have an idea. We can get more parent volunteers, increase how many students we can accommodate."

I gazed wordlessly at him. He doesn't know how difficult it is to get parent volunteers, particularly at a school where tuition should be enough to cover whatever expenses we have. And particularly when you have well-meaning parents who truly want to help, but are hopeless at the subject. They only get in the way. "I know that it would be very egalitarian to have everyone on the team, but that's not how it works. We cut, just like the football team."

I am thinking about this interaction with Mr. Morton as I face my niece in the hallway. She seems to have gotten over her hurt.

Riley reties the string on her blouse. "We just going to stand around all day, or what?"

"Or what." I note her hair is growing out brown. "Should we buy you some hair dye to fix that?"

She shrugs, then touches her head. "Does it look bad?"

"A little bit. But no one will be looking at your head. Only at my rose." I head out to the car, where the rose already sits in a cooler in the backseat. "Come on. You're going to get freeway driving experience today."

She claps her hands. "Yay! I turn sixteen in August, you know. I need plenty of practice."

"I know." I hand her the keys. "But no B average, no driver's license. Deal?"

"Deal." We shake on it.

RILEY IS EVEN MORE CAUTIOUS on the freeway than I am, never exceeding the speed limit even while cars whiz past her. "You have to keep up with the speed of the other cars," I say, gripping my armrest.

"They're going over seventy!" Her knuckles are pale on the steering wheel.

I point. "Next exit, pull over. I'll drive."

"I can do it. I can do it." She issues a chant. "I can do it, Aunt Gal."

"Just don't get into an accident. You'll crush the rose." Rose G42 is packed in its pot, which is packed into a makeshift drink holder inside the cooler so it won't rattle about. "Never mind crushing you or me."

She snorts. "Nice to know where I stand."

"Hey, I put myself last on the list."

The San Luis Obispo venue is small, in a rented church auditorium. It does, however, overlook the ocean, the water spreading beneath a steep drop-off. We park the car and stand in the parking lot, staring down at the whitecaps below. Surfers look like ants tossing around from up here. Riley inhales. "The air smells good and salty. Like home."

I think I should put my arm around her, but physical affection feels too awkward. Instead, I put my hands in my jeans pockets. "Yep. I bet you're used to the cool San Francisco weather." Another detail I'd overlooked in Riley's acclimation to her new environment. I had not given it much thought. "But the human body can adapt."

"I know." Riley sounds annoyed again. I have to say I'm not used to teens being so overtly annoyed with me. In my classroom, students usually try to control whatever disdain bubbles up.

I open the trunk and get the cooler out. "You going to help, or just stand there?"

"I didn't know you wanted help." But she lifts one end, and suddenly my load is lightened.

I pull out the handle and wheel across the parking lot. "Thanks."

THIS ROSE SHOW has only about a hundred entrants in perhaps ten categories. It's more like a local rose society display than a huge show, but it's close to home and a good place to test out G42. Here there are only the major show categories: the hybrids, the floribundas, the mini-roses, the new rose.

Other, bigger shows have dozens of subcategories, dividing rose displays into complex artistry. There are categories for single blooms in individual vases; the English Box, a box with six holes cut in rows for each rose; or a wooden artist's palette, with blooms stuck into holes where the different paint colors would normally go. There are also categories devoted to the best full arrangements, or categories giving a prize to the best blooms floating in crystal saucers of water.

Everyone else already seems to be set up. Rose show

entrants like to get there early, to snag the best vases and spots.

I don't need a vase, nor do I believe where you sit matters. Most roses are shown cut, unless they are seedlings like mine, or a mini. I have my G42 seedling in its growing pot, in all its floriferous beauty. I rub its leaves with an old piece of panty hose.

Riley watches. "What's that for?"

"Shine." I touch the leaves. "The oil from your hands gets on it, too."

She frowns. "It seems like cheating."

"It's no more cheating than Miss America putting on lipstick." I continue my ministrations, careful not to tear the foliage.

One woman comes over and wrinkles her nose. "That's not a rose, is it?"

"It's a Hulthemia." Riley crosses her arms and draws herself up to her full height. I am proud of her. "A type of rose."

"I think it's lovely," says another female voice. It's Ms. Lansing, the rose judge from those years ago when I'd met Byron. She is still wearing a lot of makeup, as she was on that day. In deference to the beachy setting, she wears open-toed sandals that show bright pink polish. She leans over and gives me a cheek air kiss. I cringe a little. "How are you, Galilee?"

"I didn't know you were coming to this little show." I pump her hand and introduce her to Riley.

"Darling, if my hotel gets paid, I'll go anywhere." She barely looks at my niece, her eyes still on the rose. "Fragrance?" She bends forward and takes a sniff. She makes no notes on the pad she carries. Her pencil remains in her pocket.

"Not too much, but it is a repeat bloomer."

Ms. Lansing glances up. She then does something odd. She pats my shoulder. "Good for you, Gal."

"Thank you?" I am utterly confused.

"I want you to know I put you in my prayer circle at church." Her lipstick is bleeding into the fine lines around her mouth.

"Thank you," I repeat. Byron must have told her about my kidney. I certainly didn't.

She gives my shoulder another heavy, overly familiar pat, then heads away.

"Was it just me, or was that weird?" I ask Riley.

"Weird." Riley is in agreement with me.

There is nothing to do now but wait for the results.

We tour the show. Byron, of course, is not here, and I am not friendly with anyone else, so there's no one to greet. This is how I like it. No obligation.

I explain the different roses to Riley, pointing out the best traits of each show rose under my breath. "Which one do you think will take Queen? Besides mine." I explain that while there can be prizes in each category, the Queen can be from any of them; it's the best rose overall.

We walk up and down each aisle, each of us examining the roses at our leisure. I'm attracted to an orange miniature giving off a spicy-sweet fragrance. Each bloom seems to have a hundred petals.

Eventually, Riley stops at a table in aisle four. "This one." Riley points to a large white rose with pink tips and a pinker center. It is in a tall vase, long-stemmed, set apart from the contestant's other blooms. Its fragrance has met us halfway up the aisle, no small feat considering how many roses are in the room. It's a Moonstone rose, a beautiful name and a lovely specimen, even if it's not a new kind of rose like mine.

"And why?" I am quizzing her, to see if she has paid attention to anything I've done or lectured her on, when she appears to be doing everything except paying attention. I expect her to shrug and say she doesn't know.

She stops and cocks her head, circling around the rose. The grower, a man in his sixties, eyes her anxiously, as if she will pounce on the bloom and rip it apart. Which would be one way to stop the competition.

Riley ticks off the attributes on her fingers. "Glossy green color. Excellent fragrance. No signs of any disease. It looks almost like a silk flower, only better." She turns to the man. "How'd you do it?"

"Secret compost tea." He winks. "Let me write the recipe."

"Thanks. I'll give it to my aunt here. She grows roses."

Wait. This man was going to just give me his secret recipe? I couldn't believe it. I hoped it wasn't sabotage, that it wouldn't contain some variant of arsenic to kill off all my plants.

"You'll need coffee grounds and alfalfa," he says, scratching out the supplies on an overturned cocktail napkin. "Been perfecting it for thirty years."

"Wow. That's almost as old as my aunt."

"Thirty is a baby," I said, thinking thirty wasn't too old.

"Oh yeah, it is. It's so long." Riley takes the napkin from the man and nods.

"I can't believe you're sharing," I blurted.

He chuckles, snapping his pen closed and tucking it into his red-plaid shirt pocket. "What are you talking about? Rose growers always help each other. Don't you belong to a rose society?"

"Only in name." I survey his other roses.

"You've been reinventing the wheel, then." He reaches out and shakes my hand. "Good luck to you. Winslow Blythe."

"Good luck to you, too." I shake his back, then his name registers. "Wait. You're *the* Winslow Blythe? *Winning Roses*?"

"That's the one." He nods. "Do you have volume six? It has this recipe in it."

"No. I have volume four. I figured they didn't change much." Also, I am too frugal to buy a new guide every year.

He shakes his head. "Nope. Lots of new material."

Riley shoves the napkin into her jeans pocket. I hold out my hand. "Oh, please, otherwise it will end up in the laundry."

"Fine. I'll fix it." She smooths it out.

12 cups alfalfa pellets
¾ cup Epsom salts
¼ cup chelated iron
1½ cups organic compost
Water (use the hose)
Large container with lid (at least 32 gallons)

I recommend putting the container near the roses before you begin; it will be too heavy to move, and it will stink to high heaven.

Fill a large container with water; a plastic trash can works fine. Add all the ingredients and give it a good stir (I use an old broom handle just for this purpose).

Put a lid on it and let it sit for between four days and two weeks. If the weather is hot, or your container's in the sun, it will likely be done faster.

Take the lid off. With a bucket, skim some of the "tea" water off the top. Each mature bush gets 1 gallon every other week. Mini roses get a half gallon. Don't give this to newly planted roses; it'll burn them.

"Well, what to my wondering eyes should appear?" I put the recipe into my fanny pack, another fashion don't for Dara, but extremely convenient nonetheless.

"You've never heard of compost tea?" Blythe grins at me. He's supposed to be over eighty, but he looks more like he's sixty. He has twinkling blue eyes and a mop of silvery hair that is only in faint strands over the top of his head. "Much less stinky than fish emulsion."

I think of my neighbor. "Maybe I like stinky."

Blythe waves us off. "We'll see you later. What was your name?"

"Gal," I tell him.

Riley and I move on. "See, I am useful." Riley grins, her cheeks dimpling, her cheeks almost filled out. The shadow of her former baby self transposes on her face. With a pang, I remember her chubby little hands and legs, never to be seen again.

I gulp. "Riley, I want to tell you something."

"What?" She spins on one Converse high-topped foot, a white sneaker covered in Sharpie graffiti.

I say it fast, before I can stop myself. "I'm sorry I wasn't there for you more when you were little."

Her good mood vanishes, blown away quicker than pollen on the wind. "Why are you saying that now?"

I reach out, touch her arm. "I just thought of it."

She steps backward, focusing out the nearby window. Riley props her forehead against the glass. Her voice is small. "You just thought of it. 'Just.' Hmmm. After how many years?" She scratches at her nose, then faces me, her eyes taking in all the reflected light through the ocean-facing window and throwing it outward. "Listen. Don't even worry about it."

I'm startled at the flat, dark edge in her tone. "Riley."

"I mean it. I'm not worried about it. No one's worried about it." She scans the room. "I'm going to find something to eat, okay?"

"I brought you a peanut butter and jelly." I dig out the baggie from my fanny pack. It's a bit squished, the jam visible through the bread. "I probably should have put it in the cooler."

She takes the messy baggie without comment. "I think I'll eat outside." And off she goes.

13

I RETURN TO MY TABLE.

Riley's mood swings—how she can seem like a perfectly rational semi-adult one minute and a screaming three-year-old the next—frighten me. They remind me of her mother. As a teenager, hell, even as an adult, Becky would be soft one minute, ready to cut you during her next exhale. As long as she was getting her way, she was okay.

Once, right before I'd gotten my new kidney, not long before I turned thirteen, Becky was supposed to go on a class trip to Washington, D.C. And then came my kidney transplant, bills were piling up, and Mom broke it to my sister that she couldn't go.

Instead of being glad I was alive, alive for her to torture another day, Becky turned from where she was putting away dishes and dropped Mom's big platter on the floor. Not just any platter. The platter my mother's mother had gotten on her wedding day from her mother, the one Grandma had brought over from Italy when she emigrated. The platter with yellow and blue flowers cascading over it, the one my mother had said I could have when I got married.

I was sitting at the kitchen table, bundled up in blankets,

still fresh from the incision on my back. "Becky!" I heard my mother say.

Becky simply walked out.

"Is it bad to say I'm relieved for the break?" my mother whispered to my father.

"I'm sure she's going to Annie's." My father hugged my mother. Annie was Becky's best friend. "She'll be back."

She didn't return for two days, walking back in when she was ready. My parents never mentioned it again.

I don't want the same thing for Riley. Which is why I'd tried to talk to her like I just had, let her know that yes, I am sorry I wasn't there. I am sorry I didn't fight her mother and her father for custody, which I surely would have lost.

A hollowness sinks into my torso. It's unlike anything I have felt before. I feel no battle cry, as I do when I have to deal with my doctor or my rebelling body. I am not even too annoyed, as I am when my students misbehave. It's a surprising and overwhelming sense that I have failed.

I cross my arms, thinking hard about how to reach out to Riley. If my mother's way wasn't quite right, and my way wasn't quite right, what should I do? Of course, Riley is not her mother. I am not my mother. A conundrum.

When rose enthusiasts come by and ask me questions about my Hulthemia, I respond with one-word answers. I make no eye contact. Eventually, they leave me alone.

Finally I remember my cell phone. I dial Riley, the first number I have programmed. No response. Of course. I let it ring again, and again, starting over each time it reaches voice mail.

I almost miss the announcement for the winner's circle gathering over the PA system. Only the mass exodus of all the contestants toward the stage area tells me there's something afoot. I pocket the phone and join the small crowd.

Due to my size, no one much minds when I shoulder my way to the very front. Next to me stand two elementary school–aged kids, one of whom is taller than I am. I am confident I'm not in anyone's sight line.

Ms. Lansing stands on a low, shallow stage behind a worn wooden podium with a tinny microphone that goes into feedback shrieks every time she speaks too loudly, which is often, as she doesn't seem to understand the electronics. From this vantage point, I can see the blue-green veins crisscrossing her legs like roads on a highway atlas. She grimaces at me as if she has read my mind, rocking back on her pink heels. "It's been an honor to be your judge," she says, lapsing into the standard spiel about how great everyone is, how wonderful our roses are, how difficult it was to choose winners in each category. Yawn. I have heard this before. I wish they would just print out a list and let everyone look at it and claim their medals on the way out.

It is interminable. Everyone is compelled to clap after each winner's announcement, even for fourth place and honorable mention. I scan the crowd for Riley's shock of black hair and light roots, the white peasant blouse. She should be easy to spot in this otherwise mature crowd.

Finally I see her, not by the stage, but on the far wall under a hand-lettered sign reading SNACK BAR. She stands, one foot behind her on the wall, her arms crossed. She will not make eye contact with me. She is eating a package of Cheetos, her fingers orange.

I call her again, though it's rude to do so during the announcements. She glances at her phone, then puts it away. "Ah." I push back through the crowd to her, reaching her just as she throws the empty bag into a big gray trash can.

"Riley." I block her from the exit.

"I have to use the bathroom." She dodges around me.

I follow. There's no reason for her to cut me out, to try to punish me. I haven't done anything wrong. "Riley. There's no reason to be so upset."

She points. "They're doing your category, Aunt Gal."

I turn. I see Ms. Lansing's lips moving. I step back into the conference space.

Ms. Lansing is gesturing to me. I climb up the stairs on the stage side. Someone thrusts a scratchy ribbon around my neck and propels me into a lineup beside Ms. Lansing. I look down at the medal. Honorable Mention. Pshaw. My first urge is to take it off, pocket it, and get out of here, but I stand and nod my head at the applause, clapping my hands until they hurt for the third-, second-, and first-place winners.

"Congratulations." Ms. Lansing squeezes my shoulders with her talons. I wince.

"Thanks."

"You keep on working, you hear?"

I nod and file offstage.

"And the Queen of Show goes to Winslow Blythe, for his Moonstone." The audience interrupts into applause. Winslow walks slowly but steadily onto the stage. Well, at least it's someone I sort of know.

I return to the snack bar, but Riley's not there.

Where could she have gone? Surely she knew to stay around. I head into the restrooms. "Riley?" I call.

No response.

Now I feel like someone has knocked a big heavy brown ball into my stomach, which happened once in second grade. I can't breathe. I lean against the bathroom tile wall.

"Are you all right?" a woman using a walker asks. "You want me to call someone?"

"No. I'm fine," I gasp. I straighten and leave the restroom without a backward glance.

No one is at the snack bar, really just a folding table with a cash box and some food. I don't see her in the audience, or at my table. I grab my rose, stick it back into the cooler, and head out to the car.

There she is, leaning against the maroon Toyota Tercel, examining her nails as though they contain the secret to life. "Hey, Aunt Gal."

"I was looking for you in there." I huff with the effort of having pulled the cooler. The parking lot is on an incline.

"Sorry. I couldn't find you. I figured you'd come back to the car."

"That's why you have a cell phone." I pop the trunk open.

"I called you."

I take out my phone and look at it. Two missed calls. "Oh. I must not have felt it in my pocket."

"It's easy to miss a call." She picks up the cooler and hefts it in. Though she is young and healthy, she struggles with the weight of lifting. It was easier to get the thing out. I resolve to give her more lean protein, build some muscle on her. When my sister sees her again, Riley will be unrecognizable.

In the car, Riley snaps her seat belt. "I take it you didn't win."

"Honorable Mention." I start the engine. I don't want to talk about it. I haven't even had time to process the rose show results. Byron was correct. When isn't he correct? I should listen to him. He knows what he's doing. And I, what am I? I'm an overly optimistic dreamer.

Not only a dreamer about roses, but about my kidney, too. Who am I kidding?

Something I've been holding at bay washes over me. I do

not move the car. I sit and stare at the ocean, at its fuzzy blue flat horizon. All my blood flow tests have been inconclusive. I am never going to get a new kidney. Not ever.

I am too dehydrated to even squeeze out a single tear for relief. But sobs threaten to escape. Occasionally, throughout my life, I have suffered what Mom calls a Blues Day, when the despair of having this chronic disease gets the best of me and I'd retreat into my room and cry for twenty-four hours or so.

I need to stave this off as best I can, until we get home and I can crawl safely into bed. If I am aware of my irrationality, I wonder, does this make me rational? The waves move back and forth on the water. I imagine the ocean is a pool of my tears instead, visualizing my sadness getting washed away from my body. I breathe in and out slowly twenty-five times. All right, I tell myself on each exhale. I'm all right.

Riley turns up the radio to a rock station. Lady Gaga drowns out all. Clearly Riley doesn't know what is really bothering me, or particularly cares. I should not expect her to. She's only a kid, not my confidante, and certainly not my caretaker. I feel more alone than ever.

"Honorable Mention is better than a kick in the face, as Grandpa would say." Riley's voice snaps me out of my meditation. She's correct. That is what my father would say. I can imagine his dry tone saying it, too. I smile in spite of myself.

She's right. Who cares if Winslow Blythe won? He's been breeding roses for, what, sixty years? I am a mere pup compared to him. There had to be another chance for me. I am already planning to go to the Pasadena rose show in June. Dara said she could probably go with me, said she always wanted to go to the Rose Bowl swap meet. I was going to go whether or not I had a good rose for show, just so we could have an excuse to get down there. I turn off the radio and step out of the car. "Why don't you have the first turn, Riley?"

AT HOME, I get inside as quickly as possible. "I'm going to have a shower and a nap," I say to my niece, kicking off my shoes.

She eyes me silently. Throughout the ride, an occasional tear has slipped out despite my dehydration. Once I begin to get down, it's hard to rise again. I'm a deflated soufflé. I try as best I can, treating Riley to the fast food of her choice and letting her listen to whatever music she liked. I complain loudly about pollen affecting my eyes. But she might have noticed something amiss anyway.

"I really am sorry I ran off, Gal."

"Water under the bridge." I'd forgotten about that hours earlier. I am not about to burden her with my kidney fears. She will only worry. There's nothing she can do to help me.

"I'm going to go to Samantha's to do homework." She fidgets with the string on her hoodie. "She's helping me a lot."

"Biology, I hope." I have assigned them work to do over the weekend. Samantha would be a good one to study with. I am enthusiastic about this idea. "There's a bike in the garage." It's still light out. "Be home by dusk."

"You ride a bike?" Riley is incredulous.

"Nope. But Grandma and Grandpa left it."

She shoulders her backpack. "See you later, Aunt Gal."

AFTER MY SHOWER, my mental state improves. The house is blessedly silent. I dress in soft sweatpants and a T-shirt.

No one else is breathing in the next room, no television, no sounds, and no sullen child staring in the corner. Though I enjoy Riley, I haven't realized how much I've missed this. Being alone. I am a creature of routine, of silent habit. People like Dara always seem to assume I must be miserably lonely, a spinster living even without a cat (I'm allergic to all things furry). I am not. I am happy like this.

I go outside and unload my rose from the car. Old Mrs. Allen is out watering again, her grass green and knee-high. She glares at me from under her black straw hat.

I leave the rose cooler in the driveway and walk over. "Afternoon, Mrs. Allen. If you want someone to cut that grass for you, I can recommend a student of mine."

"I don't need your help." Mrs. Allen directs a fierce spray of water toward my side of the fence. Mud splashes onto my plastic clogs. "Who's that girl always hanging around?"

I back away. I would have told her about my niece, but now I won't tell her one thing. I get angry despite my best efforts not to. I am always prone to being crankier when I'm tired, anyway. This is the wrong time to mess with me. "Why do you have such a problem with me? What have I ever done to you?"

She glares, her watery and red blue eyes suddenly focused. "Roses."

"Roses?" I'm confused.

"Your damn rose vines come over my fence." She points down the property line to where my climbing roses are indeed climbing over a six-foot lattice wall.

"The fence is on my property line," I point out. My father took great care to assure that. "If you don't like how it looks, build a fence on your side."

"The roots come up under the grass. It's ruining my

lawn. And your lawn is an eyesore. Looks like a hillbilly farmer lives there."

The roots certainly do not affect her lawn. I shake my head, seeing the futility of arguing with someone like her. I could show her the climbing roses entry in the rose encyclopedia about roots, and she would think I'd secretly written the entry and sent it in. "Have a nice day, Mrs. Allen."

"It's nice evening, now. It's five o'clock!" she barks after me, sending another spattering of muddy particles against my ankles.

Back in the greenhouse, G42 has produced another open blossom. I sniff. Not fragrant, either. I will breed it again and get something better next year. Or the next.

Truly exhausted now, I go back into the house. I will get a little nap in before dinnertime. I'm not hungry anyway. I lie on the bed and immediately fall asleep.

The phone awakens me a few minutes later. At least, I think it's only a few minutes later, until I look at the clock. Nine o'clock. I answer. "Hello?"

"Gal!" It's Mom, sounding relieved. I was supposed to call her at seven. Obviously, she got worried. "How was the rose show?"

"Didn't win." I sit up and put on my glasses. Sheesh. I was more tired than I thought. Good thing I didn't drive. I silently thank Riley for not waking me up when she came in.

"There's something wrong. I can hear it in your voice." My mother's voice gets progressively more frantic. I picture her waving to my father to pick up the extension even though he's in the middle of his crime show. Indeed, I hear a click and the drone of lawyer-type television voices in the background.

"Hi, Dad."

"Gal."

I take in a breath. "I'm just having one of those days, is all."

"Oh." One syllable from Mom, containing a world of understanding. "Let me talk to Riley. I want to let her know what to do."

"She shouldn't have to do anything, hon. She's only fifteen," my father says.

"Fifteen is plenty old enough to pitch in. I had a full-time job when I was fifteen, and took care of my younger brother and sister." Mom sniffs. "Go get her, Gal."

I tell Mom to hang on and go out to the living room.

It's dark. No television. No light in the kitchen. No light in Riley's room. I turn on her lamp to check. No Riley.

I go out to the garage. The bike sits where it's been sitting since my parents left it, still dusty.

I return to the bedroom. This is the second time today Riley's gone off doing whatever she likes, without regard. I'd told her to be back at dark. I get back on the phone with Mom. I don't exactly wish to relay this to my mother. Admit I might have lost their only granddaughter. I think I know where to look for her.

"She's in the bathroom right now," I say instead. I force every bit of brightness I can into my tone. "Washing her hair."

"You tell her to call me tomorrow." Mom buys it.

"Listen, I'm super tired. Let me get off the phone."

"Good night. Love you."

"Good night. Love you too, Mom. And Dad," I add. There's no answer on his end.

"He hung up while you were out looking for Riley," Mom says. "I'll tell him."

Immediately after hanging up, I call Riley's phone. No

answer. I get out the school directory and look up Samantha's phone number. Her mother answers and tells me Samantha's not home. "She told me she's studying with you, Ms. Garner," she says, sounding surprised and immediately anxious. "You and Riley."

The plot thickens. I tighten my grip on the phone. "I think I know where they are," I say grimly. "Don't you worry. I'll get her and bring her home safe."

14

BRAD LIVES A FEW MILES AWAY FROM ME, ON A street with small lots and even smaller houses. The lights are all on at the low-slung house when I pull up. His father's truck is gone, I note as I step out of my car onto the cracked concrete driveway. Brad's there. This girl is going to catch it when I get her.

I knock sharply on the painted green door. The house is not so well kept for the home of a custodian; gray paint flakes, and there's visible dirt even in this porch light. The porch itself is covered in a fake grass carpet.

Brad creaks open the door, his face registering shock. "Ms. Garner!" He probably wants to make a joke, but stops at my face.

I push him aside with my hand. "Where is she?"

Brad moves backward, not acting as if he has anything to be ashamed of. He shakes back his hair. "Riley! Your aunt's here."

She comes out of a back room, her hair wrapped in a towel. The collar of her shirt is soaked. Samantha follows. Both girls look extremely guilty. Samantha can't even bring her eyes up to meet mine.

I gasp. "Why were you taking a shower here?"

"I can explain." Riley holds up her hand. "It's my hair."

"What about it?"

"We were dyeing it." Samantha steps out from behind, chewing on a cuticle. "It looked pretty bad. My mother doesn't approve of hair dye, so we came here to do it."

Riley shakes out her hair. It tumbles down, an array of blond and brown once again. No more black. And it's considerably shorter, now shorn just below her ears. Brad looks on admiringly.

"We had to cut it. The ends were all damaged." Samantha lifts up a hunk of hair to show me.

"So you've been dyeing hair this whole time?" I am not sure whether I should believe this. I've never dyed hair. I suspect they were doing more than dyeing hair; they are teenagers, after all. Brad does not seem to me like the type of boy who would be content with hair dyeing. Though I have no personal experience with males in this capacity, I've seen it plenty of times in my classes and with, of course, my sister. I purse my lips disapprovingly at him, but he merely gives me a small grin, his face innocent of all sin.

"We had to bleach the black out first, then dye it back." Samantha sounds proud of herself. "It's a two-step process."

"You sound pretty knowledgeable."

She shrugs modestly. "I do all my friends' hair."

"My dad's the only parent who doesn't care about the mess in the bathroom," Brad says.

"I see." I tear my gaze away from the boy. "Samantha, your mom wants you home."

She looks shocked.

"Yeah, you might want to get your stories straight before you tell them." I jerk my head toward my niece. "I called your mom looking for her."

"Oh, shit," Samantha breathes. She rushes back and reappears with a backpack and an arm full of books.

"So, how much studying did you get done?" I glance at Brad and at Riley. She looks at the wall.

Brad looks at me. "Enough to get by."

"What did you tell my mother?" Samantha takes my arm rather roughly. I remove her hand.

"That I'd come get you."

"Please don't tell her where I was." Samantha's eyes are reddened. "Please."

I step back resolutely. "Samantha, I can't hide this from your mom. Come on. Let's go."

"You don't understand!" She backs up behind Brad. "She will kill me."

These teens. Always so dramatic. I assess her, standing behind Brad, who has his arms raised as if he wants to protect her. Riley stands behind him, too, behind Samantha. I wonder exactly what sort of relationship the girls have with Brad. "She won't." Though lying and being at a boy's house and shaming her family in front of a teacher can't be good. My heart softens for a second. Then I get a grip. "Let's go." I shepherd Riley and Samantha into my car. Samantha sits in the back, hanging her head down low into her lap, her hair covering her face like two planes of dark water.

ON MONDAY, I see Brad walking alone. Samantha follows him several paces behind, several random students between. Then Riley, in the same manner. They pass me in the hall without glancing up, continuing down to the adjoining church for our monthly school Mass.

Samantha's mother showed no visible reaction when I

dropped her off. She only apologized for putting me to any trouble. Samantha stood silently next to her mother, her gaze directed down.

"No harm done," I said, though I thought Riley certainly deserved some sort of reprimand or punishment for being where she was not supposed to be, and staying out later than I'd said to boot. Reassured that Samantha's mother would not do anything worse than I would, I left with Riley.

I still hadn't thought of a suitable punishment for my niece. Not for dyeing her hair, but for staying out far later than she was supposed to and for not telling me where she was and ignoring my calls. "You're a minor. What you do falls on me," I'd said to her several times the next day.

"I know. I know," Riley said, her voice low.

Now I slip into the back pew onto the hard wooden seat, pulling down the padded kneeler. The nearest student is six rows ahead of us, but I don't have supervisory duties at the moment, and I want a break. The church is modern-looking, built in the 1960s with oak and mahogany paneling, and is used for the community as well as our school. Big clear windows slant into pyramids toward a clear sky above the pulpit. Along the side walls, angular stained-glass depictions of the Stations of the Cross form windows fourteen feet above the congregation. I stare blankly at Christ carrying the cross, the faces all acute angles and the robes sharp. The organist, our music teacher, plays a melody I don't recognize.

"Sorry I didn't call you back this weekend." Dara kneels beside me with difficulty, wearing a green Chinese-style sheath dress with a high collar and silken frog buttons in red. I'd tried to call her all day on Sunday, after the Riley-Brad-Samantha fiasco, but she never did answer or return my call.

"I have a cell phone now. You can call me anytime." I keep my voice lower than hers. "Where were you?"

She squints up at the sky. "I went out with George."

Acid from my breakfast burns my throat, though I can't remember what I could have eaten to cause it. Mr. Morton sits with the kids, kneeling in a pew. The back of his neck has a fresh haircut and looks soft above his green shirt collar. I swallow. "Finally taking my advice. Did you have fun?"

"I did." She allows herself a small smile. I wonder how much fun was had. My friend is not known for her saintliness. She sits through the Mass only as a courtesy to the school, not because she feels any great religious need. It has never bothered me. "How was the rose show?"

I look back up at the stained glass. "You don't want to know." I didn't call her to talk about the rose show. I called her to talk about Riley. I fill her in now, as we rise and the processional into the church begins with the priest walking down the aisle.

She steps out of the pew and motions me to follow. I dip my knee and make the sign of the cross as I leave, which my friend does not.

We go into the front alcove, closing the heavy double doors behind us. Dara stands before the bulletin board, with notices of roommates needed and gas guzzlers for sale. "The only part that sounds really terrible is you telling Samantha's mother."

I gasp audibly.

She holds up a hand. "Samantha comes to the after-school art program. She's only allowed to do academics. No socializing. No friends. Certainly no male friends."

"I'm pretty certain Brad is more than her platonic male friend."

Dara cocks her head. "That's probably true." Her abdomen expands and contracts in her dress. "But do you know how badly she's going to suffer for something as innocent as helping Riley with her hair? She probably won't come out of the house until she leaves for college!"

"I happen to think Samantha's mother deserves to know. What she does with that information is not my concern."

"It should be."

"I don't control other people."

"No, but you know how some people react better than others." Dara crosses her arms.

"That is not the point. The point is the girls were lying and breaking the rules."

"What were you doing while Riley was gone?" Dara paces the floor.

I hesitate. "Taking a much-needed nap."

Dara turns back to me, her face sympathetic. "Gal. Do you think you've taken on too much?"

I shake my head. Unbelievable. "I'd expected you to tell me what Riley's punishment should be, not get into this whole other moral debate."

"It's not my place to tell you."

"Yet it's your place to tell me I was wrong about everything else." I put my hand on the door to go back into the church. I need simple support, not criticism. I feel like she's slapped me.

"Gal." Dara's shoulders slump, but she makes no move toward me. "Don't be like that."

I go inside.

The priest prepares the Eucharist, the biscuits and wine. Body and blood. I lean against the wall, unwilling to go back to the pew yet. Is Dara right? Should I have not told Samantha's mother? Does Riley not deserve punishment?

A simple restriction should do. One, maybe two weeks. No recreational computer use, no venturing out with her friends. Riley sits with her sophomore class, apart from Samantha. Indeed, apart from the others. Samantha sits flanked by the pre-Riley posse, the girls who remain unsoiled and perfectly studious. I realize Samantha is not going to be allowed out with Riley again, no matter if Riley is my niece, a relative of a woman who could write a stellar college recommendation. Yet, what else is there to do except tell the whole truth? It's not for me to decide what is good for Samantha's mother to hear and what is not. Just as during my parent-teacher conferences, I tell the parents both the good and the bad. I will not hide details.

I decide to go out and tell Dara what I'm thinking. I crack open the church door and hear her voice.

"She just can't stand to be told she's wrong. Ever. No matter what. She has to get her way." Her voice rises in frustration. "And you feel so bad telling her she's wrong, anyway, because she's already sick."

Dr. O'Malley's voice returns in a rumbling baritone. "They're not bad kids. You're right. There are worse things to worry about."

I sink back, my hand closing the door silently. Dara is the one person at this whole school who has bothered to see beyond my cracked exterior shell and be my friend. I thought. I go back to my pew just as the students begin lining up to get the Eucharist. Mr. Morton gets in line behind them, his back straight and tall. He glances back at me and gestures for me to join him. Instead, I move down to the kneeling pad, my mind roiling and my knees protesting. I stay like that until the church is empty once more.

15

After school, I break the restriction news to Riley, and she takes it with a single nod.

I hesitate before I ask. Do I really want to know this? "Was Sam's mother very angry?"

"Does it matter?" Riley cracks her math book open on the coffee table. "I haven't talked to her. She hasn't e-mailed me. I have no idea."

I don't pry further.

"Can I call my mother?"

"Of course." Though you shouldn't, I add silently. Because your mother's only going to agree with you because it's easier.

That night, I drive myself to the hospital. At the dialysis center, I collapse into a chair. Perhaps I should switch to daytime dialysis. I hate leaving Riley alone, especially now that I know she'll go off at any moment. Are there kids coming over while I'm gone?

Dialysis for me now is nothing more than an endless middle ground. The light at the end of the tunnel is always a kidney for a dialysis patient. When that is gone, what is there? It's like telling a kid Santa's dead and there's never going to be another Christmas. My next appointment with Dr. Blankenship is not until mid-May, and I doubt anything will change between then and now.

A rustle of a newspaper makes me look up. Mark Walters folds the paper into his white-jeaned lap. The man looks not much the worse for wear, despite his dialysis. His skin has a new brownish glow, as if he just climbed out of a hammock strung between two palm trees on a warm beach. Today he wears a gray V-neck T-shirt instead of a white one, and my surprise is so great I can't help but blurt, "Wow. That's almost a color."

He glances down at his chest and laughs.

Furious with myself for breaking my vow of silence to this man, I pick up a *Newsweek* and turn my body away from him. I don't want to have a conversation. I've promised myself often enough I wouldn't. Everyone thinks he's so terribly charming. There's nothing charming about him. He reminds me of the popular girl in high school who pretends she is dumb to get praise and male attention but is smarter than the rest of us. "Fake" is the word I'm looking for.

Before I know it, he's sitting in the vacant seat next to me. "Excuse me, young lady. Have I done something to offend you?"

I shrink away from him, shocked that he's talking to me still. "It's 'pardon me.' 'Excuse me' is for when you want to be dismissed from something, like the table during dinner." I am buying time. What has he done specifically to offend me, besides exist?

"What?" He blinks, the gray reflecting into his eyes and making them bluer than usual.

I put down the magazine. I have had enough. Dara and

Riley and the rose show and the kidney. Especially the kidney. "I just think it's funny how some people are born with a disease and need help to fix it, while others bring it upon themselves and get more help than they perhaps deserve."

He twists one side of his mouth. "You're talking about me?"

I stare at him, daring to deny it. "I know all about you. Everyone does." Alcoholic, non–blood-pressure-medicine taker, ruining his perfectly functional organs. With a shudder, Becky comes into my mind's eye. This could be Becky in ten or twenty years.

He laces his fingers over his crossed knees. "And that's why you hate me?"

"I don't hate you, exactly." I take an enormous breath, aware of the nurses behind the glass partition watching this exchange carefully. I hope they will still be gentle with the needles later. "I got bumped off the list."

His impressively shaggy brows knit together, casting a hairy shadow over his cheekbones, like a dark caterpillar is marching across his face. "I'm sorry to hear that. I know the wait is difficult."

"I've done it before. Twice. I know what's involved." I will not be talked down to. Not by him, not by Dr. Blankenship. "I happen to think there should be criteria for treatment."

"So only the morally deserving get served?" His tone is pondering, not angry. "Perhaps if a motorcyclist refuses to wear a helmet and gets a head injury as a result, we should refuse treatment? Or an obese person who gets diabetes should not be helped?"

I consider this. "I hadn't thought about it, but perhaps we should all take responsibility for our actions, and the results of those actions."

"Are you not considering the frailty of the human condition?" Walters gives me a sad smile. "I started drinking, Gal, at a low point in my life. My wife had just passed away. I lost my business. I was in a pit I could not quite climb out of alone."

I search for something to say. "I'm sorry."

He sits back in his chair and I think I detect a note of triumph in his demeanor. His smile looks smug to me.

This riles me again. "So you think that it's excusable for someone to hurt themselves because of a tragic event? Others have bad things happen to them without destroying themselves, or others, for that matter."

"I'm not saying it's an excuse. It's simply something that happened. A reason."

I sputter. I'm not a believer in explaining away misdeeds by shirking responsibility. "I bet you think all the murderers on death row should be let out because they had bad childhoods."

He raises his hands. "Not at all. I am simply saying," he puts his hand on my forearm, "that none of us is perfect, Gal."

I remove my arm from him. "How do you know my name?"

"The same way you know mine. We all know you around here, Gal. And contrary to popular belief, we are not all against you."

"It's not just popular belief," I mutter.

A nurse calls his name.

Walters pats my arm, retracted though it is, and gets up. "Chin up, Galilee."

It is difficult for me not to throw the *Newsweek* at his back.

Winslow Blythe's *Complete Rose Guide* (SoCal Edition)

May

Can you believe summer is almost here? Your roses are in full bloom by now and subject to attack by various forces: bugs and fungi.

Wash the rose undersides daily to get rid of critters. Do this in the morning; doing so at night will lead to mildew or fungus.

Deadhead the spent blooms, unless you want them to produce rose hips.

Now is the time when roses use the most food. Don't be stingy and they will repay you by reblooming again in the fall.

If you do see signs of powdery mildew, it's important to spray a fungicide and kill that before it gets out of hand. The foliage will turn pale gray and crinkle up like a piece of old tissue paper. There are other types of mildew, too, like downy mildew, browning the leaves. Either type spreads like a bad flu through a nursery school, and you can pretty much forget those rose specimens.

16

THE FOLLOWING DAY, I AM AT SCIENCE OLYMPIAD practice, getting my group of students ready for their task: Disease Detectives. In this event, the students look at a real-life report of a food-borne illness, then must decide which disease it is based on the clues.

Mr. Morton is doing Crime Busters, which is like forensic science. Mr. Morton has set out some sneakers he's laced with fingerprints and hair for the students to analyze. I watch them, wishing I could do the experiments, too. I love watching *CSI*.

We're both doing the Storming the Castle event.

I give my Disease Detectives students the handouts for the food-borne illness. Jim Hillyard, a basketball-tall senior with long brown hair, grins and rubs his hands together comically. Samantha looks at the handout with distaste. I tell them to make a list of symptoms and what the people had eaten so they can narrow down what the culprits may be.

"I already know which disease it is." Sam's voice is flat. She drops her handout onto the table.

"Don't say it aloud," I say, not wanting her to ruin it for the other teammates. "Pretend you don't know. And you certainly don't know how the health department figured it out."

"It's not that hard." She won't meet my eyes. Oh, yes. Samantha is unhappy with me.

My temper flares. "No one is twisting your arm to be on the science team, Samantha."

She reaches for the handout. Not even a sigh or an eye roll escapes. What self-control. I lean down, not very far considering her head comes up to my chest when she's sitting. "Everything all right, Samantha?"

She gives one quick nod.

I should know she will not talk to me.

I survey the students. They are all involved in their tasks. I watch them ask each other for help, and the trebuchet kids raise their hands for Mr. Morton. I tell myself I am achieving the ultimate goal of a teacher: to become unnecessary to a student's success. But I have to swallow a lump as I stand in the back, feeling my redundancy.

Mr. Morton tells the trebuchet team to go outside and launch their beanbags, then measure the distance. We both go into the courtyard.

"We could have one more kid on this team," Mr. Morton says. "For backup. The Olympiad requires two people per team."

"Someone from another area can cover. We probably won't get two people dropping out." I watch Brad launch a beanbag into the air, then yell for the other kid, a junior, to get the tape measure.

Mr. Morton's forehead wrinkles. Today he is wearing flat-front khakis, brown leather slip-on shoes, and a light gray shirt patterned with something that, on closer inspection, appears to be small airplanes flying about. "It doesn't hurt to plan for the worst, does it? I called the other people on your alternate list. None of them want to do it."

I know he's still talking about Riley joining the team. If all the people on the wait list decline, then I don't really have any reason to say that my niece can't do it. Except for my belief she won't perform, and doesn't want to.

She did less than stellar on the recent biology test about cell division, never once showing up for help, though I could see she did not understand the concepts. The students who did come for tutoring, who sat quizzing each other with the flash cards they'd drawn, these kids all got at least a B. Riley got a C minus.

"It's passing, isn't it?" she had said, acting as though she didn't care. I truly could not tell if she did care or not, the way she crammed the test so casually into her backpack. If it were up to me, I would post all the students' grades in public, for everyone to see. Public shaming can work wonders. Though in this day and age, it's possible no one has any standards anymore.

"It's barely passing." It was an embarrassment to me, her aunt and her teacher, for her to get such a low grade. Dr. O'Malley would tut over it, think it was another example of Gal Garner's poor teaching ability. Never mind all the others who did pass. "You must come to tutoring."

She had tried for a bargain. "If I don't do well on the next test, I'll come."

"By then your grade will be too low," I had said sharply. "It's May. How much time do you think you have? Then you won't be able to drive."

She had no answer then.

Mr. Morton waits for me to respond to him. The afternoon sun glints like candlelight on his face. I don't really want to get into all this with him, explaining everything about my niece and her little quirks. "Trust me. You don't want Riley on the team."

"Sometimes kids respond better to teachers who aren't related to them." His tone is mild, but I take offense.

I squint up at him. "How long have you been teaching, Mr. Morton?"

He takes a breath. "One month."

"I see."

"But I have taught . . . kids . . . who are related to me. I mean, she's still very young." His voice gets husky.

I want to ask him who and I don't want to ask him. He doesn't want to tell me, either, because he strides away to Brad, instructing him on how to correct the trajectory. I watch for a moment. The male students, outdoors, their sleeves rolled up, fixing the catapult, nearly vibrate with health. With their matching uniforms and tans, it looks like a school recruiting ad. I return inside, to my anatomy and my violent vomiting-and-diarrhea scenarios.

17

A WEEK PASSES WITH RILEY ATTENDING TO THE details of her grounding like a patient prisoner. "I did not use my phone today," she reports every evening, showing me her Calls list. "You can check yourself."

"Hmmm, yes." I make a big show out of checking, though I can barely work my own phone. "Good job, Riley."

Each day after school, Riley involves herself in all the clubs available to her that will give her an excuse to do something valid with her peers, exactly as Samantha does. She joins Key Club, the community service club; Art Club; Spanish Club; and even the Chess Club. At these clubs, she laughs and jokes like any other kid who's been going to a private school her whole life. Gone is the Riley who arrived here, punk makeup and all. I try to be happy; she wants to fit in, but something about how thoroughly the old Riley has disappeared unnerves me. She's trying awfully hard. Maybe too hard. I say nothing, not wanting to seem critical. Arouse the sleeping dragon.

After our post-school activities are done, I take her home, where we make dinner in relative silence.

Every evening that I'm not at dialysis, Riley does her homework. She stares at the dark TV and her turned-off phone, looking so dejected I almost let her use them. "Would you like to play a board game?" I ask her halfway through her week of no electronics.

She gives me a look like I'm an alien from outer space.

"How about cards?" I suggest.

She straightens on the couch, her posture looking the best it has in weeks. She flips back her new hair. The colors are somewhat dull, the shininess probably bleached out by all the processing, but it looks much more normal than it had before. "For money?"

"How about for pennies?" I get out my jar of pennies. My parents and I like to play cards when they visit. Usually it's long games like bridge, if we can get a fourth. Dara sometimes submits, but the card games are too long and boring for her. I tell her it's a mental exercise, and we can still chat while we're playing. "Texas hold 'em. And then blackjack."

I deal the cards, explaining how the game works. I'm a pretty fair poker player, and I've got no problem with gambling as long as you have the money to lose.

Occasionally, my parents take me to Vegas, where we stay at one of the cheap places off the main strip where my mother gets the rooms comped in return for all the money she loses on slots. Dad and I hit the poker rooms, then blackjack tables.

"This is awesome." Riley taps the table. I deal her another card.

"It's better with more people." We play a few more rounds. Then I show her blackjack, how to get to twenty-one and when to hold and when to double down, when to hit. "Now, this is all important to know. What you do here can mess up your whole table. Some people, like me and your Grandpa, would get mad at you."

"Can we have popcorn?" she asks, sounding like a little kid again.

"Sure. Go ahead and make some." I'll bet her mother has not played games with her, not even Candy Land.

Becky was never one for board games. She was always on the go, always wanting to be out, out, out while I was perpetually stuck indoors. During my long periods of confinement, Mom sent Becky to a neighbor's, who practically adopted her. I remember going days without seeing my sister. "Where's Becky?" I'd ask my mother. I'd wanted Becky to stay and play board games with me, or watch television, or sit on the bed and play Barbies. The answer varied: Becky was out whale watching, or at the Wild Animal Park, or simply outside playing. As she got older and could choose her social schedule, she would be out every weekend night. Eventually, Becky became more like a person we saw only on random weeknights and holidays than a true family member.

That Becky felt left out did not occur to me until many years later, before Riley was born and after both of us had ventured out into the world. Mom invited me over for her world-famous tacos. Me, and not my sister.

Becky had shown up that night, dropping off a load of laundry. She froze when she saw us. We froze, too, hunched over our dripping crunchy taco shells as if we'd been caught with gold bullion in a bank.

To my amazement, Mom got a guilty look on her face and began explaining it away as coincidence. "Your sister just dropped in. Would you like a taco?" This clearly wasn't true, and I was confused for a moment until it hit me. They hadn't wanted to see Becky.

Becky knew it, too. The air whooshed out of Becky's step as though someone had whacked her kneecaps with a base-ball bat. She sank into Dad's recliner and retied her shoes, which did not need retying.

"No time, thank you." Her voice was too chipper, crack-ing; her hair hung over her face to hide her expression. How could I see such tiny things in my sister when I never even knew what to buy her for Christmas? And why couldn't my parents see it?

Mom relaxed, going back to her taco. Dad acted as if he had barely heard the exchange at all, his eyes still trained on the football game in the other room.

Only I, confronted with the evidence that I was my moth-er's favorite, reached out to her. How can a mother have favorites among her children? At the time, I still harbored hopes that one day I would find some man who could look beyond everything I appeared to be, see who I was. "They're really good tacos, Becky."

Instantly she reared back, a cobra attacking. She stood. "What part of 'no' don't you get?"

"Fine." My throat caught on a piece of shell. I swallowed. "Don't eat the tacos. I don't care." I would not offer again, not offer anything. Couldn't she see that none of this was my fault? Why did Becky have to punish me?

"There's no need to be rude." I thought Mom was speak-ing to me, but no, she was speaking up for me, to Becky, her tone even more cutting than my sister's.

I sat thinking of all this now as my sister's daughter, play-ing a good-girl role, made popcorn. I had been unlucky in some ways, lucky in others. I wanted, more than anything, for Riley to be lucky in everything.

. . .

ON FRIDAY EVENING, Riley comes in, her chores discharged, wiping her brow dramatically as if I'd just asked her to complete the seven labors of Hercules instead of clean our common bathroom. "My restriction is up. May I go out?"

So it was. Curiously, this week had felt less like a restriction week than a small vacation with my niece. For a moment the word "no" presents itself on my tongue. I flicked it away before I could say it aloud. "Where, with whom, and for how long?" I tick these off, feeling as if something has again slipped away from me before I can hold it. "With Samantha?"

"Are you kidding? Not with her, probably ever again. With some kids from art class. You don't know them."

"I know everyone." The school is not that big.

"It's just to Rory's Diner." She names a popular hangout for the high school kids, a fifties-style joint with an old Corvette turned into a dining table. She slides what look like sleeves cut off an old T-shirt, with thumb holes in them, over her forearms. I realize that's exactly what they are. "I'll be back by ten."

My stomach clenches. I understand, suddenly, Samantha's mother's concerns. How much easier it would be for me if I kept Riley at hand, under my roof, in my sight, at all times. But I can't do this during my dialysis and I cannot do it now. "All right."

She disappears into the bathroom, and as though on cue, a car pulls up and honks. Riley opens the door. Her black eyeliner is back in place, her hair is slicked down. She wears black jeans and oxblood Doc Marten boots, and a T-shirt with a lacy vest over it, along with those weird gloves. She looks like what I think a typical art student would look like, except with fewer piercings. "See you."

Her armor is back. I sit upright on the couch. "Wait. Who else will be there?"

She leaps out the door, a gazelle escaping from a lion.

I ponder how she made these plans without using her cell phone or computer. And how she would know I'd say yes.

The phone rings. It's Dara. I have spoken to her only in passing since I heard her gossiping with Dr. O'Malley.

"Dara." I try her name out gingerly, not sure how I feel about it.

"Hi, Gal. I haven't seen you around school this week."

"My class is still in the same place."

"So's mine, oddly enough," she says drily. "Listen, I'm sorry about the whole Riley and Samantha thing. I know you're doing your best."

"I always do." I consider whether or not to apologize. I decide to do a half apology. "I'm sorry if I upset you."

She hesitates. "How'd you like to go get some food?"

"Love to," I respond. I nearly wither with relief that my friend is free.

We avoid the burger place with the kids, though Dara could own that joint, with her wide cream circle skirt and her ballerina flats. Her hair is up and out of her face, and she wears no makeup except for lip gloss. "You look classy," I say to her.

She tosses her hair back. "I *am* classy, Gal."

"Hey, classy is a compliment to some people."

After a discussion about what I can eat, we choose a soup and salad place, which has enough variety for the both of us.

I pile a plate with soft French bread and pasta with white sauce, and another with Romaine, zucchini shavings, cucumber, and celery. I have to avoid high-phosphorus veggies, and I'm allowed just three half-cup servings of each permissible vegetable. However, I can eat as many bread products as I like, provided they are not whole-grain, because those contain too much phosphorus.

Dara eyes my plate as she adds a high-bran muffin, no butter, to her plate of greens. "I wish I could have that pasta."

"Maybe so, but you probably don't want the rest of the package." I avoid the tomatoes and the soups, all of which seem to have some kind of potato in them, which are also banned.

We sit at a wood table so heavily lacquered I can see up my nostrils when I glance down. I move my plates of food in front of me. I consider whether to tell her I heard her talking to Dr. O'Malley in the hallway about my stubbornness. The only reason I think I'm right, I want to point out, is because most of the time I am. I shouldn't have to change my mind simply because someone else has a different (and wrong) opinion about a situation.

Dara should know by now that I don't avoid doing things because they are easier. It would have been easier for me not to involve Samantha's mother, for me to cover up for her daughter. But then if something else happened later—say, Samantha went out again without her parents' knowledge and got into serious trouble—surely I, as the adult involved and a teacher to boot, would bear responsibility. Samantha's parents would say I should have told them at an early stage.

I don't want to get back into any unpleasantness with Dara. The sting of her words with Dr. O'Malley has worn off. I've heard worse about me. Sticking to a position, in my opinion, is a character virtue, not a flaw.

"Excited about the rose show in Pasadena?" I ask.

She nods, but grimaces. "I am."

I grin. "You know, Byron will be there."

"Byron the great and powerful?" She takes a small bite of bran muffin. "I can hardly wait. What am I supposed to do with a guy in another state?"

I shrug. "Same thing you'd do with a guy here, probably. Not get serious about him."

She ignores this jab. "Gal. I'm still not sure I can go. It's pretty tight for me right now. I'm saving for a house." She shifts uncomfortably in her chair, tucking a strand of hair behind her ear.

"Oh." I can't fault her for that. Still, I don't want to think about the possibility she won't go. "But you'll probably come, right?"

"I'll have to see after our next paycheck. I have a lot of credit cards to pay off." She changes the subject. "How's the science team coming?"

Dara just has to come with me. I wait until I swallow before responding. "Just fine."

"George says you need another alternate for the trebuchet." She focuses on her plate.

I put down my fork. "Don't tell me you're trying to put the pressure on, too. Riley is not coming on the team."

She holds up her hand. "One, chill out. Two, you are not the Grand Poobah. You don't have final say in everything."

"I do in this." Science Olympiad is my territory. "Why don't you start an art team?"

"There can be no art team. Art is too subjective."

"I thought you always said you know good and bad art when you see it."

"But that's only me." She heaves a frustrated sigh. "Gal,

has it occurred to you that if you do let Riley on the science team, she might be inspired to work harder in your class?"

I waggle my finger. "That's not the way it works. First she works hard, then gets rewarded. Not being lazy, and then getting special treatment."

"Who is it going to hurt?" Dara asks.

I stare at her. She should let this go. The only answer for why she won't is Mr. Morton. Mr. Morton is pillow-talking her, complaining about me. The thought of Mr. Morton and Dara pillow-talking is too much to bear, and I get up abruptly, shaking the unsteady little table. "I'm going to get more pasta."

I take my time at the pasta station, watching the cook heat up the sauce and the rigatoni in the big wok pan, waiting for a fresh batch although more than half a bowl is still in the serving area. Whatever happened to people proving themselves first, then getting rewarded?

I see Dara on her cell phone, talking away. Mr. Morton. How much do they see each other? Are they calling each other boyfriend and girlfriend yet? Dara hasn't seemed to mention any of her other hangers-on these days. I get my fresh pasta plate and return to the table as she hangs up.

"It's like credit," Dara begins.

"What's like credit?" I burn my tongue on the pasta and take a gulp of water, which uses up all my water for the day.

"People get into trouble with credit. Maybe they lost a job and couldn't pay a bill. Then the credit companies jack up the rate and make it harder to pay off. They can't get credit because the rates are too high. But these are the people who need a break, so they can pay off their bills." Dara looks pleased with herself.

"People should live off what they make, not use credit

cards," I say piously, blowing on my pasta. I know she's talking about herself.

"Not everyone has parents to help them out, Gal," she says, her tone hard. "That's not the point."

"Yeah. I get it. Riley needs a break because she's so far behind. I get it. Did Mr. Morton just tell you to say that?" I jerk my head toward her cell, lying on the table.

"No." She eats her salad quickly. "You know what, Gal, you're impossible sometimes." She gets up. "I'm going to get more bread. You want anything?"

I reply in the negative. Impossible. Yes, I am impossible. Everything about my life seems to be one grand impossibility after another.

I play with the pasta, thinking about Dara. I never did tell her about the rose show results. Nor has she asked. It would be like Dara getting married and me not asking her how the wedding was. Sure, I could just tell her, but shouldn't she ask if she really cared?

For the first time, I get that my friend has a different agenda than I do. Different opinions. We are possibly two people that should not converge so much any longer. I want to weep.

I do not. Instead, I wait for Dara to return, then tell her I'm not feeling well. I leave the restaurant before she can voice a protest or a concern.

LATER THAT NIGHT, I'm in bed reading the Winslow Blythe rose book, waiting for Riley to return home. I've left on the porch light and two lamps in the living room, plus the light in her bedroom. Now I skim the words over and over; I already know them nearly by heart, and the book only serves as company. The paper rustles comfortingly under my fingers as I listen for a car to slow. All I hear is the refrigerator, my old companion.

At last, at precisely ten, the front porch creaks and the front door clicks shut. "Riley?" I call.

She closes her bedroom door without answering. Uh-oh. I get up, shoving my feet into slippers.

"Riley?" I knock, then enter. She's lying on the bed, facing the wall, her back to me. "Everything okay? Did you have a good time?"

She does not answer. Her breathing is ragged. Crying. I sit on the bed next to her, touch her back. "What happened? Talk to me."

She turns over. Her makeup is smeared all over her face in garish streaks, her eyes streaked with red. It reminds me of finding her outside, gripping that golden retriever's fur, when she was a toddler. "Nothing. I'm just sad."

I lean into her. "Why?"

"You wouldn't understand." A sob chokes her.

A smell like sweetly rotting fruit comes off her breath. Alcohol. I lean in and smell her jacket. Cigarette smoke and pot. I fight the growing panic rising inside. "Riley. Tell me where you were and what happened. You were drinking and smoking."

"I didn't smoke anything. Other people were." She covers her eyes with her hands, not denying the drinking.

Fear tumbles my stomach. I put my hand on her. "Did someone do something to you?" A million possibilities rush through my head. Someone giving her booze on the sly. Rape. Roofies. Who knows?

"No. No one did." She takes her hands off her eyes and blinks at me. "We were out in the field behind the old

Schaeffer place. A bunch of us. Samantha, Brad, pretty much half the school." Tears fall again. "I only had a few sips, Aunt Gal. I swear. I . . ." She trails off, turns away again, covers her head with the pillow.

I want to smack her. "Don't you know the trouble you could have gotten into?" She's turning into Becky. Who knows what she and Becky did together. Maybe she already is like Becky. Frustration gets the better of me. I hit her wall with my palm. "This is unacceptable. You know that."

Her shoulders shake. She's hyperventilating.

I rub her back. "Riley. Take deep breaths."

She tries to say something, but she's hiccupping now. She turns over to face me again, taking one giant breath to steady her diaphragm. "I'm sorry, Aunt Gal." She is so sorrowful, my heart breaks.

I exhale. "I'm going to have to punish you again, Riley."

She nods, her eyes squeezing shut. "Aunt Gal. Why did my mother send me away?"

My heart catches. This is why she's done this. "She didn't want to, sweetheart." I don't know if it's true, but it's what she needs to hear.

Her face crumples again. "I was good. And she didn't want me."

"She does want you." I stroke her hair. I am close to crying, too.

She shakes her head. "Not enough." Her breath shakes her body. "Can I . . . can I call her now?"

"Sure." I get up and leave, shutting her bedroom door.

In the living room, I sit on the couch, putting my feet on the coffee table. Wondering how I can stop Riley from becoming Becky. Being with Becky has screwed her up. Becky leaving her has screwed her up, too. Riley is going to have problems either way. I take off my glasses, rub my eyes. Something hard is in my throat, something that won't be swallowed away.

Riley opens the door. "She didn't answer." She's taken off her jacket, her posture slumped. She looks like the Little Match Girl.

I am a little glad her mother didn't answer. I'm not sure Becky would have helped. I pat the couch next to me. "How about some late news?"

She sits next to me, close but not touching. Her makeup and tears have dried. I reach over and grab a tissue out of the box, wipe her face. She does not move.

I turn on the television, and we watch until Riley's eyes begin to close.

18

I turn my water wand on the roses, looking for small reddish brown specks. It's Monday of the second week of May and the spider mites have come out to play, as they always do this time of year. I call them red vampires. I'm supposed to be a biologist, interested in the circle of life and everything having its place, but I hate anything that will hurt my roses. If I were a true Darwinist, a believer in survival of the fittest, I would leave them alone. Of course, if I were a true Darwinist, I also would have died a long time ago.

A row of hybrid teas has a few mites, though their numbers are mitigated by my daily morning washing. It is exactly as annoying and time-consuming as it sounds. The early sun beats down on my unprotected brow. I will have to remember to wear a hat. The weather has heated up, and is now averaging in the mid-eighties by noon.

Inside, Riley is getting ready for school. We hadn't talked about the incident all weekend. Instead, we'd gone to the nursery, to a movie—some comedy I've already forgotten—and to church yesterday. Throughout, I'd watched her. For what, I didn't know. Some sign that she needed to talk, or cry again.

"I'm here if you want to talk," I'd said, clumsily.

She had shrugged. "I'm fine."

I have decided not to punish her for drinking. I'm certain Riley had acted out only because of her mother's leaving her. I mean, if my mother had sent me away abruptly, who's to say I wouldn't do something like that? I can't imagine it.

I OPEN THE HOSE UP MORE, soaking my navy blue sweats through. Next door, the neighbor peers through her window. She drops back when I wave. The water spray must be powerful enough to wash away the mites, but not so powerful the roses are damaged. I bend and search under each bush, waving the wand until my arm aches. It's a good workout. An insecticide would be easier, but I like to avoid spraying various chemicals on my roses, not because I'm particularly against poisons from an environmental standpoint. I'm against poisons from a hazardous-to-Gal standpoint. I simply believe that with all these other cards stacked against me, I certainly don't need to add "exposure to hazardous chemicals" to the mix, even if they are supposed to be benign to human life. Do you know how many things throughout human history scientists have asserted would hold no harm against humans? I rest my case.

At last I finish the rinsing and wind up the hose on the huge reel. I have a soaker system, but I also have this regular big green hose for tasks like this, requiring real water pressure. I am not used to the physical labor and begin huffing before a quarter of the hose is collected.

This is the time when Brad normally comes, in the morning before school starts, so he can clean the roses and we can let them air-dry during the heat. With school and dialysis and getting ready for the next rose show, I have no time to do this.

I have one major problem, though.

Brad quit today.

He simply texted me this morning, instead of showing up. Just like that. No warning. Nothing. Only words coming through a little tiny phone screen.

It had to be because of the drinking. He thinks, rightly so, that I will be angry.

Brad probably did not want to hear the hundred lectures I had planned for him about underage drinking and corruption of underclassmen. Nonetheless, I'd expected a bit more notice. I'd expected him to face me in person. I was wrong.

Now Riley comes outside, dressed in her uniform, her hair neatly brushed. "Aunt Gal, you can't do all this by yourself. You're all dirty. You have five minutes to get ready." She looks worried, her arms crossed and her forehead wrinkled. "Let me help."

I wonder what the gossip will be at school today, and if any of it will be directed at Riley. "You going to be okay today?"

She looks down, scuffing the toe of her sneaker into the dirt. "Of course. Why wouldn't I be?" Then she meets my eyes directly, her eyes flashing green. "Nothing happened at the party, Aunt Gal. Nothing except drinking."

I straighten from the hose winder. I can feel specks of dirt all over my face, though I was only watering. My breath comes fast and heavy. "Good. Finish winding it for me, and we'll get to school just fine." I walk into the house as she gingerly grabs the handle and begins turning the crank.

IN AP BIOLOGY, I confront Brad as he walks in right before the bell. "Hallway. Now."

He follows me out. He says nothing. I'd thought better of him.

Down the hallway, his father is emptying a trash can. He glances up, looking exactly like Brad will look in thirty years, except I hope Brad won't look so hangdog-defeated. Bags swirl under the man's eyes. He nods at me and I nod back.

Brad holds up his hands and, seeing his father, leans forward in a whisper. "I am sorry, Ms. Garner. I have to help out my father."

"What do you mean?" I'm confused. I glance toward his father. "In the morning?"

Brad flushes. "Dad has a paper route. Dad works a night shift, too, and he's too tired in the mornings now. He's saving up money for my college."

I glance down the hall at his father again, wondering several things at once. One, why the school doesn't pay a living wage to its workers. Two, why Brad's father, who appears to be a fairly intelligent, capable human, can't get a better-paying job. Three, whether I can start paying Brad so he doesn't have to leave.

Brad passes his hands over his face, leaving fingerprints on his cheeks. Down the hall, his father empties a dustpan noisily, shuffling away without a backward glance toward his son. The confident Brad disappears for a second, and I see a new Brad. Unhappy, afraid, alone. This Brad I see comforting his father when his mother didn't come home, getting the free secondhand uniforms from the school, the one who doesn't pay into the class field trip fund, who's earned his peers' respect through the luck of his good looks and athletic abilities. I see that I don't know the half of this kid.

So I don't say anything to make him feel bad about texting me or quitting. I know I can't pay him. For a moment I consider asking my mother for help; I know she will foot the bill without question. It's tempting, but I want to be a stand-on-her-own-two-feet adult too much to ask.

I am aware of the class inside rustling about. It's far past bell, and they know we are out here. "Okay, Brad," I say, after a long silence. "Thanks for letting me know."

He nods once, begins to turn, and pauses. "I can't come after school, either. I have too much studying to do for finals. I don't want to mess up."

I nod once in return. He goes silently into class.

I GET TO SCIENCE OLYMPIAD a little late, because I'm trying to organize my curriculum for the next day. With the competition in two weeks, Mr. Morton is in a tizzy, but I have no worries. My teams are more than well prepared. The kids could do these tasks in their sleep.

Mr. Morton, on the other hand, thinks his students will forget everything as soon as a little pressure is on them. Maybe his teams aren't well prepared enough.

When I arrive at his classroom, the trebuchet kids are outside. Mr. Morton is nowhere to be found, neither inside nor out. My kids are efficient as an ant colony, with their supplies all set up. I look in earnest for my co-coach. His briefcase and metal water bottle are still here, the water bottle forlornly on its side.

I am bending over helping my anatomy student identify a kidney ("Surely you jest," I say) when I hear another voice join the kids outside. A familiar female voice belonging to my young niece. I peer through the bank of open windows lining the room.

Sure enough, it's Riley, clipboard in hand, watching the

action. Brad hands her a tape measure. "I'd rather not do that part," she demurs. "I'm here to watch."

He sputters the exasperation I feel. "What good is being an alternate going to do if you don't know how to step in? What if somebody's sick?"

I call out a rejoinder. "Yeah, what if someone's sick?" I step forward. So Mr. Morton has decided what I think does not matter, and so has my niece. But really, what else is new around here? I feel resigned more than anything.

Riley's eyes widen. "Hi, Aunt Gal."

"Miss Garner," I remind her. Riley fumbles with the tape measure, unable to get the metal to uncoil. Brad holds down one end by the trebuchet, and she walks the tape measure out to where the beanbag sits in the middle of a brown, dead patch of grass.

"Five meters and . . ." Riley's voice trembles. "Two centimeters?"

"Can't you read one of those things yet?" I ask in what I think is my mild voice. I stride over and read it. "Five meters, twenty centimeters."

"You don't have to yell at me." Riley turns away, chewing her lower lip.

"This is nowhere near yelling." I glance around. Still no Mr. Morton. "Has anyone seen Mr. Morton?"

They all shake their heads, except one. One of the trebuchet team, a female junior, points. "He went back there."

Odd. There's nothing behind the science building except scrubby hillside. I walk around the building.

Indeed, there he is, talking on his cell. Cell phones, I decide, should get some kind of award as the most accursed invention of the modern age. You can never be unplugged.

I'm about to say something, but his back is turned, and what I hear next stops me cold.

"I have given you everything," he says, his voice loud and full of more emotion than I've ever heard out of a male, except at a Shakespearean play. "I want to see her. I'm her father."

At this, I drop back behind the corner, unwilling to listen to any more. Mr. Morton is a father? Who is the mother? Dara doesn't know about this. That's the kind of gossip that spreads fast. Who is he talking to?

What do we know about this man? I ask myself.

I go into the classroom. Mr. Morton comes in shortly after. His hair seems to be electrified, which makes me smile momentarily, but he shows no sign of being upset.

"Sorry about that." He sits at his desk, straightening papers that need no straightening, and only then do I notice the flush in his cheeks. I decide not to confront him about Riley just then.

But I don't have to, because my niece herself materializes next to him. "You said you were going to tell her," she says accusingly. "She went all crazy on me."

Teens sure have a different reality than I do. "Riley. Define crazy."

Mr. Morton raises his hands. "Hey, hey. Peace. I'm doing the trebuchet, I can have her as an alternate if I want."

His direct snub of not only my teaching authority but my guardian authority stings. "I thought we were both doing the trebuchet," I say. My father built the contraption, after all.

He shakes his head. "My name's on the form as the adviser. You know you only need one coach per event."

"And Mom signed off on my form," Riley chimes in.

"That's why I let her on the team."

"You kept her a secret!" I cannot believe it.

"It just happened." Mr. Morton is going to make this All About the Principle. I can tell he's hunkering down, ready for a long-term battle.

"How?" I'm certain Riley has forged the signature. "Show me the permission slip."

Mr. Morton makes a show of leafing through his files.

Riley stands resolute, her fists at her sides. This team is important to her, even though she's just an alternate and she can't read the darn tape measure. I suspect its only importance comes from the fact that I said she couldn't do it. Her cheeks burn carnation pink, making the freckles stand out on her nose. "She said I could sign it for her."

"Forgery. That is perfect." I sit down at an empty table opposite Mr. Morton. He twists his mouth into something resembling concern.

Riley crouches next to me. "If you call her, she'll say she signed it."

This is the last conversation I want to be having. People always seem to think I seek conflict. I don't. It seeks me. I put my forehead in my palm. It feels hot, or my palm is cold. I can't determine which.

I have had enough. All I want to do is go home and watch *Wheel of Fortune*.

"Obviously, both of you are going to do as you like. I might as well not be here." I pick up my tote bag, a pink one imprinted with multicolored DNA molecules that my mother bought me last Christmas. The DNA molecules roil before my eyes. I focus on a corner of the room, waiting for the dizzy spell to pass.

"Don't be like that." Mr. Morton exchanges a look with Riley that says, *We must manage her before she has a true fit.* This I really cannot stand. Before I say something I will probably regret forever, I hustle out of there, dizzy or not.

19

It's not until I arrive back at home that I remember I left Riley there at school, when I am the one who drives her home. Well, she's a big girl. She can figure out a way home. She has before.

Everyone else wants to make things too easy for the kids. No one has to work for anything, figure stuff out. Mr. Morton's niceness will be the downfall of him as a teacher. He'll probably let all his students take the final three times until they get the grade they want.

I push aside my feelings that I'm committing neglect, and get on the computer to check my e-mail.

One from Byron. Finally.

> So sorry about your rose show. Terribly busy with the
> season now. Good luck to you.

And that was all, no signature, no chattiness. He's had enough of this quasi-friendship, no time to give me a how-do-you-do. Or he is in fact busy, as he says.

First Dara, then Brad, then Riley and Mr. Morton, now Byron. Not to mention the kidney doctor and powers-that-be. Is there no one *not* conspiring against me? I let out a breath, a long one whooshing the dust off my keyboard. Then I sneeze.

I have to laugh at my own pitifulness. There's nothing else to do. By this time next year, I promise myself, I will have:

1. A new kidney
2. A successful Hulthemia, with scent
3. A new couch

I write the list down on a piece of scrap paper emblazoned with a Realtor's picture. I pause. It seems like Riley ought to belong on this list someplace. But what do I want for her? Do I want her to leave or stay? I write:

4. Riley?

I put the list away.

My phone pings with a text. Mr. Morton, not Riley, because Riley knows better than to use the text feature. I am going to have to change to the unlimited text plan, unhappy as I am about that prospect.

Will give Riley a ride since you left, it reads. Jesus God.

That reminds me of overhearing him on the phone. Dara and I know next to nothing about Mr. Morton, except that he used to work at some chemical company. He and Dara have been out several times, but all they've done is see a movie, get coffee afterward, and talk about the movies. Hardly getting-to-know-you scenarios. That's more like conversational avoidance.

I think about the morning I'd asked Dara if she liked Mr. Morton, when she dropped in to have her coffee with me. I've always hated coffee; tastes like bitter dishwater, but I've watched her drink gallons over the years.

"He's a nice guy," she said. Her mug was shaped like the face of a winking woman; it said BAILEY's on one side.

"Does Dr. O'Malley know you're advertising liquor on campus?" I said.

She blinked. "Come on. I got it in an antique store."

"That makes it perfectly acceptable?" I settled back into my chair. I'd brought in some of my newly blooming roses off my nonbreeding bushes, the burnt red Hot Cocoa, and had them arranged in an old pasta jar in a big cloud. "I know he's a nice guy. But what does he like to do?"

She took a sip of the coffee so light it had to be mostly cream. Dara never ate breakfast; said her coffee had more than enough calories and calcium to count for food. "Build things. Watch movies."

"Heck, I know that much." If it were me going out on dates, I would have the man's mother's maiden name, Social Security number, religion, and childhood dreams by the second one. I made a noise of disbelief, which sounded more like an unattractive snort. "Dara. Come on. Quit bringing me second-rate information."

"I'm sorry!" Dara laughed, smoothing out her capris printed with large roses. "I prefer to let things take a natural course, not force them."

"At that rate, you're going to get married at about the same time the sun burns itself out." I sharpened my jar of number two pencils, something I did every morning for the students who forgot theirs at home. For a while I told every-one that if they forgot a pencil, they were just going to be out of luck, but then half the students did no work for a solid week because they'd left their pencils at home. Dr. O'Malley was not so happy about this.

Dara took a rose out of the jar. "Can I take one?"

"Looks like you already did." I kept sharpening as she stuck it behind her right ear.

"Not behind the left?" I indicated her other side. Left ear would mean her heart was taken.

"Nope." She held her now-empty cup. "I'm still seeing Chad, too. It's all still light."

Any lighter and Mr. Morton would think she wasn't interested at all. I stuck another pencil into the sharpener, raising my voice against the satisfying mechanical hum. "Whatever makes you happy, my dear."

At home now, I open Google on my computer. If Dara is not going to find anything out about George Morton, I will. It's so easy to find out stuff about people these days. Once, a man advertised a set of large pots on Craigslist. He'd e-mailed me back, told me it would be first come, first served, and then didn't answer his phone. All I knew was his first name, his neighborhood, and his phone number, and I found his house and got in his driveway seconds before another woman. Yes, I got those pots.

I type "George Morton, San Luis Obispo" into the search engine.

Instantly (this still surprises me, after all these years of having the Internet; I still half expect to have to use a card catalog when doing research) a number of hits come up. Most of these are not his.

I look over the image search. On page four, one photo sticks out. George Morton with another woman and a baby girl.

"Acrimonious divorce pits Alchemy Tech founder Morton against his wife," the caption reads. *"Lara Stratton-Morton, a former lab technician at Alchemy Tech, has filed for sole custody of their two-year-old daughter."*

My fingers feel frozen. I rub them together. A baby girl? An ex-wife? Why did they split up? An image of Riley's father flashes into my head, a man now so distant I honestly have to look up his name or ask my mother if I want to know it.

Now that I know his company's name, it's easier to find another article. Most are his research papers; he deals with synthetic polymer chemistry, it seems. This encompasses non-natural rubbers, plastics, and fabrics like neoprene and nylon and, of course, polyester. Because many polymers use petroleum as a starting point, and we're running out of oil, companies are trying to develop new ways to produce these materials. I find myself impressed at his body of work. Why would he leave something like this to teach at our nothing school?

Then I come across this nugget. Nugget, nothing. More like a piece of coal that I must swallow.

Shares of Alchemy Tech plummeted today at the news that CEO and founder George Morton is stepping down. Amid rumors of a takeover, Morton sold his majority shares last week and has no plans to remain in operations. "I have every confidence that our teams will continue to produce the best work and fulfill all our contracts," he said in a statement. The company primarily deals with developing new synthetics for the polymer industry.

Dara should know about this. I'd want to know. I reach for the phone.

The door slams. Riley pauses dramatically near the entrance, holding aloft the chrome Craftsman tape measure my father left here. "I learned how to read it. Want me to show you?"

I have the phone in my hand. What should I say, good job for learning how to do something everyone else learned in sixth grade? Is she going to learn how to skip rope next? The mean thoughts make me flush. I'm still angry at her for joining the science team behind my back, though the fault really lies with Mr. Morton. I decide I won't bring up the science team at all. "Not right now, Riley. I have to make a phone call."

Disappointment crosses her face. I was supposed to want to see her read a tape measure? I suppose a real teacher would. I put the phone down. "Measure the couch. Show me." The couch would be easy; I know it's exactly eight feet, two and a half inches.

"Maybe later." She tosses her tape measure unceremoniously on the couch, where it bounces off and crashes into the TV remote on the coffee table, knocking it off. "Oops."

"There better not be a ding in my table." I get up and inspect its white paint. It's what Dara calls a Shabby Chic table, one with curlicued sides. I found it by the side of the road. Dara painted it pink, then white, scratching away part of the top to reveal the color underneath. It reminds me of some of my pink and white roses.

"It's made to look old, Aunt Gal." Riley flops down in the chair, sending small clouds of dust into the shafting sunlight, where they hang glittering in the air. "Sorry."

I run my hand over the table. Smooth. I check a sigh, pointing instead to the dust. "You used to call those 'dust fairies' when you were little." I smile at the memory, of little Riley sitting at my parents' house, absorbed by watching the "fairies" that sprung up from the dust my mother could not be bothered to clean up. My mother had jumped up, got wet paper towels, and wiped down all her furniture.

"I did?" Riley smiles.

I nod.

"Do you remember any other stories from when I was little?" She leans forward, her elbows on her knees.

I honestly can't think of any at the moment. My head is still wrapped around George Morton and Dara, the image of him with his wife burning behind my eyes. The fairies were incidental, a result of seeing the dust motes. "You were a terror," I say finally, thinking of something general, things my mother related. "Never wanted to nap, or put away your toys. You climbed high up on my parents' bookshelf when you were not even two, and gave my mother a heart attack."

"Anything else?" Riley, so hungry for stories of her child-hood, continues to watch me with her large eyes. No matter how I try to fill her up, she will always be empty of these, which I cannot provide.

I have no words to express it to her.

Instead, I pick up the remote from the floor, and the phone, trying to be gentle when I tell her. I am not the one who should be telling her these memories. I have too few, and most are hearsay. "I can't remember anything else at the moment." I put the remote back on the coffee table and leave Riley sitting there, still staring at the spot where I'd been sitting moments before.

· · ·

DARA ISN'T HOME, it turns out, so I put her dilemma out of my mind and instead head over to dialysis a bit early, leaving Riley alone with a can of chicken chili and the TV.

I hesitate, keys in hand, seeing Riley at the table solo, glad to see she has actually bothered to pour the chili into an ancient melamine bowl. Before I can say anything, she raises a hand. "Don't worry," she says, her eyes on an open textbook. "I've got a biology test tomorrow I must study for, oddly enough." She smirks at me.

"Remember your flash cards."

She nods, spooning another bite into her mouth.

I point to a lined list I've tacked to the well-used bulletin board on the wall. Her chore list. If I give her enough to do, then she won't have time to get into trouble. "And this."

She squints up. "Chores?"

"Wipe down the bathroom with the Clorox wipes, vacuum the living room carpet, use the Swiffer on the hardwood, start your laundry, and empty the dishwasher." I tap each item with my index finger.

"No problem."

I wish I could tell her to go next door if there's trouble, but of course that neighbor cannot be trusted in particular, and I don't know the others. Instead, I tell her to call Dara, who's agreed to be the designated go-to emergency person. For a moment I consider texting her the important George Morton info, springing it on her unavoidably, but I decide it can wait until the next day. I am not a coward like some when it comes to relaying information in person.

On my street, the neighbors are courteous, but not social.

We wave to each other in our yards and watch for burglars. On Halloween, I hand out pencils instead of candies because I don't want their soft young teeth to fall out of their heads. They probably don't like me that much, those kids. One picked a rose on her way to school, as I sat at the window having my tea. I popped out in my robe, explaining that I certainly did not mind her picking a rose, as long as she asked first, because otherwise it was stealing, which was wrong. She threw it at my feet and never returned.

I plan to be back extra early in the morning to rinse my roses. Once more I give a little mourning cry for Brad and his punctuality. I might have to scale back my operations, if I am thinking realistically, maybe grow roses only in the greenhouse, but I avoid considering this seriously. Because if I scale back, there's no way I'm ever going to be more than a simple rose hobbyist, and that would be unacceptable.

The dialysis clinic is quiet this night, so silent I can hear the buzz of the energy-efficient lights on the ceiling, the nurses clicking the keyboards from behind their partition. I almost don't want to go in. The entire operation seems pointless, endless, if I have no chance of getting a kidney. For the rest of my life, however long it is, I will be coming here every other day. I can't think about it. I think about fungus instead, the Hulthemia, how I need to call Byron. These are the only items keeping me sane.

Nurse Sonya looks up from her computer screen. "Gal. How are you holding up?" Her face, for some reason, is sympathetic. She lowers her voice and leans forward. I lean in, so close I can see the stray hairs under her eyebrows. "Dr. Blankenship can be a real hard-ass."

Warmth spreads in my chest. I smile. "Tell me about it."

She straightens and gives me a wink that tells me she's pulling for me. "Have a seat. I'll call you back in a minute."

I turn to the waiting area. The only other patient in the whole place, surprise, is Mark Walters.

I want to avoid him, but then I decide I will not. He does not hold that much power over me. I sit down not on the other side of the room, but on a chair opposite and to his left.

This time he has an electronic reading device instead of a newspaper, with a rich-looking leather cover on it. He grins. "Ever use one of these?" He hands it over, spanning the aisle with a long arm.

It feels impossibly light to contain so many books. I squint at the screen. "There's glare from the overhead light."

He repositions it in my hands, his arms brushing mine. I see that he, too, has a fistula in his arm, the plastic heaving under the skin like a long-forgotten parasite. "You're imagining that. There's no backlighting." He adjusts the reader.

"I like paper books." I hand it back to him, freeing myself of it.

He wags his finger at me. "Don't be afraid of change, Gal."

"I'm not. I simply have a preference. Is that a crime?" I consider telling him about all the ways I'm not afraid of change. Having Riley with me, for one. For another, breeding a whole new rose. I'm certainly not opposed to change there, am I?

He looks expectantly at me, as if he can see these thoughts forming on my tongue and is waiting to hear them in the air.

I bite them back. I leaf through a magazine, but don't see the words.

He passes his hand over his mustache. "Gal," he says finally. "There's an article I found you might be interested in."

"About what?" I expect him to say roses.

"About kidney transplants." He touches his screen and hands the device over to me.

I take it from him with a frown, not knowing what he's talking about. *The New England Journal of Medicine.* The article tells me that a kidney transplant can be done even if there is limited blood flow on one side; you simply transplant the kidney on the opposite side. So my problems are on my left, and the doctor needs to put the new kidney on the right.

A million thoughts rush through me and I say the first one, the most important one, the only one that will affect my outcome. "Dr. Blankenship won't care."

"She has to care." He closes the screen. "Even she can't ignore *all* the research."

His emphasis on the word "all" makes me smile. "Tries her best though, doesn't she?"

He folds the cover over his device. "I e-mailed this to her. Told her to take another look at your case."

I pause, surprised. Why would he do that, after I've been so, well, rude to him all this time?

"You're right. Me being on the list higher than you is unfair." He shoots me a half smile, crooked and tired. "All of it's unfair."

I have no response. My throat tightens.

Walters lowers his voice to a whisper. "The chief of surgery here is an old friend of mine, Gal. We went to elementary school together."

"No wonder everyone likes you," I breathe.

He guffaws, slapping his knees. "That's not why. They like me because I'm a nice guy."

I grin.

He looks around, apparently content to do the talking for

the both of us. "The people here are nice, your company no exception, but boy, I can't wait until I never have to see this place again."

I put my chin on my hand. I had never thought about it. "What do you think it will be like, when we don't have to come here anymore?" I say so softly he has to lean forward. "When we don't have to worry about who we leave at home and we can eat what we want?"

He moves across the aisle next to me. "Don't you re-member?"

"It's been," I squeeze my temples with my thumbs, "a very long time." I move my head back. "How long has it been for you?"

He holds up six fingers.

"Six years? Nearly as long as me." I am impressed for a second.

"Months." He gives me an apologetic smile.

"Months?" I shake my head.

"If there's one thing I've learned in my life, Gal, it's that you need patience." He crosses his legs. "If you have patience and faith, good things will come. Back when I was a young man—"

I snort, interrupting him. I've had enough. Is this why he showed me the article, so he could have permission to lord his knowledge and pomp over me as I sit, a captive audience, in a waiting room? I don't care if his patience story involves a war, or the Great Depression, or the gas crisis of the 1970s. I simply don't give a damn. "Who are you to tell me about patience? I've got more patience in my . . ." I cast about for something small, "my earlobe than you have in your whole body. I've been on dialysis eight years, Mr. Walters. Eight years. Sick my whole life. Who are you," I am standing now without realizing it, "to tell me?" I'm sobbing now, these tears coming more often, unbidden and uncontrollable.

He looks at me, shocked, as the nurse rushes in and takes me by the arm and leads me away.

I have to get in one more thought. "You don't know a thing," I say to him, my acrimony hanging in the air, visible as a shroud.

20

AT HOME IN THE MORNING, VERY EARLY, I AM RINS-
ing the roses when Riley comes outside. I didn't bother to
come inside, just shut down my car and went right over to
the greenhouse.

The nurse who led me away said not one word about my
altercation with Walters. She hooked me up to the machine
as she always did, put a warmed blanket over me, and asked,
"Do you need anything else?"

I shook my head no.

She closed the door and left.

It took me a long time to go to sleep last night, and when
I did, I awoke every hour on the dot, jolted to high alert by
some invisible force, surprised continually that I was not at
home in bed.

The sun is barely up, orange in the distance. I didn't think
Riley would be, either. I always have to go into her room and
awaken her. She has an alarm clock, a Hello Kitty one that
appeared one day, but she hits snooze over and over.

She is already dressed in her school uniform, pants this
time, which the girls usually avoid because they think pants
aren't cute, with sensible-looking athletic shoes and a white

blouse with a Peter Pan collar and a navy blue hoodie, emblazoned with the St. Mark's logo of a lion standing over a book. Her hair is combed and tied back at the crown with a navy blue ribbon.

The morning light slants across the left side of her face, casting her right side into shadow. For a second, she looks undeniably like her mother, and also, to my surprise, my mother, as if they are one unbroken line of female clones.

"I didn't think you'd be up." I close the brass spray nozzle, wiping my hands on my pants.

"There was a cat fight that woke me up at five." She pulls the hoodie tighter around herself.

"Zip that. You'll get a chill." I drag the hose to the next row of roses.

"I can do that." She is beside me, her hoodie already zipped, taking the hose out of my hand. She gives it a gentle tug. "Let me."

"Go eat breakfast." I won't release it.

"I did." She gives it a harder tug. My dirt-stained hands give way.

"Don't get muddy." I relent, only because my stomach lets out a gurgle so loud Riley hears it and grins. I open the nozzle so that a medium-hard stream of water sprays out. "Not too much of a hard spray, or it could damage the leaves. We don't want to power-wash the roses, only knock the spores off. Wash the undersides. Then go to the next row and do it again."

"Got it." She looks pleased with herself, like a toddler helping a grown-up with an important chore.

I walk slowly to the house, my clogs catching on the mud I've created, cool on my toes, my socks soaked.

Inside, her biology textbook and notes are scattered on

the coffee table. A plastic mixing bowl full of popcorn kernels sits on the floor, next to the television remote. I pick up the remote; it's greasy. I hope she's ready for the test today, at least. I pull off my socks and put them into the small laundry room at the end of the kitchen. Piles of laundry await there, dirty and clean baskets, and I can't tell which is which. The clean ones are supposed to go into the living room for distribution, not left to sit and get more dirty clothes thrown carelessly on top. I throw a load in, not bothering to sort, washing everything on cold.

I go into the bathroom to wash my hands, flipping on the overhead light. My skin looks as pallid and gray as the mourning doves who nest in my springtime garden. I slap some cold water on my face, hoping to wake it up.

The off-white Formica counter, run through with veins of false gold, is still dirty, rivulets of dust and water and who knows what making rivers of nastiness. I grit my teeth, get the wipes out from under the sink, and wipe down everything.

I change my clothes and finally get to the kitchen, pouring myself three-quarters of a cup of puffed plain brown rice cereal. I pour one-half cup of fat-free milk over it and sit down with a big clunk at the table.

The newspaper is already spread out before me, turned not to the comics section but to the business section. The classified ads, to be exact. Riley's circled some jobs. Office clerks, work from home scams, and, for some reason, dental assistant jobs all bear a heavy black mark around them. I smile at her ambition and naiveté.

Riley comes in through the back door, letting it slam. Though her pants are dark blue, I can see the dirt on them. I glance at the clock. We have to leave in ten minutes. "Riley, get changed."

"I was about to." She kicks off her shoes, returning in a few minutes (she can surely be quick if she wants) and tossing her dirty clothes into the laundry room. "Do you know where my P.E. uniform is, Aunt Gal?"

I eat the last bit of cereal. "I'm not in charge of your uniform. Why didn't you wash it last night?"

"I put it in the washroom two days ago." She picks at the newspaper, shredding a corner.

"So what have you been wearing to class?" I frown. Students get marked down for not having uniforms.

She shrugs.

"A shrug isn't an answer."

"Regular clothes."

"Unacceptable. Your grade is going down."

She puts her chin in her hand. "Are you ready to go yet?"

"Are you ready to go?" I nod toward the coffee table. "Your books are not in your backpack."

"Whoops." She gives me an angelic grin, sloping off to gather her things and thumping the bag on the table.

I slip my loafers on. "Riley, I'd rather have you do the chores I listed for you than my roses."

"I'd rather do the roses."

I angle my neck, feeling it crack. Hospital beds, even the adjustable ones, are not the most comfortable things ever invented. "Riley. Can you do what I ask?"

Her nostrils flare and her face flushes. "No problem." She shoulders her backpack. "Can I drive?"

"After school you may. I'm too tired to supervise at the moment." This isn't exactly true, she requires little supervision, but the driving feels like a reward to me she hasn't earned today, despite her help with the roses.

She holds the door open for me, her back pressed against it to prevent it from automatically closing. As I pass her, I look at her downcast face, her pale arms, the way she always stands with one foot ahead of the other. I realize she does not look so much like Becky, she looks like me. Or what I would look like, had I not been stunted.

I press the car keys into her hands. Our cold fingertips touch momentarily. "Go ahead."

ALL DAY, I search for Dara. She does not come to the lunch room. Mr. Morton eats with the physics and math teachers. He avoids eye contact with me. So this is how it's going to be. It's as though he knows that I know all about him, suddenly. I take my lunch back into my empty classroom and eat alone, my Internet browser open to the Pasadena rose show and convention.

I am excited, because not only will it be a larger show and farther away so it will be a mini-vacation, but Byron will be there. Dara will finally get to meet him.

I pore over the categories, though I have them memorized and already sent in my entry forms. Perhaps I should try to do more than one category, not just the new breed of roses. I have a few good mini-roses coming in, or maybe one of my hybrid teas will be ready. There's also the hotel to consider, with discounted rooms available. I'll have to check with Dara.

A knock sounds, soft, at my locked classroom door. "I'm closed!" I yell back around a mouthful of salad greens (one cup of lettuce with an ounce of tuna).

Dara's painted face peers through the glass transom and

I unlock the door. "I didn't see you in the cafeteria." She sips from a can of Diet Coke through a straw. She wears a full brown skirt and matching blazer with a nipped waist.

"Nor I you." I wipe my hands on my slacks.

She sits in the guest chair by my desk, crossing her ankles as delicately as royalty. "What's new and exciting? I saw you called."

I want to blurt out the whole story of Mr. Morton, but something is holding me back. Dara leans back in her chair, her eyes scanning the desk, the room, her lap. She looks everywhere except right at me. "I sent in my entry for Pasadena." I point to the screen. "Where do you want to stay?"

Her last sip of soda is a loud slurp. She crumples the can and tosses it into the blue recycling trash. "About that."

I wait. Her throat moves in a swallow. She laces her fingers. At last she continues. "I don't think I'm going to make it."

I blink. I feel strangely calm. "Why's that?"

She furrows her brow. "Remember? I said I was a maybe. I'm going to make an extra payment on my credit cards instead. Gal, I'm sorry." She hasn't moved her hands off her lap, where they appear to be holding each other for comfort. "Are you mad? You're mad."

I search for my lost voice, willing it to show itself from the bottom of some kind of deep pit where it fell. She *had* told me she was a maybe, at dinner. But surely she *knew* she wouldn't be able to make it. Why didn't she just say no? Then I wouldn't have made these plans. My brain freezes. "I'm not angry," I say at last. "I just wish you had been clearer."

Dara's body already fidgets toward the door like a bad student. "I really did want to go, Gal." She opens her mouth as though she wants to say something else, her eyes wide circles, but doesn't. She looks at a crumpled piece of paper on the floor, throws it in the trash.

"I'm glad you're being responsible," I say, sounding exactly like my mother. "Maybe Riley can go with me."

She relaxes, her shoulders slumping in the chair. "I bet she'd love that."

I nod, once.

The bell rings. Dara springs up. "Have a good afternoon, Gal."

"You as well." We sound like a bank teller talking to a customer, interchangeable and shallowly polite.

She leaves the classroom as my AP Bio students trickle in.

I still haven't told her about Mr. Morton. "Wait, Dara." I go to the doorway but she's gone, down the hall, talking to Mr. Morton. She nods and he glances toward me. I step back into the classroom before she can turn around.

Perhaps it's not my place to tell her anyway. I shut the door to my room as the last bell rings.

21

After school this day, I have nothing to do except tend my roses. It's my favorite kind of day. Just warm enough to wear short sleeves, but not so hot that same shirt sticks. Sun block optional, not required.

With Riley in the house studying, I put on my grubby clothes and my big straw hat and go outside. I found an aphid the other day, the ladybugs I released are not enough, so this evening I go around checking every single plant for the little green critters. It is a critical time, May. I want the roses to keep going all summer. Aphids secrete a sticky substance called "honeydew" that causes fungus, as well as sucks all the life out of the plants. If you see a plant with curled and yellow leaves, chances are aphids are the cause. They're a rose breeder's nightmare.

The outside roses have a considerable infestation. I'm particularly worried about the English roses closest to the greenhouse. I hold a Victorian Spice in my palm, a peachy pink David Austin rose that has always done well for me. It almost looks like it's got green polka dots on it.

I go into the greenhouse. More blooms have appeared on my seedlings. I run my hands over them, checking for aphids.

None have gotten inside here yet, thank goodness for that. A few of these seedlings are absolutely one hundred percent no good. One has withered leaves and ugly blooms. I yank it out of the potting mix, tossing it into my recycling bucket before it can contaminate the rest of my flowers.

I check my mother plants, the ones I have just crossed. These will wither and ripen into rose hips, which look like red seed pods. Most casual rose growers never see these, because either they deadhead the roses before it happens or their roses are sterile. If I didn't need the hips for breeding, I'd eat them. They're full of vitamin C.

Rose G42 is looking splendid. I turn it around to better see it. Plants, all plants, stretch toward the sun as they grow. This was something I learned through observation of my mother's fern houseplants as a child. "They're lopsided unless you turn them," she said.

This is true in the greenhouse, where the sun beams on it indirectly. I have to change the position of G42 daily. There are several more blooms on now. The one blossom it had at the rose show has made more petals, making it even fuller. The colors are so bright they nearly hurt my eyes.

I bend over and sniff it, hoping it somehow magically has gotten fragrant. Nothing. My nostrils itch. Nothing much at all except the regular pollen-y smell of a plant.

I don't much like to use insecticides, not when they might get the good bugs, too. But I can't risk the aphids getting into the greenhouse. Usually the water spray works great. There are too many of the critters this year, though. With regret, I get out the insecticide and mix it in the special bucket with its attached sprayer I keep just for this purpose.

"What are you doing?" Riley is standing behind me. I jump about two feet into the air.

"Lord, Riley, you scared me."

"Sorry." She leans on the table, her bottom touching the G42.

I push it back from the edge. "Please be careful."

She picks up the small plastic pump bucket of aphid poison. "What's this?"

"Poison. Put it down."

"For those green bugs?"

"You saw them?"

She nods. "This morning."

"Didn't you wash them off the roses?"

"Was I supposed to? I thought I was washing fungus, not bugs." She absentmindedly pulls on the trigger. A squirt of poison shoots out onto the floor.

"Be careful." I take the poison away from her pointedly. Is she really fifteen? "Yes, you were supposed to wash those off. And now they've gone crazy." I calculate. A few days without getting washed away properly accounts for a number of aphids on those English roses. I go outside and spray.

She follows me out. "You're destroying their organicness."

"Technically, all carbon-based life forms are organic." I keep spraying. "'Organic' really isn't a very descriptive term." I am being difficult, I know.

She frowns. "Whatever. You won't be able to eat those."

"Nobody's going to eat them."

"You're poisoning our water supply."

I stop spraying and cast an evil eye on her. "Riley. What is it you want?"

"Have you graded my bio test yet?"

I turn back to the spraying. "I'll do it tonight. After dark. When I'm done with this."

She doesn't give up. "I really really want to know how I did."

"You'll get it back tomorrow." It's one of my hallmarks of teaching that I do all my grading the same night they take the test, for almost immediate feedback.

"What's for dinner?"

I ignore her. I step back from the rosebush, satisfied all the bugs have been saturated, then begin on the next one.

"Aunt Gal?"

I spray the bush a bit more vigorously than necessary. "Riley, it is four o'clock. If you're so worried about dinner, go get started on it."

"What?"

I spray the rose bush. "In my house, when your mother and I were growing up, she who complained about dinner had to cook it. Believe me, eating Becky's dinner when she was eleven was interesting, to say the least."

Riley follows me to the next rose. She's wearing sweat shorts, her legs pale and cold-looking under them. Of course she's wearing the ever-present hoodie. "What did she make?"

I think back. Becky had complained about Mom's roasted broccoli, tossed with olive oil, cooked in a 400-degree oven for thirty minutes until it was almost black, the roasting rendering it crunchy-sweet. I still love Mom's broccoli, as I called it, only I can't eat it now. I told Riley this. "Can you imagine, someone not being allowed broccoli?" I chuckled.

"What did Mom say?" Riley can't resist touching the rose leaves. I smack her hand away gently.

"She said they were too oily. So Grandma had her make dinner the next night." I grin and Riley mirrors me, eyes shining. "Some kind of weird mix of tuna and way undercooked pasta and a can of peas, with some Ranch dressing."

Riley laughs delightedly. "It's pretty much the way she still cooks."

"Is it? What's your favorite thing for your mom to make?"

"Frozen food." We both giggle. Riley thinks. "Once, when I was five or so, she made me a cake for my birthday. From a mix, but still, it was sooo good. Devil's food. I thought I was going to hell for eating devil's food."

I laugh. "I like devil's food better than angel food." I reach the final rosebush. This one isn't so heavily infested, but I make sure I spray it in case some aphids decide to move over.

"Oh no." Riley bends and picks up something. A dead ladybug.

"Friendly fire casualties, I'm afraid."

She drops the bug, like a miniature slice of watermelon, onto the earth and kicks dry leaves over it. "I'm sorry, Aunt Gal. I'll do a better job."

"Not your fault."

"I was supposed to wash them off. I'll do better."

"Riley. Please. Do the jobs I put out for you, like I said, and I'll do this."

She reaches to rub her eye and neither agrees nor disagrees.

"There's no poison on your hand, is there?" I catch the offending appendage and examine her eyeball. "You were just touching the leaves." Her eye is reddish, but then, so is the other eye. Light purple crescents shine underneath.

"I'm all right. I'll be fine." She pulls away.

"How late do you stay up when I'm at dialysis?"

She shrugs. "I read. I lose track of time."

"Riley, you have to get to bed by ten, lights out by ten-thirty." I gather up my poison pot. "Interesting fact. Teenagers, though they always tend to get less sleep, actually need more sleep. That's why you all sleep in forever on the weekend. We should start school at nine-thirty, not seven-thirty."

She heaves a sigh, then squeezes her eyes shut and speaks rapidly, as though she's afraid she'll forget her spiel. "Aunt Gal, I really really need help with the trebuchet event."

"The tape measure?" I put down the pot again. "I thought you got it. You just have to memorize the increments. I know the metric system is different, but it's actually a lot easier than inches."

"That's not it." She shifts her weight from foot to foot. "The part where we use our graphs to predict where to set our targets."

I nod. In the competition practice, students use projectiles of varying sizes and weights, along with counterweights, to try to knock over some blocks representing a castle. In the actual competition, the students are given these weights and counterweights and then have to figure out their best use. Part of the score is this calculation, using all the data they collected during their practice runs.

"Brad tried to show me, but I didn't get it." Her voice is low, ashamed.

"Mr. Morton has you on the team. He's supposed to teach you."

"I might have told him I understood." Riley's voice gets even lower, forcing me to lean into her to hear it.

"Oh." I give her a gentle smile. This is not uncommon among the kids. How many times have I stood up in front of a classroom and asked, "Are there any questions?" and gotten two dozen shaking heads, only to have a quarter of those kids turn in incorrect work? "Let's go inside and work."

I stick my poison pot into the greenhouse on a random table, and lead Riley into the house.

. . .

Riley's biology test grade is, once again, not so good—a D plus. The same grade most of the class earns. I hand back their graded exams facedown on their desks. When you get a test facedown, you know the grade is less than a B. The students slump in their desks and groan. The A students get a high five from me.

"If you find your grade has gone down," I say, walking to the front of the classroom, "then you will need to do extra well on the final to pull it back up."

A strapping sophomore named Javier raises his hand. "Can we do extra credit?"

I cluck gently. "All the extra credit in the world can't make up for the meaty chunk of a final grade."

I don't meet Riley's gaze, which burns on my skin. Riley should have gotten a better grade. I told her what to study. I told her how to study. The only thing I didn't do was take the test for her.

I shouldn't have to point out to Mr. Morton how silly it is for a C minus student, her class average, to represent what's supposed to be an academically gifted school in the Science Olympiad. Even if she is my niece. Especially if she's my niece. People are going to accuse me of favoritism, when it's really all on Mr. Morton.

The bell rings. Javier, perhaps only now comprehending that he will be dropped off the wrestling team, groans and shoves his test into his pocket for his parent to sign. "This sucks ass," he mutters.

"Mr. Gutierrez, please refrain from using that kind of language in my classroom. Surely you can come up with some synonyms."

He sneers. "For 'ass'?"

I count them off on my fingers. "Booty, bottom, derriere, rump, fanny." He gathers his backpack and begins exiting. The other students, despite their black moods, laugh as I follow him into the hallway, calling out to his back, "Backside, posterior, rear."

He turns with a grin. "It doesn't mean the same thing."

"Then just say, 'How awful.' No 'sucking' and no 'ass.'" I wave him off and he recedes into the sea of students.

I glance around for Riley, but she has already left.

Dr. O'Malley is standing before me. I jump. "Do you lie in wait behind the lockers, Dr. O'Malley?"

"A word, Ms. Garner." He goes into my classroom. It's my prep. I square my shoulders and follow him.

"I take it you saw the test grades." I entered them into the school computer last night. It's a system we have so that everyone has immediate access to grades, and no parents can say they were blindsided by Junior's failing grade.

He sits behind my own desk as if it's his. The sun hits him square in the face and I think he would have been better off if he'd sat at a student's desk. He gets up and closes the blinds.

"I know what you're going to say. And you know what I'm going to say. So why do we have to have this conversation all over again?" I stare at him, waiting for an answer.

"Parents want you removed." Dr. O'Malley's voice is soft and level.

I sit down behind the first desk.

"Ms. Garner . . ."

"Miss. I've never been married." Fired? The parents want me fired? "Did they start calling you today?"

He nods. "Oh, it's been a long time coming, Gal. You know that."

"You can't fire me. I haven't done anything wrong. It's not my fault if the students don't put in the effort." But then I think of Riley. Riley did seem to put in the effort, didn't she, with her flash cards and her worry?

What if I really was the problem? Was there something I could do better?

Dr. O'Malley stretches his palms flat across my desk. "Listen. The way you teach is the way a lot of science and math teachers teach. You teach like you expect them to have a certain degree of knowledge already, like you don't understand *why* they don't understand. It's easy for you. It's not easy for them."

He lets this sink in.

I think back to my teaching methods. To Dara and Dr. O'Malley talking about me in the hall. They are conspiring and this is the result. "Dr. O'Malley, you've seen me teach. Why would you never point that out before?"

He grins a little. "I have, albeit more indirectly. You are less than open to criticism, Miss Garner."

I lean back in my chair. "So. If we're being blunt here, what now? I've been doing things this way for eight years. How can you suddenly do this?"

"We'd like to move you to a part-time position." His hands relax and he places them back in his lap. "I think it will be better for you overall."

He's thinking about my kidney. He's thinking about the time I missed because my leg graft got clogged, because of the IVP dye, because of all the various small things I have go wrong all the time.

I bristle. "It's discrimination. I am a capable person. You can't do this. I'll fight it."

"Then at the very least, consider making your tests more accessible."

So it's an ultimatum. "Accessible? These students don't have anything holding them back except their own desire and willingness to learn." I go over to the desk and grab my big black gradebook. "I know one thing. The kids who came in for extra tutoring all got at least a B. What does that tell you? If they ask for help, they shall receive."

"What about Riley?" Dr. O'Malley asks mildly. "You help her and she's still not getting a great grade."

"I help her a bit." Riley hadn't come to tutoring. I think for a moment. Who knows if she actually used the flash cards I'd told her to make? I was at dialysis, not sitting there making sure she studied. "Students have some responsibility for their own learning."

He nods. He gets up. "Think about the part-time offer, Gal. It could work out for the best."

He leaves, shutting the door behind him.

22

I set Riley up with her homework before I leave for dialysis. "Call me if you have any questions about biology," I tell her.

She nods, once. She has not talked about her grade, simply sitting there through the afternoon, paging through her biology textbook quickly, as though she has a photographic memory.

"Or about math, or about life in general," I continue. "But probably not about boys."

She doesn't even crack a smile.

"Riley?" I venture. "Are you okay?"

"Fine. What's not to be fine about?" She shuts her biology textbook. "I'm fine." She smiles only with her mouth.

I frown, trying to decipher why she is so upset. "Is it the biology test? You can still pass the class."

"No. It's not that, though, yeah, I did study for it."

"Did you really? Did you study while I was at dialysis?"

She plays with her notebook binder, hot pink with orange flowers all over it. "I thought I studied enough."

"Maybe what you think is enough and what is actually enough are two different things. Heck, it's nothing to be ashamed of. You know how hard I had to study spelling? I still can't spell to save my life."

She appears unpepped by my pep talk. I try to think of what else could be bugging her. I feel bad about leaving her alone again.

Then I get an aha moment. Riley hasn't seen Samantha—or anyone, for that matter—since that night she had a drink. She just goes to school, comes home, studies, hangs out with me. I personally don't see a huge problem in this for a high school girl, having no social life. But I have to admit Riley is isolated.

"If you want to go visit Sam, that's fine. As long as you stay at her house."

She stretches ostentatiously. "Too tired. Besides, she's not allowed to see me or anyone." Then Riley crumples in on herself. "I haven't made a single friend here."

My head thrums, the beginning of a headache. "That's not true. I see plenty of kids saying hi to you in the hallways."

"Yeah, but I don't do anything with them." She holds a throw pillow under her arms, this one embroidered with a large rose by my mother during one of her sick-Gal visits.

"You can invite kids to do stuff."

"Like what? Hang out here, in this tiny living room with their biology teacher breathing down their necks and telling them to take off their hats inside and they're too stupid for her class?" Riley squeezes the pillow fiercely. "The kids around here like to party. Drink. Is that what you want me to do?"

"Not everyone does that, do they?" I know she'd told me half the school was at that party, but I'd thought she was exaggerating. I try to reconcile my vision of these studious kids, well, mostly studious kids, or at least well-behaved kids, with what Riley is telling me.

"All the ones I've met do. The other ones never talk to me." Riley wipes tears off her cheekbones. "I just don't fit in around here, I guess. I can't pretend to be someone I'm not."

I think now of all of Riley's almost costumelike clothing changes, her black eyeliner, her preppy clothes. I put my hand on her shoulder. "I'm sorry, Riley. You should just be who you are."

She shrugs me off. "Do you think my mother will be home this summer?"

"I hope so." I gaze at her, thinking of my own mother. Riley might be better off with my parents, where she wouldn't have to spend even more time alone than she did with Becky. Raising herself, essentially. A sudden vise squeezes my heart so quickly that I gasp for air. It's all in my head.

"I better get to dialysis," I say at last. She hasn't noticed my physical distress. I'm awfully good at hiding things.

Trish, a nurse who's worked there longer than I've been a patient, sits behind the reception desk. She slides open the glass transom window, shoots me a grin that creases her well-smiled face, and crinkles her eyes into merry slits. "Checking in, sweetheart?" She's one of those people who calls everyone sweetheart. It's easier than remembering their names. She's also my favorite nurse there, fast and efficient, her fingernails always clipped short on her strong hands.

I nod.

"Don't worry. One day, you won't have to look at my mug again. Bet you won't miss that." She gives a hearty laugh.

I force a smile. She says that often. And it's true. Either people get a kidney or, eventually, they die. They have heart attacks, get infections, or develop other problems. No one comes through unscathed.

I turn away from the window, my stomach clenching.

Mark Walters watches me. His expression reminds me of the dog we had when I was little, a black Lab with a white spot on her chest named Daisy. Daisy would lie at my door whenever I was sick, which was so often, her head on her paws and her eyes rarely leaving me. Whenever I stirred, Daisy raised her head, her black dog eyebrows working up and down as if trying to decipher my needs. If Daisy thought that someone was making too much noise, she'd go into the hallway and bark three short times. "She's your guard dog," Dad said. Daisy had been his dog, accompanying him to job sites in the truck. Somehow she took it upon herself to change into mine.

My heart gives a little wrench of sadness. I hadn't thought of Daisy in years.

I meet Walters's eyes for the first time. His are luminously blue under the briar patch of eyebrows casting shadows over them.

I inhale to speak. No idea of what I'll say.

"Gal?" Trish comes out of the reception area. "Come on back now."

I follow Trish to my room. When I glance back at Walters, he is holding his reading device as if I was never there. It would be creepy if he were still watching me, I think, but I'm still oddly disappointed.

I ARRIVE HOME the next morning a bit later than usual. The irritating thing is, I shouldn't be late. It is like I got sucked into a time warp. I looked at the clock in the car when I pulled in and it was twenty whole minutes later than I expected it should be.

It must be the many small things adding up: extra traffic around town, the nurse coming in at a snail's pace to remove my hookups, the molasses feeling of my tired muscles in the early morning. I stretch in the car, yawn. Blink at the red-orange dawn, so like a Hulthemia. It will be a warm day. I can tell already. The air feels heavy, more humid than usual.

I need to wake up.

I head for the roses before my car door shuts.

The first thing to do is check under the roses outside for aphids and mites. Nothing there. The spray worked. The underside is sticky. A few petals are brown on the underside of the pink rose. Evidence of too much spray. I hadn't used too much, had I? I always make sure to use exactly the correct amount.

I examine the next bush. The blooms on this one are brown, too, even worse than the first. "Oh no," I breathe. So is the next one, and so on down the whole row. These roses are done for this bloom cycle.

A clattering sounds in the greenhouse. The hairs on my neck stand up. I walk as quickly as I can, huffing a little. "Riley? Is that you?"

Riley straightens and turns toward me. I gasp. She has the poison can in her hand.

"What are you doing?" I bellow. I have a voice that can rival a basketball coach's, if I choose. "What did you spray in here?"

She points to the one entire table of seedlings. "They have aphids all over them."

"Oh no." I snatch the poison can out of her hands. "How did you mix this? How much did you put on?"

"Calm down. I followed the directions."

"I have my own directions." I gesture toward my note-book shelf. "I don't agree with the manufacturer recommendations. It burns the roses." I rush toward the G42, the rose I'm taking to Pasadena. "Did you touch this one?"

"I didn't know ..."

"Answer the question! Yes or no!" I am shouting again. It's early and I'm probably waking up Old Mrs. Allen, but I do not care.

"Stop yelling." Riley's eyes fill.

"Then answer the question." My voice is still loud, but not as shrill.

"No. I didn't do that one yet."

"Thank God." I pick up G42, looking at it in the light. Yes, the underside has aphids all over it. I take it to the big laundry sink and rinse it gently, using a soft cloth to wipe away the aphids.

Riley stands frozen to her spot. I replace G42 and take several deep breaths. "Did I not tell you to stay out of the roses? To do the chores inside?"

She looks down.

"Didn't I?" I stamp my foot. Childish. But I'm so frustrated I'm afraid I'll splinter into a hundred million fragments if I don't do something. "Why didn't you do as I asked?"

She shrugs.

"That is not an answer." Oh, this is far worse than dealing with a student in school. At school I am generally calm. I don't take misbehaving personally. This feels like a punch to the gut.

"I don't know, okay?" Riley wipes her nose. I notice, finally, that she is wearing her Polarfleece pajamas, my Crocs over her thick white tube socks, and an overcoat. Her hair, parted on one side, covers one eye.

I put the poison pot back where it belongs. "Did you do your chores? Your homework? I hear you have a math quiz today."

She gulps so loudly I can hear it.

I swivel back to her, slowly. "Riley. You did study, didn't you?"

Her mouth corkscrews. "I'm going inside."

I raise my hands into the air, hoping for divine intervention of some variety. Taking a breath, I am about to unleash another torrent of useless reprimands when I see Riley is trembling as if there's an earthquake underfoot.

I put my arms down by my sides. "Go ahead."

Dismissed, she heads for the house.

I sink onto my rolling stool. What am I going to do with her?

What will I do with me?

23

THE DAY DOES TURN OUT TO BE WARMER THAN normal, making the kids want to ditch and go do something wildly physical. It's almost as bad as a rainy day, which any teacher will tell you also turns students into restless beasts. My classes will not shut up, will not concentrate.

Instead of forcing them, I give into the flow. I put on a video I have ready for such occasions, a BBC-produced romp about diseases, hand out worksheets asking them a few questions about the movie to encourage them to pay a bit of attention, and then I sit at my desk and look up roses all day.

At least I'm not failing them for their muddle-headedness. That ought to please Dr. O'Malley. This worksheet will be worth ten measly points, but they will be able to take home a paper reading 100 percent to their doting parents, who will think, "At last! Miss Garner is recognizing my child's superior intellect!"

I giggle to myself.

I hadn't seen Dr. O'Malley except in passing since he made my classroom visit. He nodded to me in the hallway this morning, gravely. "Did you think about what I said?" he asked.

I nodded back. "You are going to have to use all the powers of the board to kick me out, and I will have to use all the powers of the law to stay in." I smiled my sweetest smile at him.

I wanted to tell him that no matter what I'd thought of him, I'd never taken him for a weak man, like I did now, one who would bend to politics. But even I know when to keep my mouth shut. Sometimes.

I steal a glance at my AP Biology class. They appear absorbed in the video. It's a good one, with a guy from Monty Python narrating. I log into my Gmail.

Byron is online.

I type:

Are you coming to Pasadena?

Yes. U?

Of course. Showing G42. What about you?

Surprise.

Do you have a breakthrough?

Can't talk about it.

Oh.

My fingers pause over the keyboard as I think. Then I type:

Did you get fragrance?

He ignores this.

Have you selected which specimens you'll breed next year? I have a mother to give you. Performed well last two years with growth, reblooming. All it needs is fragrance. Do you have a fragrant rose yet?

I don't answer. No.

I think about the mother rose and get excited. We have not exchanged seedlings before. The truth is, we keep the best for ourselves.

Both of us want to be the first to have the best Hulthemia ever. Why would we give away our greatest specimens to each other?

Besides, Byron would always win. Always, with his larger operation. I am at a disadvantage so enormous it's like a mom-and-pop hamburger stand competing against McDonald's. But I happen to be a big believer in David over Goliath.

The chat shows he's typing, but nothing appears. Then there's a pause and it shows typing again. He must have erased his thought. Then he types:

Fragrance. That is the missing element, isn't it?

That and ease of growth. I'm going to give a bush to my friend Dara. If she can't kill it, no one can.

Good thought.

He signs off.

I sit back in my chair, thinking. What has he got up his sleeve? Why's he being so secretive?

I find Dara after school, not having been able to find her at lunch again. She's in her classroom.

I've barely seen her since she told me she wasn't going to the rose show. Perhaps she is avoiding me. I admit, I have been avoiding her, a little bit. Waiting for her to make the first move. I say hello to her, but I haven't sat with her and Mr. Morton in the lunchroom. Nor do I roam around searching for her after school. Really, outside of our friendship, there is little reason for our two departments to interact. And I am very busy.

Dara's room is a little wing of its own, with wide windows and natural light coming in on both sides. She has drafting tables that can be adjusted to various angles and tall stools. Easels stand folded and ready at the sides.

She has a little yard for ceramics, with dirty canvas-covered tables under the patio awning and a brick kiln some long-ago donor funded. Clay pots and sculptures dry on wooden shelving. It is out here that I find her, surveying the ceramics and touching each. "Firing up the kiln today?" I cross the lawn and sit at one of the worktables in the shade.

"You remembered. I'm impressed."

"I do pay attention, sometimes." A hunk of wet clay sits before me.

She takes the seat across. "Do you want to build something? I just kneaded the air bubbles out of it."

"Air bubbles?"

"It's like bread. I think of clay as a living thing." She gestures to the gray clump. "Go ahead."

I pick up a piece. It's slimy. I grimace. "I can't figure out what to make."

"So make anything." She crosses her arms on the table. Today she wears a big stained apron over jeans, rolled up to her calves, and an old T-shirt. Her hair is loose around her shoulders.

I think about Mr. Morton and how I should broach the subject.

Dara breaks off a piece of clay, rolls it between her palms into a ball. "How's Riley?"

"Fine." I consider telling Dara about Riley almost killing my prize rose and tanking the others, and that odd feeling seizes me up inside again. "She's just fine."

Dara nods. "Is she looking forward to the Science Olympiad?"

I nod. What kind of lame small talk is this? I might as well be talking to a parent of a student.

She clears her voice and I can tell she's getting down to some nitty-gritty business. Dara always clears her throat beforehand. "I talked to Dr. O'Malley."

I keep moving the clay in my hands. It's drying out. I dip my fingers into a plastic water bucket before Dara can tell me to. "He told you about the part-time ultimatum. I mean, offer."

She nods, holds up her hand. "Before you go off the deep end, let me say that I think it's a good idea."

I slap down my clay. "Why does everyone think I'm always going off the deep end?"

Her gaze is level. There's a small streak of mascara under one eye. "Because you do."

"Well, I do not, nor do I think it's a good idea. I don't want to be relegated to some part-time position with no health or retirement benefits. Ever think of that?" I pick up the clay, my fingers moving without my notice.

She leans forward. "Gal, if you don't take this, you might get pushed out and then you'll get nothing at all."

"I'm willing to risk that." I stand up. "I thought you'd take my side, Dara."

"I want what's best for you. We all do."

"No. You want what's convenient. That's the whole problem." I plop down the piece of clay. I haven't mentioned Mr. Morton. I don't want to. Not anymore. If she wants to be high and mighty and right, then she can do that all by herself. "You don't understand. You would rather pass a student than give them a bad grade. I bet you never give your students less than a C, do you?"

"Art is subjective, but I do have grading criteria." Dara has made a pinch pot out of her clay. She places it on the table. "The point is for students to learn the material, isn't it? Why not let them get some extra credit?"

"Because they have to get the work done on time. Their employers won't wait around for them to do extra learning."

"But this is high school. They *are* learning." She wipes a stray strand of hair, leaving clay behind on her forehead.

I go back to the part-time question. "I am not going to just be a part-time coach for Science Olympiad. Eighty-five percent of my students pass the AP Biology test, Dara. Eighty-five. That's well above average. Those are real measurable numbers, not subjective." I stand, holding my clay in my hands. "I'd rather get a whole new job than work here part-time. Maybe at a company in San Luis Obispo." This is my shot to Mr. Morton, but Dara shows no recognition.

She appears unflustered by my small tirade. "Maybe your rose will get to market and you can retire."

I cannot tell if her tone is sarcastic or not. I decide it's not.

She indicates the clay. "What'd you make?"

I look down, having made whatever this is unbidden. I hold it between my thumb and forefinger. It appears to be a large bean. "It's a kidney." I smash it back into the big pile of clay.

She sits frowning.

"I'll see you around, Dara." I brush off my hands on my pants. The clay has sucked the moisture painfully out of them. I won't stop to wash. I go on home with Riley.

24

I SHOULD BE RELAXING OR WORKING IN THE ROSE garden, cutting away all the dead English roses, but instead I am lying on my bed, my head under my pillow. From my stomach escape great big juicy sobs that I hope will be muffled by the comforter and fake goose down and the walls, not to mention the television.

It might have been hours or seconds before Riley knocks on my door. "Are you okay, Aunt Gal?"

I look at the clock's green display. Six-thirty. I've missed dinner. I sniffle. I have worked myself into a hyperventilated state. When I get like this, I can barely talk, barely think.

"Aunt Gal?" Riley is insistent.

What do I tell her? I don't want her to see me like this. She'll be alarmed, call for help. "I need to be alone," I call back.

She pauses. "All right." I hear her footsteps shuffling into the kitchen, hear the phone being taken off the hook.

I blow my nose. What is Riley, if not alone? She was alone last night during dialysis, alone after school for the most part, alone with her mother. Alone with me. Always alone. It's a shame for a kid to grow up that way.

I drink a bit of water. I'm having another Blues Day. The

emotion must occasionally be released out of me like a too-inflated tire or I will pop. It's been too much. Dr. O'Malley. Dara. Walters. Dr. Blankenship. Dialysis. I look ahead and all I can see is unfulfilling part-time work, losing roses, and endless machines hooked up to my body.

In short, this shit wears you down.

I take a deep breath and give myself a pep talk. This feeling will pass. It always does. My eyes dry. I sit all the way up. Riley's voice comes through the wall. I wonder who she's talking to, and then she knocks on my door. "Grandma wants to talk to you," she says.

I pick up the extension.

"Gal?" Mom's voice is tense. "Gal, are you all right?"

"Fine."

"You're not. You're having a Blues Day." She clucks softly, trying to soothe me through the digital phone lines as though she's stroking my hair. I close my eyes. "Gal, Riley thinks you're crying because of her."

I focus on the wall. "I'm not."

"I know that. But she ruined those roses, and she thinks you're mad at her, honey." She clucks again. "I can be up there tomorrow morning. You need help, don't you?"

I inhale, thinking. Riley's been here, what, only a little more than a month? It hasn't been long. It seems like longer. A lot has happened.

"Gal?"

"Maybe Riley ought to live with you, Mom." I exhale at last, lightheaded.

"Maybe so," my mother agrees, without missing a beat, as though she has expected and prepared for this call. "It is a lot to handle for you, isn't it? It's hard enough having a kid, but getting one that's already a teenager . . ."

Tears start again. "I tried, Mom."

"I know."

"It's the kidney and the roses and everything all together."
I lie back on the bed. "She's not getting the attention she
needs. She's alone too much. I'm not enough for her."

"You're more than enough for anyone, Gal," Mom says
loyally and predictably.

"No. I'm not. I am not capable of taking care of her like
she needs." I wipe my nose. "Riley got a pretty bad deal,
didn't she? First her mom. Then her dad. Now me."

"I'll be there tomorrow, Galilee." Mom hangs up gently.

I go out to the living room. Riley has her feet up on the
coffee table, pink socks on. She is eating a microwaved
carne asada burrito wrapped in a paper towel and watching
Wheel of Fortune. She looks up at me expectantly.

I sit in the chair. "I'm not mad at you, Riley. Not at all."
Vanna White is wearing a gold gown with a Cinderella skirt.
The contestants clap and all have wide, white smiles and a
thousand teeth. "I'm going through a lot. It's not you. In fact,
it's unfair to you."

"What's unfair to me?" Riley takes a bite of her burrito,
holding her mouth open to let the steam escape.

I spread my arms apart. "This whole situation. Leaving
you alone so I can go to dialysis. It's too much to ask of you."

Riley shakes her head. "It's not. I told you, I'm fine."

I lean toward her. "You say you're fine, but you're not.
You need more people around you, Riley."

She takes another bite, focuses on Pat Sajak. "Free market evaluation!" she says to the television.

"Focus, Riley. I'm trying to have a serious conversation
here." I tap her knee gently.

She glances at me. "I am focused. You want me to go."

"No. I don't. I like having you here." I realize this is true. Having another person here is comforting. But what is comforting to me may not be what Riley needs. "It might not be best for you, Riley."

She eats the last of her burrito with her fingers.

"Riley? Are you okay with that? Living with Grandma?" My eyes are trained on her face.

She nods carelessly, still trained on the television, as though it doesn't matter one whit to her either way.

I sit awkwardly until my stomach rumbles. "Is that all you want to say?"

She swallows her final bite. "Yeah."

I rub my hands with my fingertips. They're still dry from the clay. "How about we go over the trebuchet some more? Make sure you know how to read the metric ruler, do the equations. What do you say?"

She nods, wadding her paper towel up and throwing it across the room into the open kitchen trash can.

I stand up. "Let me get something to eat. Then we'll work."

She nods again, stretching out on the couch like a big cat.

I go into the kitchen and stare into the cupboards for a full five minutes, transfixed by all there is and isn't to eat, listening for Riley with one ear, wondering what I could have done differently.

My mother arrives alone in the morning. She brings only a small overnight bag plus a pillow, because she is particular about her pillows and needs a special one made of foam and contoured to fit her neck.

She has more trouble than usual getting out of the car. I gesture to Riley to lend Mom a hand. She rises with a hearty *oof.* "How are my girls?" She envelops us both. Mom smells of vanilla and something fruity—pear, perhaps, along with

the linseed oil she uses in her painting and which is probably stuck on her clothing someplace. Her hair is a fat dough-
nut on top of her head.

"I like this perfume better." I sound muffled, my cheek
pressed by Mom's hand.

Half of Riley's face is smooshed into Mom's shoulder.
Her one open eye meets mine and we both giggle.

"Let me breathe, Grandma." Riley steps back.

"You look so nice!" Grandma takes her by the hand and
spins her around, ballroom dancer style. "I love your hair."

"Thanks." Riley touches it proudly. "My friend cut it for
me." At this mention of Samantha, Riley grows still. I know
she's thinking "former friend," and I think of Dara.

Mom looks from me to Riley and back again. She grins.
"Who wants ice cream?"

"It's ten o'clock in the morning, Mother." I pick up her
bag. She takes it from me roughly.

"It's ice cream time someplace in the world." She hefts
the bag, clutching the railing, moving with a slow limp into
the house.

I INSIST ON WAITING until after lunch for ice cream.
Riley makes herself the smallest meal possible: two frozen
chicken nuggets and a handful of baby carrots. "That's a
toddler lunch," I say. Riley downs the food before I can sit at
the table with my salad.

"I don't want to get filled up." She beams.

"Good idea," Mom says, and ruffles Riley's hair. "Gal,
don't you have any soda for Riley?"

"Of course not." I have never bought soda. Expensive
sugar water. Mom buys it by the case. I fear if Riley lives with

Mom, she will gain two hundred pounds and her teeth will fall out. I'll simply have to remind Mom that she won't be able to spoil her grandchild like that when she lives with her.

Mom makes herself a small plain green salad, iceberg lettuce. "Rabbit food," she says. "Doctor says losing weight will help my hip."

"You need nutrition." I scoop baby carrots on her plate. "And protein."

She wrinkles her nose. "I'm saving my calories for ice cream."

I sigh.

We go to the locally made ice cream shop in town, a place called Bub's, next door to the movie theater in a strip mall. The walls and floors are covered in dark wood paneling, thick with yellow lacquer. Hanging yellow glass and wrought-iron chandeliers from the seventies complete the scene.

"What'll it be?" Bub himself is working the counter today, a small older man known for contributing to local schools.

Riley salivates at the menu, which stretches all the way across the back wall and features customer-created concoctions as well as Bub's own. "Get what you want," Mom says.

Riley does a happy dance. "I'll have the Dream Boat hot fudge sundae." Two scoops of chocolate and raspberry cheesecake ice cream, followed by hot fudge and sliced strawberries on top, whipped cream and a cherry, too, of course.

Mom frowns. "Let's see. May I get a child cone of vanilla?"

"All those calories saved up and you're only going to get a vanilla?" I laugh. If I could get anything, I'd have what Riley is having.

"I like the pure flavor of vanilla. It's very complex."

"We use real vanilla bean. It's delicious," Bub agrees. He

peers at me from under his baseball cap, green eyes bright in his sun-reddened face. "What will you have, ma'am?"

"Ma'am" makes Dara feel old. I feel respected. I smile. "Nothing, thank you."

"I can give you a sample." He holds up a tiny spoon. "Anything you like."

I shake my head regretfully. My favorite flavor used to be butter pecan. Here Bub has a macadamia butter nut with caramel streaks, which appears to be a close approximation.

My mother squeezes my shoulder. "If I had your willpower, Gal, I'd weigh eighty pounds less."

I nod, once.

"I'm sorry. I should have come here with Riley alone."

"No. I don't mind." They get their treats and we sit in the sunshine at a black wrought-iron table on the front patio. It's unusually quiet for a Saturday.

As I sit and watch them eat their ice cream for a few minutes, I think of what it will be like when Riley leaves with my mother. To sit alone again.

At least I won't have to go to the ice cream parlor. I smile ruefully.

Mom senses what I'm pondering. "Have you talked to her?" She nods her head toward Riley.

"If I hadn't, then it would be mighty awkward right now." Mom is sometimes not very subtle.

Mom gets down to her sugar cone and begins crunching. "Riley. You're coming home with me at the end of the weekend?"

"I am?" Riley wipes her face with a paper napkin.

"Aren't you?" I shift my legs on the hard chair.

Mom holds up her hands. "Everyone stop answering questions with questions. Riley. Do you want to come back with me tomorrow night, or stay here until the end of the school year?"

Riley stirs her ice cream into soup. "I can't decide. Whatever Aunt Gal wants."

"That's not an answer. Make a decision."

"But I don't know!" She lifts her head up. Her cheeks and nose are pink. "I thought you meant at the end of the year, but if you want me to go now, I will."

"Riley. It's not that I want you to go." I put my hand over hers. "It's that I don't think I'm a very good guardian for you. I have dialysis every other night and I have those roses." I take a deep breath that hurts my chest. "I just want you to be safe and comfortable."

Mom watches us, her head moving back and forth as though watching a tennis match. "I think she should stay and finish the year," Mom says at last. "It doesn't make sense to go now. There's only a month of school left."

Riley brightens. "Okay." She pours the melted ice cream into her mouth from the silver bowl.

Mom nods slowly at me. I nod back. "Why are we nodding?"

"I can stay with you until the end of the school year. Help out." Mom smiles. "Would you like me to do that?"

I think of Mom on my pull-out couch for the next month. Not one, but two extra bodies. Dad alone down south. "I'll be fine."

A black Audi pulls into the parking spot in front of us. My heart speeds up. Sure enough, Dara exits, not waiting for Mr. Morton to come around and open her car door as he is trying to do. She swishes up in her circle skirt and sweater set, looking like an extra from *Grease*, except she's got on strappy heels instead of saddle shoes.

"Mrs. Garner!" Dara bends and embraces Mom. Mr. Morton shakes her hand.

"Dara. So nice to see you." Mom gestures to the table next to us. "Why don't you join us?"

"Can't. We're seeing a movie." She stands apart from Mr. Morton. I see that she is indeed quite a bit taller than he is, with her heels on. This gives me a measure of satisfaction, for some reason.

Dara nods at me. I nod back.

He checks his watch. Wearing a sports coat to a movie, over jeans. Dating Dara must be difficult. If you ever wore shorts and a T-shirt, you'd look hopelessly underdressed. "Come on, Dara. We'll be late."

"Don't do anything I wouldn't approve of," Mom calls after them.

They laugh, Dara waving her off.

Riley picks up her dish. "Guess that means they won't be doing much of anything."

"Hey, I have plenty of fun. Painting and traveling. You'd be surprised how much fun you can have, and how much you can get done, if you don't fritter away your time watching trashy movies and the like." Mom hands her napkin to Riley, who throws it away. She grins. "Now, how about a Costco trip for you?"

25

After the Costco trip, I insist again that I will be okay, that Mom can leave as scheduled on Sunday afternoon. She has bought me enough warehouse supplies for the next several months. I have toilet paper stored under my kitchen sink, in various crevices in the garage, as well as in the actual bathroom.

"Are you certain you can handle Riley?" Mom says to me as we unload the dishwasher.

I shrug, then nod. "Yeah."

"Heard from Becky?"

"Not recently. Riley talks to her sometimes, but I don't think she's been able to contact her for a week. She hasn't said when she'll be back."

"I'll pin her down." Mom closes the glass cupboard with some force. "It's important for Riley to have stability."

"I agree."

"Becky should either let Riley spend the rest of high school with me, or come home and be a real mom." Mom wipes away some excess water from a bowl.

"You mean, not take pills or drink?" I clank silverware into the drawer. "You might be asking too much."

"I don't think she does that anymore." Mom begins work on the egg pan in the sink. "I know she still has a drink every once in a while, but it's not as bad as it was."

"You just can't stop doing something like that, Mom."

"At least she's functional. Holds a job." Mom hums a tuneless song, a furrow forming between her brows. She doesn't like to hear anything bad about her kids, true or not.

"For now."

"I know you've given up on your sister, but I think she's improved. Give her a chance." Mom dries her hands, reaches into her purse. "Before I forget. Here's a check. Becky wired money into my account. I'm to give it to you." She hands me the check. It's for a pretty good amount, I have to admit. More than enough for Riley's food and extra utilities and the like. "Or you could give her your account number, so she can transfer it directly to you."

I pocket it. "There's no way I'm giving Becky any access to my account."

"Dad will wire the next one from our account into yours." Mom finishes cleaning the pan, puts it on the drying rack.

"If it comes," I mutter darkly.

"It will. It will." Mom kisses me on the cheek. "Have a little faith, Gal."

ON TUESDAY AFTERNOON, Dr. Blankenship wants to see me. We meet in her regular office, with her leather chairs and computer and desk, instead of the exam room. She never sees me in there unless she's handing out news. I clutch my tote bag nervously.

Dr. Blankenship sits behind a great big cherrywood desk with an L-shaped return against a wall overlooking a parking lot. She has a Chinese money plant, lucky bamboo in a vase, and a miniature Zen sand garden with a tiny wooden rake all set up along the return. There's a red lantern hanging in one corner of the room, and a mirror opposite her entry door. There are so many of these things I wonder for a second if she's part Chinese.

She sees me looking at her collection. "Feng shui," she says. "Good health and wealth. Helps energy flow."

I purse my lips. She believes in energy flow, but she won't believe in IVP dye allergy? She must see my surprise, because she shrugs. "Hey, I have a lucky rabbit's foot I rub before surgery. I have some superstitions. Can't hurt, can it?"

"I suppose not." I regard her warily. Today she's wearing a bit of makeup, blush to make her white skin glow a bit healthier, better concealer over the dark under-eye circles, mascara on her light-colored lashes.

"Mark Walters sent me something interesting." She throws down a printout of the medical journal article. The pages fan out across the desk.

I gulp, bracing myself. "Let me guess. You read it. You disagree."

"Nope. I read it and met with my surgery board, and now," she takes a breath, "now I'm thinking all we need to do is put the stinking kidney on the right side instead of the left, and blood flow won't be an issue."

I swear at that moment all my bodily functions cease. I am suspended in the air. I hope it won't hurt when I fall.

She continues as if this is an entirely normal and everyday conversation. "I'm not one who can't admit that there are other ways of doing things, that she might be wrong. It's all in there."

I stare at her, uncomprehending.

She shuffles the report back together in a neater pile. "You're back on the transplant list, Gal."

Somehow my brain revives. "You're serious?"

She nods, giving me what I think is the first genuine smile ever. "You have Mr. Walters to thank, Gal. And the review board."

Of course. When you can no longer come up with reasons not to do something, you have to do it or get the pants sued off you. I don't ask her why she wasn't keeping up with the research, why she needed another patient, for heaven's sake, to tell her. The only thing I have to hold on to is that Dr. Blankenship's surgery skills are actually pretty damn good, with high survival rates. "Thank you. What's my priority number?"

"Top ten. You know, we go down the list and whoever is the best match gets it."

I nod. It's been so long, I've forgotten how it works.

Dr. Blankenship stands. "The kidney transplant coordinator will be in touch with you later today. She'll go over any questions you have and also make sure the match is right for you." It sounds like she's talking about a matchmaking operation, not a kidney surgery. I smile.

I hold out my hand. "Thank you."

She hesitates before taking it. "Gal. You're the most challenging patient I've ever had."

I laugh drily, because what else can I do? "Thanks."

"That can be bad. And good." She takes a breath. "What I'm trying to say is, I'm going to do my best for you, no matter what. Okay?"

"I appreciate it." I grin.

She waves me off. "Have a good session. Go call your mother."

· · ·

MR. WALTERS is in the waiting room, alternating between humming and chatting up the various old and young ladies around him. He wears white shorts today, with a white long-sleeved button-down shirt and brown leather sandals. I walk right up to him.

"Thank you." I extend my hand.

He takes it. "So she did agree."

"You didn't have to do that." I sit down next to him. The awful truth is I'm not sure I would have done the same for him. "I could get a transplant before you."

His chipper attitude is unabated. "It's out of our hands. The best match gets it. You and I do not require the same kidney, Gal. It's all up to fate now."

"I hate fate." I cross my arms.

"Fate's a bitch." He grins, then slaps me on my arm. "Tell you what. As long as we've got to be strapped to these machines, how about a game of Scrabble?"

Would the nurse move one of us out when it was time for sleep? "Can't spell worth a darn."

"Then it will be even more fun." He grins.

I pat my tote bag. "I've got lessons to plan." This is only partly true. I've had my lessons planned for weeks, because I decide on the plan at the beginning of the semester. It's basically the one from last year. "Maybe next time."

He nods. Do I detect a note of disappointment? Does he like me? He can't. He's old enough to be my father. But maybe he thinks I'm his age.

"I'm thirty-six, you know," I blurt. Everyone in the room, young and old, snaps their attention to me.

Mark smiles slyly. "Congratulations. I'm fifty-nine."

I sit straight up in my chair. "I just thought you might like to know that."

"I will remember. Thirty-seven candles for your next birthday cake. When is that?" His eyes twinkle. They remind me of how I try to hold in my laughter when a student does something especially funny while they're trying for utmost seriousness.

"January thirty-first." I flush.

He bends his head in a nod. "And what is your favorite cake?"

"Depends on what I'm allowed to eat."

"Let's be optimistic. By your next birthday, you shall have a new kidney." Walters crosses his legs. "Pick a cake, any cake at all."

I consider, scrolling through all the cakes I've ever tried in my mind's eye. I settle on one. A complicated concoction. "Baked Alaska. Over a chocolate cake with vanilla ice cream."

One eyebrow shoots toward the ceiling. "Impressive. And shall it be a flaming baked Alaska?"

I nod. "Of course."

"Had it before?" He actually takes out his BlackBerry and types something in.

"My mother made one for me after I got my first kidney, when I was twelve." I smile. "Twelve egg whites for the meringue. She couldn't bear to throw out the yolks, so she made a custard the next day. She put on five pounds from that event alone." Worth every pound, Mom had said. Would have been worth twenty.

He laughs so hard he dissolves into a cough, a hacking, choking one, turning his face into the color of a beet, little white lines appearing around his eyes.

"Can you breathe?"

Walters holds up a hand, a wheezing noise emitting out of his mouth. Nurse Sonya rushes over with a Dixie cup of water. He gulps it. I see how skinny his neck looks as the water goes down. I wonder what he looked like when he was healthy.

He thanks Sonya for the water, then continues talking to me as if he hadn't just nearly choked to death. "I think the candles might sink into the meringue."

"Use bigger candles."

He laughs again. "You're a problem-solver."

Sonya calls my name. I get up. "See you in the morning, probably."

"See you." His BlackBerry is out again. I hesitate. Maybe I could play one game. I could suggest Sequence or cards instead of Scrabble. But now the nurse is calling my name, insistently, and I don't want to make trouble by rearranging rooms and pushing around beds. I leave Mr. Walters, bent over his little black phone, his big lean fingers mashing down the keys.

26

THE SCIENCE OLYMPIAD IS HELD IN PASO ROBLES, because we're too small-time to host a shindig like this. On the next Saturday, the last weekend in May, Riley and I awake at five and drive in. I turn off the car stereo. "It's too early for that noise."

She yawns big. "Is anyone sick, do you think?"

"You shouldn't wish people sick."

"I'm not. I'm just wondering if Mr. Morton called you this morning."

"No." I haven't spoken to Mr. Morton since that day in front of Bub's.

Riley gives me a sidelong glance. "I know how to use the tape measure now."

"That is good."

"So even if I don't get to do anything else, I did that." She fidgets with the zipper on her hoodie, zipping it up and down, slowly and quickly, until I'm afraid she'll catch her skin.

"Did you know that I didn't know how to read time until I was in seventh grade?"

"What on earth do you mean?" I think of the digital displays on the oven and computers and microwaves.

"A regular clock, with hands. I didn't know how to read it. We never went over it in school. I guess each teacher thought the last teacher had told us. I don't know." She smiles down toward her feet. "I've never been too good at this kind of stuff."

A little cloud lifts and bursts from somewhere above my head. I'm simultaneously happy and sad. "I should have taught you how to read the tape measure, even if you weren't on the team."

She shrugs. "I like shooting the trebuchet."

"It is pretty fun." I pull into the parking lot at the high school, where the meet will occur.

Mr. Morton stands near his car, carrying a clipboard and looking very official. His hair looks like errant brambles in the wind. "You're late." His tone is crisp.

"Then why are you standing outside?" I glance at my watch, a Swatch imprinted with geckos. It's eight. True, he had said seven-fifty, but eight is close enough considering the event actually begins at eight-thirty. "We're perfectly on time."

"Brad and Samantha are sick." He makes some kind of mark on a piece of paper. "Riley, you're covering for trebuchet."

"What?" Riley and I say at the same time.

"Why didn't you call me?" I ask.

"I did."

I whip out my phone. "Oh. You did. But I was driving! I couldn't answer."

The flu season's over. Both kids were fine yesterday. I just cannot believe Brad would miss this, or Samantha, with their concern for grades and the extracurricular. Maybe Brad; he's a senior and doesn't give a flying fig anymore. But Samantha, the junior? Is she having a mid-high-school rebellion?

"Aunt Gal?" Riley's at my side. She blinks rapidly. "I'm nervous."

I put my hands up on her shoulders. "You will be just fine, Riley."

THE HIGH SCHOOL AUDITORIUM is really more like a gym, built for basketball games, with hoops at either side and hardwood floors and bleachers. It's impossibly noisy, everyone's voices echoing. I pull out my little red-foam earplugs from my fanny pack, take a stadium cushion out of my bag, and perch on the bottom row.

The trebuchets are already set up in a row along one end of the room. Some are made out of metal, but most are wood, like ours. Our whole team wears dark blue T-shirts emblazoned with our mascot and team name, St. Mark's Lions. The back features a white lion rearing up on its hind legs toward the competitors.

The judge hands out the weights and launchers. They're beanbags, probably filled with metal BBs. I hope none of them land in the audience. They should have done this outside. The students have to calculate how far those things will fly, based on their previous tests.

Riley, armed with a calculator and a notebook of graphs and tables, searches the stands. Who is she looking for? Oh. Me. I wave. She waves back. I give her a thumbs-up. "You can do it," I say, though she will never hear me from this distance. She nods like she's reading my lips.

It's odd. I see the other parents around me, waving to their children. I've cheered kids on in a teacherly role, sure, but this is the first time I have felt so rawly nervous for a student.

Because she's mine.

I lean forward, my elbows on my knees. "Come on, Riley. Come on."

She scratches her head with her pencil, then crouches down and writes furiously. She adjusts the trebuchet, places the beanbag, and holds the string. When she pulls the string, the catapult will release and fire the beanbag.

"Fire one!" the judge calls.

The first team fires. The beanbag flies nearly to the other basketball pole.

"Fire two!"

That's us. Her teammate Jim releases the trebuchet. It flies a little further. Riley raises her hands in victory.

Once all the teams have launched, they each send a member with the tape measure. A judge will double-check that they measured accurately. If the student didn't, points will be deducted.

I pray Riley remembers her metric system.

"Riley, Riley, Riley." I am chanting loud without realizing it. The other parents look over at me. I am the only one chanting. Oh Lord. I've turned into one of those annoying parents I hate, the ones who stand up and clap at graduation after we've asked everyone to hold their applause until the end, the ones who yell at the soccer coaches from the sidelines. How easy that transformation was.

She measures, looks at the tape. She straightens and gives me a thumbs-up and the biggest smile I've seen on her.

I can't help it. I stand up and cheer.

She is not embarrassed. She gives a little jump and claps. Second place. It doesn't matter. I hoot as loudly as I can. Everyone stares, surprised at the noise coming out of the short lady.

Mr. Morton, looking on from the other side, shakes his head with a smile.

BACK AT ST. MARK'S that afternoon, the parents who didn't drive come pick up their kids. I leave Riley chatting with Jim, and go over to Mr. Morton.

He sits alone under a Chinese flame tree. It's a young one, the trunk still studded with thorns, yellow flowers barely starting to show. As it matures, the thorns will smooth out into green bark.

Mr. Morton's hair, so wild in the parking lot, has been combed down to an unrecognizable Ken-doll helmet. Even his beard is unnaturally still. His face is drawn and tight, as though he's been sitting there grinding his teeth and clenching his fists.

I sit down beside him. "That went well, considering. I've never needed an alternate in all the years I've been doing this." We acquitted ourselves well in Disease Detectives and the other events.

Mr. Morton squints out at the quad, his face bare of sunglasses. "We should probably name alternates from now on."

"Probably." I think of Dara, and I want to ask him how the movie date went. I fear it will be taken wrong, as jealousy or prying. "Sometimes we make mistakes. We're human, aren't we?"

He gives me a sideways, puzzled glance.

I take a breath, decide I might as well ask. "Why did you leave your company? And your wife and child?"

Mr. Morton shifts away as if I've developed symptoms of the Ebola virus. "Please, don't be so indirect."

I tap my foot. "No. Really. Does Dara know? Does she know about all this?"

"Maybe you should tell her, since you seem to know so much." He sets his mouth back into a firm line. "Hell, you probably know more about it than I do."

"I'm watching out for her. Someone has to." I think of Dara, our new coolness, and tears prick my eyes. I haven't even told her about my new kidney transplant status yet.

"I haven't talked to Dara since the movie last week, if you must know." He shakes his head. He stands. "I make it a point not to discuss my love life, past or present, with anyone except the parties involved."

I spread my hands apart. "Hey, I'm just trying to figure out whether you're a jerk or not."

He laughs. Sticks his hands into his front pockets, stares at his brown loafers. "I am not."

I picture his little girl, alone with her mother in another city. Riley and Becky and her father all over again. "Do you ever see her?" I ask. "Are they still in San Luis Obispo? That's not far."

He gulps. "I don't see her as much as I'd like."

I want to ask him why. Did he abandon them? Use drugs? Before I can think of a more socially appropriate way to pose the question, he asks me one.

"What about you?"

"Me?" I crumple my lunch bag.

"You. Are you a jerk, or not?"

I blink at him. No one's ever accused me of being a jerk. At least, not openly.

He nods toward the Chinese flame. "You're as prickly as this tree. You take pleasure in it. But underneath," he shakes his head, "I don't know yet."

I don't think of myself as prickly. "Correct" is a better term. Protective. "Maybe you never will." I remember the day he came over to make a trebuchet, how well we'd gotten along then. I sort of wish it could go back to that. But ever since he crossed me with Riley, I have only been looking for the worst in him. Perhaps I'm missing something. I know he's missing something with me.

"Listen. I'm sorry I brought that up," I say in a low voice. "It's between you and Dara, and you and your ex. Not me."

"You're only looking out for her." He smiles quickly. "Don't worry. I'm not a jerk. I don't think." He runs his hand through his hair. "I'm a private guy, Miss Garner. I don't like to talk about my personal life."

"Bet that drives your mother crazy." I notice he's calling me Miss Garner again. Establishing distance.

As he well might. He may not be here past the school year. I expect he'll want to move back into the city.

Riley jogs up, her eyes bright. "Ready, Aunt Gal? All the kids have been picked up."

Mr. Morton gets up with a nod. "I'm on my way out, too."

I swallow. "I'll see you."

"Yup." He waves.

We part to our opposite sides of the lot, each disappearing into our cars.

THAT NIGHT, I hear Riley talking to her mother. Describing the tournament, her triumph. Glossing over, understandably, the Disease Detectives.

"Your daughter was the hero of the day," I say, loudly, from across the room.

"Shush, Auntie." Riley laughs. It's good to hear her laugh.

Then the conversation gets around to other topics. I'm trying not to listen, but at the same time, how can I not listen in such a small house?

"School's over the third week of June, Mom." Riley listens. "She wants to talk to you, Aunt Gal."

I notice Riley's more likely to say "Aunt" while she's talking to Becky. "Becky. How's Asia?"

She ignores this. The connection is scratchy and it sounds like we're talking in 1911 instead of 2011. "Gal, I know I said I'd be home this summer."

I brace myself. "So when are you coming home?"

Riley pricks up next to me on the couch. I get up and go into the bedroom. I don't want her to hear this, whatever this is. I sense it's not going to be good.

"They want me to stay on this job through the summer. Go to China and Japan from here." Becky's voice is hoarse. I don't sound that bad unless I have a flu.

"Are you using?" I hiss into the phone.

"How dare you ask me that," she says angrily.

"I think you are. You sound like hell."

"I am not. I have a cold. I talk a lot." She clears her throat and her voice sounds better momentarily. "If you don't want her, send her to Mom's right now."

"It's not a question of *wanting* her, Becky. It's a question of you doing what you're supposed to do."

"I'm *supposed* to be earning a living. That's all I'm supposed to be doing."

"You're not conscripted into that company. It's not military service. Find a job close to home." I am whispering now, sure Riley's got her ear to my door listening.

Becky pauses. "This is what the company wants me to do. I have no position stateside. I'm doing all I can." She is emotionless in her delivery. I consider arguing with my sister. Then I remember Riley's got more meat on her than she probably has in years, that her hair is no longer that depressing ultrablack color, that she has actually voluntarily participated in a Science Olympiad.

Becky continues. "You want me to quit this job and come home to nothing? In this economy?" She sniffles. "I can't have Riley here in Asia. I'm traveling too much. She'd be alone."

I stop her. "All right, all right. Calm down."

"Don't tell me to calm down."

I laugh at the sheer cliché of our conversation. One of us is always telling the other to calm down.

"I'm hanging up now," Becky says.

"I'm not laughing at you."

"Good-bye." She hangs up.

"Bye," I say into the buzzing receiver. "Good-bye, Becky."

Once again, it's up to me to break the bad news to her daughter. I square my shoulders and fling open the bedroom door.

Winslow Blythe's *Complete Rose Guide* (SoCal Edition)

June

It's almost time for the second grow cycle and the June rose shows! To get ready, your roses are going to need lots of food. Ever see a teenaged boy at an all-you-can-eat buffet? That's what roses are like. They will eat as much food as you give them, and then some.

- Give them a nice weekly fertilizer as their main course.
- Pep them up with organics, like the fish emulsion and maybe the special organic tea you made.
- Clean 'em up daily for mites and such. Spray if you must.
- Continue your hybridizing experiments, if you're into that sort of thing.

27

THE CALL COMES EARLY IN THE MORNING, WAKING me before dawn on the following Tuesday. It's the first day of June, the day after Memorial Day, the end of the school year winding up, when students worry over finals and term papers and I worry over my next big rose show.

"We have a kidney. Do not eat anything today." It's Joanna, the transplant coordinator.

I'm number two on the list. Walters is one. The doctors run a bunch of tests to see if the kidney is a match. The blood type is only one way of matching. They try to match as many criteria as possible.

My stomach flutters. "When will you know?"

"This morning."

I knock on Riley's door. She rolls over, her face bearing the wrinkles of her pillowcase. I give her a thumbs-up. "Today might be the day."

I expect her to roll back over and go to sleep, but she sits up. "You better call Grandma. She won't forgive you if she's not the third to know."

. . .

AT SCHOOL, I keep my cell phone on, though this is frowned upon. There are always exceptions. This is definitely an exception.

All morning, I'm a frazzled bundle of nerves. I jump at every noise and sound. Me or Walters? Walters or me?

During Riley's biology class, Dara shows up. "Riley told me." She takes my hands. "I didn't even know you were back on the list. How'd you manage that?"

I drop her hands and smile wryly. "Long story."

She lowers her voice. "I know you're mad at me for siding with Dr. O'Malley, Gal, but really all I want is what's best for you."

I'm reminded of my own words to Riley. "Maybe I know what's best for me, Dara."

She blinks, smoothes her skirt nervously. "Are you excited?"

Not at all. "What do you think?"

She laughs. "I think you're nervous as hell."

"No cursing in my classroom, please."

"I'll help with Riley until your mom gets here."

I give her a quick smile. "Thanks."

My phone finally buzzes. We all freeze. I pick up.

"It didn't go to you. I'm sorry." Joanna sounds sympathetic.

My pulse slows. "To Walters?"

She hesitates. "I'm not supposed to say. But I will say he's not available today."

I hang up with a small grin. I picture Walters at the hospital, getting congratulated, prepped for surgery.

Riley stands next to me. "It's a go?"

"No."

"Then why the heck are you smiling?" Riley is tensed up,

perhaps ready to fight or cry on my behalf. Behind her stands Dara, appearing to be exactly as fearful as my niece. Two sentinels.

I shrug. "I just am." I reach down into my consciousness and feel around for jealousy or rage. Nothing. "I guess it went to the next-best person, right?" I shake off my nervousness, literally shaking each leg until the kids stare, and pick up my whiteboard marker. "Let's get back to business, shall we?"

AP BIOLOGY IS DOING all review until the AP test the next week. I hand out the copies of review sheets as they walk in, thick packets twenty pages long. "I hope your study groups are meeting," I say.

Samantha and Brad come in, a few paces apart from each other. I step in front of her to stop the two at once. "You got over your flu quickly."

"Stomach virus. Twenty-four hours." She grips her stomach, slouching so her long hair covers her face.

"Did you know there's no such thing as a twenty-four-hour stomach virus?" I hand her the review sheet. "Must have been food poisoning. Should we do Disease Detectives to find out what caused it? What did you guys eat?" I look from her to Brad.

Brad pushes past Samantha, who goes to her seat. "We're fine now." He moves his hair out of his face, his tanned cheeks flushed. He is angry. I can feel it. Angry at being called out. I think the appropriate feeling would be shame.

"I'm glad." I watch as Brad studiously avoids glancing at

Samantha as he sits next to her. She turns her body away from his. Ah, young love. Forbidden love. Messing up Science Olympiads. I hope it was worth it. For Brad it didn't matter, but for Samantha, a junior, a win could have made a big difference on her college applications, especially because she might have gone to the state championships. "Let's begin." I turn on the overhead projector.

SATURDAY, THE DAY of the Pasadena rose show begins, as usual, before daybreak. I am up and moving G42 into my car before the paper boy (really, a paper deliveryman in an old Toyota) cruises by. Riley gets up shortly after, excited about the prospect of a road trip and spending the night in another city.

"Can we go to Disneyland?" she asks.

"Do you think I'm made of money?" I load a bag with snacks for her. Pudding cups, apples, granola bars. "Haven't you ever been?"

She shakes her head.

I pause, a bottle of water in my hand. "We'll have to remedy that. Even I've been to Disney a few times."

"Cool." She smiles and brings her backpack out to the car.

Pasadena is smoggier than I remember. It hangs over the background mountains, the convention center in the foreground, its brittle white the color of a bleached bone.

There are far more people here than at the San Luis Obispo show, with dozens more categories, including all the fancy displays with specially built rose boxes. I explain this to Riley as we walk in. "This show will be a fun one just for that," I tell her. "For wandering the aisles."

"Scoping out the competition." Riley smiles. "This will be a lot more fun than Science Olympiad, that's for sure."

We check in. I see Ms. Lansing at a far table and we wave to each other, but she doesn't approach me, thank goodness. I find my table, number 20, which I take as a good omen, and set down my cooler.

I plan to leave it there until judging time. For one thing, I don't want anyone else ogling my rose. For another, I want to keep it a surprise. I've entered it into the New Breed category.

I sit on the folding chair and wiggle my toes. "I've got an intuition this is going to go really well today." I grin.

Riley sits on the table, tipping it a bit. She jumps off.

"Careful, Riley."

"I've had intuitions about stuff before." Riley sits on the chair next to mine. "Sometimes I know which song is going to play on the radio before I turn it on."

"Maybe it runs in the family." I smile at an elderly man going by on a walker. I hope I'll live to be so old.

"Sometimes I feel like my dad's going to come back for me. That never happens." Riley shrugs. "Guess we can't all be right all the time."

She slumps down in her chair until her head is on the flimsy back. I put my hand on her shoulder and give it a little shake for emphasis. "He doesn't know what he's missing."

She smiles.

I clear my throat, reach for my purse. I dig around and pull out some cash. "This is for you."

"For what?" She stares at the two twenties as though it's a fortune.

"Whatever you like today. Food, souvenirs. Heck, you

might even want to buy your own rose." I press it into her hands.

She opens up the small black purse with a gold chain strap and takes out a tiny cloth coin purse with a kitten sewn on it.

"Don't lose it."

"I'll be careful." Riley grins. "I'm going to walk around, okay?"

"Remember. Table 20." I wave as she flounces away. "Just ask someone if you get lost, all right?"

"I'm not two, you know," she calls back, still flouncing.

I shake my head.

"Teenagers. I don't envy you," the lady at the next table says. She's about my age, I assume, and her table is crowded with roses. She has four minis, two hybrid tea bouquets, and three arrangements of old-fashioned roses. I can barely see her behind it all. She stands and tugs on her carefully tailored blazer.

"Have any kids?" I ask conversationally.

She grins. "I wouldn't have the time for all this if I did."

I simply nod.

"Teenagers are all right, I've found." I wheel my cooler under the table, trusting that in this rose show no one will disturb it, then go off to find a snack bar.

THE ROOM BUZZES with activity. All around me I see people shouting greetings, hugging, slapping backs. I don't do much networking at shows, but I almost envy these folks their enthusiasm.

Why don't I talk to more people? I might learn some-thing, as I did with Winslow Blythe, who gave out the fertilizer recipe. Sure, I say hello to strangers, compliment them on their roses, but when have I ever really tried to make a connection?

Only with Byron. And he's the one who approached me.

I reach the snack bar and see nothing that I want, or can, eat. I make a circuit of the room, going up and down each aisle. The area seems to be the size of a small stadium, everyone's voices rising up into the ducting and crystal chandeliers above and floating away.

At last, as I circle back up my aisle, I see a crowd of ladies around a table and suspect Byron must be behind them.

I grin. Byron, holding court, dapper in a navy blue blazer with a white shirt underneath. The ladies swoon and touch his shoulders and arms. I cringe. They're hungrier than prepubescent girls at a teen idol concert.

I smile serenely. I go up and take his arm with a big flourish, giving him a kiss on each cheek. "Byron! Dah-ling! I haven't seen you in ages."

"Since when did you turn into Zsa Zsa Gabor?" he murmurs, kissing me back. His cheeks are as smooth as a baby's.

"Let me see your roses." I grin backward to the women, who range in age from about twenty-one to sixty-five. "You have a diverse demographic."

"I do." He smiles at them, gives a dismissive wave.

"Show's over, ladies. Nothing to see here." I wave at them, too.

The ladies disperse, still not believing an upstart like me could hold Byron's attention. They'll be looking for my roses for sure, assuming I'm a genius breeder. Which I am.

He points out one of his roses. "A mini-Hulthemia seedling I've named Larissa, after my sister's daughter." It has light pink petals but no blotch. "The blotch will come out as it gets older," he says, reading my mind. "No fragrance, unfortunately, but excellent color and reblooming qualities."

I stop and look at him. "Are you ever going to go pro, Byron? Just mass produce your own rose plants and sell them directly to the public?"

He puts his hands behind his back and grins like a schoolboy. "Later this year."

I give him a congratulatory punch on the arm, as I would a brother. "I knew you'd be the next David Austin! The David Austin of Hulthemias."

I expect the next words out of his mouth will be him asking me to come work for him. I wonder how much houses cost in his neck of the woods in Texas. This could be the perfect opportunity, I realize. Getting out of my teaching job that I might get shoved out of anyway, working for Byron. If I could go there after my transplant, after Becky reclaims Riley, it would be perfect. I'm sure he'd let me.

Byron gestures to the next rose on the table. "I also have an apricot mini, named and registered this year."

I lean over and sniff. It smells delicious. "It actually smells sort of like apricots, Byron."

"That one will be a hit, I'm sure." I admire its very glossy, dark green leaves.

"Do you know what I've named it?" He hems and haws. "Gal."

"Yes?" I wait for him to tell me the name.

"It's Gal. The rose is called Gal." He smiles, waiting for my reaction.

I pause. "After me? Galilee?"

"Just Gal, because that's what I call you. I hope that's all right." He peers into my face.

I freeze. "Gal" is what I'd planned to call my G42. Gal, after me. My name. And now it's going to be a mini-rose that I had absolutely zero to do with.

He points to the tag. BYRON MADAFFER, "GAL," APRI-COT MINI. There it is, already done and officially registered. Not a thing I can do about it. I might as well be pleased. Some moments pass before I finally say, "It's an honor."

It is. Really. I bet any one of those ladies, no matter what their station in life or how many rose titles they had won, would love to switch positions with me. I smile and extend my hand. "Thank you, Byron."

"It's my pleasure." He shakes my hand.

I take a breath. "So. How many new employees are you going to hire?"

He goes behind his table and busies himself with straightening. "Probably none."

"None?"

"None."

His assistant, a tall young man wearing a white shirt with a tie, hands him a polishing cloth. Byron gets to work on his roses, though they already appear perfect.

I linger by his table. Byron is hard to read. One minute he's into you, the next he's done and on to the next thing. "If you're ever in the market, give me a call. You know I'd love to work with you."

He nods shortly. "I can't make any guarantees."

I get the hint. I step away. "Of course not." Humiliation, I decide, tastes like dish soap. His assistant flashes me a sympathetic smile. I gesture behind me. "I better get to looking for my niece. It's almost time for judging."

Byron finally stops his polishing. "Did you bring G42?"

"Of course." I expect him to say he'll stop by and look at it. He's seen it only in pictures.

Instead, he extends his hand, his brows crinkling up in the middle. "Good luck, Gal. I'll see you later."

"Okay." I turn and walk away, wiping off the residue of his hand, which had suddenly turned sweaty.

28

RILEY IS SITTING BEHIND MY TABLE, EATING A chili cheese dog out of a paper bowl. She's got chili all over her face and some has dripped onto her jeans, but I'm immeasurably cheered anyway. "You know you should eat those with a fork and knife," I say.

"Oh." She glances at her mess. "Ew."

I reach into my purse for tissue since she doesn't seem to have taken any napkins with her. "Here." I mop up the beans from her lap, wipe her mouth. She takes a swig of cola from the bottle on the table.

The lady next door shakes her head exaggeratedly. I smile.

I decide to take out my rose. Forget Byron and his odd ways. Naming a rose after me without asking. What if I wanted to name a rose after myself? That might be considered unspeakably egotistical. I decide to be flattered. It will do me no good to be mad, will it?

I grin at Riley. "Do you know there's a rose named after me?"

"There is?" Riley hoots. "Hot dog. No pun intended. You're famous!"

I shrug. What was it going to say on the tag? "Named

after Gal Garner, a quasi-good rose breeder who couldn't get this done herself so I did it for her"? I remind myself to be grateful again.

"People will be buying your rose at Valentine's Day."

"Probably not. Red roses are the most popular Valentine's roses, and they're usually shipped from South America."

Riley stops. "You don't have to work so hard at deflating me, you know."

"I didn't mean to deflate you." I clap. "Hooray for me! I only meant it's not the biggest deal on earth. On the other hand, if it were a rose that I'd bred, I'd be doing a cartwheel down this aisle."

"You can do a cartwheel?"

Probably not. I could never do a cartwheel when I was a little kid. Couldn't do the monkey bars, either. No upper-arm strength. "A metaphorical cartwheel, then."

"Okay. How about if I metaphorically do the chores?" Riley wiggles an eyebrow.

"That *is* how you do the chores, isn't it?" I grin. She laughs.

I spot Byron standing at his table and try to catch his eye, but he will not turn my way. Ms. Sourpuss at the next table glances at us instead, her brow furrowed as though we're making merry in a library instead of in a noisy room.

I wave to her, Miss America–style, shooting her the most smug smile I've ever mustered. She looks away.

OUR JUDGING does not take place until after lunch. I indulge in a portion of a high-salt hot dog, as I am occasionally allowed to do, giving most to Riley, who eats it though she has already consumed the chili dog, a soft pretzel with cheese, fries, three cans of soda, and two apples that I insisted on.

"You must be going through a growth spurt," I say. I am watching Ms. Lansing make her way down my aisle, stopping at the other displays, making notes on her clipboard.

"My mother says it will catch up with me. She works out like a maniac." Riley considers her half-full can of soda with regret. "Says it'll show up on my hips on my sixteenth birthday."

I search for something remotely nice to say about Becky. "Your mother doesn't know everything, Riley."

She looks surprised. "I know that." She turns the soda can over in her hands. "I got plenty of exercise by our house. Where we used to live. I walked everywhere."

I try to picture where they lived. I can't, because I haven't seen it. My sister is essentially a stranger. She shouldn't be.

"I wonder where we'll live when she comes home?" Riley finishes her soda.

I do, too. I rub the bridge of my nose under my glasses, which suddenly pinch. "Take that to the recyclable trash, please."

Riley has turned morose again. I put my arm around her. "Hey, kiddo, your mother's doing the best she can. I'm sure of it. And all this is only going to make your college applications a lot more interesting than a kid who grew up in one house his whole life and never had to do anything."

"I guess." She rises, picks up her soda can, and heads in search of a trash can.

Three other judges follow Ms. Lansing, two men and one woman who all appear to be post-retirement age. These are the largest demographic, the folks who have the time and inclination and free income to devote to rose growing.

Ms. Lansing pauses at Byron's table. Her peal of laughter cuts through the other chatter. I grimace.

Riley sits down. "That lady is loud," she observes, following my gaze.

"She's one of the judges. Be nice."

"I'm always nice." Riley crosses her ankle over her knee with a grin.

"Extra nice. Like meeting the queen nice." I am on hyper-alert, full of energy.

"Sheesh. Should I curtsy?"

I think she's kidding, but not entirely sure. I'll call her bluff. "If you must."

Ms. Lansing reaches us. Riley settles on a slight bow from the waist with her hands pressed together, as though she's Japanese. Ms. Lansing eyes her doubtfully.

"Dear! How are you?" She presses one cool cheek against mine. It feels like one of my old leather boots pressed against my face. I'm sure there will be powder and blush residue on me.

"Very well, Ms. Lansing."

She clucks sympathetically. "All things considered, I expect. What a little trouper you are." She turns to the other judges. "Poor thing needs a new kidney."

I flush.

"I'd give you mine, but I only have one," the dapper gentleman in the charcoal blazer pipes up.

"The rest of us are too old," Ms. Lansing says.

I hate these over-majestic displays of sympathy. They make me feel about a zillion times worse than I do on my very worst day. When I say I'm fine, I wish people would reply, "Me too. Let's get on with life," because that is all I want to do. Get on with it.

Now Ms. Sourpuss is looking less sour and more like she wants to give me a hug. I want to slap her.

Ms. Lansing turns G42 around. "Same rose as San Luis Obispo, I see." She glances around the table ostentatiously. "Did you happen to bring another rose, Gal?"

"No." She can see that I didn't. Riley sits upright.

Ms. Lansing blinks her false eyelashes rapidly. "The thing is, Gal, you can't have this particular rose as a new breed."

My head, already spinning somewhat, increases in velocity until it feels like I've stepped off a spinning carnival ride. "I don't understand."

Ms. Lansing leans forward. The other judges, who apparently all know what's going on, shuffle to the next table. Her eyeballs are now only inches away from mine, so close I can see every red blood vessel and the blue and green irises. "Gal. Byron registered this rose last month. Didn't you know?"

"What?" My voice is so low I barely hear it myself.

She stands up straight. "He registered it with the American Rose Society. It's named the Gigi."

"Gigi?" I repeat it as though I've been struck dumb.

Ms. Lansing turns the G42 around. "I thought you were friends. I thought he'd tell you." She smiles regretfully. "I'm sorry this was a waste of your time, Gal."

She continues, vanishing in a cloud of lavender scent and my own defeat.

"Aunt Gal? What was she talking about?" Riley is at my side.

I look toward Byron.

He stares back at me.

I feel the blue of his eyes like lightning arcing through my body to my feet. If this were a movie with special effects, there would be blue sparks shooting between us, like casting magical spells at our worst enemies.

He turns away. Strides away from his table, away from me. Coward.

I head after him, following his blond halo of a head for a while, before he disappears into the crowd.

I stand panting. I brush my hair back.

This whole show is pointless. The whole weekend is pointless.

In college, one of my professors—I don't remember which one, but it wasn't science—talked about the gift of forgetting. How you can forget that you have a paper due so you feel no guilt about partying. Or, in my case, how I can forget I have kidney junk so I can keep doing whatever I'm doing, at least for a little while.

I remember this as I get buffeted by a couple of older folks. Elbow to the ribs. Ouch. Right now, I want to forget all this rose business. Just for a little while.

"Aunt Gal?" Riley's shaking my shoulder. "Earth to Aunt Gal. What happened?"

I collect myself, reshuffle my thoughts into a semblance of order. "Pack up. We're blowing this Popsicle stand."

I HAVEN'T BEEN TO DISNEYLAND since my parents took us there when Becky was in eighth grade and I was in sixth. Becky took a friend with her, a perky, wild Gidget type, and the two had disappeared for the day. Fine with me; I had my parents all to myself. It was a few months before my transplant, and my parents rented me a wheelchair so I wouldn't have to walk. All in all, it was a pretty great trip.

Until Becky and her friend got put in Disney jail for cutting too many lines. The trip home wasn't so pleasant.

I told Riley the story as we wound our way through the greater Los Angeles/Orange County area. It takes about one hour, depending on the traffic. I'd managed to get a hotel refund, which I now planned on applying to one of the hotels by Disneyland, after a quick check of my coffers to make sure I could afford the trip.

Riley appears mortified. More mortified than I'd intended. "I didn't know my mom would do something like that."

I had meant it to be humorous. "It was a little shocking at the time. But it's funny now, don't you think? Your mother was a typical teen." More or less.

"That's typical?" Riley's brow wrinkles. "You think that's typical? You teach at a Catholic school. Aren't you supposed to tell me not to do that kind of thing?"

"I wasn't telling you to do it. I was only telling you about your mom." We exit on Disneyland Drive. It's changed since I was last here. We're routed through a mile or so of side streets, past the hotels, until we emerge at a gigantic parking structure. "My goodness. You used to be able to walk in. Now you have to take this tram."

"Well, I wouldn't do it." Riley crosses her arms. "I would never do something like that."

"It doesn't matter. It was more than twenty years ago." I wish I had never brought up the subject. "Let's have some fun. It's open until midnight."

Disneyland is filled with teens on date night. Of course. Saturday night, and if you live in Anaheim, what better thing is there to do? I'd buy passes if I lived here. We get in line for the Matterhorn ride, a bobsled roller coaster that climbs a giant fake snowy mountain past a robotic Yeti. I can't help but wonder how many of them met moments earlier and now have their hands in each other's back pockets, like the young couple in front of us. I can see Riley's got the same thing on her mind. "You're right. Becky wasn't a typical teen." We inch forward. "She had a lot of problems."

"I know. You don't have to pretend she didn't." Riley hugs herself. "Or that she doesn't. I'm not a little kid."

She defends her mother to others, points out Becky's weaknesses herself. It's all right for you to pick on your family member, but not for someone else to. I personally never objected when others pointed out Becky's problems, when our high school teachers asked in hushed tones how Becky was getting along, knowing full well she skipped class regularly. It was all true. I can't change the truth.

OVERHEAD, A PETER PAN DOLL flies as we go on what is apparently a never-ending journey on "It's a Small World." It feels more like the journey to the center of the Earth, given the cavernous setting. Riley tugs my arm and points. The dancing marionette-like dolls sing in stereo. "Creepy!"

"Cute!" says Riley.

"This is going to give me nightmares for a year. They're as bad as clowns." I settle back and close my eyes. It's been a long day. Tomorrow, we will sleep in, hit the parks for a little bit, then drive back in time for my dialysis. "Can you imagine being the worker who has to clean up in here alone? What if they all come to life?"

"Aunt Gal. I thought I was the one with the overactive imagination." Riley giggles.

My phone buzzes. I feel sufficiently secure that we won't

tip over into the drink and answer without looking at the number.

"Gal."

I'd recognize the voice anywhere, and especially his delivery. "What do you want, Byron?"

"You left."

"Of course I did. There's no reason for me to stay." I raise my voice, thanking the ride gods we're alone in this boat. "You ran away."

He ignores this. "You left before they announced the results."

I ignore that. I don't care who won what. "Did you hear me? You ran away."

"I didn't *run* away." He clears his throat. "I had other business at the time. Then I looked for you."

I make a harrumphing noise. "If I were going to screw you over, mister, I'd do it to your face."

At last, he sounds humbled. "I'm sorry, Gal. You're right. I didn't want a scene."

I wished he was here so I could shove him off the boat into the water. I hate modern life sometimes. "Do you have fragrance, at least? Did you get that much?"

He gets louder. "Are you at Disneyland?"

"I'm surprised you recognize the song. You who have no soul."

He sighs. "You know we talked about the parent roses for breeding two years ago. I just happened to get to the end product first."

"You could have warned me." I shut my eyes, thinking of G42. Of course Byron beat me. He of the endless resources.

"I never talk about which roses I'm going to register before I do it. Neither would you. We're not partners."

Heat rises to the surface of my skin. "I would tell you if I knew you had almost exactly the same rose." I would. Wouldn't I?

I think of all the things I purposely didn't tell him. The seeds and cuttings I didn't send.

"I don't think you would. You're too competitive. Like me."

I would like to think he's wrong. If I were in his shoes, with his capabilities and money, would I not be more generous? I don't know. I'm not sure he *is* wrong.

"It's not personal, Gal."

Echoes of Dr. Blankenship. "It never is, is it?" I hang up.

Perhaps it's better we didn't have the conversation face-to-face. It is distant, as all our interactions are. Even our face-to-face interactions are detached on his end, I realize. Byron is not a man who is ever really present. Little wonder he's unattached.

Riley leans over and speaks directly into my ear. "So, does Byron's rose have fragrance?"

"He wouldn't say." I look at her. I didn't think she cared. She admires the robot dolls. Her skin glows, lit by the many colors of the artificial carnival we're passing through.

She leans out of the boat to let her hands trail in the water. A booming voice sounds, "Keep your hands inside the boat!" She puts her hands in her lap with a small yelp.

"Don't you get put in Disney jail, too." The heat leaves my skin. I grin. "I keep forgetting you haven't been here before. We'll have to get you a mouse-ear beanie."

"With my name sewn on it?"

"With your name sewn on it." I settle back and watch Hawaiian dolls doing a hula. "How long is this infernal ride, anyway?"

"Aunt Gal, were you ever a kid?" Riley leans over the bench in front of her. "Relax."

RILEY FALLS ASLEEP on the tram ride back to the parking lot, her big adult-sized head heavy on my shoulder, her breath smelling of pineapple from the Tiki Room. The tram itself is quiet, save for the low roar of the engine. The small children are on their parents' laps or shoulders, strollers folded up at their feet, parents with dark shadows under their eyes.

A father holding a little girl with a mouse hat identical to Riley's sits on the bench across from us, the space so small our knees touch. Next to him is a boy of about twelve, wearing a skull-and-crossbones black hoodie pulled over his head, his eyes squished closed. The father catches my eye and grins. "They grow up fast, don't they?" he says in a low voice, smoothing his daughter's wild red hair.

I blink. I remember Riley as a girl that small, small enough to go on someone's shoulders. All the space in between our visits filled up by years. How she grew without my notice. My presence.

The tram rounds a corner. I feel Riley lifting away from me. I put my arm around her so she doesn't fall out, holding on as tight as I can. "They do." I smile back at him and he closes his eyes, as if now he can go to sleep, reassured by my response.

29

THE FOLLOWING WEEK, I VISIT WALTERS IN THE hospital. He is looking pretty good for someone who just had an organ from a dead body implanted into him. I tell him as much.

"You really know how to dish out a compliment, Gal." He gives me a weak smile.

I glance around his hospital room. Flowers, one of the standard arrangements from the grocery store, stand in a glass vase. I have my own tucked behind my back. Roses from my garden. "Have room for a bit more green?"

His unkempt eyebrows leap. "Holy shit, Gal. Those are gorgeous."

"I didn't know shit was holy." I take the jar I've brought along, just in case, fill it with water and flower food, and arrange the roses. I've brought him Hot Cocoa, the hybrid tea, fourteen of them, so they form a solid cloud.

"Bring them close. Let me smell."

I comply, taking care not to let the water spill.

He takes a deep whiff. "Damn. Somehow everything smells better with this new kidney."

I quell my jealousy. "Apparently the new kidney makes you curse more, too."

"Sorry." He raises his bed and winces. "I'm just really happy. And a bit out of my mind."

I nod slowly, looking everywhere but at his face.

"Your turn will come, Gal. I know it." He reaches out, maybe for my hand, but I pretend not to see and spin away.

"How are your functions?" I look for his chart, but a doctor's got it or it's in the computer. They don't hang it off the end of the bed like in the old days.

"They're impressed. Kidney's working great. Peeing like mad."

"Great." I am happy for him. I must be happy for him. Or I will be officially the Worst Person in the World, my face appearing on television on that news guy's show. "I can't believe I'm jealous of peeing," I say at last.

Walters lets out a mighty guffaw.

"Speaking of which." He nods toward a plastic container sitting bedside. "I'll need privacy."

"I'm on my way out." I pause again. "When do you go home?"

"Next week, most likely."

"You have help?" Odd question for me to ask. It's not like I'd have him stay over, sleeping on the couch while I nursed him to health. I don't even really know the man.

"Staying at my son's." He gestures to the other flowers. I assume his son brought them. "Imposing on them for a bit. Hate to do it. Makes more work for my daughter-in-law."

I like Walters more and more. I edge toward the door. "Let me know if you need anything."

"How?" He smiles. Suddenly he looks pale, his older body tiny in the bed. "I don't have your number."

I write it down on a scrap of paper I find in my purse. What if he does ask for something big, like staying with me? What will I do? "I mean, if you need a ride, or something."

"Scrabble game? This daytime television is rotting my brain."

I grin. "I prefer cards. Remember, I can't spell."

"Cards it is." He waves me off. "Hell, I'm a lot better at cards than I am at Scrabble, too."

"Cursing, cursing." I make a *tsk*ing noise as I exit.

My sophomore biology students listen to me go over what will be on the final. We're at the urinary system, a quiz most did not do well on. "On the final, you'll have to draw and label the system from memory," I say. They look at me blankly. "Write it down." They do.

I go to the whiteboard and quickly draw the system. "I myself always want to draw the kidneys near the stomach, since that's where mine are now." I draw two kidneys, mirror images of each other.

"Your kidneys are in your stomach?" The girl named Sarah is bewildered.

"Duh," says John. "Someone was paying attention all year."

I smile. "They put the kidney transplant near your stomach."

More students raise their hands. "When did you lose them?" "Why?" "How do you live?" "What happens?" The questions come faster and faster.

I put down my marker. Who knew the key to holding their attention would be to couch science in personal drama? "Hold on, everyone. I'll tell you." I do, starting at the beginning, when I was small.

Riley has her mouth open wide enough for a kitten to get inside. I realize I have not told her the whole story, either, figuring it was simply family lore, that my mother or Becky had told her. Apparently not. As the story progresses, her mouth closes, but she shrinks down, looking incrementally more miserable until I am sure she wishes she could melt away.

"Will you die without one?" Sarah asks.

"Sarah! Shut up." Riley at last raises her head. "That is the stupidest question I've ever heard."

The classmates murmur in agreement. No one wants to talk about the possibility of death.

I think about heart attacks. Infections. Other organs shutting down. My nose is running today; who knows if it will blossom into a new sinus infection, enter my bloodstream, and land me in the hospital? "Maybe." I am shaking a bit as I pick up my marker and finish labeling. "There will be one point for drawing each part correctly, one point for each label. Total of ten. Memorize this, if you haven't already."

The bell rings, and I dismiss the class. Riley remains in her seat, gathering her papers in an overly slow manner. I walk over to her. "Riley, I'm going to be perfectly fine. Don't you worry." As I speak these words of optimism, as I have so often, I believe them. I will believe them for now, until something else happens to make me doubt their truth. Though I try to be an optimist, I am only a half-assed one.

She nods, standing with her backpack bowing her crookedly over. "But you don't know that, do you?"

I blink, stalling for time. Riley waits, her face guarded,

all her vulnerability evaporated. Instead, she is as calm as a secretary of state receiving news of a war, her eyebrows drawn together in an expectant, intelligent frown. The next class is coming in and I walk Riley to the door. "No one knows anything, Riley. Ever. A steel beam could fall out of the ceiling while I'm teaching and crush me."

She draws in a long, shuddering breath then, and I know she is thinking about me and Becky and about how the adults in her life have failed her in ways big and small. "That's what I thought." Then she walks away to her next class, taking strides so long I know I can never catch up, even if I run.

30

At our school, we have a tradition of a graduate banquet the week before commencement. Never mind that by the time graduation rolls around, the last thing any kid wants to do is sit around with his tired-out teachers talking about the good old days of high school as we gnaw on the dried-out prime rib provided by the parent-teacher association.

Nonetheless, all the other teachers and especially Dr. O'Malley are very into the occasion. They dress up in their good clothes, they get out crystal goblets culled from various people's collections, and they rent some tables for the library. Crisp white tablecloths and bowls of flowers complete the look.

It's also the day when we give out awards, one last enticement for the students to show.

Dara and I are in the cafeteria working on the food. There are supposed to be other teachers showing up to help, but of course, no good deed goes unpunished, so we are the only ones making tiny canapés on toast with fresh mozzarella, a slice of cherry tomato, and basil on top, drizzled with balsamic vinegar and olive oil. This will be followed by a salad.

Parent volunteers are bringing the prime rib and the desserts.

I've missed my friend.

I'm in a good mood. Finals are over, and I graded Riley's before I came. A solid B. She will pass my class. I couldn't resist telling her.

My ears still ring from her screams of joy.

I smile at the memory as I cut the tomatoes. "Whoever thought of slicing cherry tomatoes was wrong," I say. There are tomato innards all over the stainless countertops, not to mention my hands and forearms.

"Whoever thought of this idea in the first place should have the decency to show up and make the dish." Dara slides a pan of toast out of the oven. "Darn it. These burnt."

"Use less time."

"Obviously." She grins. She wears a fuchsia halter dress with white polka dots all over it. The halter part is wide enough to cover most of her shoulders. She has a little white jacket hung up over a chair, and a big white apron on. I'm wearing navy slacks and a pink sweater. I don't bother with an apron.

Dara steps back and surveys the tray we've completed. "Looks good."

"Lot of work for something that will be gone in sixty seconds."

She laughs. "Now that I'm done with the senior show, I finally feel like I can breathe."

"Is that why you were hiding?" I'm only half serious.

"No." She sits on a stool. "No, that's not why. And you were hiding from me, too."

"I wasn't trying to." I'm not being completely truthful. I slice more cherry tomatoes and put down my knife, wiping my hands on a paper towel. Why pussyfoot around anymore? "Dara, what's really going on?"

The oven pings. She takes out the new toast, plops the baking sheet onto the counter, then faces me. "Gal, do you know why I didn't just come right out and tell you I couldn't go to the show?"

I slice the mozzarella. "As a matter of fact, I don't."

She gives a little laugh. "Sometimes you don't listen to me. You get so mad when people don't do what you want." She looks down. "I was scared of how you'd react."

She may as well have burned me with that tray. "I don't get mad."

She raises an eyebrow. "After I told you I couldn't go, you never called me again."

I put down the cheese knife. "I was waiting for you to call me!"

"I thought you were still mad." Dara tears up. "Maybe you don't realize it, but you only call when you want me to do something for you, Gal. I'm the one who takes you to your appointments, helps you when you're sick. And I don't mind doing it, because you're the closest thing I have to a sister." She wipes her nose with the back of her hand. "But I felt like I gave and gave, and the more I gave, the more you wanted. I want you to give a little bit, too."

I take a step back. I feel as though I'm choking. "I need to get some air."

"Don't run away from conflict. You always run away." She gets louder.

"I don't." I sit on another stool. Dara is crying now, weeping into her toast. I want to tell her it's all right, but it's not.

I take from her. What do I give? A hard time? My wit?

When was the last time I had done a favor for Dara?

I cannot remember.

"I'm sorry, Dara." I am sincere. I take a breath so deep it hurts my ribs. "I'll be a better friend."

She smiles. "I know, Gal." She wipes her hair off her forehead. She blows out a sigh of air. "Whew."

At last I know what to do. I reach out and hug her, awkwardly. She hugs me back, her tears warm on my shoulder.

I admit. I was scared to confront her. I wanted Dara to step up, not me. But look how little time it took for a wrong to be corrected. I am grateful that Dara thinks enough of me to tell me the problem and give me the opportunity to fix it, instead of simply walking away. Ignoring it, like I try to do.

I break free. "You better go blow your nose and wash up before we finish making these. It's a biological hazard."

She laughs, going to the sink and splashing water on her face. "Good thing I wore the waterproof mascara."

I watch her for a moment, thinking of what Mr. Morton said after Science Olympiad. "Are you and George not dating anymore?"

She shrugs. "Nope. It just didn't work."

I drizzle a little too much oil over the toast. I should tell her anyway. "It's not because of his daughter, is it?"

She dries her hands and face on brown paper towels. "No, that wasn't it."

The oil drips over my hands. I put the bottle down. "His having a daughter didn't bother you? Did he tell you what happened?"

"We didn't get that serious, Gal. He didn't tell me what happened. I'm still seeing Chad." She throws away the paper towel.

"Am I supposed to know who Chad is?"

"The accountant." She grins, and her cheeks bloom. "Turns out he loves art."

"Sounds like the perfect man." I slice more cheese.

"George is really nice." She chops some celery into small pieces. "Boring, but nice."

"Boring?" I hadn't thought of him as boring.

"Fall-asleep boring." She giggles. "All he wanted to talk about was science."

I am offended. "That's all I ever talk about."

She shrugs. "He does like music. Opera."

"Really?" I'm intrigued.

"Why are you so interested?" She moves the celery and cucumbers into separate bowls.

"I'm not. I just . . ." I shrug. I have no answer. Maybe the guy isn't a jerk.

She chops up two carrots expertly quick, putting them into yet another bowl.

"Just put everything in the salad bowl and we'll toss it."

"Not everyone likes the same thing. That way, everyone can add what they want."

"It's a sit-down dinner, not a salad bar. They will deal. They're all adults now." I dump the ingredients into the lettuce before she can protest.

She sighs. "Guess some things don't change."

THE LIBRARY-CUM-BANQUET-ROOM is candlelit, the warm yellow flames throwing attractive light over the faces of the metal bookcases, the laminated posters with grinning celebrities holding books, and the seniors and teachers. They're already seated at the long tables when Dara and

I bring in the appetizers. Besides the mozzarella and tomato canapés, which Dara informs me is *caprese*, we have mini premade quiches and crab cakes. Salad, mashed potatoes, macaroni and cheese, and prime rib sit in chafing dishes. One table holds a dozen different kinds of desserts, artfully arranged by a parent into tiers. It's not five-star gourmet, but these kids will be filled up at the end.

I'm glad our school is small, with only fifty seniors. "Just what a library needs. Flames and food crumbs," I murmur.

Dara raises her eyebrows.

Mr. Morton is seated near the table's head, to Dr. O'Malley's left. He has his head low, listening to Ms. Schilling the math teacher talk. She's wearing a scandalously low-cut green dress, way too much cleavage for a student event. She looks more like she's going to the Grammy Awards.

"Hey." I poke Dara. "How is Schilling's dress not flying all the way open?"

Dara, taking a sip of water, chokes. I pound her back. "Taped," she manages to gasp.

For an instant, I imagine how I would look in such a dress. I giggle. Ridiculous.

Mr. Morton glances up at me. The corners of his eyes wrinkle in a smile. He is much more appropriately dressed in a white shirt, a dark blue tie, and a dark blazer.

"Is he going to date his way through the teaching staff, do you think?" I take a bite of *caprese*. This cheese will be my phosphorus intake for the day. It's delicious, creamy and sharp with the balsamic. I nod at Dara. "This is good."

"I told you." She eats one herself, quickly. I take one more small bite, chewing as slowly as I can, before putting it down.

Dr. O'Malley gets up and pings his water glass with a

fork. The prime rib sits in front of him, with a big carving knife and serving fork. I wish we would hire a caterer and let someone else do all the carving and cooking.

"Ladies and gentlemen. Thank you for coming to the last student-teacher event of your glorious tenure at St. Mark's."

"Has he been drinking?" I whisper to Dara. She shushes me.

Dr. O'Malley winks. Actually winks at me. The students snicker. "And our own Miss Garner. Come up here and do the honors." He waves up me up. The students clap uncertainly.

I pick up the knife and fork. Slowly I begin carving small, thin pieces. The meat is surprisingly moist and pink. Steam wafts up. "Everyone pass their plates down," I say.

Dr. O'Malley puts his hand over mine. "Miss Garner. The awards, not the meat. We're doing all the awards first."

"Oh. I thought people were hungry." I raise my hands up to the students. Heck, if I'm going to be quasi in charge, I'll be in charge all the way. "Get some food on their plates, and we'll yak while they eat. Don't want the food getting cold and dry."

"Yeah!" Brad pumps his fist in the air. The other students cheer.

I pump my fist, too. "Eat eat eat."

Dr. O'Malley looks at me helplessly. I begin cutting again, bigger pieces this time, slapping them on the plates. I grin. "Relax, Doc. It's all under control."

He hands me a plate. "I'm going to need two pieces tonight."

"You shouldn't drink on an empty stomach, you know." I put two thick, fatty pieces on his plate. "Hope you took your cholesterol meds."

He begins to laugh. The most genuine laugh I've heard out of him. Around me, anyway. "You better pass this one down to one of the young men."

. . .

AFTER THE DESSERTS have been picked apart and the coffee drunk to the dregs, the students begin filtering out. It is only us old fogeys who, with nothing better to do on a Friday night, linger and chat.

Brad comes over to where I sit in one of the comfy padded armchairs under a window. "Ms. Garner." He extends his hand. I shake it. "Thank you for everything."

"You're a fine young man, Brad. You'll go far." I sound like I'm about a hundred years old, but I don't care. "Come say hi before you leave for college."

"I will." He nods, his blond hair shaking down in front of one eye. "I gotta get going."

"All right." I feel a twinge of nostalgia as I watch him leave. Last year, I would have known his summer plans, what he planned to major in, his opinions on the rose mite situation. He used to be more like a nephew. Now he is a stranger. It's like we were never close at all. Maybe we weren't.

"You look lost in thought." Mr. Morton sits in the other armchair, only a small round marble-topped table between us. A large lamp obscures most of his body up to his face.

My mind is still on Brad. I forget I still am not supposed to like Mr. Morton so well. "You ever think you know someone?" I wipe a bit of something sticky off my hands. I don't think I've gone over my limits on any food type, but I wouldn't be surprised if I had. "I mean, you think that they're your friend, shown you everything there is to know, but then it turns out you know nothing? That they don't consider you as good of a friend as you thought?" I'm talking about Brad. About Byron. About almost everyone I've ever known, I guess.

He wrinkles his brow. "Absolutely." He smiles ruefully and holds up his naked wedding ring finger. "I have this to prove it. I still have a tan line from my ring."

I peer closely at his hand, take it to better see. A faint ring outline is on his finger. "It looks like you took it off a few minutes ago. Women will think you're trying to pull a fast one."

His hand is rougher than a teacher's hand usually is. I drop it.

"Yes." He takes a sip from the white mug of coffee he holds. "She left me, you know."

I glance at him. He stares into a dark corner of the library. Everyone else is away from us, by the food tables or the exit or at the table.

"Sometimes you think you have everything. Turns out the other person had a different idea." He sinks lower into his seat.

"Why did you become a teacher? Leave such a good job?"

He puts his mug down and his elbows on his knees. I scoot closer to him. He takes a deep breath. "I'd always wanted to try teaching, and my wife agreed it would be a good change of pace. Live in a smaller town. I'd have more time. I got a teaching credential. We made all the preparations." He takes a breath. "Except, after I accepted this contract, when we were packing up the house, my wife left me for my business partner."

"What?" I put my hand on his arm without thinking.

He has tiny brown freckles on the bridge of his nose and small lines around his mouth; he is not as young as I'd thought. "It had been going on for a while. I guess she didn't feel so guilty, knowing I was going to a brand-new town anyway." He pauses. "But that wasn't enough, you see? She wants our daughter, too. Abbie. She told the custody judge I'd abandoned them for a low-paying job in another city. So for now, I can only see my daughter every other Saturday afternoon." He crumples, as if this admission is his breaking point. "I used to brush her teeth and read her a bedtime story every night. Every other Saturday . . ." He trails off, smiling sadly. "I'm nothing more than a stranger."

I take this in. "When did all this happen?"

"Earlier this year. Before I came here." He straightens. "My ex has tried to erase me. As if I never existed. She's rewriting history." He clenches his fists, then relaxes them.

"You're still fighting for her, then? You won't give up?" I wish I knew why this is so important. I need to hear something concrete from someone.

"I won't give up," he says, very quietly.

I believe him.

ONCE THE LAST BELL RINGS on the final day of school, I drive Riley home with a sense of dread. My mother will drive up the next day and retrieve Riley for a summer of grandparent spoilage. And then, then they want her to stay on, until such time as her mother decides to come back.

"I think the public school will be too big for her," I told my mother on the phone.

"You went there. You made honor roll."

"But I didn't like it."

The truth of the matter is, imagining my house empty frightens me. No strange cartoons playing, no loud music.

No other presence. Only the quiet sounds of my own solitary existence.

I think of this as Riley sits in the car next to me, playing with the strap on her backpack. "It's fraying," she says.

"You'll need a new one next year."

She nodded, her fingers mindlessly pulling at the shredded material. I reach over and stop her. "You'll rip it all the way."

"It doesn't matter."

"Then you won't be able to use it at all."

She tears it.

"Riley." I skid to a halt in my drive.

"I don't want to go." Her voice is loud. Old Mrs. Allen, out watering next door, glances up, the spray of water hitting my plants on my side of the fence.

I remove the key. "Riley, I think it will be better if you go to Grandma's."

"I don't want a new school. I want to stay here. With you." She bends her chin down to her chest.

"Riley." My heart pounds. "Of course I'd rather have you stay here. But I need to think of you."

She crosses her arms. "I'll be sixteen in August. I am old enough to decide. I could be emancipated if I want."

"But you don't want that. We want you to have friends, Riley. You don't go out."

"I have friends here."

"Who?" I challenge her. She hasn't hung out with anyone since Samantha.

"I know kids."

"You never call anyone."

"I will. This summer." She lifts her chin. "I promise."

I regard her in silence. Then I say, "Grandma will be here tomorrow."

Riley lifts up a finger. "I have an interview tomorrow. At the nursery."

This is news. I admire her entrepreneurial spirit. "Are you even old enough to work?"

"Yes. It's assistant work. Sweeping and stuff." She leans toward me. "Twenty percent discount, Aunt Gal. Think about it. All that potting soil you could buy."

I'm not thinking about a discount.

I'm thinking about Riley and her grandparents. Could I make this work with Riley? Wouldn't it be better if my mother and father took her? They would be strong and stable in ways I could not.

"Please, Aunt Gal?" Riley grins. "Please?"

I take a breath that I feel in my toes. "All right."

"Yes! I knew that discount would push you over the edge." She gets out of the car with a whoop, slams the door, pumps her fist in the air. Next door, Old Mrs. Allen is spraying her hose indiscriminately.

"Keep your water on your side!" I yell to her.

Winslow Blythe's *Complete Rose Guide* (SoCal Edition)

July

Deadhead all the old and spent blooms. It's important to note that not all blooms, when left alone, will turn into rose hips. Many will not. The only way to know is to watch, and wait.

Water roses daily. They need plenty of hydration. If you think you've watered enough, increase it by 15 percent. Unless you're an old pro, in which case you might be right.

Feed the roses high-quality organics. Now is the time the composting you started in the spring will pay off. If you neglected to start composting, simply buy the good stuff at your local nursery, or ask a more forward-thinking friend for some.

31

SCHOOL IS OUT AND THE FOURTH OF JULY HAS JUST passed. I always think of the holiday as the midpoint of summer. This is the crux at which vacation begins going by too fast, days tumbling down like a toddler's block tower.

This summer Riley is here.

It's not even eight a.m., and already I've done more than most people do all day. I've risen early to putter in the rose garden before it gets too hot. Temps can reach into the one-hundred-degree mark during the season, and the outdoor roses need water every day.

The roses in the greenhouse are thriving, as if they don't know it's really too hot for their delicate beauty. G42, I've decided, will become a mother plant next year. It's too late in the season to hybridize. I wish I had bred it in the spring, when I had the chance. It would have been better than wasting my time at rose shows.

I wipe my hands on my pants and take a drink out of the hose, though that's supposed to be bad for you. Riley is at the nursery. I head over to buy some fish emulsion and compost.

It used to be that after the roses, I could take a nap, work on some craft or rose research, and then work in the garden again as the day cooled down. Sometimes, Dara and I would hit a movie or play cards or go to the air-conditioned mall, where I'd sit on a bench and wait for Dara to flit in and out of the stores.

This summer, Dara is teaching an art class and seeing her accountant Chad, who is now, I suppose, her official boyfriend. Not that she will admit it.

And I'm chauffeur to Riley. Three days a week, Riley drives to the nursery to work. I drive with her, allowing the extra practice. I've promised she can take the driver's test on her birthday, August 5. Tuesdays and Thursdays, Riley takes Dara's art class.

The nursery where Riley works, Cranston Farms, feels hot and sleepy. It's built on a few acres of land. There is a green shade cloth over the more sun-intolerant plants, which are kept closest to the central building. The cacti and other succulents are set out in vast rows that shoppers walk through in the blazing sun.

I go into the air-conditioned building, where they sell houseplants and orchids and furniture. I wonder who around here could possibly buy orchids; they're so difficult to grow outside of the tropics. I would never attempt it. I eye a tiger-striped bloom as a teenaged girl calls up Riley over the loudspeaker.

"You're Riley's aunt?" The girl's name tag reads ZOE. She's got two red Pippi Longstocking braids and a wide grin with a gap between her front teeth.

I cock my head. "You're the famous Zoe." Zoe is a senior at the public high school, has her own vehicle, and she and Riley are becoming inseparable this summer.

Riley rushes in, sweat stained. She takes off her big straw

hat and wipes her forehead. "Aunt Gal! You here for the fertilizer? I'll get the guys to load it in your car."

"Thanks." It's good to see her so animated. Healthy-looking.

She takes a small Moleskine notebook from her back pocket. "We have a cool new flower. I drew it." She shows it to me. It looks like a sea star, five petals, with exposed stamen and buds in the center.

"Wow. That is really cool. What's it called?"

"*Stapelia flavorpurpea.*" She looks to Zoe, who nods. "I got it right."

"The weird thing about the *Stapelia* is that most of them smell like rotting meat." Zoe sits on the counter by the register. "To attract flies."

"Lovely."

"Not this one, though. It smells like sugar." Riley beams. "And it's all shades of pink."

"Interesting." My heart pounds as it does when I look at a rose. I want to get one of these. "Are they easy to grow?"

"I have an idea." She snaps her notebook closed. "I want to make a garden. A garden that looks like it's under the sea. All succulents, real water-tolerant. What do you think?"

I'm taken aback. "Where? There's no room in the rose garden." Does she want to remove some of my roses?

"No, no, no. In the front yard. There's only some deadish grass patches there." She opens the notebook again, shows me a sketch. Flowers that look like sea stars, plants that look like a kelp forest, sand for the ocean floor, all composed prettily in front of the porch. "I wrote down everything we need."

I raise an eyebrow. "How much will it cost?"

"I get a discount." Riley deflates.

"Give me a price total and I'll consider it."

"I'll buy the plants. I'm working."

"I want you to save your money, Riley." Her face is streaked with brown dirt. I wipe it away.

"It's okay, Aunt Gal." She moves away. "I can do it."

Sudden agitation flows through me. "It is not okay, Riley. Save your money."

A wave of sudden nausea hits me. My head pounds. I need to sit.

She holds up her hands. "Okay, okay, Aunt Gal." She and Zoe exchange a look.

"What are you looking at?" I am mad, and I don't make sense. I am not afraid, for some reason, though I probably should be. There's a white chair behind me. I sit.

Riley grabs me. "Aunt Gal, what are you doing?"

I am flat on the ground. "Who moved the chair?" I feel around for it.

"You're super hot." Riley kneels, her dirty face worried.

"Your boss is too cheap to turn on the air." Darkness is closing in at the corners of my eyes. How very strange.

I listen for my heart in my ears. Nothing. No pounding. Just cool darkness closing in, like a microscope out of focus.

"It's quiet," I yell, but I hear silence.

"What should we do?" Zoe sounds far away.

"Call 911." Riley's hands, cool as ice packs, soothe my forehead. The darkness finishes expanding. I tumble down.

I AM IN THE HOSPITAL, in a room that looks like any other of the dozens of hospital rooms I've been in. Pastel-patterned curtain hanging on a curlicued rod from the ceiling, around my bed. Another patient, unseen, groaning indistinctly next to me. Blankets piled high, still hot from the warmer. An IV and blood pressure cuff on me. At least I'm near the window, though all I can see is the blank wall of the building next to this one.

"Gal?" A dark shadow appears before my uninspiring view.

"Doc?" I squint. Light comes in around her, like a halo. Ironic.

"Do you know where you are?"

I glance around, holding up my bound arm pointedly. "Hmmm, I don't know. Is this some kind of trick question?"

She makes a note on her electronic pad. "Knows where she is."

"What happened?"

"Dehydration. Heat stroke."

That makes sense. Dialysis involves getting all the liquid sucked out of you, the same amount on hot days as on regular days. The last thing I remember is talking about sea plants. Or did I imagine that? It seems like an odd thing, an undersea garden. I watch the cold saline flow through the IV into my neck, where I feel it pulse down toward my pumping heart. I'll need a few bags of this.

"On hot days when you're out and about, you have my permission to drink more water." Dr. Blankenship fusses with the coverings at my feet, tucking them under. I don't like having my feet trapped.

"I hadn't even thought about it," I admit. "I didn't think I was doing much physical work."

"You gardened, you drove, you walked around in the heat. That's plenty for someone like you." Dr. Blankenship stops her tucking, thank goodness, and walks to my other side where I can see her clearly. Her wavy bob is crazy frizzy.

In this daylight, the fine lines all over her face are visible, and I think irrelevantly she could use some hydrating lotion.

"How much more?" I hate her unspecificity. Does she expect me to read her mind?

"An extra cup. You'll sweat it out in this weather." She puts her hand on my bed railing. I stare at the short filed nails on long fingers, her impeccable cuticles.

"Write that down for me." I hope my memory is working fine again, but I can't be sure. Dr. Blankenship writes it down on a yellow Post-it and sticks it to my nightstand.

"I'll put it in your discharge instructions, too. Don't worry."

"Don't forget." I pull the blankets up to my armpits.

"I won't." She backs up toward the curtain exit. "You rest."

"It would be easier to rest if you guys didn't wake me up every half hour to see whether or not I'm dead." I point to the machines. "Or turned off this cuff."

"Necessary evils." Dr. Blankenship smiles at me. I can't muster a return smile.

Footsteps approach, high heels and sneakers, from the sounds of it. In the next second, Riley's and Dara's heads poke through the curtains. "Can we see her now?" Dara asks.

Dr. Blankenship nods, waves good-bye. I lift my fingers in return.

Dara swishes in, kitten-heeled sandals and a full navy blue skirt, and sits on the hard guest chair. Riley follows, sitting on the vinyl-coated recliner. She still has streaks of dirt on her face, so at least I know I haven't been in here too long. "Haven't you made her wash yet?" I say to Dara.

"We were too worried to think of appearances." Dara puts the emphasis on appearances.

I look pointedly at her clothes.

"I was dressed for a date." She crosses her ankles primly.

Riley smiles timidly. Her face is sunburned. I point my finger at her. "You need to wear sunblock, miss, not just a hat."

"I did."

"Did you reapply after an hour?"

She shakes her head.

I spread my hands. "I rest my case. You sweated it off."

"I'll stay with Riley until your mother gets here." Dara untucks the blankets from my feet. I wiggle them gratefully.

"My mother is coming?" I don't know why this is surprising. Maybe because I feel like everything is handled. Dara is here and I'll be out tomorrow, I bet.

"Did you really think Grandma wouldn't?" Riley asks rhetorically.

"I convinced her you were stable, so she's driving. She should be here this evening, depending on traffic." Dara pats my ankle.

I nod, putting my head all the way back on the pillow. I press the button for my bed to lower. "I'm getting sleepy, girls."

"Let's hit the road, Riley." Dara stands and exits.

Riley hesitates. "Do you need anything else, Aunt Gal?"

"No, Riley. I'm covered." I'm already drifting to sleep.

"I'm sorry," she whispers.

"For what?"

"I don't need to make a sea garden."

I laugh. "So that wasn't a dream."

She grips my hand. "I won't do it."

I shake my head. "Riley, quit thinking everything is your

fault." I manage to open my eyes to deliver this. "Nothing to do with me is your fault, okay?" She stares at me, at the IV in my neck. I probably look kind of horrible.

"Repeat it." I squeeze her back.

"Nothing to do with you is my fault."

I drop her hand. "Good. Now let Dara get you some chow." I turn my head away and listen. It is several moments before I hear her rubber soles squeaking across the room.

IN THE MIDDLE of the night, I awaken to my mother sleeping next to me, upright in the chair, only one thin thermal blanket over her. Her hair is so very gray now, her jawline softer and jowlier than I remember. She's getting too old for this. I say another quick prayer for a kidney transplant.

As if she can feel my wakefulness, Mom sits up. "Gal? What do you need?"

"Nothing." I whisper, not wanting to disturb the person in the other part of the room.

Mom gets up, feeling my hands, my forehead, looking at the blood pressure readings with the expertise of a registered nurse. Which she practically could be, after all this experience. "You're cold." She puts her blanket over me.

"No, Mom, that's your blanket." I try to give it back, but she pushes it down.

"I'll get another from the nurses' station." She smoothes my hair back, her eyes crinkling. "Feeling better, love?"

"What about Riley?"

"Dara's with her."

"You should be with Riley, Mom. I'm fine here."

"You need me more. Riley's just sleeping."

I close my eyes, waiting to hear Mom walk to the nurses'

station. Instead, the recliner squeaks. She will sit there cold all night, unwilling to take her eyes off me.

My mother marks time waiting for me, painting and traveling with my father, but really all she wants is for me to come home so her life can begin again. I am her main concern.

This is why I moved away, I think. I fall asleep.

THE FOLLOWING AFTERNOON, my mother leaves to pick up Riley from art class. Dr. Blankenship wants me to do a lap or three around the floor to prove I won't keel over again. Then, I might be released.

I wheel my IV around past the nurses' station, down the hall past various people either doing the same thing or being pushed in chairs, and back to the station again. "Good job, Gal," one nurse says. I thank her. I've never seen her before. If I go into the hospital again, I'll get to know them all.

The whiteboard behind her catches my eye. GARNER RM 314, it reads. WALTERS RM 320.

"Mark Walters?" I say involuntarily.

She nods.

I doubt she'll tell me why he's here, and I don't want her stopping me, so I wheel my contraption over to room 320 as quickly as I can go.

"Ms. Garner!" the nurse calls after me. "You can go ahead and rest now."

"One more lap." I pause by room 320. The door is open, the curtains closed over both beds.

I shuffle cautiously in. "Mark?" I call.

A pause, then a grunt. "Who's there?"

"Gal. Where are you?"

"Door number one." He coughs. I part the curtains.

He looks terrible. He is swollen with fluid, puffy nearly beyond recognition. Like a balloon someone has drawn features on with a marker. Only his hair and mustache give him away. "Shit, Mark, what happened?" I don't bother closing the curtain behind me.

"And you tell me to watch my mouth." He manages a weak grin. "Liver infection."

"Oh." I sit down.

"I'll be okay in a few days." He pats the side of his bed. "You bring cards?"

"I'm in the hospital, too." I point to my IV.

"I didn't catch that. I'm not too swift at the moment." His eyes, bleary with drugs, peer at me. "You're okay, walking around."

"I am." I nod. Especially compared to him, I want to say.

"Next time, bring cards. I can still beat you even if half my brain's clogged." He laughs.

"I will." My mother has cards in her purse. Always does when she comes to the hospital. "We'll play."

But he is asleep.

The nurse pokes her head in. "There you are. Your mother's looking for you." She shakes her head.

I get up. "Is he going to be all right?"

She doesn't meet my eyes. "I'm sure he will be." A nonanswer designed to protect privacy. I get it.

"Help me with the IV, please." We walk into the hall, where my mother and Riley are waiting.

32

BEFORE I LEAVE THE HOSPITAL THE NEXT MORNING, I check in on Walters. He's asleep. I promise myself I'll call him in the next few days.

On the weekend, I awaken to sounds of digging outside. Mr. Morton, my father, Riley, and Zoe have my father's truck backed up to the front yard. It's full of dirt. They are busily digging out the patch of grass.

"What's all this?" I wave to Mr. Morton.

"How are you feeling?" He shades his eyes with a hand and looks up at me. He's wearing a tank top, the hairs of his chest poking above the collar line. I blush. My body betrays in so many ways.

"The undersea garden, of course." Riley doesn't stop digging. "Sheesh, Aunt Gal, this is pretty cruddy earth you have out here."

"I know. I had to amend the entire backyard. Remember, Dad?"

Dad, in his big straw hat, doesn't stop digging, either. "I remember. We rented that little backhoe. Should have done that with this project."

"We'll get it done. It's not that big. Seven by twenty." Mr. Morton spreads out his hands. "It's going to look fantastic. People will be driving by your house to take pictures."

"Just what I wanted." I pull my bathrobe tighter.

Mom sticks her head out the door. "Gal, what are you doing up?"

"I'm perfectly fine, Mom. That's why I got to come home."

"Come eat your breakfast." She addresses the little crew. "I made coffee, too. Take a break and have some."

Dad and Riley and Zoe wave her off. But Mr. Morton abandons his shovel and leaps up to us.

I am acutely aware of my hair sticking out at all angles. "How'd you get roped into this?"

We follow my mother slowly into the kitchen. Mr. Morton wrinkles his forehead. "I was buying plants yesterday and Riley told me. So here I am. Your resident free labor."

"You don't have to."

"You forget. I have the summer off. I am acutely bored. I need a distraction." He smiles tightly and I know he's talking about his custody battle. George sits at the table, kicking his legs out at an angle. His boots are dirty. He sees where I'm looking. "Sorry. I'll take them off."

I shake my head. "It's fine. Dirt's already in here." Mom puts a mug of black coffee in front of him, tea for me, and a little white cow-shaped pitcher full of cream. He pours about a teaspoon in. "You mean you aren't enjoying your summer of leisure? It's why I became a teacher." Mom sets a plate of scrambled eggs in front of me. Mr. Morton waves off her food offer.

He grins. "I'm not one for sleeping in. I've been landscaping my yard. Maybe I'll grow roses next year."

"Find your own flower." I laugh.

He laces his fingers. "I'm building a chicken coop. Room for twenty chickens."

I brighten. "Chickens? I've always been interested in chickens."

"I'll bring you some eggs."

"Forget the eggs. I want the poop. It's incredible fertilizer." I take a sip of tea. Mom has already sweetened it the way I like. I smile at her gratefully. She stands at the sink, washing the breakfast pans.

"Maybe Dad can build you a coop next time," Mom says.

I shake my head. "No more room."

"They'd eat the bugs, too." Mr. Morton stares out the window thoughtfully, picturing, no doubt, where he'd place such a coop and how it would work. I recognize the look. A look of dreaming. He turns back to me. "Anyway, I'll have Rhode Island Reds and Araucanas. Those lay blue eggs. Great for Easter."

"I bet your daughter will like that," I say without thinking, only picturing the delight of a young girl discovering a blue egg.

Mom stops her dishwashing, listening. Mr. Morton takes a very big gulp of coffee and sets his mug down. He gets up. "Back to the grind, then." He smiles, but his eyes aren't in it anymore. He goes outside.

"What was that about? He has a daughter?" Mom wipes her soapy hands on a dishtowel.

"He does. It's complicated." I sigh. "I shouldn't have mentioned her."

"He can't not mention her," Mom says reasonably. "It'd be like people not mentioning your kidney condition. It's worse when they ignore it, believe me."

I pick up my mug of tea and go to the front room, sitting

by the window. I watch them work outside, wondering why I can't control my mouth better.

"I'm sorry," I say to him through the pane of glass.

He laughs at something my father says. Only I can see, from my angle, the sad slump of his shoulders.

IN THE AFTERNOON, they are finished digging and are ready for plants.

My parents take Riley out for pizza. I need to stay home and rest some more.

My computer pings with a notice from the school. The AP test results. Only three students who took the test got less than a three, the minimum passing score. "Yes!" I whoop. This ought to show Dr. O'Malley that my teaching methods are up to snuff. Another year, another burden of proof.

Samantha got a five, the highest possible score. Smart girl. Brad got a three.

I double-check. Brad got a three?

I frown. Based on his grades, not to mention his science project, I would have had him pegged as a four or five. Perhaps he slacked off in his prep because it was senior year.

I shut my computer down.

OUTSIDE, I PONDER the dug-up soil for the new garden plot. They have amended it with plenty of black earthy soil, from the smell of it fish manure, too. The neighborhood dogs will be over here shortly. The ripe scent doesn't bother me as it does most people (I fervently hope Old Mrs. Allen will be downwind of it). It smells of fertility, of good things to come.

Something blue sits on the white picket, near the sidewalk. It's Mr. Morton's sweatshirt. I pick it up. It's old, softened through a thousand washings. Faded letters say "Cal" in yellow cursive. Without thought, I wad it to my face. Some cologne I can't identify, something green and citrusy, wafts up. And musky sweat. Man sweat. Much, much different than my father's smell. I inhale involuntarily.

Embarrassed, I put it down. I glance about to make sure no one saw me. The street is empty except for a few far-off neighbors taking their big trash cans out to the curb.

I pick it up and take it to my car. Before I know it, I am backing out onto the street. I don't remember grabbing my keys.

33

THE LIGHT IS ON IN THE LIVING ROOM OF MR. Morton's bungalow. His is a Craftsman style, with stone-graced pillars and abstract stained glass over his window tops, the kind of house I could only imagine owning.

Apparently I really am quite a natural stalker.

In the dimming sun, I see he has been hard at work in his yard. He's planted lilac bushes at either end of the porch, with a bedding of greenery that hasn't budded yet. I can't tell what kind of flowers they will have.

His silhouette gets up. No curtains. A flat-screen television is on, playing some movie. He looks out, seeing me standing on the flagstone path. He opens his big oaken door. "Gal!"

"What kind of sprinkler system you using?" I gesture to the plants with his sweatshirt.

"Underground."

I nod. "I like drip myself." I hold up the sweatshirt as though I've forgotten it. As though it's not burning my hands as if it's possessed. "You left this."

He holds the door open. "Come on in."

I enter, wiping my feet ostentatiously on the welcome mat.

He points to a small ceramic plaque with a picture of flip-flops on it. ALOHA. PLEASE TAKE OFF YOUR SHOES, it reads. I slip off my Crocs. "Now why couldn't you remember that at my house if you do it at yours?" I ask.

He shrugs. "Too excited about the coffee, I guess."

"You from Hawaii?"

"No. California. But I like to visit the islands. Warm water." He glances back at me. "Have you ever been?"

I shake my head.

"You should go."

"There are lots of things I should do." I don't have to explain the difficulty of doing things. He gives a quick nod.

I follow him into the living room, sitting in a chocolate-colored leather armchair. He sits on a rust-colored couch and flips off the TV. His hands are bandaged.

"What happened?" I indicate his bandages, wrapped up several times around his palms like a mummy.

He holds them up. "Blood blisters. From the shovel."

I wince. "Did you ice them?"

He shakes his head.

I shake mine. "Don't tell me you're a typical stubborn man."

"No one's ever accused me of being typical." He puts his hands in his lap.

I move over to the couch next to him. "Let me see." I pick up one hand. It is clearly swollen. I cluck, unwinding the bandage. Sure enough, there are two blood blisters per palm, right below his fingers. "You should have worn gloves."

"I left them at home."

"I'll get you ice." I go into his kitchen. He follows me.

"You don't know where anything is."

"Um. Could it be? Ice in the freezer?" I open it. He has one of those French door models, no automatic ice maker. I take out an ice tray. "Ah, elementary, my dear Watson."

"Indeed." He sits on a stool at an island.

His kitchen is spacious for a bachelor, with a five-burner gas stove and double oven. The Craftsman theme has been carried out here, too, with honeyed wood cabinets and shiny golden hardware. I glance around. "Do you not have a microwave?"

He gets up and presses a paneled wall. It slides open, revealing a microwave and food pantry.

"Oooh. What'd you do, buy out the home show?" I scoop some ice out of the tray. He hands me a small plastic baggie.

"The house came like this."

I glance at the stove. "Are you a good cook, at least? It'd be a waste to microwave everything."

"All these questions suddenly." He crosses his arms, resuming his perch. "Fair, I'd say. Out of necessity."

"Did your wife cook?"

His face darkens. Oops. "No."

I sit opposite him. The light from above makes his eyebrows cast shadows on his face. It doesn't help that he is staring down the countertop. "Hey. I'm sorry I keep bringing them up. But you can't pretend they don't exist. It'd be like me pretending I didn't have," I gesture to myself, up and down, "this disease. It's there, in your face."

"I don't think of you as a person with a disease." He folds his hands. "You're Gal to me."

"And I don't think of you as a jerk who ran away from his family." I put my head on my hand, elbow on the counter. "Not anymore."

"I'm still getting used to it. Telling people."

"Openness is best."

He shoots a sidelong look at me. Then he starts laughing.

"What?"

"You're not exactly the most open person I ever met, Gal."

"What are you talking about? I'm a darn open book." I laugh, too. "You know, there are degrees of openness and closedness. I'm about midway for me."

"Me too." He grins.

We sit for a minute.

"How're your hands?"

He picks up the ice pack. "Better."

"Don't they teach you chemistry teachers anything?" I stand up. "Basic first aid. Seriously."

"Chemistry teachers *are* barely human," he says with a straight face.

I walk to the door.

"Thanks. It's my favorite sweatshirt."

"I could tell." I smelled it, I think, and I blush all over again.

"You all right?" He is next to me.

"Fine." I grip the door, open it. "See you around."

"See you." He watches me get into the car, watches me turn over the engine. Doesn't move back inside until I'm pulling out of the driveway.

I put the car into gear. He raises his hand. I raise mine. "Good night, George," I say. The name feels comfortable in my mouth.

ON TUESDAY, I am sitting in a lawn chair looking at the new sea garden. It looks, as Riley would say, totally awesome.

Riley and Dad have gone to town on the project. There are cacti that rise in waves like kelp, the sea-star flowers, orange succulents that look so much like anemones I am forced to touch them, and rocks resembling coral at the bottom of the ocean. The floor is lava rock and sand.

"It's not done," Riley says. "I'll add to it over the summer."

"It's fantastic." I admire it.

Dad comes out of the house, rubbing his hands together. "Ready to get down to business, Riley?"

"Doing what?" She takes a sip of her sweating Diet Coke. Of course Mom bought the stuff while she's in town.

I nudge her. "The roses, remember?"

Riley and Dad are to go through the seedling pots and pull out the remainders. I've gotten the ones I want to keep. If they are flowering, they may also cut them for bouquets.

"Right." My father pulls her up with a hand and they go out to the greenhouse.

Mom comes out on the porch with a glass of iced tea, wearing an enormous purple and white flowered muumuu. "Not going with them?"

I shake my head. "It's depressing to pull out the seedlings. Like putting away Christmas ornaments."

Mom nods, the ice in her tea jangling. She glances toward Old Mrs. Allen's house. "I bet I can win her over." Mom takes a sip of tea.

"Be my guest." If anyone could do it, it would be my mother. "I guess I rub her the wrong way."

"Aunt Gal?" Riley comes around the side of the house at a run. "You better look at this. In the greenhouse."

I get up, panicked. "What is it?"

"Just come on!" Riley returns to the greenhouse. I begin speed-walking, causing my mother to yell, "Slow down!

You don't want to fall." I feel like a toddler running ahead of her mother.

Riley leads me to the seedling tray. She points to a single seedling left.

"What about it?" All I can see is the back of a purple flower. "It's a plain old purple. I have a half dozen like it."

She turns the bloom over so I can see it. Not only is it purple, it's a light purple with white spots, plus the red splotch. I make a noise. A delighted noise.

"Smell it," she commands.

I sniff.

Sweetness wells, singing up into my brain and eye sockets. I inhale again, greedily. This time I detect notes of spiciness, like it's spiked with paprika. It smells delicious.

I have to sit.

An image comes into my head. My sister, Becky, and me, holding hands in our grandmother's garden. Eating peaches dripping onto our dresses, making our faces sticky. My mother wiping us clean with a gentle scold. My grandfather presenting each of us with a small wooden car, whittled by his own hand.

My eyes fill.

Suddenly I miss my sister.

I don't think I have before.

I always complain about her not being a good sister to me, but what have I done for her? What kind of sister have I been? I have no answer.

"Aunt Gal? Don't you like it?" Riley bends over me.

"I thought it smelled pretty good myself," Dad, who barely comments on any smell, good or bad, says. He wipes his hands off on his jeans.

My mother finally arrives at the greenhouse door. All

three of them stand and regard me, their collective breath held.

I gulp the cooling early evening air. I examine the glossy green leaves, all perfectly formed, and the purple blossoms. "It's perfect," I manage. I push my bangs off my head. "It is perfect."

They shout and clap me on the back. My family, all there. One missing.

She probably wouldn't be happy for me anyway, I tell myself. She wouldn't understand all the fuss.

But maybe she would.

34

I HAVE TO WATCH THE HULTHEMIA. IT SHOULD rebloom with more roses. If I'm lucky.

I think I am.

I make a decision. The American Rose Society is holding its annual fall convention in Los Angeles this year. I'm going to enter it to be considered for their International Test Garden, a two-year process that puts the roses through different climate rigors.

I haven't decided on a name yet. Its cross number is G213, but it deserves a name.

"Can you register it like Byron did his?" Riley asks. She sits at the desk, flipping through my growing journal.

"Too expensive for me. My best hope is the American Rose Society trials. See how it does in colder areas."

"How do you think it will do in other places?"

"I don't know. We'll have to make some more of them and find out."

"What if it doesn't make it into the trials?"

"I'll do it myself." I think about replicating freezing temperatures by putting them into the freezer.

She stops her flipping. "Do you think Byron will pay to register it?"

My heart stops. This is a possibility I haven't considered. Byron, with his new company, could certainly back me if he chose. But whether I want him to is another question. "I don't know, Riley."

A knock sounds. Brad enters. "Your mother said you were back here. Hi."

"Brad! Long time, no see." I saw only a glimpse of him at graduation, long enough to shake his and his father's hands. "I was hoping you'd get the valedictorian speech." The school has several students with straight A's, GPAs higher than 4.0 due to the heavily weighted advanced placement courses. The speaker had been a girl named Alicia, voted by the seniors.

He sticks his hands into his khaki shorts pockets. "Ah. Alicia practically cried all year for it."

"That's no reason to let her do it."

"I just didn't care." Brad looks me in the eye. His face is expressionless.

"What can we do for you, Brad?" Riley has closed my journal and put it back into its desk drawer. She sounds like she's conducting a business transaction. She sounds like me.

She crosses her arms and legs and regards him. He barely glances at her. He hands me a cream-colored note. "I'm having a good-bye party. My dad thought you'd like to come."

Not him. I swallow my pride and examine the note. "At the country club?" I raise an eyebrow.

He scratches at his nose. "My dad knows a guy."

"I see." I smile at him, this kid whom I've mentored for the past four years. As a freshman he'd been small and skinny, more like a sixth-grader than a ninth. And here he was, nearly six feet tall, off to college.

He points his thumb toward the door. "I have to go. I'll see you."

"See you." I pin the invitation on my bulletin board.

Riley sighs.

My fingers pause. "What exactly is your problem with Brad? You have disliked him from the instant you met him. Then you seemed to like him. Then you suddenly didn't like him. What happened?" It's the first time I've asked her so directly to tell me what happened.

She gazes out the window. "I don't know."

I spin her around to face me. "You do know."

Her mouth turns down. "Aunt Gal, I said I wouldn't tell."

My entire body tenses. "Is anyone getting hurt?"

She meets my gaze, unblinking. "Not physically." She gets up and leaves.

I consider whether I should follow and try to break her down. Maybe threaten to withhold hamburgers.

I remember an incident when Becky and I were teenagers. She was sixteen, I fourteen. She'd sneaked in one night, absolutely wasted. I could smell the whiskey on her breath as soon as she tumbled through my bedroom window.

"Shush." She held her finger up to her lips. Outside, in the moonless night, I heard a car peel away. She looked around my rose-pink bedroom, lit by the small night-light I still used in case of emergency. Her own room was dark purple. "Ah, shit. This isn't my room."

"Mom is going to kill you," I said, not unhappily.

"You'd just love that." She stumbled across to the door. "Please. Don't say anything."

I looked into her pleading face. Generally my sister's stance was to ignore me altogether. Finally I had something she cared about. I nodded.

"What do you want? I have twenty bucks." She tried to hand me a crumpled bill.

"That won't be necessary." I waved it away magnanimously. "Dear sister."

"Jesus." Becky leaned against the doorjamb, understanding that she would never be done paying me back. "I'd almost rather get punished."

And now, talking to Riley, I think perhaps I should have said something back then. Maybe Becky would have stayed off that path.

"Riley!" I call to my sister's daughter. "Come back."

But she is inside and cannot hear.

THAT NIGHT, after Riley goes to bed, I talk to my mother about the situation. "I'm afraid it's Becky all over again." I tell her my memory.

Mom grimaces, shifting in position on the couch. Dad snoozes in the chair. "Becky is Becky."

"What does that mean?"

"I mean, Becky was going to do what she wanted to do. I had too much to do with you to worry about her. She knew better. She knew right from wrong. She was healthy." Mom looks steadily at the wall, not at the television, which is playing her favorite PBS show, *Mystery!* The black-and-white cartoon people in the opening credits perform their gymnastics.

I catch on. "Did you know what Becky did in high school?"

She moves her head from side to side. "To an extent."

"You mean, you knew as much as you wanted to."

She is quiet. "Maybe. Maybe I could have done more. I don't know." She sighs, takes a handful of peanuts from the can on the table. "We did the best we could."

"You had a responsibility to her as a parent." I sound fierce. My mother looks startled. I try to clamp down on myself. "You should have done something."

"I did the best I knew how, Gal." She puts a peanut into her mouth with a hand that trembles. "Plenty of kids drink in high school, and they don't grow up to be like her. Nothing like her." She takes the remote and turns up the volume. I watch my mother watch her show, eating peanuts until her hand stops shaking.

THE FOLLOWING DAY, I try talking to Riley again, but am met with stony stares and silence.

"When you're ready to talk, tell me," I say as she and my mother leave for Dara's art class.

"There's nothing to tell." Riley does not look back.

There is nothing to do right now.

I leave my father doing a few odds-and-ends projects, fixing a cupboard door that is falling off its hinges and telling him which small plots I would like redug, and I go to the hospital to play cards with Mr. Walters.

But he's at his own home, a large ranch in a nice part of town. Much nicer than where I live. He has left the front door open. I knock on the doorjamb.

"Come on in," he calls from the couch.

"Don't you have anyone staying with you?" It's darker inside than out and my eyes won't adjust. I enter, holding a plate of double-chocolate-chip cookies my mother has sent with me.

"A nurse checks in on me. I got tired of being under my daughter-in-law's foot all the time." He waves me all the way in.

Finally I can see. Everything is neat, traditionally furnished in jewel tones of wines and teals. I get the impression he hasn't moved a thing since his wife passed away. Family photos of varying colors and eras jam the walls, almost covering every vertical surface.

Walters is wearing a robe and pajamas in the same tone as his furnishings. His slippered feet are up on the coffee table in front of him. He is less swollen, but still bloated. "Set yourself down." I put the cookies on the table and he leans forward to take two. "You make these?"

"My mother."

"Fine woman." He inhales one, then the other, fast, like he is starving. "You can't imagine how good it is to have these now."

"I can." I remember back in my pre-dialysis days, when my kidney worked and I could eat whatever I wanted.

He looks chagrined. "Sorry, Gal. I shouldn't eat these in front of you."

I wave him off. "Believe me. I'm used to it. I don't care." I speak the truth. I don't care. I will be glad when I can do the same, but I wouldn't want to feel guilty like he is.

I break out the cards. "What do you want to play?"

"Cribbage?"

"Sure." My father taught me to play when I was a kid.

We set up the board with holes in it and the pegs stand ready for scoring.

"So how are you holding up, Miss Garner?" He deals us each six cards.

"What do you mean?"

"Any closer to your kidney?"

I laugh. "It's not in my hands."

He taps his temple. "Think positive. Think, 'I will have a new kidney by Christmas.' That's what I did. Only I said, 'Fourth of July.' And here I am."

"If that kind of thinking works, then how come more people haven't won the lottery?" I look at my cards, then discard two.

"They don't do it enough. With their whole soul." He discards only one.

"Mr. Walters, I didn't have you pegged as a New Age guru."

"Hey, I'm older than you, Gal. I'm merely sharing my knowledge."

"I do pray," I confess.

"I figured. You do teach at a Catholic school." He flips over the top card on the deck. "Two," he says.

"You don't have to be Catholic, you know. My friend Dara isn't." I lay down a four. "Six."

"I myself am a proud heathen. Unbaptized, untamed. Even Mrs. Walters couldn't do it." He puts down a five. "Eleven."

"Good for you for being proud. But it doesn't stop your magical thinking, does it?" I add a queen. "Twenty-one."

"Ha. Perfecto." He slaps down a king. "Thirty-one." He moves the counting peg back to zero and we start over. "Do you know where I'm going, soon as this thing heals?"

I shake my head. "A nice warm beach someplace?"

He waves me off. "Ah. I've had enough warm beaches in my life to last me ino the afterlife. Think cold." He pantomimes a shiver.

"Where? Alaska?"

"Antarctica." He grins triumphantly, having won by getting rid of all his cards first. He raises his hands in the air. "See, I knew I was going to win."

I roll my eyes. "You're sort of impossible, you know that? One more round. How do you get to Antarctica?"

"One of those boats that cuts clean through the ice, of course." He wiggles his brows at me. "Maybe I'll meet a nice lady friend on the trip."

Antarctica. Only Mark would think of such a trip. "I wouldn't mind seeing that continent myself." I put down another card.

"So. Go." He pops the last cookie in his mouth.

"I'll put it on my after-kidney bucket list." We pause and our eyes meet. We both smile. "Mark! There were a dozen cookies and you ate all of them?"

"Tell your mother she's too good a baker."

I win this round. We keep playing until the sun disappears altogether.

35

MY PARENTS DEPART IN THE MORNING, LEAVING behind Mom's car and a big hug for Riley.

"Remember. You can change your mind about Riley," Mom whispered into my ear as she said farewell.

I nodded wordlessly. If I'd paid attention, I would have known my mind had been made up for quite a while.

I drive Riley to work, moving quickly through town. I peer up at the bright sky. "Going to be hot today."

"Better drink extra water."

I do not look in her direction. "We should go to Brad's good-bye party," I say. "I bet he'll never come back."

"Why would you say that?" She glances at me. I can see it out of my peripheral vision.

"Because there's nothing for him here. This small town."

She gulps. "Okay, if I tell you, will you promise not to flip out?"

"When do I ever flip out?"

She ignores this. "Brad and Samantha were dating."

I stop at a sign and pound my fist into my palm. "I knew it!" My instincts were right. "And her mother wouldn't let them?"

Riley nods.

I don't much want to ask Riley what else was going on that night when Samantha dyed her hair. I mean, teenagers and hormones and no adults around. There's not much to suspect. Except I really hope Riley wasn't involved. "What else?" I say instead.

Riley takes a sip from her metal water bottle.

"They were together during Science Olympiad, weren't they?"

She is surprised.

I smile. "I know. I'm kind of perceptive like that."

Riley sighs. "Samantha helps him a lot. He's smart but lazy." She fiddles with her seat belt. "She thinks it's love so she has to help him."

I feel sick to my stomach. "Are they still seeing each other?"

"I heard they aren't." She looks at her lap.

"Do you have proof?" I ask softly.

She shakes her head. "Only what she told me."

We are at the nursery. I park in the dirt lot, sending up clouds of dust. Zoe waves as she passes by and we both wave back.

I inhale. I wish Riley had said something. But what did she know? After all these years of keeping secrets for her mother, why would she rat on Samantha, or even Brad? I put my hand on Riley's shoulder, whose gaze is glued outside. "Thanks for telling me, Riley."

She looks at me. "Is Samantha going to hate me?"

I tell her the truth. "At first, yes." I hug her to me. "Not in the end, love."

·   ·   ·

I CALL DARA before I get out of the lot. No answer.

Dr. O'Malley is visiting his daughter in Oregon. No help there.

I go to George's house. I need to talk to an adult. A teacher. "Be home, be home," I chant softly.

He is. He's out back, building his chicken coop. It's a multistory affair, already chicken-wired over the frame. He is on top of it, hammering on an asphalt roof.

"George!" I wave up at him.

He clambers down, covered in so much sweat I'm afraid he'll slip. Today he's shirtless, with a hat on and shorts. It occurs to me he sure does a lot of physical work for someone so into science.

"We have a dilemma."

He listens carefully, his hand on his hip. I avoid looking below his chin.

"So there's just Riley versus Samantha and Brad?"

I nod miserably.

"And she didn't actually see any of it."

"She wasn't in their biology class, either."

He takes a breath and sits at a white vinyl picnic table. "This is how all the white-collar criminals are made."

"So. What can we do? Rescind his graduation? Call his college?" I understand now, I think, why Brad cut it off so quickly with me. George wipes at his brow with a rag he picks up off the table. "Nope. We can't do anything."

I blink.

"There's no proof," he says gently. "All you have is Riley saying what Samantha told her. And I believe it. That kid did too much for one person. Work, sports, full load of classes."

"But that means he doesn't deserve that scholarship." I

pace around the yard. "Some other kid got beaten out unfairly."

"I know."

"It's not right." My voice rises.

"No, it's not." He gets up and takes me by the shoulders so I stop moving. I'm eye level with his chest. I look up at him.

"Gal. You are a good teacher. This has nothing to do with you not catching it."

"I know that." I step back, annoyed. "Do you think I could have caught it? I am on those kids like white on rice during tests. There's nothing else I could have done."

"Sometimes there's not."

"What would you have done?" I challenge him.

He spreads his hands. "I had a student report on another student for cheating while it happened. Maybe my students trust me more."

I twist my mouth. "Are you saying this is my fault?"

"No. Not at all. Only that," he hedges, "perhaps no one felt comfortable coming to you."

My judgment of people had turned upside down. What else had I missed? Perhaps Old Mrs. Allen was not a crotchety kook at all but an archangel. "Oh, Lord. What a mess."

"It is." He picks up his hammer. "Want to hit something?"

I glance at his coop. "I don't want to ruin it."

"Not that." He points beyond, to a dilapidated shed. "I'm tearing that thing down. Care to join me?"

I hold out my hand for the hammer. "I'll need safety glasses."

Winslow Blythe's *Complete Rose Guide* (SoCal Edition)

August

Last call for summer pruning! If you want to see some big fat fine blooms in the fall, you will undertake this only marginally painful (to gardeners who hate to cut, not to the bushes) cutdown. Right now, your rose is trying to grow tall toward the sun. Cut off just one-third of your bush's height. Do not prune off the leaves! Just the height.

36

THE FOLLOWING WEEK IS RILEY'S BIRTHDAY, August 5. I get up early to assemble her gift: a sterling silver charm bracelet. To start her off, I've chosen a tiny silver palette charm, with crystals standing in for paint; a Minnie Mouse with moving legs; and a miniature silver microscope. The idea is for her to add to it as she develops new interests or visits new places.

I use the magnifying glass in the greenhouse and a pair of needle-nose pliers to attach the charms. It was a family tradition to give the girls a charm bracelet for their sixteenth birthday. Becky's bracelet had an enameled slice of pepperoni pizza and a movie-scene clapper, because she used to say she wanted to be an actress.

"Pizza?" Becky said incredulously to me in private. I was in her room, watching her look at the gifts from her party.

I picked up her charm bracelet and examined the pizza slice. It looked real, a fine brown glaze over the cheese. My stomach rumbled in response. "It's an excellent pizza representation."

She cast me a disdainful glance.

"Well, what did you expect them to give you?" I said.

"Something that has to do with my hobbies."

I wrinkled my brow. "Like what? They gave you a movie charm, and you won't even audition for the school play. How are you going to be an actress?"

She snatched the bracelet back, her long hair hitting me in the face and her fingernails scratching my wrist. "You don't understand, Gal."

I held up my wrist. Red scrapes appeared on my skin, delicate from all the dialysis. "Watch those claw fingers of yours."

She clapped her hand to her mouth. "Oh my God. I'm sorry."

"It'll heal."

She took off the pizza charm. "Here. Take it."

"I don't want it." I pushed her hand away.

"Please. Take it." She pressed it onto me.

"I think Mom and Dad will notice if I have your charm."

She wouldn't budge, her green eyes trained on me in desperation.

"Becky. I'll heal. I don't want your charm."

"Please," she whispered, her voice strange. "I want you to have it."

I saved it for two years, until I got my charm bracelet. Since then, I've added dozens of charms, commemorating graduations, jobs, trips, and things I simply liked (I keep finding adorable rose charms of different types). The bracelet is so heavy my father has had to put on a new, heavier clasp.

Becky still has only the one charm on hers.

I finish putting Riley's charms on and carefully put the bracelet into its velvet box. I put it into a gift bag, hot pink with hot pink tissue peeking out.

I rub my eyes. I haven't been sleeping well lately. Thoughts of Brad cheating right under my nose wake me out of deep sleep. I still don't know what to do. I can't do nothing, surely.

Maybe I ought to take Dr. O'Malley's offer of teaching part-time after all. I'm sure he'll let me. Then I won't have to be exposed to germs, both the microscopic and teenaged kind.

What I want to do about Brad is storm his university, write a letter to the dean, get the guidance counselor and math teachers to rescind their recommendation letters. But I know George is correct. There is only hearsay and a very real hunch.

I went back and compared Samantha and Brad's papers. I always keep a few A-grade papers, and theirs were the natural choices from AP Biology. Brad wrote about the long-term effects of food preservatives on the human body. Samantha wrote about the benefits of organic food. Similar, but not too similar. The sources were different. One seemed to be rewritten from the other.

I am a chump.

But today is Riley's birthday. We head to the DMV, appointment made, Mom's car inspected and registered in my name, and written test studied for.

The clerk hands her the test materials, still a written one with pencils and bubbles, and Riley moves to a counter with tall privacy spacers. I wait for her to glance back so I can give her a thumbs-up. She does not.

Riley has already opened the booklet, begun filling in the bubbles. She has studied the DMV handbook on her own, and I'd paid for some practice tests. She should be well prepared.

I continue to stand. I'm not sure why. I don't expect her to turn and signal for help. Someone jostles me, and I realize I'm in the way.

I sit down in a chair, each connected by metal bars so you're too close to the person next to you. Now an older man with a bad cough sits knee to knee with me. I should have brought a mask. I decide to wait outside. Secondhand smoke is somewhat preferable to a virus.

Riley pushes the smoked-glass door open a few minutes later, waving a slip of paper. "They told me to wait out here for the behind-the-wheel test." She holds out her hand. "Keys?"

They clink into her palm.

A woman with a clipboard appears. "Riley?"

I take a step back. She spins on her heel and walks firmly away.

"Good luck!" I call, my voice nearly lost.

She raises her hand, does not call back.

I should be pleased. Not having to drive her everywhere will be nice. Won't it?

I sit on the bench and wait for Riley's return.

DARA TAKES US out for hamburgers. Because it's Dara and not me deciding, we go to an overpriced joint where you can choose from among dozens of different burger toppings by checking off the ingredients. "I could do this at home for less," I point out.

"Yes, but you would never buy Gorgonzola cheese or make shoestring fries," Dara counters. I have made sure to wear my charm bracelet, its charms jangling comfortingly against my left wrist. Dara sports jeans with rolled cuffs and a plain white T-shirt, but she can't resist wearing tall black-and-white spectator pumps. Riley and I both wear shorts. Riley is getting tan from her nursery job. I'll need to remind her again about the damaging effects of the sun's rays.

We settle in at a booth with stainless tables and red vinyl upholstery, squishy to the touch. Overhead there's exposed ductwork; the walls are exposed brick. It's modern industrial meets fifties. Of course Dara loves it.

"I like it." Riley plays with the car keys. "Driving here was awesome." She speaks extra loud, looking about to ensure everyone hears. "With my new *driver's license*."

"Did you tell your mom?" Dara asks. I shake my head.

"Not yet." Riley slides her keys into her purse. Riley's mother has not called today. Riley called her, and she didn't answer. That her mood can hinge so much on whether her mother misses a call disturbs me. Her glow dims.

Dara glances at me. "Open your gift." She pushes a bright purple package across the table.

Riley unwraps it carefully, unsticking the tape. "I want to save the paper," she says. "For art." It's a set of artist-quality comic markers. "Thanks, Dara." Riley skips to Dara, hugs her.

Our burgers arrive. Mine is piled too high with ingredients; I remove more than half.

Riley chews silently. Dara and I look at each other.

I hit my palm on the table. "Riley, we should have invited Zoe."

She nods around her burger. "That's okay."

"You should invite her over to watch a movie." I sound artificially perky. Exactly like my mother, always telling me to make friends. Riley nods again.

I want to cheer her up. "Riley. Tell Dara about the driving test."

Riley grins, straightens. "You should have seen it. There was a huge accident on the road. Sirens and everything."

"Oh no. I failed my first driving test because of an ambulance." Dara widens her eyes.

"But not Riley." I beam. "She didn't buckle under pressure."

Our server appears, a sparkler candle atop a frothy chocolate cupcake. She has six employees with her and a microphone. "It's someone's *birthday* today!" she singsongs, putting down the cupcake. She begins clapping. The entire place claps along with her. "Happy happy birthday, to you!"

It's incredibly loud. Surprisingly, people sing along with enthusiasm. Clapping, I sing-shout at the top of my voice, half expecting the large windows to shatter at my sound.

I steal a glance at Riley. Her face is rosy. She wrinkles her nose and furrows her brows, but her eyes dance. She can't prevent a smile from spreading across her face. The sparkler sends disco fairylight across her face.

"Make a wish," I say.

She takes a deep breath and blows. We applaud.

WE DISCOVER A WHITE FEDEX envelope stuck between the screen and front door when we arrive at our house. "My mom's present!" Riley swoops.

"I have one for you, too." I jiggle the key in the lock. "It's right inside."

"Great." She shakes her mother's gift. "I'll open yours first."

"It doesn't matter." I find myself anxious. Of course it doesn't matter which one she opens first. But I want her to open mine.

I get the gift bag from my bedroom. Riley has turned on only the small side-table lamp. I turn on the larger lamp. I want her to see the charms. "You'll go blind in this light." I hand her the present.

She digs into the tissue, pulling out the velvet box. "Jewelry?" Riley grins and opens it up. "I love it!" she exclaims. "Thanks, Aunt Gal." She jumps up and squeezes most of the air out of me.

"You're welcome," I gasp. "Dang, that nursery work is making you strong." I show her mine, explain how it works. "So when you graduate, I'll get you a little silver cap."

She clasps it onto her wrist and holds it to the lamp.

I have a thought. "I know what. I want to give you this rose." I unclasp my bracelet, find one of my silver roses, and try to undo the hoop with my fingernails. "I need the pliers."

"Let me try." Riley undoes it without trouble. She examines the rose. It is one my mother had made specially for me, a Hulthemia, its red heart represented by etching. "Are you sure you want me to have this one?"

"You found that rose, Riley. I want you to remember it."

She clasps it onto her wrist. "Thanks."

I nod, sitting upright on the couch. I'll have to tell my mother I did that, or else she will have a fit when she sees Riley with it. If I tell her, though, she won't say a word.

Riley opens her mother's package. It jangles, metal against metal. She shakes it out. A piece of jewelry, shrink-wrapped, falls out. She rips it open.

Another charm bracelet.

"It's a Juicy Couture," Riley says. She sounds like she's trying not to be excited. The charm bracelet is gold-colored, oversized, filled to the brim with large colorful charms: a parrot, a Scottie dog, an iced coffee with a mountain of whipped cream topped with crystals, and others I can't see.

One catches my eye. A sparkly pizza box. I open its hinged lid. An enameled pizza is inside, with multicolored toppings of black olives and green peppers and pepperoni. I swallow.

"That's really cool," I say. "How clever."

"These charms cost like fifty dollars apiece," Riley says matter-of-factly. She coils the bracelet into her palm.

Holy smokes. There have to be at least fifteen charms on there. With effort, I make a neutral noise. "Maybe she got a deal in Hong Kong."

Her nostrils flare. "I would rather have had a plane ticket to visit her." She leaves the Juicy bracelet on the table and goes to her room. I brace myself for a bang, but it never comes.

37

Dara and George will go to Brad's party with me. "Don't make a big scene," Dara warns me. "Not there."

"Why not?"

She wrinkles her nose. "You want it to be exactly like a John Hughes movie. Big speech and a big audience listening in."

I smile a little. "I like John Hughes movies."

It's a lunch party in mid-August, right before Brad is due to leave. The golf club overlooks the ocean, rolling green hills meeting the surf.

Riley refuses to go. "I have to work," she says. I do not press her.

I wear a long emerald dress in cool cotton, with cap sleeves.

George smiles when I step out of my car. "First time I've seen you in a dress."

"For all you know, it'll be the only time." I hike up the skirt so I don't fall.

He has on blue and white seersucker pants, and a white polo shirt. He offers me his arm to help me over the bumpy lot. "This reminds me of the striped pants my mother made me wear to parties in the seventies. Only those were olive green and pink corduroy." He laughs. "Look at any childhood photo of mine. If I'm wearing those pants, I'm at a party."

I giggle. "Mine was a sailor dress."

"Oh, I'm sorry. That's worse."

We walk slowly to the building.

Dara waits for us at the door. "Hey, guys." She is resplendent in a white sundress printed with camellias and a watercolor cat, her hair loose and somehow not bothered by the ocean wind.

"Hey, Dara." George, I notice, does not comment on her appearance. They smile easily at each other.

I remember I am clutching George's arm and step away with a blush. Dara's eyebrows shoot up, but she says nothing.

"Miss Garner!" Brad's father shakes my hand. His hair is slicked back and his face, nicked from shaving, is earnest. "Thank you for coming."

I nod helplessly. "Uh, thank you for inviting us. What a lovely location."

He nods, leans forward to whisper. "I clean here at night. They gave me a break."

I smile despite myself. "You must be well liked."

"Please. Food, drink." He points. "Enjoy."

I glance around. Most of the people here are people I've seen at school: parents, students, teachers. Samantha is noticeably absent. Everyone mills about, food in hand. I want to kick those little plates right out of their hands and scream that it's all a scam, a miscarriage of justice.

"You all right?" Dara takes a sip of iced tea.

"Of course." I am perspiring. I better have some more liquid. I pour water into a plastic cup.

Then I see him, the man of the hour, Brad. At the window, a glass of Coke in hand, he gazes out, smoldering like the hero of a young adult romance. Except, of course, he is not. I walk purposefully over.

"Brad."

His eyes crinkle in a genuine smile. "How are the roses?"

"Fair." I don't feel like telling him about Riley's rose. I take a sip of water, watching him so intently that he blanches. "Can I talk to you outside?"

We exit through a sliding glass door onto an empty patio with tables and umbrellas. I taste salt in the air. The wind is loud, and I raise my voice. "I know what you did."

"What I did." He smirks, takes a sip of Coke.

"You know exactly what I'm talking about."

The water reflects in his irises. "I didn't do anything."

I finish my drink. His face is impassive. I feel a surge of self-righteous indignation. Doesn't he care that he took an opportunity away from another student? I stand. "Your mother would not be pleased."

He turns to me now, his face suddenly fierce. "You don't know what my mother would be pleased about."

I take a step back. He's right about that. What do I know about him, or anyone, for that matter?

He takes a breath. "I know you're pissed because I cheated you, Miss Garner. But it's nothing personal." He swivels his head back to the ocean. "It's what I had to do."

I crush my plastic water cup, considering my words. I remember him in my rose garden, working hard. Memorizing plant names. Scoring in sports. This is what I have to remember, all the good things he is capable of. I can only hope he'll keep on doing them. He didn't do this to spite me. He has only hurt himself. I inhale. "You're smart, Brad. You're better than this." I start walking toward the party, but pause to look back. The strong afternoon sun makes his face sweat, and he doesn't wipe it away. He stares at the water. I can't tell what he's feeling.

My anger is gone for good. In its place is sadness. "I wish you the best. I really do."

He does not move.

I slide open the glass to the noise of the party.

Brad's father nearly runs into me. "Are you off, Gal?"

He still has great bags under his eyes, and his face is gaunt. In fact, his entire body is gaunt.

"First one in the family to go to college." He puts his hands in his pockets and looks to where his son sits outside. "Taking that janitor job at the school paid off." He grins with half his mouth.

On impulse, I hug him.

He is stiff for a second, and then he awkwardly pats my back. "Thanks, Miss Garner. For everything you've done."

Brad has not moved from his post by the ocean. I hope he remembers me as someone who is pulling for him. I hope he sends me a card from college one day.

"It was nothing at all," I say.

I lift my hand to wave good-bye to George and Dara, across the room watching me.

Winslow Blythe's *Complete Rose Guide* (SoCal Edition)

September

Just when you think the pest danger is past, it returns. With warm summer nights disappearing, aphids may be on the rise. Look for them and the cutter bee, which will leave large circular holes in your rose leaves. Caterpillars will eat the rose buds.

In any case, you must be vigilant this month, or your fall blooms will be jeopardized.

38

THE DIALYSIS CLINIC STILL SEEMS STRANGE WITH-
out Mr. Walters. New people come in all the time, unfortunately for them, but Mr. Walters was always the constant. The
big guy in white. Now that we're friends, I see why all the
nurses liked him.

"Heard from Mark lately?" I ask Nurse Sonya, who sits
nearly hidden behind the wall partition.

She shakes her head.

I feel guilty. I haven't seen him since we played cards
almost two months ago. School has started, and I've gotten
busy again. I make a note to call him.

Dr. Blankenship walks by the nurses' station. She stops
when she sees me. She's on her way home, already changed
out of her lab coat.

"Hey, Doc." I lean through the window and call.

"Gal." Her face falls. "I was about to call you."

I observe her pale face. "It's not good news, I presume?"

We go to her office. She shuts the door and sits not behind
her desk, but in the chair next to mine.

"Gal," she says, "I have some bad news."

My body tenses. Something else happened. Kidney guidelines have changed; I am never going to get a transplant.

Her hair falls over her face as she leans her head to the side. "Gal. Mark Walters passed away yesterday."

I do not comprehend what she is telling me. I blink dumbly.

"He got another infection last week, and didn't recover. I'm sorry." She blinks rapidly. "His funeral will be on Saturday."

"But I just saw him," I blurted, though really it was six weeks ago. "We played cards."

"I'm sorry, Gal." She reaches for pen and paper, scribbling down the name of a church. Her hand shakes, so her handwriting's worse than usual. "We did everything we could." Her nose runs.

I pluck out a tissue from the generic box on her desk.

She blows. "I really ought to buy the nicer stuff. This is rough."

We both laugh in spite of ourselves.

She takes a deep breath. "I'm sorry, Gal. I try not to get personally involved, but that is impossible sometimes."

"I know." Cold floods my fingers. My heart pounds quickly in my ears. I hold on to the chair arms so I don't fall out.

Walters can't be dead.

I take the piece of paper with the church address and put it in my purse.

"Don't worry, Gal. I won't let that happen to you." She looks up at me, newly intense, and she sounds like she is speaking the truth. But all she speaks is her own promise. There's a difference.

I push my chair back. I'm sick to my stomach. "I've got to start dialysis."

"I'll walk out with you." She gets up. She turns off the lights and locks her door, checking the knob twice. I wait, realizing my hands are shaking.

I follow her slowly out. She pauses at the nurses' station, and I know she is going to break the news to them. I return to the waiting room and go into the bathroom, lock the door, so I don't have to watch.

39

It rains the day of the funeral, that Saturday. Uncharacteristic for this time of year. Rain at a funeral means something, but I can't remember what. The rain is more like a drizzle, so light I don't bother with an umbrella. The burial is a private family matter.

I stand in Walters's son's house for the wake, by myself. I have brought a dish of enchiladas and placed them on the white-lace dining table, bowing under all the food. The small house is elbow to elbow with people, mostly senior citizens, but many younger than that. Walters had many friends. Idly I wonder how many people would show up to a wake of mine.

Walters's son, Kevin, talks to Dr. Blankenship. Around thirty years old, he looks a great deal like his father, only with a mop of sandy blond hair instead of white. "He was sick for such a long time," he says. "I'm sort of glad he's not suffering anymore."

The words shock me like electricity. I know it's what people say after people have been sick a long time. But Walters, I am sure, was not ready to pass. If he suffered, he did as a fighter.

I offer Kevin my condolences. "He talked about you a lot," I say.

Kevin bends over to my eye level. "You must be Gal."

I nod.

"I know you, too." He puts his glass of wine down on top of the black upright piano. "I'll be right back."

I wait, with Dr. Blankenship standing beside me silently.

"He didn't want to die, you know," I say to her. "Suffering or not."

"I know." Her cool fingers press briefly against my arm. She wanders away.

Kevin returns, a small stuffed animal in his hand. A penguin. "He told me to buy a penguin and give it to you. Said something about a baked Alaska melting."

I smile in spite of myself, taking the stuffed animal in my hands. It's a baby penguin, the lower half gray, with large plastic eyes, made of some kind of incredibly soft material. I imagine Walters on his deathbed, concerned not just with saying good-bye, but croaking out instructions for his son to obtain a Beanie Baby for a relative stranger. How like him.

Then I picture Walters swaddled in a white snowsuit, waddling among the penguins, icicles forming on his mustache. "He wanted to go to Antarctica. I can just see your father with his white hair on the white snow. He would have been camouflaged on the ice."

Kevin laughs, then wipes his eyes, his smile fading. "That sounds like something Dad would have wanted to do. I wondered about the penguin."

"I guess I'll have to go for him." I clutch the stuffed animal to my chest.

The rain outside has picked up, at last turning into something that can properly be called rain. I clutch the penguin and watch the drops splatter the windows. Inside, the lights are on, so all of us are reflected in the glass, spectral images projected onto the trees and grass of the backyard. And I remember. I've heard it rains only on days good people are buried. But Walters was, as he said, a heathen. I smile.

AFTER THE FUNERAL, my head begins throbbing. I go home and get in bed, my clothes still on, shivering. I don't turn on any lights.

Riley raps on the door frame. "Another bad spell, Aunt Gal?"

I swallow. When I speak, my voice is so soft, she has to lean forward to hear. "You might say that. I'll be all right."

Riley disappears.

The sun goes down. I lie awake, watching the shadows change.

Mark Walters's death has shaken me more than I can admit. How am I supposed to carry on with dialysis when you die after a transplant, the thing that's supposed to save you? I want to live, but everything seems pointless. Why bother to put myself through it all?

Footsteps sound. Lights turn on. Dara and Riley appear, sticking their heads in the doorway.

"Gal? You going to be okay?" Dara whispers. "Can I get you anything?"

I shake my head.

"It's that guy who died," Riley says.

Real tears well up now, at last. They stream down my face.

Dara comes in, takes a tissue out of the box. She wipes the tears away. "You're not him, Gal."

She looks so worried, her brow wrinkled, that I want to sit up and stop crying. But I can't.

I turn over, my back to my niece and my friend. "I'll be all right. Just leave me be."

WHEN I ARRIVE at school on Monday, Dara and Riley are in the hallway, stapling up fliers. Down the hall George is doing the same thing. And Dr. O'Malley.

It's early. No other students have arrived, the front gate still locked. Strong morning light is filtering through the dusty windows. "What's going on?" I move up behind Riley. I had wondered where she went.

She jumps. "Aunt Gal, you scared me!"

Dara hits her black stapler hard with her palm. "We're in the middle of something here, Gal." But she winks.

"Something for you." Riley hands me a flier.

I am speechless.

Dr. O'Malley and George approach. "You're going to need time off," Dr. O'Malley says. "This will help."

"Dr. O'Malley and I have the wrong blood type for you," Dara says.

"But I don't." George smiles. "Type O. The universal donor."

"Yes?" I don't understand.

"I am getting tested to be a potential donor."

I am even more speechless.

Riley claps her hands together. "We did it. Finally. She has nothing to say!"

CUPCAKES
FOR A KIDNEY

WHEN: Friday at lunch and after school

WHY: To fund a kidney transplant
for Miss Garner

"And you know what? Maybe we can organize an organ swap. I give my kidney to someone with the right match, someone else gives you a kidney with the right match." Dara staples another flier to the wall. "We can make it work, Gal."

This is overwhelming. That someone—people—are helping me like this. I want to laugh and weep. Jump up and down. But instead I stand still, my mouth open, unable to move. My friends all stare at me with concern.

George grins and speaks first, to my relief. "Well, we did it. We found a way to strike her mute. Cupcakes are the secret."

I smile back into his merry brown eyes. He is patient. In a

moment, I find my voice. "I'm just glad we'll finally be putting your showroom kitchen to good use."

"Who said anything about my kitchen?" He shakes his head playfully.

"George's kitchen. Good idea, Gal." Dara begins ticking off cupcake flavors on her fingertips. "We need chocolate, vanilla, maybe strawberry."

"We can do a chocolate-dipped one," Riley adds.

"How about something more creative, like avocado and bacon?" Dara says.

"Nothing weird," I say, but she waves me off.

They all move down the hall, deep in discussions of decorations and numbers.

Only George remains behind. He indicates the others with his thumb, like a hitchhiker. "Coming, Miss Garner?"

I blink. To my surprise, my feet move of their own volition. Toward him. "Indeed, Mr. Morton."

He hands me a stapler.

Winslow Blythe's *Complete Rose Guide* (SoCal Edition)

October

Living in SoCal is a mixed bag sometimes. There are mild winters, but also occasional wildfires, not to mention earthquakes and pollution. The month of October is still hot and requires daily watering.

This month will be the *last time* you feed your roses. You want the roses to begin their winter slowdown and rejuvenation.

October sees many rose shows around the state. Try your hand at an entry, or simply go check out what's new and exciting. You might be surprised at the new varieties of roses coming out, and want to try your hand at one for your own garden.

It's also when you want to do what many rose growers dread: get rid of the underperformers. Sometimes, despite your best efforts, a rose simply will not do well in your garden. There's no shame in it. Pull it out, plant it in a different spot, or give it away. You'll be surprised at how often a simple change of venue will allow an underperforming rose to thrive.

40

THE AMERICAN ROSE SOCIETY holds its fall rose show and convention in Los Angeles this year. It is the most important rose show I have attended yet. I enter two competitions, one for the Rose Hybridizers Association Trophy, and another for consideration in the next International Rose trial.

I write the seedling's name on the form. The Riley.

Riley and I drive down the night before, my rose in hand. My stomach feels like it's tied into Celtic knots, and whenever I get behind the wheel, my foot turns to lead. I let Riley drive most of the way, forcing myself to relax. This time it's me who turns the music up too loud.

The show is at the Hilton at Universal Studios, in Studio City. "Can we go to Universal Studios, as long as we're here?" Riley asks as soon as we get into the lobby, as I knew she would. She rolls the cooler behind her with the rose inside. I have made no effort to hide the big "Riley" sticker I have made for it.

"We'll see. If I win, then definitely."

"I think I have better luck when you lose," Riley says.

"Probably so," I say. "Heck, if I lose this time I might be so depressed that I'll take you to Vegas."

"But I'm too young to gamble."

I shrug. "Guess that'll be too bad for you."

"Oh, Aunt Gal."

I immediately feel at home. The lobby has two-story windows curved inward, resembling a greenhouse. A long chandelier lights up the room and a large rose arrangement underneath.

Riley turns away the bellhop who tries to take the cooler, wheeling the thing across the lobby herself. She pushes the elevator button. "Can we at least go into CityWalk and look around?"

The hotel adjoins a colossal mall, full of pricey entertainment and dining options. "All right. But outside of dinner, you'll have to use your allowance."

THE ROSE SHOW takes place in a great ballroom the next morning. Lights glow above in two starburst chandeliers set into the ceiling. The carpet, in polka dots that remind me of black olives, makes my head swim if I stare at it too long.

Riley wears a light purple polo shirt, in honor of the Hulthemia, with khaki pants and a matching purple headband with white stripes. "You're turning positively preppy," I tease her. I put on an argyle cardigan in many pastel colors, knowing the air-conditioning will be cranked high, over my own khaki pants. For the first time, we look as though we could be related.

Rows of tables have already been set up, each with a white tablecloth and a number. I get my number, 110, and look for my table, Riley trailing behind with my cooler. There are masses of people running about, busily setting up multiple displays, and the air is thick with the scent of roses. Sweet and musky. Spicy and fruity. Peaches, pears, strawberries. Honey and cream. Loose tea. Red wine. Pepper. My nose is busier than a bloodhound's.

Every rose I see is perfectly formed, a prime example of its breed. The displays are meticulously arranged, every bloom looking as though it was just plucked from a dewy bush. The room looks like a bridal wonderland.

This is the biggest rose show I've ever attended. My Hybrid Rose category has three dozen competitors, all spread throughout the tables.

Across the room, I see Byron's head. He nods once. I nod back.

May the best rose win.

Riley and I reach the 110 table. I pop open the cooler and take out the rose. I have packed it in a base of Styrofoam and breathe a sigh to see it still upright in its pot. I take it out and place it into a larger ceramic pot that Dara has made for me. The pot is beautiful, with metallic tones of gold, silver, and green. It makes the Hulthemia rose colors pop.

"Raku?" Riley asks, turning the pot.

"That's it." I am not sure what raku means, other than it's the way Dara fired it. She took it out of the hot kiln and put it into an old oil drum filled with sawdust.

Riley runs her hand over the piece. I straighten the tag I've attached to the plant. It's all I can do to not point to it.

At last she notices. "Does that say 'Riley'?"

"If it were a snake, it would have bitten you." I move behind the table.

She is silent, regarding the pottery and the Hulthemia. The rose is at its best today. Its blooms have matured into many layers of petals, twenty-six at last count. The white stands out from the lavender like irregular stripes on candy, and the heart center is a stunning dark purple instead of red. I can see more buds appearing, and it hasn't gotten too bushy yet, like the original Hulthemia in the wild would. Its leaves are luxuriously dark green and its stamens stick out canary yellow.

I sniff the bloom nearest me. The scent has also matured. Green apples, vanilla, and an undertone of cayenne. Like being in the spice aisle of the grocery store, holding an apple pie in your hands. Sweet, but not too sweet.

Like Riley herself.

Not that I would tell her that. She would be terribly embarrassed.

I think it's the best Hulthemia I've ever seen.

Maybe the best rose.

I touch the petals gently.

"It's beautiful, Aunt Gal," Riley says.

I nod. "Thank you for saving it, Riley."

"It's you who created it." She gives me a gentle smile and comes back around the table. We sit down together on the flimsy folding chairs and watch as people drifting by stop to admire the flower. My flower. Drawn like bees.

If I have been judged, I am not aware of it. So many people have come by the table, some with clipboards, many with cameras, asking questions and jotting down notes, that I could have been judged a hundred times over and been unaware.

Ms. Lansing walks up, most definitely a judge. Today she wears a peach suit with a creamy ruffled blouse, her heels three inches too high for any human being, her pantyhose unnaturally tan. She beams, lipstick on her teeth. "Gal. My goodness. Glad to see you out and about."

"I'm not dead yet," I say, only half joking.

She blanches. What people don't know is if you don't joke about cheating death, you'll be horribly depressed all the time. It does throw some off.

"Good for you," she says faintly. She puts on the glasses from the chain around her neck and regards the rose. She makes a soft clucking noise in the back of her throat, like some strange hen. Which in fact she resembles, with her large chest tapering to tiny feet. Riley and I grin at each other.

Ms. Lansing's mouth straightens into an ugly line. She begins writing, fast, on her clipboard. She turns the judging sheet over and writes some more. I begin to feel nervous. Surely it's not a good sign, all that writing.

Three more judges walk up. Of course. They wear name tags with long green ribbons dangling from them. I smile and greet them. Ms. Lansing hasn't moved out of their way yet.

The judges see my flower and turn very serious. One of them, a man in his sixties with a great gray handlebar mustache, asks, "How did you obtain the striping?"

My phone rings. The number is George's. My heart thunders. "Pardon me," I say to the judge. There's only one reason for him to call me right now. To give me the kidney compatibility test results.

"Watch the table, Riley." I walk away, heedless of the judges, heedless of everything except the necessity of getting to a quiet place. "Hello?" I say, moving out of the ballroom at a fast clip.

"Gal." It's George. "I have the results."

I take several breaths, leaning against a wall. "Well, what are you waiting for? Break it to me."

I can feel his extreme regret before he utters another word. "I'm sorry, Gal."

I blink at the ceiling. I sink to the floor. Darn. I hadn't realized quite how badly I wanted his kidney. How much I had expected it to match. How perfect that would have been, a solution right under my nose.

"The other teachers with type O blood have all agreed to be tested, too," he says. I swallow. My voice doesn't work.

"We'll make announcements at the school, at church, on Twitter. We'll set up a chain donor system. Don't you worry, Gal." His voice, warm and worried, comforts me somewhat. Imagine. George doing this for me.

"I am very grateful," I manage to choke out. "Thank you."

I hang up and sit for a minute, drawing my knees up to my head, resting my forehead there.

Tonight I will go to a dialysis center here in Los Angeles. Our hotel room will be empty; I'm not comfortable having Riley stay alone in a hotel, away from me and from home. I will do this the day after tomorrow, and the day after tomorrow after that, and so forth forever, through vacations and work, picking up infections the way black sweaters catch lint.

I am not sure how long I can continue. How long I *will* continue. The human body has its breaking point.

I find I cannot bring myself to get up. Not one of the dozens of people walking by asks me if I need help. I don't blame them. They are all concerned about their own roses, their own judging.

"Hey." Riley is shaking my knee. "Auntie."

I raise my head to look at her. The poor girl's face is creased with concern. I'm going to prematurely wrinkle her. "Sorry, Riley." I hold up my hand. She pulls me up. "I just had to sit for a second."

She considers whether or not to accept it. I begin walking to the table. "Anything exciting happen while I was gone?"

"The judges took your rose," Riley says, skipping ahead of me and walking backward though there are people jamming every available breathing space.

I don't understand. "What do you mean?"

"They took it. The man with the mustache." She hands me a receipt. "You have to pick it up later."

I crumple the pink receipt into my pocket.

"What does this mean?" Riley asks.

"I don't know. It's never happened to me before." Our table is, indeed, empty, save for the number 110. The table-top looks large and empty and sad. I stop and stare.

Riley takes my hand. Once smaller than mine, it's now larger. She pulls on me gently. "Let's go take a break, Aunt Gal."

She should not have to lead me, this child in an adult body. I want to tell her so.

But I am too tired.

I follow her out of the ballroom.

I TRY MY BEST to lift myself up out of my funk, but I keep dwelling on George's news. I phone my mother.

"I'm on my way," she says promptly.

"No, Mother."

"Gal, at least let me do this for you. I'll stay with Riley tonight so you don't have to worry." I hear a car door bang. "I'm already in the car. You're only two hours away. There's nothing you can do about it now."

"You better hang up, then."

41

THE AWARDS CEREMONY IS HELD IN A BALLROOM. There will be a banquet after this that I will miss. I'm hoping my mother arrives in time for me to give her my ticket; after all, it's included in the price.

Riley and I get there when most of the seats are already taken. Part of me thinks this whole thing is pointless, and I might as well head to dialysis early. The only thing keeping me here is Riley. She grins, excited. "I think this is the day for the Riley!" she sings.

I muster a smile, too. "I hope so."

Ms. Lansing stands and takes the microphone. How is she always the emcee at these events? No wonder I never win. From back here, behind all these taller heads, I can see only the top of her hairdo.

"Welcome to our awards show," she says warmly, eliciting loud applause. The lights dim and a projection screen behind her shows a rose arrangement, a palette box. "Please hold your applause until the end when all the winners are up here. Third place for palettes, Mrs. Cynthia Aguirre!" She continues up through first in the category, and when all three winners are up, we clap.

Someone slaps me gently on the back. It's Winslow Blythe, fertilizer man extraordinaire. "Saw your rose. What a beaut!"

"I used your fertilizer recipe," I say. "Thank you."

"Don't mention it." He waves my thanks away like an errant bee.

"Are you a judge?"

He shakes his head. "That would take all the fun out of it. I'm a competitor. Always have been, always will be. They may be wheeling me out of here on a gurney, but I'll be happy as long as I got to show."

I take a breath. "I wish I could be happy just showing."

He leans toward me conspiratorially, so close I can smell mint, Ben-Gay mint. "Wait until you have your first win. You'll become addicted for life."

Riley does not, surprisingly, leave for a snack. She sits beside me, chewing on a hangnail, looking as increasingly agitated as I feel. "Best Hybrid Tea!" the announcer says. "Best Floribunda Bloom! Best Shrub!"

I clap until my hands hurt. Finally they arrive at my category. Best Rose Hybrid. Third place goes to someone I don't know.

Riley holds my arm. "Come on!" She is fidgeting from side to side, foot to foot.

I put my hand on her. Suddenly I am very calm, as if she has taken all my nervous energy and is burning it up on my behalf. "It's all right, Riley." Even if my rose gets no prize, it does not change this fact: this rose is a winner. I will reproduce it and enter it everywhere in the next few years. Today will not be its only chance to shine.

I turn my attention back to the stage and listen.

"Second. Byron Madaffer for his orange Hulthemia,

Tequila Sunrise!" Byron is onstage in about half a second, looking surprised.

Riley takes up my hand.

"First prize is very important today, ladies and gentle-men." Ms. Lansing pauses dramatically under her spotlight. "First place also gets a slot in the American Rose Society trials, to begin this year at the American Rose Center in Shreveport, Louisiana."

Everyone applauds and cheers. Except for me. I stand rooted to my spot on the carpet.

"First prize goes to Galilee Garner for her spectacular purple Hulthemia, Riley!" The photo of the Riley rose flashes two stories high behind Ms. Lansing. A collective gasp arises from the audience, then applause. More applause as I make my way up the aisle. I feel like a bride at her wedding. I nod to people, I high-five, some flashes go off. Only my groom is that shiny first place medal Ms. Lansing dangles before her. "Riley will be tried out for two years at the American Rose Center!

"Congratulations," Ms. Lansing says, with genuine warmth, no doubt swept away by the audience approval. She slips the medal over my head.

I take my place next to Byron, stiffly. I want to stick out my tongue and point to my medal. You can't keep me down, Byron Madaffer, I think. Both of us stare at the audience stonily.

The photographer tells us to smile, and flashes blind me.

"Smile, Aunt Gal!" Riley shouts from behind the photog-rapher, and she claps her hands down to her knees in a guf-faw. In the flashing lights she appears to be in slow motion, her hair flying about, joy on her face.

And I laugh.

All weight sheds away. I forget about my kidney and the dialysis and especially Byron. I grin with a carefree enthusiasm not seen since childhood photographs, back when I didn't care at all what I looked like, before I was sick.

The flashing ends. Byron gives me a quick, hard handshake. There is no trace of animosity on his face. Nor, really, any happiness. "Queen of Show is next," he says briskly. "Congratulations."

"Thank you." Getting Queen of Show will garner a great deal of attention. It's the best possible scenario. "But I have what I came here for. A slot in the trial garden."

"If you want," Byron begins slowly, "you could give me a cutting."

I stare at him, uncomprehending.

"You can give me a cutting and I'll start trials, too, at my farm." Byron watches me warily, his expression still hooded, expecting, no doubt, an outburst. Perhaps even hoping for one, given his audacious request. I do not understand the man, except for this: I will never understand him.

"I don't think so," I say at last.

I lift a hand in farewell. Byron is already forgotten. Instead I'm wondering how quickly my mother will get here. "See you around, then."

He gives me one nod.

I turn my attention to my niece and the people surrounding me, enveloping me in the crowd like a hug, offering congratulations.

Mom does not get to the hotel until after dinner, which for me is a quick bite at a burrito stand. We pass her in the lobby as I head to dialysis at a local clinic.

She grabs my shoulders. "Are you all right, Gal? Do you need something? Want a ride?"

"Fine, no, and no." I laugh at her concern. I will not let anything, or anyone, distract from this good mood. I've worked too hard for it.

Mom lifts my medal from my chest. "Did you win Queen of Show?"

"Nope." I tell her about the rose trials. My rose will stay with the staff. They will graft the rose onto new rootstock and send it to several gardens around the United States to be tried in all kinds of weather.

"We have high hopes for the Riley," the mustached judge told me after I claimed my medal. "This Hulthemia could be the next breakout rose."

I shook his hand more vigorously than I've ever shaken anyone's hand. "That is just the news I was hoping for, sir."

Now, my gray-haired mother lets out a shriek not unlike that of a very small girl who's had way too much birthday cake. Everyone in the lobby stares as she does a ring-around-the-rosy dance around me. Riley edges away and perches on a chair, pretending she does not know who on earth these two crazy ladies are.

"Okay, then." I put my arm out to stop her.

Mom stops, out of breath, her cheeks blown out like a chipmunk's. "Goodness. Can't a mother celebrate without people getting all in a tizzy?"

"Not like that." I smile at her.

An odd sound makes me look up. A shuffle, shuffle, *plop* sound. Winslow Blythe walks slowly through the lobby. He is using a cane with a tennis ball on the end, which is the noise I heard. I haven't seen him with a cane before. He is accompanied by a man about thirty years his junior, towing suitcases. Winslow's shoulders are stooped and skinny, the few hairs on his head all blowing askew. For the first time, Winslow is acting his age. I have an idea. "Winslow!" I hurry over to him, leaving my mother and Riley behind in the lounge area.

He stops and grins at me, the fog lifting from his exhausted gaze. "Congratulations again, miss! I tell you. What a rose. I would have given it Queen. Maybe I will have to be a judge one of these days." He cocks his head to the side. "Although, you know, winning Queen of Show isn't everything. Getting a spot in the trials is more important, I'd say."

Something about Winslow makes me glad inside. Open, quite the opposite of how I'd felt with Byron. I smile. "You're right. I'm more than happy with the prize." Queen of Show would have been great, but now the Riley had a solid chance to prove itself.

I clear my throat before continuing. "I have a question for you." I hesitate, feeling suddenly afraid. Afraid he'll say no. "Would you like to get a cutting from the Riley? Try it out in your garden?"

He bows so low I'm afraid his cane will slip out from beneath him. "I would be honored, Miss Garner."

I return to my mother, who is sitting with her ankles crossed, her arm around Riley. Riley looks considerably happier than she did when I left them, unable to control a wide grin.

Mom pats the chair next to her. "I have to tell you something else, dear. I didn't want you ruminating over it and spoiling your good time."

I sit. I wait. Mom's face reddens. She glances to and fro, on the lookout for something. "Becky's job has finally let her come back to California."

"I don't understand." My brain refuses to process the words coming out of her mouth, as if Mom has begun spouting an alien tongue.

"Your sister is coming home." Mom recedes toward Riley. "You better get to dialysis. You'll be late."

Gal's Rose Notebook

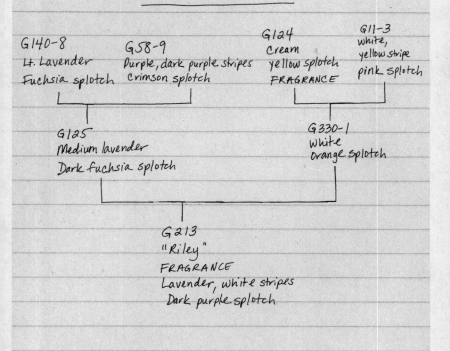

G140-8
Lt. Lavender
Fuchsia splotch

G58-9
Purple, dark purple stripes
Crimson splotch

G124
Cream
yellow splotch
FRAGRANCE

G11-3
white,
yellow stripe
pink splotch

G125
Medium lavender
Dark fuchsia splotch

G330-1
White
orange splotch

G213
"Riley"
FRAGRANCE
Lavender, white stripes
Dark purple splotch

42

BECKY ARRIVES THREE DAYS LATER, A FULL DAY past when she is expected. Constant tardiness. I check it off on the list of mental tallies I take against my sister.

A cab pulls up to my home sometime around seven. Riley, who has been sitting by the front door for the past twenty-four hours, bursts outside shouting. She wears the charm bracelet her mother sent her, plus the one I gave her on the other wrist. "Mom!"

I give them a minute to be alone. This doesn't mean I don't furtively watch them through the living room window, standing back several feet so there's no chance I'll be spotted.

Becky swings her legs out of the cab, clad in a surprisingly pedestrian pair of sweats, a matching zip-up sweatshirt, her hair pulled back in a ponytail. Her face is scrubbed clean of makeup. Her face, so skeletal the last time I saw her, has filled out again. She clasps Riley to her, pulls back, cradles Riley's face in her hands. An easy physical affection, so difficult for me to show. Riley says something and Becky throws back her head and laughs, a big easy guffaw that shows all of her wide, white teeth.

I stumble backward. I have to get away from the window.

In my bedroom, I sit on the bed with the door closed. I hear a noise like water churning, like the dishwasher is on, and I listen. It's the sound of my own blood in my ears.

I reach for the phone. I can call Dara for a pep talk. Or my mother. Or even George. He's had experience in dealing with slightly crazed, unstable people who want something you have. The image of Becky and Riley hugging outside burns in my mind. It might be me who wants something Becky has, not the other way around.

There is a knock. "Aunt Gal? My mother's here," Riley says from the other side, her voice the same placating tone my own mother uses. I hear her murmuring to Becky, probably telling her Aunt Gal has occasional fits, nothing to worry about.

I open the door.

My sister stands not two feet away from me. The whites of her eyes shine unblemished in the dim light, two hard-cooked Easter eggs. Her face dimples into a grin. "Gal!" She steps forward and hugs me.

I hug back, barely. She feels muscular and light. "Have you been working out?"

"The building where I lived had an indoor pool." She steps back and twinkles at me. Positively glows.

"You must be exhausted," I say. "You want to lie down?"

"No thanks. I slept on the plane." Becky looks around the living room, at the photos of roses on the walls, the new pictures of Riley. Riley with her trebuchet. Riley at her summer job.

I stiffen. "Oh."

"I didn't take a pill," Becky says. "I always fall asleep on planes. The altitude does it."

"Good thing you're not a pilot." Riley has ceased follow-ing her mother around, but will not take her eyes from her. When Riley was a newborn, swaddled up in her bassinet or carrier or in another's arms, she had done the same. Fixated on her mother with an intensity that surprised everyone who witnessed it, her small eyes trained on Becky as she moved about the room without her, as though she was will-ing her mother to return.

Riley offers to take her mother out to eat. "Would you like to come, Aunt Gal?" Riley says, after the fact. Hastily. She has forgotten me.

"You go ahead." I wave them off. I don't want to be the third wheel.

WHILE THEY ARE GONE, I get out my photo albums. Beginning with my childhood. Becky and I, so close together in age, so different. My moonfaced countenance peering from every photo is painful to see, the associated memories making it so. Becky grinning through childhood. Sticking out her tongue at me. Turning sullen and withdrawn by her eleventh birthday.

RILEY AND BECKY do not get home until much later, about eight o'clock. I look up from the television and its Her-cule Poirot rerun. "You better get cleaned up and ready for bed, Riley," I say calmly, though my insides dance and scream. "It's a school night."

Becky nods at her daughter, who stands reluctant at the door. "Go. Listen to Aunt Gal."

"If you need us," I say to Riley, "we'll be out in the

greenhouse." I need to talk to Becky alone, where Riley cannot hear us. I cannot take this pussyfooting around one more minute. This pretense that we are adhering to all these social niceties. I am going to explode.

Two vertical lines appear between Riley's brows as she looks from me to her mother, then back again. We both smile at her in unison, pretend we are two happy sisters, until at last Riley nods silently, retreats to the bathroom.

Becky follows me outside. The late October nights are cold, and I shiver a little in my thin cable-knit sweater, too hasty to grab a jacket.

A new moon casts dim watery light as we crunch across the gravel path. "You've done a lot with the place," Becky observes. "All these roses. I haven't been here since you bought it."

"That long?"

"I got no invitation."

My mother and father spent every Christmas with me, figuring that at least Becky had Riley, while I had no one at all. I had told Becky, when Riley was small, she could come along. "There was always a standing Christmas invitation."

"There's not enough room."

"I would have given you my bed."

Becky makes a noise like a disappointed field mouse. "Mom wouldn't have allowed it."

I switch on the greenhouse lights.

Becky stands blinking in the sudden brightness, walking down the aisle of roses. "This is impressive, Gal. A real operation you have going on here."

"That's what they tell me." I feel suddenly proud, pleased at my sister's compliment. I sit on the rolling stool as she makes her lap around, not bothering to give her the tour. Just watching.

She does seem clean, I have to admit. Her mind is the sharpest it's been since she was pregnant with Riley. Not that I have seen her too often, I remind myself.

She gets back to me and sits on another stool. We are face to face, my height comfortable on the short stool, Becky looking somewhat crunched up, as though she is in a kindergarten classroom. "So," she says.

"So," I say.

I know what her next words will be before they're out of her mouth. "I want Riley to come back with me."

"Back to where?"

"San Francisco. I'm back home."

I turn away, staring at the empty containers for the seedlings. Next month, these will be filled and planted with new seeds. Another cycle begun. "You've got to be kidding me."

"I'm not." Becky scoots closer to me. "Gal. I don't take pills anymore. Not a drop of alcohol, either. Or pot."

I move away.

"Gal, I'm clean. I've been clean. I'm good." She looks down at her hands. "I've missed her. More than I knew I would."

"Like you did when her father had her?" I can't look at her or I will break. I put my hand on the wooden frame, feeling its splinters on my palm. "You haven't been there for her for years."

Becky says nothing, is silent for so long I swivel to see if she's asleep. She is looking at me steadily, her eyes big and wide. "That is true," she admits.

I stand. "You know what I don't understand? How you, who has everything, all the health, intelligence, and looks anyone could ever need in three lifetimes, how you can just throw it all away." My voice is loud but steady.

"Gal." My sister swallows. "I know it was hard on you, but it was hard on me, too."

"What was so hard on you? Not having anything wrong with you?" I cannot keep the sarcasm out. Becky, playing the victim. No more. I won't have it.

"Your disease." Becky stands now, moving away from me. "You always got whatever you wanted, no matter what it was. For Mom and Dad, you could do no wrong. Hell, if I wanted extra allowance, all I had to do was get you to ask. They'd say no to me but never to you."

"And you gave me a cut." I smile, a little ashamed. My parents were so easy to manipulate, I couldn't tell I was doing it. It was all I'd ever known.

Becky laughs bitterly. "Yeah. Me, I was left alone. I wasn't sick, so it didn't matter if no one came to my school concerts or took me to soccer practice. There was always next year." A look of anguish passes over her. "Do you know how much time I spent alone, in front of the television, while you were at the hospital?"

I remember being jealous of my sister for getting to stay home, not having to go to the doctor every other day. "At least you weren't in the hospital getting things cut out of you or poked into you," I point out. "At least you got to grow up to be a normal size. Have a kid."

Becky stares at me. "Do you know how much trouble I had to be to get any attention at all? Heck, when I fell out of that tree, all Mom said was, 'Stop your whining. At least *you're* going to get better.'"

"She did not say that." I refuse to face the truth of her words. It still does not excuse what she did.

Becky sighs. "I'm paraphrasing."

"Is that what your therapist told you to say?"

She blinks. "Gal. Don't be hurtful."

I press on. "It's not hurtful. You can't explain away messing up Riley's childhood, Becky. It is your fault. No one else's. You should see how far she's come. You can't throw it away again. Not now."

"You think I don't know that?" Her voice rises now. "You think I don't understand how messed up I've been? I do. But I've got news. I can't go back in time and fix it." Her voice breaks. "All I can do is fix what I have. In the present."

I look into my sister's face, expecting to see tears. There are none. She has her head up high, her jaw set. Ready for extended battle.

"I am her legal guardian," I say.

"I am her parent," Becky says. "She is old enough to choose."

I look around the greenhouse. The roses forming their hips, getting ready to give me their seeds. I think of all the hours Riley has spent in here working with me. I swallow. "Just so you know, I would have preferred to be a little bit bad when I was a kid, too."

She smiles wistfully. "I know."

I stand undecided. For the first time in many years, I want to hug my sister. Doing so feels like admitting something, my wrongness, my culpability. I have done nothing wrong. I never asked for any of this. But Becky stands there trembling, vulnerable. If I don't, she might shatter.

I hug her.

43

THE NEXT DAY, MY HEAD IS CLOGGED WORSE THAN a sink at a beauty school, but I go to work anyway.

I stop by the doctor's on the way home to get antibiotics. Dr. Blankenship shakes her head as she takes my blood, a task she used to leave for the nurse. "You need to take it easier, Gal."

"If I took it any easier I'd have to give up living, Doc," I say.

At home, I find Riley sitting at the dining table, doing homework. Becky reads a novel beside her, a Phillippa Gregory with a queen on it. "I didn't know you liked to read, Becky." I put my bags down beside the door.

"There's a lot of downtime in my job." Becky doesn't look up. "I read two a week, at least. More when I was in Hong Kong." She closes her book, smiles at her daughter. "I was lonely."

I make no comment. Becky saying she is lonely is like the Earth saying it's lonely when there are all those stars orbiting around it. But maybe that is apt, I think. Maybe she does drift, unconnected from anyone, everyone close but not touching her.

I take the first of my antibiotics with a glass of milk and a piece of bread, watching Riley and Becky from the kitchen.

If Riley leaves, I will be alone again. The thought does not cheer me. I go in the bedroom to lie down.

A bit later, Riley knocks on the door. She comes in and sits on the bed beside me, her weight making me slide over. "Don't worry," she says. "I already told her I'm not going."

I blink. The expected relief I should feel at her statement does not come. I can think only of my sister, and my niece, their foreheads touching. "Are you sure about that?"

"You need me more than she does." Riley flashes me a smile. "You've done so much for me."

I struggle to sit up. "Wait a minute. This is not a tit-for-tat relationship, Riley. You are not obligated to me in any way."

"I want to stay here and help you, Aunt Gal."

I shake my head. "No."

What I have known on some deeper level for some time becomes clear. This should not be the role of a sixteen-year-old. Caretaking. She should not have to worry about me and my sinus infections, or how I'm doing at overnight dialysis. Be responsible for me if I should fall ill. Think it's her fault if I get depressed. This is not a good role for her, either. Riley is not my mother. She needs to be a kid for a little bit longer, before she grows up for real.

Besides, I admit, I might not make it for much longer.

I think of Becky out there alone, the prodigal mother returned. In some ways, my sister has always been alone, more than I have been during my whole life.

Riley is Becky's daughter. Not mine. I love her like a daughter, but I cannot take her away from my sister. I cannot keep punishing Becky forever, not when she's finally done what I wanted her to do. She has taken responsibility.

Even if it terrifies me, the thought that Becky's responsibility could be temporary. There's no way to know if it will stick, no way to know except to let it play out.

I take a minute to find the right words. I inhale. "Riley, I love you. But I don't think it's great for you to be here, taking care of me like you're the grown-up. It's not right."

I watch her face. She is listening.

"If you want to stay because you like it here, you like the school, you like the people, then I would love to have you stay with me." I smile at her, squeeze her forearm. "But I don't want you thinking you have to stay because of me. I will be just fine. You will not be letting me down. Okay?"

She nods, once.

"Think about it, Riley."

She nods again. "I'm going back out to my mother."

I lie back on the pillows.

ALL WEEK, I can see Riley's answer building. Her bonding again with her mother. When she is at home, an almost-grown-up young lady of driving and dating age, she will not release her mother's hand.

I wonder if this is how foster parents feel, giving the child back to their real parents, hoping against hope that the biological parents will step up the way they're supposed to.

"How can you let that woman waltz back in and take her? After she threw her in your lap?" Dara demands of me during lunch on Tuesday. Dara and George and I sit outside, away from the others, a motley trio on a bench under a tree in the still-hot October afternoon.

Dara is so irked that she can't open her chocolate milk

carton properly, ripping it nearly in half. "How can Riley want to go back?"

"Because Becky is her mother," I answer.

"Is she even clean?"

I nod. "I haven't given her a blood test, Dara, but she says she is. She seems like she is. She looks healthy. Different." As I speak, doubt wells inside anew. What am I sending Riley back into? "Riley's old enough to decide what to do. I can't ban her from living with her own mother."

Dara finishes off her milk and throws the empty carton away. "I still don't like it."

"I have no choice, Dara." I think my voice will break, but it holds. I take a deep breath from my abdomen. "I am far from liking it. But this decision isn't mine."

Dara shakes her head. "I have to go set up ceramics. I'll see you later." She strides away through the lunch crowd.

"You'd think she was the one with the problem," I observe.

"She cares." George chews ruminatively on his sandwich. I know he is thinking of his own daughter, how his wife should have done what was best rather than what she felt like doing.

"Am I doing the right thing, George?" I ask suddenly. "Should I tell Riley to stay here for her own good?"

George leans on his elbows and regards me gravely. In the shade, he takes off his sunglasses. "If you fight your sister and Riley wants to go, it'll make things worse. Let her go. She can always come back. You are her safe haven."

I sigh. "I wish I had a guarantee."

He laughs gently, puts his arm around me. The gesture is friendly, I think. His arm is as warm as a blanket on my shoulders. "There are no guarantees for anything, Gal. I thought you, of all people, knew that best."

I sigh, take a sip of water. George does not move his arm.

The only comfort I have is this. No matter how many organs fail in my body, or what works or doesn't work with the roses or with my friends and family, this moment will be the hardest thing I have ever had to do. This giving up of Riley.

The warning bell sounds. George reclaims his arm. With his other hand, he gently tweaks my nose. "You okay?"

I nod. Such a brotherly gesture, this nose tweaking. I am disappointed, but this is all I ever expected from him. A brotherly touch.

But then he holds my gaze longer than he needs to. "Gal."

"Yes?" I brace myself for his asking me about ordering Bunsen burners, or Science Olympiad.

He clears his throat. "There's a play about Marie Curie. Do you want to see it with me?"

"I'd love to." I bend my head to let my hair hide the flush on my cheeks. "How much are tickets?"

He will burn a hole into me with those eyes. "No. Nothing. I'm paying."

"You're paying?" I'm confused. "I can't let you do that."

He laughs now, taking up my hand between his two large ones. "You can if it's a date."

"Oh." I let this sink in for a moment. "Oh!"

Almost all the students have gone inside. We scramble up. "Call me if you need anything," he says. "Or, actually, I'll call you to find out if you need anything." He moves a piece of hair out of my face.

I am blushing again. I smile. "Thank you, George."

I run to class as the tardy bell rings, late as any truant student.

ON FRIDAY EVENING, I'm in the greenhouse, talking on the phone to my mother. "I don't like it," she says. "Dad, what about you?" Tomorrow, Becky needs to return to the city. A broker has found her a nice apartment, with two bedrooms. The movers will take their things out of storage.

Dad is silent on his end. "Gal's right. It's up to Riley."

Mom draws in a noisy breath. "I'd rather have Riley come here than back with Becky."

"Aunt Gal." Riley finds me.

"I have to go," I tell my parents, and hang up. They're not telling me anything I don't already know.

I have the bright light on, the seed pod on the table, removing the pellets that I will plant next spring. A magnifier sits on my head. "Riley." I have been expecting her. She has grown more and more quiet throughout the week, and though I do not know for certain, I have warned Dr. O'Malley about the potential release of one of his students.

"Aunt Gal?" I look up, putting my tweezers down. "Is it already seed time?"

"Yes, Riley." I wave her in closer. "Would you like to see?"

She nods. I show her the hard red-orange pellet formed by the rose, and how I've cracked it open to reveal the seeds. "This is the one I pollinated right around the time you showed up," I say. "I can't wait to see what it will look like."

Riley smiles. "Me, neither." She is close to me, smelling of apples and shampoo, the same baby scent she had when she was small enough to sit in my lap. Tears prick my eyes. She will not see what it will look like, not right away.

I take off my glasses and wipe them. "Too much eye strain." I smile at Riley through my haze. Tomorrow she will drive away with Becky. I will watch the car disappear, waving until I cannot see them anymore, until they are so far beyond sight they might as well be in space.

"Aunt Gal?" Riley sits on the stool next to me. I sort the seeds into a small labeled plastic container with the tweezers, then put a lid over it.

"Yes, Riley." My heart is thumping.

"I've made a decision." Riley puts her chin on her hand. I can feel the regret coming off her as surely as I can feel waves when standing in the ocean.

"It's all right, Riley. I understand."

"Can I talk?" She shows a flash of her old anger.

"I'm sorry." Chastened, I put down all my tools again. It hurts to look her in the eyes.

"I want to stay here." It's Riley's turn to avoid my gaze. "If that's all right."

"Stay here? With me? Are you sure?" I lean forward.

She nods.

"What about your mother?"

"I'll spend next summer with her." Riley picks up the plastic seed container and shakes it around. "It doesn't feel right to leave now, Aunt Gal. I know you're worried about me taking care of you, but I can handle it. Grandma says it's good for me." Riley grins slyly.

"She would," I say. I grip her hand to stop mine from shaking. "Are you sure this is what you want?"

Riley nods again. She blinks tears back. "Aunt Gal, I've been thinking about this a lot. I've learned so much here.

Tons about roses and gardening. Art. I've even learned to like science." She spreads her hands apart and inhales. "I guess, most of all, I've figured out how to be a person. I mean, a real person. A person who messes stuff up and fixes it. A person who keeps on going." She smiles a little. "Like you."

Like me? Tears spring to my own eyes. I smile back, overwhelmed, thinking of what to say. All I want to say. It's all mixed up inside of me, and I can't get anything out.

Riley waits for me to speak, her eyes now downcast. I take a shuddering breath. At last, I cup her face as I would have when she was small. "Riley, I'm proud of you. I'm so happy I've gotten to know you. It's meant more to me than anything." I gulp down the lump in my throat. "I am honored if I've had any influence."

Riley nods quickly. "My mother says if I change my mind, I can go up there anytime." She blushes. "I just want to see if this new 'mothering responsibly' thing sticks with her, you know?"

"I know." I release her face and pat her head.

Tears fall down her cheeks. "That's not bad, is it?"

"Of course not. It's very wise, Riley." I stand up. I will not give up, I think. I will keep on going for Riley. "Come here." Finally I hug her to me, her bones no longer tiny and fragile, but strong like they ought to be. I give her a kiss on the forehead, wishing it would protect her like Glenda the Good Witch's kiss to Dorothy. "You are going to be just fine, young lady." We stand and go inside the house, where Becky is alone.

Winslow Blythe's *Complete Rose Guide* (SoCal Edition)

November

The final blooms of the year are here. Cut them, give them away, make potpourri—you might as well enjoy them while you can. If you leave roses on the bush, pull off the petals instead of cutting them to see if they will form rose hips, which are full of vitamins and make a great tea (of course, these are edible only if you haven't been spraying poisons all over the place all season).

This month, check your potted roses. The root-bound ones should be repotted into larger pots, or else they will die in their small pots. If the roses aren't root-bound yet, then you can wait until next year to change their pots.

44

On Thanksgiving morning, I awake early to the smell of pumpkin and apple pies and coffee. My parents are here, their motor home parked in front of the house, where Dad will drive it around the block once every forty-eight hours so that Old Mrs. Allen does not call in a parking violation.

I yawn. There is still no kidney for me, but I'm hoping there will be better luck soon. By spring, I tell myself, I will have a new kidney. Dr. Blankenship says I'm a difficult match, my body so worn out from its previous infections and kidneys. Dara is still working on her double kidney trade idea with the doctor. Mr. Walters's penguin winks at me from the top of my dresser, reminding me. Anything is possible. Or keep dreaming until you can't dream anymore. I haven't decided which precisely. Maybe both.

I stretch, listening. I've forgotten to shut my blinds, making my room brighter than I'm used to this morning. Mom and Dad's voices and coffee cups clink from the kitchen. From the living room, behind another wall, Riley and Becky's higher voices chatter away.

I throw on my robe and push my feet into my fuzzy boot slippers and go out into the living room.

Becky regards me with an eyebrow raised. "Go get dressed!" she stage whispers. "George is here."

"George is here?" I look around. His voice wasn't one I heard. Becky points outside. There he is, tramping in from the front yard, apparently admiring the sea garden and rearranging some rocks.

He pauses at the front door. "I thought you'd be up watching the Macy's parade by now."

"Ahem." I point at his dirty boots. He bends over and quickly unlaces them, placing them outside. "Why don't you come have some coffee?"

He can't stop grinning. "I got her. I got her for Christmas. And every weekend after that."

He doesn't have to tell me who he's talking about. I let out a whoop and reach out my hand for a high five. He doesn't connect. "Don't leave me hanging, Morton!"

Instead, he picks me up and swings me around, fast, like I weigh nothing, until I'm dizzy, as if I'm on an amusement park ride, and I laugh.

IN THE EARLY AFTERNOON, everyone has gathered on the front porch, spilling out of the small interior to the extended living space. Dara is here now, in a brown shiny cotton dress with white polka dots all over it and saddle shoes, with her genial accountant boyfriend, Chad. I'll have to get to know him. He seems to be sticking around. Mom and Dad sit on the porch railing, sipping their wine and arguing about how long to let the turkey rest. "Twenty minutes!" Mom says. "An hour!" Dad counters. Becky tips her sparkling cider toward me. And George Morton salutes from his perch on the white Adirondack chair, another mug of coffee in his hands. Still in his stocking feet.

"Too much caffeine is bad for you, you know," I say.

He takes a sip. "But it goes so well with the pie."

"You let him have pie already?" I ask Mom. "You never let us have pie before dinner."

She shrugs. "He asked very politely."

George grins at me. I grin back. Are we dating? I'm afraid to call it that. But it's something. Something is happening.

"Do you want to cut the roses for the centerpiece?" Dara gets up from her seat. "I can do it."

"I'll do it. You don't know which ones to get." I climb down the porch steps.

"Whichever ones are left?" she calls after me.

"You relax," I shout back.

First, I tend to a few of the roses in the greenhouse. I find the potted roses whose roots begin to peek out of the bottom of the pots. These root-bound plants must be moved to larger pots. There are only three of these, all thriving miniatures. I wonder how Byron's Gal rose is doing. If anyone has purchased the rose and is pondering who this Gal person is.

I put on my rose gloves and loosen the first mini, a pink one, and lift it out of the pot by its top. The roots curl at the sides like mangled, coiled spaghetti. Contrary to popular belief, this doesn't mean you've done something wrong. It means the plants love your care so much, they've thrived, getting bigger and bigger. But you have to remember to move them only when necessary; it's stressful for the plant, and they need recovery time. That's why November is a good month to repot. They have all winter to hang out, not trying to do anything new.

Riley appears, running in from the house in bare feet. "Dara wants to know if you have the roses for cutting. Grandma says the turkey will be done in ten minutes."

"Cutting is next." I finish tamping the new soil into the larger pot. "Help me with these two and I'll finish faster."

She pulls on her own gloves and we get to work on the other two minis. She works silently and efficiently, just like me, pulling out the plant and gently teasing the roots loose, then cutting off the wildest tendrils. "Is this good?" She shows me her handiwork. I nod.

I don't know how long Riley will stay with me, if she will finish high school at St. Mark's or move back to be with Becky next year. I can only enjoy her while she is here. She will spend Christmas with Becky, their relationship still moving forward. Tentative, but growing steadily. Like so many other things.

Finished with the repotting, I move on to the rose cutting. Riley hands me my rose cutters from their peg on the wall. I pick up my rose basket. Outside, I bend and cut orange and yellow and red, a combination of hybrid teas, the Hulthemia, and English roses in fall colors. Dara and Riley will assemble these into a grand arrangement for our harvest table.

These are the last blooms of the year, the final gasps before the roses turn into ugly thorny sticks. Ugly to people like Old Mrs. Allen. Their bare, forlorn branches give me something to look forward to all winter, something to hang my daydreams on like ornaments on a Christmas tree. In the spring, they will bloom again.

Riley and I cut a basket each full of roses, until their blooms threaten to be crushed by one another. "Enough?" I ask, lifting up mine.

Riley screws up her mouth in thought. "One more," she says, stepping through the nearly naked rows of plants to the climbing rose arbor. A pink old-fashioned rose, the Abraham Darby, of pinky apricot and golden tones. It is ostentatiously pretty and overblown, with more than one hundred petals in a full head.

"That doesn't match the others," I say.

She puts it in her basket without hesitation. "It's the last on the vine. I can't leave it alone. It would be wrong."

"It's your centerpiece." I smile.

We head back to the house, where everyone waits for us patiently.

Acknowledgments

This book would not have been possible without my sister-in-law, Deborah Dilloway, a three-time kidney transplant recipient. If you don't think a dialysis patient can do as much as Gal does in this book, then you should have met Deborah. She who held down a full-time job, ushered for the Royals baseball team, and earned a master's, all while undergoing dialysis. Deborah patiently explained (and re-explained) every detail of her experiences with dialysis, IVP dye allergy, and transplants. Unfortunately, Deborah lost her battle just before Christmas 2011. Please consider becoming an organ donor to help people like her.

Thanks must also go to Jim Sproul of Sproul Roses by Design, for introducing me to Hulthemia roses, and answering myriad questions about rose breeding. Any errors made are mine alone. If you're interested in hybridization, Sproul's website is a good place to start; he provides many essays on the subject.

I am appreciative of the San Diego Rose Society and its president, Bob Martin, for letting me attend and bend the ears of its members. Member Linda Clark came up with the Queen of Show soil mix, made by Hanson A-1 soils.

Thanks also to Fara Shimbo, who told me about her roses with spotting and striping. I am also indebted to the Rose Hybridizers Association, whose online forum allowed me to get in touch with

Jim Sproul and Shimbo. The "rose tea" recipe is a variation of the one created by famed rosarian Howard Walters.

My editor, Marysue Rucci, thrilled me with small suggestions that made huge differences. Thanks for making me a better writer. Diana Lulek, your invaluable assistance made everything easier. Thanks also to Dan Lazar, for looking out for me. I am also grateful to Elaine Markson and Gary Johnson.

Last but not least, thank you to my children, for making everything worthwhile; and to Keith, for your bottomless patience and pep talks. A writer (or anyone else, for that matter) couldn't ask for a better family.

READERS GUIDE TO

The CARE *and* HANDLING
of ROSES *with* THORNS

DISCUSSION QUESTIONS

1. Consider the title of the book. What multiple meanings might it convey?

2. In the early chapters, as we're getting to know Gal as a character, what is your opinion of her? Does her struggle with kidney disease affect your perception of her character?

3. Gal often views the world in black and white, and is inclined to stick to rules in the name of order and fairness. But, at times, other adults in the story question or undermine her decisions, believing that individual circumstances merit a special response. Who did you agree with during these conflicts? Do you see rules more as guidelines that should be flexible, or do exceptions make rules meaningless?

4. The book highlights the complex and fraught system of organ donation, where in the face of a limited supply of organs, potential recipients must be ranked according to criteria that may not always seem fair, and this ranking can mean the difference between life and death. Do you agree with Gal's implication that she's more deserving of a kidney than Mark? What criteria would you take into account if you were doing the ranking?

5. Riley comes to live with Gal at a fragile time during her teenage years, when she's still trying to identify interests,

solidify skills, and find her passions. How does living with Gal help her grow in these respects? Which other adults and peers also influence her development?

6. Irresponsible, flaky Becky is an interesting foil to Gal, who is rigidly consistent in both her outlook and actions. Did your opinion of Becky change over the course of the novel? Do you sympathize at all with the struggles she faces and the choices she makes?

7. As we learn in the book, rose breeding and cultivation is both a competitive endeavor that can lead to financial gain and a collegial undertaking in which fellow hobbyists share tips and information for mutual benefit. How do Gal and the other breeders handle the fine line between sharing and competing? Do you think Gal's anger toward Byron was justified?

8. In what ways does Gal become transformed by the end of the story, as a teacher, sister, friend, and stand-in parent?